Fused

Book Six of Millennial Mage
By J.L. Mullins

Copyright © 2023 by J.L. Mullins

All rights reserved.

No part of this publication may be reproduced, distributed, or transmitted in any form or by any means, including photocopying, recording, or other electronic or mechanical methods, without the prior written permission of the author, except as permitted by U.S. copyright law.

The story, all names, characters, and incidents portrayed in this production are fictitious. No identification with actual persons (living or deceased), places, buildings, and products is intended or should be inferred.

Contents

- Chapter: 1 - Tight Spaces 7
- Chapter: 2 - Draining Her Reserves 21
- Chapter: 3 - A Long Night 33
- Chapter: 4 - Through-Spike 45
- Chapter: 5 - Memories 57
- Chapter: 6 - Crazy 75
- Chapter: 7 - Adjusting Your Senses 87
- Chapter: 8 - Kannis 101
- Chapter: 9 - Master Avian 115
- Chapter: 10 - Just a Minor Change 131
- Chapter: 11 - That Unleashed a Flood 143
- Chapter: 12 - Embarrassing for Everyone 157
- Chapter: 13 - Surprisingly Reasonable 171
- Chapter: 14 - Not Surprised in the Least 185
- Chapter: 15 - I Really Want To 199
- Chapter: 16 - Genuinely Shocked 213
- Chapter: 17 - Explain Everything 231
- Chapter: 18 - Dissolution 247
- Chapter: 19 - Alat, Ignored 261
- Chapter: 20 - Uneventful 273
- Chapter: 21 - You'll Never Guess 287
- Chapter: 22 - Family Claims 301
- Chapter: 23 - Nalac and Leighis 313
- Chapter: 24 - I'll Be Fine 331
- Chapter: 25 - A Tea House 343
- Chapter: 26 - Exceptions Aside 357
- Chapter: 27 - The Marliweather Constructionist Guild 369
- Chapter: 28 - A Fun Idea 387
- Chapter: 29 - A Wonderfully Peaceful Time 401
- Epilogue: 1 - The Reason 419
- Epilogue: 2 - Found You 431
- Author's Note 445

Chapter: 1
Tight Spaces

Tala walked out of the Constructionist Guildhall and into the wintry late morning air. She took a deep breath and let it out, a smile blossoming across her face.

"Well, I might as well go to the Culinary Guild." She glanced to Terry. "Thoughts?"

He cracked an eye, then opened his mouth.

Tala grinned and tossed him some jerky. "Fair enough. You just want this done with, so you can join in the training."

He let out a happy, quiet trill around the jerked meat.

That settled, she went to the only Culinary Guild office she was aware of—the one that she'd picked up the most recent batch of jerky from.

Her arrival caused a mild panic.

As Tala walked in, the assistant stood up from behind his desk to greet her, but his words froze in his open mouth before his teeth clicked together in surprise.

First, he seemed to take in that she was a Mage. Then, his eyes flicked to Terry but didn't stay long. A small, sleeping bird wasn't that much of a threat. At that point, his gaze clearly dropped to her left hand.

While Tala had been doing a fairly good job of keeping the newly painted hand, and the glowing spellforms, out of sight for the most part, at the moment, the painted appendage was just hanging by her side, clearly glowing with seemingly active magic.

Well, I didn't think of that as that big of an issue.

Millennial Mage, 6 - Fused

The assistant's eyes widened to an almost comical degree, and he opened his mouth to scream.

Tala raised both her hands in what she thought of as a placating motion, but he didn't seem to take it that way.

He tried to scream in abject terror, if his expression gave any indication, but no noise seemed to come out.

Rather than realizing that his heightened emotions were affecting him, he likely assumed that the raising of her hands had silenced him, somehow.

Thus, he fainted, collapsing to the floor in a crumpled heap, out of sight behind his desk.

"Well, that could have gone better." She moved her left hand behind her back, pulled her iron Order of the Harvest token into her right, and then, she raised her voice. "Hello? Can I get some help out here, please?"

She considered going over to help the man but realized that that could easily compound misunderstandings.

Another young man came out and took in her arrival. "Mistress? Is everything alright?"

He looked around more carefully but couldn't see behind the desk. "Derrn is supposed to be at the desk. My apologies for the wait. What can I do for you?"

She tossed the token to him. "I'd like to speak with the branch manager if at all possible."

He caught the iron coin, and his eyes widened. He looked back and forth between her and the coin before swallowing and nodding. "Certainly, Mistress. I will be right back."

Tala waited for a while, growing a bit more concerned as time went by and Derrn didn't wake up.

When the other man returned with a woman who was, presumably, the head of the local branch, Tala decided that she needed to do something about the unconscious fellow.

Before either of them could speak, Tala pointed at the desk. "I think there is someone back there, but I didn't want to startle them."

The other young man walked over to investigate and exclaimed in alarm, rushing around the desk and lifting his friend. "I'll get him to the back room to lie down. If he needs it, I'll get a healer."

The guild head nodded. "Thank you." She watched the two leave, clearly concerned, but schooled herself before turning to Tala and bowing. "Mistress Tala. I apologize for the irregularity. I was told to expect you at some point."

"I quite understand, and I hope that he is alright."

The woman bowed her head in acknowledgment but didn't say anything further.

"Are you aware of why I might be here?"

"Well, you could be here to kill us all, but I think that unlikely." She frowned, glancing Tala over, head to toe, and seemingly noticing that she had her left hand behind her back, even if just slightly. Even so, the woman didn't make an issue of it. "I believe it is more likely that you tested out your theory and wish to report the results."

"I did. Do you wish to talk more privately?"

The woman waved that off. "Here is fine. I'm Valry, if it matters. These things seem much above my level, so I doubt it will."

Tala immediately felt sympathy for the woman. *She's been thrust into this mess because I happened to choose this Culinary Guild location.* "I'll be brief. There is no injunction against research into the consumption of harvests. If you were to go inquire with the Archive, you would be welcomed and dealt with fairly."

"I'm not walking into a Mage stronghold on your word, Mistress."

Millennial Mage, 6 - Fused

This city is a Mage stronghold, you idiot. But she didn't say that. "Then, would you consent to my sending an Archivist here to talk with you?"

The woman looked incredibly uncomfortable, but after a moment, she stood up straighter, swallowed visibly, and nodded. "Yes, I will meet with an Archivist."

"Do you want me here for the meeting?"

Valry laughed ruefully. "Oh, I think one Mage at a time in my facility is quite enough. Thank you for the offer, though."

Tala scratched the side of her face. "Well, when Derrn wakes up, he might be under the impression that I used magic on him. I didn't, but I think I gave him a good scare."

Valry stiffened. "Oh? How so?"

"Well, with this." She hesitated, then added, "This is not active with outwardly directed magics." She pulled her left hand out from behind her back.

Valry's eyes widened a bit, but she contained herself. "I see. Thank you for forewarning me. I can see why that might have startled him."

"I do apologize for that."

"I'll pass that along." She swallowed again. "Now, is there anything else, Mistress?"

"No. I'll leave you to your day. I'll go talk with the Archivist shortly, and I believe that she'll come by when she's able."

"Thank you."

Without another word, Tala turned and left.

Well, that could have gone better, but it definitely could have gone worse, too.

She needed to drop through the library, now, but she was closer to the blacksmith. *Probably hasn't been long enough. I'll come by later to pick up my order.*

So, off to the library she went.

She passed through the Archon compound with ease, entering the library to find Ingrit waiting for her, as was standard and expected. *You can get used to anything, I suppose.*

"What have you done to your hand, Mistress?" It was not an unexpected first question, all things considered.

Tala lifted her left hand. "I found a more effective, passive training method?"

Ingrit gave a half-smile. "I'll be interested to see how well it works. Now, as I assume you intend to use it on more than your hand, may I offer a bit of advice?"

"Please."

"I suggest that you be ready to placate others whenever you enter any of the more defensive facilities, as the automated scripts won't like you very much. Most will have secondary triggers, which will alert a high-level Archon to scan you, and they will easily detect your gate, but automatic defensive measures won't necessarily be able to do that."

Tala scratched the back of her head. "Noted." She'd have to balance that and other inconveniences against the benefits that she could already feel from the paint.

"So, shall we get a booth?" Ingrit smiled as she drew Tala's attention back to herself.

Tala shrugged and followed the woman into the library proper. They were soon seated in a booth, behind a privacy screen, and Terry was munching on a large section of jerky.

Ingrit again broke the silence. "What can I do for you?"

"I want to grant you full access to the Culinary Guild's records, temporarily."

"Why?" Then, she hesitated, her eyes closing in an expression of almost exhausted realization. "Mundane human consumption of harvests. Of course."

"Do you need anything from me?"

"Just a request to look through those records. If you have access, I will be granted such for the term of our discussion."

"Then, please, review the Culinary Guild's records."

Ingrit's eyes immediately began flicking back and forth as she clearly read something that Tala couldn't see. Tala, in turn, pulled out one of her books and passed the time productively.

Finally, after what was at least an hour, the Archivist sat back, glowering. "Well, that is quite illuminating. We've certainly tied ourselves in knots to please the false king."

Tala frowned. "What?"

Ingrit waved her off. "It's an old saying." She blew out a long breath. "This is a tangle. Your inquiry gave me full access to all records available to you, associated with the Culinary Guild, and there is a *lot* in here… I can't take it to anyone or do anything about it, though…" Her eyebrows rose. She was clearly still going through records at an incredible rate, even as she talked, and one had caught her attention. "They tried to kill you?"

Terry lifted his head to look at Tala with sudden interest.

Tala just shrugged. "One of their members panicked and stabbed me. It didn't even break the skin."

Terry squawked an irritated exclamation and settled back down.

Ingrit grunted. "So the report states. Apparently, it is incredibly uncommon for a Mage to ask such pointed questions, and they've not killed a Mage in living memory… That will make that side of things easier." She let out a long sigh and shook her head once. "How many things like this do we have hiding throughout humanity?

How often are we tearing off our own toes out of fear of stubbing one of them?"

Clearly, with the pursuit of knowledge being so key to who she was, Ingrit hated the complete segregation and isolation of knowledge, no matter how necessary.

She turned, locking gazes with Tala with a ferocity that had the younger woman leaning back involuntarily. "Can I meet with the branch heads here? We need to clear this up. The sooner the better."

"That—" Tala swallowed, settling herself after the intensity of the woman's attention. "That was the plan, actually. Valry is expecting your visit. I can give you directions if you like."

Ingrit's eyes flicked to the side once. "No need. I know which guild office she leads." She leaned back, clucking her tongue and talking almost to herself. "There isn't anything truly groundbreaking in their pursuits, but there is a lot of ancillary information that could help so many other guilds and research units. We could probably even arrange for the sale of such information by the Culinary Guild to increase their capital."

"I think that such a meeting will be perfect. I honestly had no idea what to do about any of this, and it sounds like you do. Please, do as you see fit."

Ingrit arched a single perfect eyebrow at Tala. "You handed a rope enthusiast a rat's nest that is a mile wide and which has been being tangled and added to for centuries."

Tala gave a guilty smile. "But hey! Think of all the rope you'll have in the end?"

Ingrit let out a genuine laugh at that. "True enough. Now, was there anything else?"

"No, Mistress Ingrit, thank you."

The Archivist stood, deactivating the privacy scripts. "I will keep you apprised of the progress with the Culinary

Guild." After she was clear of the booth, she bowed deeply to Tala. "Thank you, Mistress Tala, for trusting me with this information. I shudder to think of the number of small groups that exist, hoarding bits of knowledge that could benefit so many. I am sure their reasons vary, but whether they do it out of fear, greed, or ignorance, we are all worse for it. Thank you." She bowed again.

Tala was taken aback by the gesture, as well as the outpouring of words. "I... You're welcome, Mistress Ingrit."

The woman smiled at Tala, turned, and left.

Tala scratched Terry's head. "Well, I guess we're done here."

* * *

Tala dropped by the blacksmith and picked up her items, storing the three triangular contraptions first.

The other item looked like nothing so much as a steel, three-fingered claw, perfectly sized for her spheres.

Out of the back of the claw were two small steel bars that clearly manipulated a simple mechanism.

"Pull the one with the slot." The blacksmith seemed quite proud of his work.

Tala did so, and she was able to lift the claw while it kept a tight grip on the tungsten ball.

"Now, the other."

Tala grabbed the other—this one had a simple hole in it—and the claw opened, allowing the sphere to fall free.

She let out a happy laugh. "Oh, thank you, Master Aniv."

Master Aniv waved her off. "None of that, Mistress. I just made it to your specifications." He hesitated. "Can I see what you're going to use it for?"

Tala paused. "Maybe? I don't know of anywhere I can safely test it, now that I think about it."

He sighed. "Very well. If you do find a place, let me know what you use it for and how it works, will you?"

"Of course!"

Tala paid the man, and he added a simple rope to the secondary tab so that she could pull that to allow the claw to open.

"Take care, Master Aniv."

"And you, Mistress Tala. Be sure to come back if you need anything else."

"Oh, I will, don't you worry."

* * *

Tala stood within Kit, an old knife around a hundred feet from her as she stood just inside the entrance, the door closed behind her. She had set up the knife so the handle could be the target of her working.

On the ground before her, a gravity neutral tungsten ball sat in the claw, and in the slot in the primary tab rested one of her dimensional anchor darts, locked in place by a clever little catch.

As she concentrated, dumping power into the pull of the sphere toward the knife handle, the claw began to slide across the ground, pulled away from her by the ball.

As the dart reached ten feet from her, or more specifically from the dimensional anchor at her belt, it stopped moving away as the dimensional anchor began to work.

Another minute passed, and the ball and claw slowly lifted into the air, seeming to float as they tried to fall toward the knife handle at the far end of the long hallway.

The slowly building whistle of wind currents began to permeate the space as the air tried to fill in the expanding space and leave the contracting space in equal measure. In these tight confines, that stirred up quite the gale.

Unfortunately, with Kit's limited space, the best she had been able to manage was a one-hundred-foot-long hallway that was three feet wide and six feet high. The remainder of Kit's space was taken up by all her physical possessions, though how Kit made them fit, Tala had no idea.

As the *increase* continued to ramp up the acceleration, the air also started to heat up considerably, shortly before the tungsten ball and front of the claws began to glow bright red from wind whipping across them.

Good enough. Tala grabbed the thin rope that she'd tied to her belt and which led to the other tab on the claw and pulled.

The claw moved back, opening and dropping to the ground with a ringing, bouncing series of impacts. In those impacts, Tala thought she heard the subtle sound of bending metal, but she was otherwise distracted.

The instant it was freed, the sphere plummeted across the intervening space, crossing the ninety feet to the target faster than Tala could track.

The sphere must have slammed through its target and continued on to the back wall because it struck with an impact that seemed to shatter the very air within Kit.

Tala was thrown backward, blasted out of the door at the end of the hallway and into darkness.

*   *   *

-Ding.-
-Unbelievable. How often must you lose consciousness?-

Tala groaned, sitting up.

-Loss of consciousness detected due to full-body exposure to a pressure wave and the following impact with the magically reinforced gate of a dimensional portal. Discrete regenerative systems activated to their fullest capacity to restore consciousness and mobility.-

"I thought you were unavailable."

-Well, apparently, you losing consciousness overrides anything else and brings me back to perform my most basic function. Please stop interrupting. I'm just getting to the good part.-

"Really?"

-Stop talking out loud to yourself. It makes you look crazy. Reinitiating mental delve per last recognized command. All other functions will be offline for the duration.-

Tala sighed, blinking to clear her vision and looking around.

A cloud of dust surrounded her, seeming to be billowing out of the wall nearby, even as it was settling down.

In addition to her slight disorientation due to losing and regaining consciousness, she felt the aftereffects of a *lot* of her bones being rebuilt. Several of her organs seemed to have been ruptured as well, though they were back in order when she checked on them. *Well, that's a successful test… and successful proof that I shouldn't do such tests in enclosed environments.* She really did need to make Kit bigger.

She staggered to her feet and over to the archway, which was all that was left of the doorway into Kit.

She placed her hand on the doorframe and dumped power in. Kit was near empty—likely due to internal damage.

Well, I now know what it takes to break through Kit's door. It seemed like she'd been thrown against the door with just barely more force than was required to break through it, as she'd woken up in the middle of the alley, and the wall that had been across from Kit's opening was undamaged.

As she considered, though, that wasn't a good measure of how much it would take to break in. A blow from the inside, pressure from the inside, was far more destructive than the same force from the outside.

"I'm sorry, Kit. I didn't mean to cause any damage, let alone this much."

Kit did not respond, but it did continue to greedily drink in the power that she provided.

Tala noticed that all the dusty air had been pushed out through the arch, leaving the air within Kit clean and clear. "Good to know."

As she recharged the storage device, a few small items clattered seemingly out of nowhere, through the archway.

Tala quickly identified the items as the remains of the sphere, knife, and claw.

The sphere was little more than twisted splinters of tungsten, still glowing with heat.

The knife was handle-less, the blade kinked and distorted, likely from bouncing around inside of Kit after it was struck.

The claw was bent and twisted but not shattered. *Oh, right. It was picking up the same speed and then dropped to the ground. It effectively skipped across the floor within Kit, while already hot. That's what bent it.*

Tala was left feeling incredibly grateful that she hadn't tested the idea anywhere in the city. The cost to repair the damages would have been exorbitant.

Even now, she was standing in an alley and getting strange looks as the dust settled enough for people to see her from the streets to either side.

With nothing else that she could do, she pulled Kit free of the wall, hanging it back on her belt as a pouch, and left out the less trafficked side of the little space between buildings.

Note to self: This works and is incredibly effective. However, it is not for use in tight spaces.

Chapter: 2
Draining Her Reserves

Tala headed for home. She was a bit irritated that she was coated in dust, but there wasn't really a convenient place to bathe, and she was still dumping power into Kit to the point that she felt quite hesitant about stressing the item by opening a door inside and willing a bathing room to be ready for her.

Maybe when I get home.

It was late afternoon, and the light was painting the snow a golden orange, revealing the playful trails, snow forts, and snowmen, both full and partial, that bore testament to a wonderful day of play for the neighborhood children.

Tala felt a smile tug at her own lips at fond memories of playing with her siblings—and her parents on occasion. *Thank you, Alat.*

She sent her gratitude to her other interface, knowing that she would receive it when she was free once more. Though Tala didn't like that the memories had been dredged up, she found them more pleasant than painful, much to her surprise.

The last rays of the sun were already fading from the sky when she turned down the short front walk and approached Lyn's front door. It was locked, of course, but that was solved by Tala's iron key. With a quick turn, she unlocked the front door and walked inside.

"Is that you, Tala?" The voice floated down the short hall to the entry room.

Millennial Mage, 6 - Fused

"If it isn't, then you're much too free with keys to our place." Tala smiled at the knowledge that her friend was home.

Lyn laughed. "I just grabbed some food. I don't have enough for your appetite, but I can spare some if you'd like."

The mention of food sent waves of hunger through Tala. She'd been a bit mangled by the blast from her tests and had used more of her stores than she'd have liked in the healing.

Though, I'm not going to side-eye the regeneration. Even if I could have gotten to another Mage, paying for a healing would have been much more than the food I consumed for the stores used to allow my scripts to do it.

Over the months of training and monitoring her store levels, she had gotten the impression that she used up about as many days' worth of food from her reserves as it would have taken to heal a given wound. The amount was lessened by the percentage of her body that was actually being healed by the scripts, and the exact nutrients and substances used were different depending on exactly what was being repaired.

Things got more complicated from there, like when she healed something that would never actually heal naturally, but it was a good rule to guestimate what her regeneration would require.

After her overly successful test, Tala had needed to heal basically all her body from a plethora of damage. In the end, it would likely have taken a couple of months for her to recover from the blast… if she even could have.

All told, she was lucky to have any reserves left at all.

Though she'd adjusted to it unconsciously, she was positively light on her feet. *I'm almost halfway back to the weight I should be without my magic, and that doesn't bode well.*

"Since you're offering, I'll take a few bites while I make some of my own." She wiped her feet on the mat that Lyn had out for her, though she felt it was a bit futile. "There's some things I wanted to talk with you about, actually."

As she walked into the room, Lyn glanced her way and blanched. "Tala? What happened?" She stood and quick-walked over, starting to look Tala over. "Did you fall into a flour silo?" She started coughing as some of the dust came off. "No. To the bath with you. Eat after."

"But—"

"No buts."

Tala groused but knew her friend was right. "Fine, fine."

Half an hour later, she left the bath room of Lyn's house and found quite a bit more food awaiting her. "I know it's still not enough, but I thought I'd grab at least a little something more while you were cleaning up."

Tala thanked Lyn profusely and sat to eat.

"Why's your hair up?"

Tala glanced up, taking in the towel wrapped around her head. "Oh. I lent my comb to someone."

Lyn grunted, clearly not understanding, but not caring enough to ask further either.

In truth, Tala was pretty irritated by the need, but she hadn't wanted to take the time with the hot air incorporator to dry her hair more quickly, so she was letting nature take its course.

Lyn gestured to the food, taking the first bite of her own dinner. "So, what did you want to talk about? What happened to you?"

Tala took a moment to examine the grilled meat-and-vegetable kebabs, selecting the one that seemed to most call to her inner hunger. It was mostly meat, though a few mushrooms and a tomato were scattered throughout. "As to what happened to me: I tested out a new method of attack, and it was more effective than I expected."

Lyn hesitated, but when it was clear Tala wasn't going to continue, she shook her head with a sigh. "Not going to tell me more?"

"Anything more would just be boring technicalities." Tala shrugged, tearing into her food.

"Fair enough."

Around a mouthful, she continued, "As to what I wanted to talk to you about…" She pulled Kit from her belt and threw it at the nearby wall, wishing for a door. She'd finished filling the dimensional storage's reserves before finishing her bath, and she was confident in using it again. "I don't really need a room anymore."

Tala turned to look, juices dripping down her chin, along with Lyn, and watched as a door seemed to suddenly be there in the dining area's wall, fully integrated with the house and looking for all the world like it belonged and had always been there.

Lyn blinked, her kebab stopping just before her mouth. "There's a new door."

"My dimensional storage got an upgrade."

"I can see that." She went back to eating.

"So, I don't need a room anymore, though I do like living here. I just need a blank section of wall to use when I'm about."

"Huh. So it seems."

"So, how much to rent a wall in your house?"

Lyn huffed a laugh. "Let's call it one silver a month and be done with it."

"Sounds more than fair. Does that mean you're going to find another person to rent the room?"

Lyn sighed. "Maybe? Against my better judgment, I ended up taking the Archon-level position with the Guild. Pays better, and the work is more varied." She laughed.

"Not like I actually needed the money to begin with. It's just nice to have some help with expenses, and the company is usually a plus." Lyn narrowed her eyes at Tala. "I'm not giving any of your rent back."

Tala held up her hands. "Not asking you to."

"Good. See that you don't."

She grinned at her friend. "I wouldn't dream of it."

They fell back into comfortable silence as Lyn took measured bites, enjoying every careful mouthful, and Tala gorged, only really stopping to go into the kitchen and make herself more to eat. Even then, she was eating jerky, tossing bits out to Terry.

The venture food was coming in handy once again, and she found herself quite satisfied with the purchase for the umpteenth time.

Lyn and Tala did occasionally chat about small things but nothing of real consequence.

As a result, Tala let her mind mostly wander. *I want to apply the body paint tonight, so I don't have to mess with it tomorrow.* As she considered that, and the evening moved toward true night, she realized that she had a problem.

"Lyn?"

"Hmm?" Lyn had finished eating and moved to one of her reading chairs, a book casually open before her.

"You didn't ask about my hand." Tala held up her left hand.

"I figured you'd tell me when you were ready." Lyn didn't look up from her book.

Tala took a moment to shake her head before sighing. *Infuriating woman.* "Fine, fine. So, it's a paint— the gray is, anyway —and I plan on covering myself with it."

"As one does."

She glared, but her friend still hadn't looked up. "As I was saying, I plan on complete coverage, but I realized that I have a problem."

"Your hair?"

"What? No. I'll shave it off, paint my head, then regrow through the layers."

"Sounds like a great way to get ingrown hairs, if you ask me."

Tala frowned. "The scripts include a breaching element. I don't get ingrown hairs anymore, not anywhere, but that's not the point."

"Lucky."

Tala grunted. She certainly didn't miss them, that was for sure. "But, as I was saying, I've realized that I have a problem."

"Just one?"

She took a deep breath and let it out in a rush of irritation. "Can you please stop interrupting?"

Lyn looked up. "As you wish." She put on her best attentive smile.

"I can't do my back."

Lyn just looked at her, waiting.

Tala cleared her throat. "So, would you be willing to paint my back, after I've done the rest of me? I need three coats, but it dries fast and should only take around ten minutes of your time."

Lyn continued to watch her for a long moment before shaking her head. "I don't know what I expected, but painting my friend's hard to reach places wasn't it. Sure, fine. I'll paint your back with whatever nonsense you've cooked up this time."

"Well, to be honest, an alchemist came up with this stuff. I'm just going to use it."

"An alchemist."

"That's right."

"Aren't those the people who prey on people too poor to get proper healthcare?"

Tala bristled. "My family are alchemists."

Lyn blinked, clearly taken aback. "Oh. Oh, Tala, I apologize. I didn't know."

Tala hadn't realized that tears had immediately come to her eyes until they began to fall.

Lyn was up and embracing her again without hesitation. "I truly am sorry. Work's been…" She shook her head. "No, now's not about me. Will you forgive me?"

"You didn't know."

"But I could have."

Tala gave a rueful laugh. "I don't talk about my family. No, you couldn't have."

"Why is that?"

Then, without really deciding to, Tala began to talk.

She told Lyn about her older brother—well, half-brother—and their childhood together, followed by his death; her mother's death at her own birth; and her step-mother, who'd raised her. She told Lyn about her other siblings, and about her father's injury and self-medication, leading to addiction and debt.

She told her everything.

Then, she told her about Alat, in brief, and about the memories that were now being dragged back into the light.

Through it all, Lyn listened intently. She asked some questions, but for the most part, she kept her silence.

In the end, they sat in that silence for a good five minutes, only slightly marred by Tala's continued munching, before Lyn broke it.

"Tala." Lyn breathed in deeply. "This is a chain around your neck."

"Don't I know it."

"You need to address it."

Tala stiffened.

"Go to Marliweather. See them. Reconcile or rail against them, just don't kill anyone. Put it behind you one way or another."

Tala threw up her hands. "That would be great if I can actually do it."

"I can get you a route there and back. It can probably leave in the next week or so. It's a common enough route, without any prominent fringe benefits, so the slots shouldn't be contracted too far in advance. You need to take a contract or two soon anyway, after the long hold-over in Makinaven."

She gave Lyn an irritated look. "You know very well that I'm not talking about the logistics of getting to Marliweather. Terry could have me there in less than two days if we wanted to."

Terry lifted his head from where he'd been sleeping in one of the chairs. He gave her a flat, mildly offended look.

"Sorry, Terry. One day. He could have us there in one day if we wanted."

Terry breathed out a satisfied trill and curled back up.

"The point is: that's not the point."

Lyn mostly contained her smile of amusement. "I see. I'm dazzled by your brilliance."

Tala closed her eyes and huffed a self-deprecating laugh. "You know what I mean."

"I do, I do, but Tala, you need to face this—to face them."

Tala put her head into her hands. "I know, but I don't want to."

"It's easier to simply hate them for what they did than give them a chance to explain?"

"Exactly." She wasn't surprised at her own honesty. Not really. Tala had been dancing around this issue for years, and it all seemed to be coming to a head at last. "Fine. I know you're right. I know that's what's best."

"I'll set up the route, but you'll have to take it from there."

Tala just grunted.

Lyn leaned forward and hugged her again, and Tala accepted the embrace for a long moment before pulling away.

"Now, I need to get naked, get clean, and paint myself."

"Don't let me keep you from a good time."

Tala rolled her eyes and walked to Kit's door, where it still sat in Lyn's living room and dining room shared wall.

"That can't stay there, by the way. Find a place in the hall before you sleep tonight. Alright? It messes with the feel of the place."

She smiled back at Lyn. "Will do."

Without further discussion, she walked inside and closed the door behind her.

Ten minutes later, she was scrubbed clean.

Twenty minutes after that, she was hairless and painted with three layers across every area she could reach, her elk leathers now reshaped into the outfit that most neatly exposed the places she still needed assistance with.

She was keeping her hair from regrowing, so she was effectively bald for the moment. As such, when she walked back out of Kit, she could only imagine how she looked.

A white halter-top, leaving the entirety of her back, shoulders, and arms exposed, was the only color contrasting the dull, metallic gray of most of her skin. The top definitely exposed more than she needed uncovered, but it was the only one that left everything she needed open, exposed.

Across all of that gray, golden light twisted and glowed in powerful, clearly magical lines.

Her eyes felt like they were glowing a brighter red than usual, adding to the aesthetic.

Lyn glanced up when Tala exited Kit and froze in obvious alarm, color draining from her face.

"Lyn! It's me."

"Yeah... I gathered that." She swallowed. "Tala... I don't know that you should go out like that..."

Tala waved that off. "I'll take some precautions, but come on. I need help."

Lyn tentatively came to her as Tala turned around, setting the paint container and a brush on the table as she did so.

The older woman was a bit hesitant at first but calmed as she took up the task of painting Tala's back.

It tickled a lot more when someone else was doing the painting than it had when she did it herself, but Tala had borne through much worse.

In less than half an hour, they were done, the paint was dry, and Tala was regularly clothed once again.

"You still look rusting terrifying."

"One moment." She released the hold on her hair growth scripts, and it grew to the desired lengths. She left it free, allowing it to fall around her face. "Eh?"

Lyn sighed. "Now you don't look quite as daunting, at least not at first glance, but you are glowing, Tala. That might trump any skin coloration."

Tala glanced down, and sure enough, the spellforms were manifesting all across her body. They weren't shining through or above the elk leathers, but her magesight could see them everywhere, visible to others or not. And the external, glowing lines were nothing compared to what was going on inside.

Holly had been right when she had likened the results to a pressure cooker.

Within the nearly impenetrable iron shell, Tala thrummed with power. It had taken a minute or two to really noticeably build, once Lyn had finished, and only now was it getting to a level that felt extreme.

"Oh, wow." The words carried pulses of magic with them out of her mouth that caused the very air to quiver before her magesight.

Lyn was giving her a searching look. "How is the power not leaking out through all your follicles?"

"I'm not sure?" The magic took her every utterance as a momentary chance to equalize with the power in the room around her. *My very voice is shaking the world.* She started to laugh, the world reverberating to that as well, making her laugh harder.

After taking the time to calm down and get herself under control, and then taking more time to convince Lyn that she wasn't going crazy, Tala sat down to continue examining the changes.

Everywhere she looked, she could see power subtly starting to swirl and move.

It took an embarrassingly long time for her to realize that she was losing power from her eyes, if at a *much* slower rate than from her mouth when she opened it.

Similarly, her breath contained more power than it ever had before, even when exiting through her nose.

So, tighten my aura. She did so, closing off those gaps. It wasn't perfect by a long shot, but it at least made her look more like an untrained Mage, rather than a fount made flesh.

Well, all humans are founts in the flesh... So, it wasn't a perfect analogy.

Millennial Mage, 6 - Fused

She could feel her scripts working, remaking her flesh, upgrading it per their prescribed patterns. Before, it had been a subtle thing, only noticeable if she delved deeply and focused her full attention on it. Now, it was almost impossible to ignore.

And it was draining her reserves.

Tala sighed. "Well, I need more food."

Lyn barked out a laugh, having watched Tala closely for the last few minutes of silent introspection. She seemed to relax a bit, apparently deciding that Tala was still herself at the core. "That doesn't surprise me in the least."

Chapter: 3
A Long Night

Tala woke bright and early the next morning—at least, according to her illusory landscape.

Much of the time, magic was just a background part of everyday life, but there were still moments when it really hit her how amazing the power was, such as staring out at a vista that didn't exist, created simply because she wished to see it.

I really do love waking up to that view. Which was probably exactly why it was there. She grinned. Things were looking up. She had money; she had a place to live; and she was growing in power daily, even if just a bit.

Well, I still need to see how the iron body paint has affected things.

Lyn had gone to bed the night before while Tala had made herself another large portion of the venturing food. Once she'd eaten as much as she could stomach, even with her incredible capacity, Tala had placed Kit's door in the hallway, per Lyn's request, and gone to sleep.

Now, as she stretched into wakefulness, she casually checked the time, simply by desiring to know what time it was.

Midnight.

What? She would have sworn she had laid down just a couple hours before midnight. How could she feel this well rested with only two hours sleep?

The answer was obvious as she looked down at her hands.

Millennial Mage, 6 - Fused

The most prominent spell-lines glowed brightly to her mundane eyes while being little more than flickers to her magesight. There were several oddities as she looked closer. The lines didn't actually exactly mirror the golden lines that laced through her flesh. Instead, as she considered and compared, she would guess that the lines of light were the same *magically* but with the medium of air and the line composition of magical power itself.

They were horribly inefficient, hence the glowing, but they were there.

She frowned. *No, they aren't actually there.* As she examined more closely, she could see that the spell-manifestations existed within the dimensions of magic, surrounding her and affecting her without regard for the iron.

The light was simply a physical manifestation of their inefficiencies, so it manifested in the physical world in the closest approximation to the magical dimensions in which the spellforms actually existed.

Tala bent over and rubbed the sides of her head. *Extra-dimensional thinking was never my strong suit...*

All that said, the result was that she basically had a second set of highly wasteful inscriptions perfectly mirroring her first, running purely on the waste energy.

As Holly was good at her job, there wasn't a lot for the secondary set to work with. Even so, with the iron keeping it all contained, even a small amount built up rapidly.

As she examined herself further, diving inside with her magesight, she noticed something that she never really had before: Her flesh wasn't able to take in all that the spell-workings were trying to do.

It was as if many of these spellforms had been designed for a body with higher capacities, and while her form was being remade to meet that demand, slowly, it couldn't yet.

So, as the power washed over a particular part of her, that organ, system, or cell could only take in so much of it. The rest simply dispersed.

She would bet that it had been doing that since she had first been inscribed.

Now, her iron was catching that and perfectly reflecting it back, giving her physiology a second chance to integrate the power. What was missed would disperse and be reflected back, again.

And again.

And again.

All the while, her inscriptions were continuing to add power. This built a resonance within her being, where each aspect of her spellforms became, essentially, standing waves, steadily growing in amplitude.

Pressure cooking indeed.

She hesitated. *I'm mixing metaphors. That doesn't really make much sense...*

She pulled back her minute examinations and took in the look as a whole.

Given the glowing magical lines, combined with her near-metallic-looking gray skin, she probably looked like an animated metal statue.

You know, I've only heard of those in stories, but I bet they're real. Animated metal warriors would be amazing. *I should ask about them at some point.* It was probably a good question for the Archive.

She continued to examine her own hands. She could see the individual lines, and while they didn't really cast light, they were clearly alight.

Tala frowned. *But I have* much *better sight than most people.* She'd have to ask Lyn's opinion.

Millennial Mage, 6 - Fused

Speaking of my eyesight. She felt like it had heightened yet again, if only just, likely due to the reflection of the magic of the enhancements.

She carefully stood and stretched, her body moving more easily than ever before. A part of that was her reduced weight, due to her lower than ideal reserves, but she was also at least a bit stronger than she had been even the night before.

This could get interesting, given enough time. It was also draining her reserves marginally. If her guestimations were correct, she'd need four times the food of a normal person going forward, just to maintain.

Alright then, doubling the meal budget. Six silver a day it is! She hadn't been using even her normal budget, but that had to change. *Especially if I'm going back on the road soon.*

She needed time to think, so decided to go out to the main room for her stretching and exercises. She didn't really take into account how different she might look, however.

As she walked out into the main space where Terry was sleeping, the terror bird's head jerked up, and he immediately vanished.

A pulse of dimensional energy and a blow across her back told her where he'd gone.

She stumbled from the blow, which had oddly felt more bludgeoning than slashing. *He's probably a bit hesitant of unknown threats, given the Leshkin blood that was just recently so prevalent in our enemies.*

She tried to call out to her friend. "Terry! It's me!"

But Terry had flickered again, nearly the size of a horse and with his talons closed around her neck, already constricting her airways.

Tala tried to gasp or pull in a breath, but nothing came past the crushing restriction. His grip was so tight that she thought the blood to her brain might be cut off soon despite her much more resilient physiology.

She pulled Flow from her belt, shaping it into a sword even as it whipped past the bird's extended foot, toward her hand.

As expected, Terry flickered away, avoiding the attack, but in that instant, she sucked in a desperate breath, eyes frantically darting around the space until she found Terry, crouched low in one corner, eyes narrowed in hostile scrutiny.

Tala moved away, putting her back to a wall, and holding Flow before her in a warding stance. "Terry." Her voice was raw, and she hacked out a cough as her trachea reformed, helped by her attempted word, which reinflated the airway as she'd forced it out.

The voice hadn't sounded like hers, but Terry clearly realized something was not as expected, likely given that she'd used his name.

He lifted his head slightly, tilting it to the side as if puzzled.

His eyes moved to Flow and then widened in recognition.

He trilled questioningly.

Tala nodded vigorously, still coughing a little as the regeneration finished its work. "Yeah. It's me."

He walked across the intervening space, showing more caution that she'd seen from him before. He trilled again.

"I thought you saw me last night before we turned in."

He waggled his head side to side, then half-closed his eyes.

"You were too tired to pay much attention?" *Seriously?* Her voice was fully recovered by that point, but it had taken some of her stores. *Great. Need to eat even more, now.*

He bobbed his head in a nod.

She gave a rueful chuckle. "Well. No real harm done, I suppose…"

He let out a bit of a mournful squawk, flickered to her shoulder in his smaller size, and headbutted her cheek.

"Yeah, yeah. I know you didn't mean to hurt me."

He bumped her again, then flickered back to curl up in the corner to await her departure.

Hmmm, I guess I look and feel vastly different with this on. Obviously, it is much more extreme than I expected. I might need to get some sort of solution ironed out before something drastic happens. But it was still very late… or early. *Standard stuff, first. Then, I'll deal with what's new.*

As she moved through her normal morning routine, she had time to think and consider. Inevitably, the more she thought, and the more she considered, the more it became clear that she had something that she had to do.

Thus, once she'd recharged her items, stretched, and exercised—physically, mentally, magically, and spiritually—Tala had decided what she needed to do first. *Well, next.*

She set out for the Archon compound, Terry on her shoulder for the trip.

It was still in the dead of night when they came out of Kit within Lyn's house.

There was a creepy stillness to the place in the dark dead of night.

She glanced to Terry. "Anything off to you, bud?"

He shook himself lightly.

"Fine. It's just me, then." That decided, Tala didn't focus on the odd feeling as she quickly traversed the space and exited the building, carefully locking the door behind herself.

The trip through the city was similarly odd, as there was almost no one around.

She was almost all the way to the Archon compound before she realized what had her so on edge. Her mundane sight had been enhanced to the point that it *almost* looked bright enough to be day, but there was still no one around. Therefore, it gave the city a decidedly abandoned feel.

If it was dark and empty, that would be explainable, but since it looks bright to me, it feels a bit creepy. Satisfied that she had her reason for the odd feeling, she quick-walked the last bit to the Archon compound.

When she strode down the last part of the entry tunnel, she felt a scan pass over her, not through her, and she sighed. *Well, let's get this over with.*

After an instant's hesitation, things became... chaotic.

The air filled with power as it thickened around her, taking on the consistency of cold molasses in an attempt to restrict her movements.

Terry flickered away to the recesses of the atrium before the working fully settled around her. *Good, he'll stay safe.*

Tala was inconvenienced by the thickening of the air, but not that much as it didn't really stress her increased strength, at least not at first.

She did not draw Flow. She wasn't there to fight.

Instead, she raised her hands above her head in the most exposed, unthreatening posture that she could think of.

As if triggered by her continued movement, more power wove through the air around her, and it was suddenly as hard as stone.

Tala thought that she *might* be able to break free, if she had to, but she was sure that whatever had sensed her movement and increased the power of the restraint would just do so again, and she was having enough trouble breathing as it was.

Millennial Mage, 6 - Fused

Behind the counter ahead of her, the assistants had crouched down, and a dome of magical energy too complex for Tala to comprehend easily or quickly flickered into place, clearly projected from an intricate circle of copper scripts beneath the floor, surrounding the front desk.

I really hope I don't have to pay for the use of all these defenses...

A moment later, she felt a magical probe that bypassed her iron, clearly indicating that an Archon was directly behind it, and a voice filled the space, laced with power, "Stop!"

The air became normal once more, and the magically created shield, whatever it was made of, vanished.

A blue—maybe even slightly indigo—aura filled the space, though it seemed to bend and distort to avoid contacting the people in the room, including Terry, if what Tala saw from the corner of her vision was correct. Into the sudden silence, both auditory and magical, a woman strode from one of the side passages coming to stand in front of Tala, looking her over. "Child, dear child." There was a mirth-filled smile obvious across her features. "Even with warning, you still managed to cause us quite a bit of shock."

Tala had the presence of mind to look sheepish, even as she didn't lower her hands. "That is why I'm here, actually. I wanted to see if anything could be done to mitigate misunderstandings or if I should just scrub it off."

"Oh, no! Don't do that. Your progress will be astronomical in that fascinating... suit. We wouldn't want to lose that potential. Humanity needs every edge we can get." She glanced up at Tala's arms, her smile gaining a bit of a grandmotherly bent. "You can lower those, child.

You will not be harmed unless you act completely out of character."

Tala did so. "I'm Tala, though you likely know that. What is your name, if I may ask?" She felt it was best to find out sooner, rather than later.

"You are right, I do know who you are, though we've not had the pleasure of meeting in person. I am Jenna, wife of the city lord of Bandfast."

Tala's eyes widened, and she reflexively asked before she could stop herself, "If you're Reforged, how powerful is he?"

Jenna grinned. "Oh, he's Refined, but he enjoys administration, where I decidedly do not." She shrugged. "It works on every level, actually. I do love that man." Her eyes had gotten a far-off look, but she seemed to shake herself, coming back to the moment. "But we're not here to talk about our relationships."

"I suppose not." Tala swallowed, trying to get some moisture back into her dry mouth. "I... Thank you for not being upset that I tripped the alarms."

Jenna waved that away. "Honestly, ever since Mistress Holly let me know about your plans, I've been expecting there to be an incident *somewhere*." She glanced at Tala. "For future reference, it would have been better for you to come here, first, before painting yourself. We could have helped you, monitored your internal power, and ensured there weren't any unexpected side effects. That said, coming here as your first stop after your experiment is certainly an improvement above what I feared. You are maturing nicely."

Tala blushed, but it was an invisible reaction, only obvious to her because she could feel her own cheeks heat. She immediately tried to distract herself from her own embarrassment. *Oh, why aren't I overheated? This*

Millennial Mage, 6 - Fused

body paint has to trap some; plus, I can't really sweat through it.

The answer was obvious the instant she thought about it: Holly had improved her heat-dissipation scripts after she'd cooked her own muscles by overworking them. *I'm glad those are in effect.*

"Now, we need to do something about your look and how you show up to passive scans. Follow me, please? And bring your friend. I'd hate for the city's defenses to misidentify him." Jenna's eyes had locked onto Terry, where he waited off to one side.

Tala nodded and followed Jenna from the room, Terry flickering to her shoulder at her second step.

As they walked, Tala examined the woman surreptitiously but found she was unable to get a read on her power.

Jenna had pulled her aura back in and seemed to be wearing it like a suit. It wasn't held at her skin like Tala had seen so many other Archons do. Instead, it was extended roughly three inches in every direction, filling in the gaps that might be expected between her feet or between her arms and her sides.

The result was a mostly ovaloid bubble, with the occasional protrusion from the extension of a hand or foot as they walked.

Tala cleared her throat, partially to get the woman's attention and partially to give her an extra moment to think. "So, if I may ask, Mistress Jenna, how are we going to do something about my look?" She tried to mirror the woman's words so as to not overstep.

Jenna glanced back toward her. "Have you ever seen an Archon who didn't look precisely human?"

Tala blinked in confusion at the seemingly unconnected question, then she realized what Jenna meant. "You've developed items to help those with less-than-clean soul mergings function in society."

"That's not an answer to my question, but you did get the point. Several Archons at your raising did petition for you to receive a mitigation, but we thought your changes were not sufficient to warrant it. Besides, at some point, we need to ensure the mundanes are accustomed to the realities of magic." She laughed at her own words. "Though, we've been saying that for centuries. We're too set in our ways, truth be told. Hastel has done a fantastic job in Audel, this iteration. Twenty-seven years in, and no riots. A whole generation has been raised up with a better understanding of how the world really is, though some secrets are still required."

Tala frowned. "Hastel?"

"That's Master Hastel to you, child. He's lord over Audel. He's a bit younger than the rest of us, a bit less set in his methods." She smiled. "He's testing out a new way of doing things, and it seems to be working. I suggest you drop through Audel on one of your routes. It's a lovely picture of how we could be in another few hundred years." She shook her head and sighed. "I wish it were easier to change norms in established cities, but the mundanes don't like it much." She laughed a little. "And if I'm being honest with myself, *I* don't like change that much either, but I will do what is best for us all."

Tala nodded, though she thought she likely didn't understand everything implied by the woman's words.

"But listen to me chattering on. One does seem to talk more as one ages. After you." Jenna gestured at a blank section of wall that they'd stopped in front of.

"The wall?"

"Yes, child. Walk through."

Like all the walls in the Archon compound, there was a thin barrier of power, seemingly designed to increase the integrity of the stone and hold the walls together regardless of the stresses they might be subject to. The fields of power didn't seem to be meant to block a person passing through, though. *An illusion?*

No, she should be able to see that.

Mind magic?

No, Alat would have activated in irritation if they were under the influence of mental manipulation.

I suppose someone could have made the stone permeable.

In any case, the Reforged had given her an instruction, so she should obey.

Tala stepped forward and smacked her face into a hard stone wall, bouncing off.

It didn't hurt, but it was startling. "What?" She looked over to Jenna, who was hiding a smile behind one hand.

"Oh, that was amazing."

Tala frowned.

"It's this way." Jenna pointed to the door behind them both. "Thank you for the smile, though. It's been a long night."

Chapter: 4
Through-Spike

Tala followed Jenna into the room on the other side of the hallway, rubbing her nose after the impact with the stone wall.

Honestly, Tala was a bit irritated by the incident. "Was that necessary?"

Jenna shrugged. "Necessary? No. That said, it was entertaining; it lightened the mood; it conveys an important lesson; and I'm tired. You woke me up."

"I thought you said you had a long night."

"I did, then I finally got to sleep, and..." She cocked an eyebrow and gestured to Tala.

"And I woke you up."

"And you woke me up."

"My apologies."

Jenna waved that off. "Nonsense. It was better for it to happen in the middle of the night than in the middle of the day."

"That is what I had hoped." Tala finally looked around the plain room. Aside from two chairs, most of the space was filled by a huge black box. "What was the lesson?"

Jenna walked in and sat in one of the chairs, Tala following and taking the other.

"Don't always trust those in authority, or with power over you."

It was Tala's turn to cock an eyebrow. "Look at me, Mistress Jenna. What part of this came from following the dictates of authority?"

"Yes, child, you are very rebellious. Good for you."

"That's just insulting."

Jenna hesitated. "It was, wasn't it?" She tapped her own jawline a few times, then shrugged. "I apologize. I did not intend to insult, but the point is still valid."

"Which is?"

She sighed. "You seem to treat people either with complete and utter trust or complete and utter contempt."

Tala opened her mouth to protest, but Jenna raised her hand to stop her.

"I don't mean in the sense that you hate them, simply with how you treat their words, advice, and instructions."

Tala closed her mouth and considered what the other woman had said. *Is that true? Do I consider the source more important than the content?* The more she thought about it, the more she thought it *was* true. *Rust.*

The older woman glanced at the still-open door and gestured, closing it, though Tala didn't see any power connect her to the door.

Alright. That's interesting. At that point, she finally took a good look at Jenna.

While Tala knew that the other woman was older, likely by centuries, Tala would have placed her in her early thirties. *Yet more evidence that I am horrible at judging the ages of Mages.*

She had dark red hair, falling in big curls around her shoulders without poofing up on the top of her head overmuch. She was short, shorter than Tala even, and curvy. The woman was fit, as all Mages tended to be, and she had an almost aggressive tone to her stance and manner of movements, as if she was ready to come out ahead in any interaction, whether verbal, martial, or magical.

Jenna wasn't visibly armed, but that meant little, except that she didn't wish to look armed.

She wore very traditional Mage's robes of some sort of black silk with bronze swirls and no visible clasps. From the toes Tala caught a glimpse of, the Archon wore simple, black leather slippers.

Tala's examination of the Reforged had been quick, barely a glance, but she'd clearly noticed, though she seemed disinclined to comment on it.

Instead, Jenna simply lounged back in her chair. "So, your look isn't actually that great of an issue. We can fix that with any number of little artifacts. The real problem that we should discuss is how you appear to passive scans."

"Couldn't I use something like a collar for arcanous animals?"

"What? No." Jenna gave Tala a searching look. "You know how those work, right?" She glanced to Terry. "I'd have thought that you did."

"Of course I do." Tala felt vaguely insulted. "They change the magical signature of the wearer to one that won't trigger the defenses."

"Ahh, so you understand, you just didn't think it through."

"What?"

Jenna shook her head. "You are a clever girl, and I do mean that. So, you tell me."

Tala took a moment to think and realized the issue. "I've basically no magical signature to alter."

"Precisely." Jenna nodded in approval.

"So, what can we do?"

"The simplest would be to have a breach in your iron layer so that scans could penetrate through and get a good look at you, but that is unideal for many reasons."

Tala nodded.

"We could give you a beacon that would effectively give you a false magical signature. That might work."

"But isn't that dangerous? Couldn't it be taken and used for nefarious purposes?"

"Possibly? But as it wouldn't suppress anything about you, just give off the magical signature, someone else using it would appear pregnant." Jenna grinned. "They'd look like they were pregnant with an Archon at that. So, it would be pretty obvious that it was being misused."

"Pregnant?"

"Two magical signatures in one body. I know it's late, child, but you really should think a bit more before asking questions."

Tala shrunk in on herself, feeling her cheeks heat.

"Now, now, don't do that. An admonition to be better should not be seen as a reprimand."

Tala sat up straighter, feeling somewhat irritated by the woman. "Oh? And should I thank you for the rebuke?"

"Don't be childish. If I thought you an idiot, I wouldn't say anything. Use that mind of yours. It was incredibly capable even before it was enhanced. I've seen your record. You are better than these lazy questions."

Tala felt anger build within her, but she grabbed ahold of the emotion, bent it to her will, and smiled. "I didn't know that pregnant women showed two signatures."

Jenna cocked an eyebrow, then shrugged. "I suppose most probably don't go investigating that type of thing very often, and it's subtle as they are usually close mirrors of each other." She smiled again. "That's why having your signature, or one like it, overtop anyone else's would stand out so starkly."

"That does make sense."

"Now, we're getting rather off track. Do you want one that looks like you, magically, or just one that will keep Guild and Archon facilities from reacting poorly?"

"Why would I need a custom one?"

"Well, there are two types of custom ones we could create, and they each have different uses, aside from the main one, which all have in common."

Tala waited for her to continue.

Jenna pulled a teacup from the air and took a sip of the steaming liquid before placing it back into, well, nowhere. "My apologies, I am still a bit scattered. Where was I?"

"The two types of custom magic beacons?"

"Right! Yes. The first mimics how you are, now, and will always be exactly that, unchanging. It is useful for static defenses and locks, which have been created based on how you are now, but that is almost like creating a key that anyone can use for those. So, we don't usually recommend that one without other, extenuating circumstances. The second is basically a constant mirror of how you should look, just much, much fainter. That allows your current signature to be used for… well, everything as it normally would be."

"How would that be accomplished?"

"In your case, I believe that the easiest way is with a through-spike. I would also recommend it as the best solution."

"A what?"

"A through-spike is an artifact that looks a bit like a very, minutely small grommet. We would tap it in place and remove the center. Your power would then have an outlet, but the through-spike would only let through the barest fraction of a percent of the power, taking from that to color your skin back to your natural shade and render its texture back to looking like flesh, instead of dried paint. It would, of course, be a magical effect, so anything that could disrupt your magic would reveal your actual appearance, and anyone with roughly your magical weight or greater and looking at you with their magesight might be able to see through it."

Millennial Mage, 6 - Fused

"Might? Why only might?"

Jenna paused to consider, taking another sip from her teacup as she did so. "Well, the spellforms are highlighted by the Mage's aura radiating from behind them. The through-spike causes your aura to radiate out from in front of the spell-lines, acting more as a mask than a spotlight." She frowned. "That wasn't well explained."

"Even so, I think I understand." Even as Tala said that, she felt herself flinch internally, expecting Jenna to rebuke her and tell her that she couldn't possibly understand.

Instead, Jenna simply nodded. "Good. It's an esoteric concept, but not really a hard one." She huffed a short laugh. "Any other thoughts?"

"Yes, actually. Why are my eyes and mouth not sufficient?"

"Excellent question, actually. Passive scans don't look for *any* instance of human power, otherwise an enemy could just hold a human-made item and be done with it. The scans look for the magic given off by a creature."

"My aura."

"More or less, yes. But aura is more a function of soul than magic, and passive scans are *notoriously* bad at making judgment calls based on souls. So, we design them to look at the magical portion of a Mage's aura."

"Which my iron blocks, even though I have some power leakage from my eyes and mouth."

"Exactly. Incidentally, even those points of 'leakage,' as you put it, are minute to what they really should be, given your build-up of internal power. Your aura control is ridiculously excellent for such a new Archon."

Tala smiled at the compliment. "Mistress Odera gave me some good pointers, and Master Jevin helped me quite a bit."

"Ahh, I've heard good things about Mistress Odera. She is making quite interesting strides in the study of Archon Stars. It's a shame she isn't suited for advancement. And Jevin? He does take an interest in the Mages in his realm of influence. I'm glad for your extended stay there, though the circumstances were hardly ideal." She took another sip of her tea. "But we're off topic once again. Do you have further thoughts?"

Tala considered, then nodded. "Yes. The through-spike seems... very specifically tailored to me. And as a solution, I should be able to see through them with relative ease, too. So, that doesn't actually explain why I haven't seen non-human-looking Archons about."

Jenna waved that away. "I said this was the best solution for you, child, not the best solution for everyone. Even the manner of this solution would be tailored to you. Others would have their hair or eye color changed or the three-dimensional texture of their skin, rather than the texture as regards to light. They might also need to have certain bodily proportions masked, though those would usually be on a different style of artifact. Through-spikes are generally only used for this when paired with things like living armor or Archons who have reached a level of aura hardening so as to present similar to how you do now."

"You can do this with aura control alone?" Tala gestured at herself. Then, she hesitated. "Wait. Living armor?

"I'll address the first question first: No, child. Some can *look* like that. They do not get the same multiplicative benefits that you do. Honestly, if you work out as I hope, we may try to steer more Academy students toward your style of body enhancements and flavor of offensive powers. Mistress Holly has hinted that your gravity manipulation could be swapped out for all sorts of abilities, depending on the student."

Tala didn't really know what to say to that.

"There would be requirements, of course, and drawbacks. We cannot rule out that your inscriptions were part of the cause of the… fervor with which the Leshkin pursued your caravan. We'll have to test that theory, though, before we raise up a generation with that handicap."

Jenna looked to Tala and seemed to notice something on the younger woman's face.

"But I'm rambling. Your second, mostly implied question: Living armor."

Tala leaned forward.

"It's nothing more than what you are wearing right now. Though, obviously, what you have is not the breadth of all possibilities. It is armor that self-repairs and protects the wearer in some manner. Some have bound creatures to serve in that capacity, though it rarely works very well because either the creatures are very solid, physically, and therefore it is gruesome to manipulate them to be able to be worn, or they are more flexible and therefore less good at being armor." She shrugged. "What you have, with imbued magical defense, is accepted as the best practice."

"But why would this require a through-spike?"

"If you merged it with a being, harvest, or item capable of complete magical isolation, in one form or another."

"Ahh, that makes sense."

"Now, as lovely as this conversation is, would a through-spike meet with your satisfaction as a solution to the current issue?"

Tala shrugged. "I honestly have no idea, but from what you've conveyed, it seems like exactly what I need."

"Wonderful. Now, such things aren't free."

Tala glowered.

Jenna laughed. "I'm not going to up-charge you, child. I remember how tight money can be in the early years, even with as lucrative a career as you've chosen, not to mention the secondary role, and then there are your other side ventures. We only ask for a reimbursement of our costs. We don't even charge you for my time in consulting. I promise you, you couldn't afford me, even with a loan." She gave a mirthful wink.

Tala sighed. "How much?"

"One gold."

She scrunched up her face but nodded. "That's fair, I suppose."

Jenna handed over a tablet with the transaction.

After Tala had confirmed it, Jenna changed what was displayed.

"Here are the places that Mistress Holly said you could have the through-spike implanted without it interfering with any of your inscriptions. I'm partial to inside the nose, but some find that disturbing. Below is a text overview that will explain it clearly enough that you should be able to power the device. I'll give you a booklet with more details before you go, so you can improve efficiency at your leisure."

Tala looked over the available options, read the description, and sighed. "I'll take this one." She pointed to the illustration of the back of her neck, roughly halfway between Alat's core spell-lines and her gate. "I think this will be the least obtrusive. Why wouldn't my regeneration push it out?"

"Your body will push out foreign substances that are embedded into your skin. That is magically enhanced. The through-spike will match your magical signature from the moment of true activation, so it won't be rejected."

"I hadn't considered that side of it. It makes sense."

Millennial Mage, 6 - Fused

"I'm glad I could explain satisfactorily. Now, are you ready?"

"As I'll ever be. Let's do this."

"As you wish." Jenna reached out to pat Tala on the shoulder.

Tala felt strangely warmed by the gesture, but at the last moment, the woman's hand moved with a quick flick, and Tala felt the smallest little sting on the back of her neck, more like a poke than a puncture. She glared for a quick instant before letting the expression fall away and sighing again, shaking her head. "You could have just told me."

"I couldn't have you even subconsciously resisting, or it wouldn't have taken hold."

"And my noticing and trying to flinch away?"

"Yes, your perceptual and reactive speeds were greater than I was counting on, but it doesn't seem to have negatively affected the device."

Tala opened her mouth to ask if it had worked, then simply glanced down at her hands. They looked perfectly ordinary to her mundane eyes.

Her magesight showed her lines of power weaving through the air just outside her body-paint, subtly altering the light as it bounced off of her. Over that, she felt like she was looking at her naked power, unobstructed by inscriptions or workings, though it was much dimmer than she'd have expected.

Tala grunted. "Seems to have worked."

"Indeed."

Tala considered for a moment. "This wasn't developed for disguise creation, was it? If the illusion were replaced with a defense of some kind, then that defense would be devilishly hard to detect."

Jenna's features morphed into a wide, genuine smile. "Well considered. The through-spike's original purpose was the generation of additional defense while letting your magical signature through and allowing it to appear normally distributed. Sadly, through-spikes tend to interfere with one another. One day, when you no longer need an illusory one, you might want to look into the defensive variety."

"I definitely will. Thank you."

As they stood to go, Jenna handed Tala a little booklet. "For your reading—when you have time."

Tala took it with a smile, then glanced at the large black box that had been sitting next to them through the entire conversation.

"What is that, by the way?"

Jenna froze, eyes widening just slightly. "You can see that?"

Tala looked between the woman and the black box. "Obviously. There's no magic to it, but it's a big black box. My eyes work just fine."

"No human should be able to see that box."

Tala hesitated, sighed, and rolled her eyes. "You're trying to mess with me again, aren't you?"

Jenna paused, then shrugged. "I laid it on too thick?"

"Just a little, yeah."

"Fine."

After a moment's silence, Tala cleared her throat. "So, what does it do?"

"What does what do?"

Tala felt her eye twitch. "The black box."

"The what?"

Her face heated in irritation. "The black box that we were just—" Then, she stopped herself and took a long, deep breath.

Jenna grinned. "That *was* much better. Thank you for the feedback."

"You're not going to tell me." It wasn't a question.

"Tell you what?"

Tala closed her mouth, bowed to the woman, and turned to leave.

"Oh, Mistress Tala?"

She paused and looked back. "Yes, Mistress Jenna?"

"Don't paint over the through-spike, please. That would rather defeat the purpose, and I don't actually know what having those magics trapped and reflected back into you would do."

"Thank you for the warning, Mistress. Good day to you."

"And to you."

Chapter: 5
Memories

Tala exited the Archon compound, Terry on her shoulder, looking more normal than she had in a long time.

Except that I'm barefoot in the snow. Yeah, that was telling. She felt a smile pulling at her lips.

With a thought, she dove into her elk leathers and gave power to the path that would give her shoes.

She lifted each foot just a bit as the tendrils grew out of her pants leg around the foot and filled in. After that, the shoes disconnected from the pants, seemingly separate pieces of clothing.

There. Now, I don't look quite so odd.

She wasn't wearing a coat, and it was actively snowing. She sighed.

And it's coming up on five o'clock in the morning. She really shouldn't be out and about if she was any sort of normal.

Good thing almost no one will be out and about to see me.

The snowfall wasn't nearly blizzard proportions, but it was steady and far from sparse.

White flakes drifted down through the nearly completely still air. A silence of a type utterly unique to new-fallen snow blanketed the city.

Tala felt a warmth in her chest at the environment and decided to go for a walk through this seemingly private winter wonderland.

Millennial Mage, 6 - Fused

Terry occasionally shook himself free of snow and flickered to grab all the jerky that Tala tossed for him, but otherwise, he was content to rest on her shoulder.

The streetlights were thoughtfully spaced but dimmed in truth due to the late hour and to the human eye by the steadily falling snow. Nonetheless, the omnipresent white surfaces allowed what little light there was to reach farther than otherwise, giving the whole expanse a nearly mystic glow at this early hour.

Still, Tala had no trouble whatsoever. In fact, she found that it helped offset the wrongness that she'd felt during her trip to the compound earlier that morning.

As she walked, she didn't really have a destination. She just strolled and thought.

She wondered about her family, about her brothers and sisters.

When she tried, to her shock, she realized that she couldn't bring their faces to mind.

That's not right. I have a perfect memory now. But she hadn't seen them in seven years, and she hadn't had her inscriptions then.

I can perfectly recall my imperfect recollection. It was a sick joke.

She had already decided to go resolve things with them.

But what does that mean?

It would certainly involve some exchange of words.

What should I even say to them? She didn't know.

She ran a thousand scenarios through her head but had no reason to believe that any one of them was more plausible than another.

-Ding.-
-Memory recovery complete.-
Alat?

-Tala, these two are... heavy. And I found a few others besides.-

Let me sit down.

-I don't know, what you're already thinking about is pretty important.- There was a slight hesitation. *-Oh, you've been up to some fun things. I like Jenna, and I like the increases I'm feeling from this new body paint.-*

Nonsense, you're getting off track. I need to know what memories were taken. She moved over to a nearby park and found a bench, clearing it of snow before settling down. *I'm ready.*

-Alright, lighter ones first.-

Tala was then forced to relive some of her worst memories of her time at the academy, as well as her departure.

I had suppressed my memory of arriving naked on purpose.

-Yes, but it qualified as one of the memories you commanded I search for.-

I really should track down Phoen. She was kind to me, and I never thanked her properly.

-That would be the civil thing to do.-

That settled, Tala closed her eyes and was treated to a few flickers of her more reckless decisions since graduation, and she felt quite a bit of embarrassment for how foolishly she'd acted. *Well, if you look upon your past actions with shame, it shows that you've grown, right?*

-That sounds like something embarrassed people tell themselves to feel better.-

You're kind of a jerk.

-I am literally you.-

Fine. I'm kind of a jerk.

-Recognizing the issue is half the battle—or something like that. This is character growth in action.-

Millennial Mage, 6 - Fused

Tala narrowed her eyes but had no one to direct her ire-filled gaze at, at least not externally. *You're stalling.*

There was some hesitation, then, finally, Alat sighed within her head. *-Yeah, I am. This isn't great.-*

Well, let's get it over with. Tala swallowed to wet her dry lips and closed her eyes.

-As you wish.-

*   *   *

Tala was in Bandfast, a short walk from the teleportation tower.

As her eyes scanned those she passed, she was able to pick out the occasional Mage by their bearing and fluid manner of movement, not to mention the spell-lines evident across their exposed skin. Most also wore Mage's robes, but not all.

To her surprise, she also saw an arcane—a humanoid arcanous creature.

What had caught her attention at first was the leather collar he wore, though it was tucked low, almost entirely hidden by his shirt's collar. As she'd looked closer, ensuring that her eyes hadn't deceived her and that it wasn't just an odd fashion choice, he'd turned to regard her. She hadn't noticed his gaze until after she'd seen the metallic spell-lines on the leather collar.

When she had felt his gaze, her eyes flicked up, meeting his, and she felt frozen to the spot.

His eyes were blood.

No comparison holds the weight of truth save to say that his eyes were spheres of fresh, liquid blood, unbroken save small circular scabs in place of pupils.

Tala swallowed involuntarily. *He's looking at me.* She tried to smile politely and turn away, but she found she couldn't force herself to turn.

Around his eyes, true-black, smooth skin forced the orbs into starker contrast, making their deep shades seem almost to glow. Subtle hints of gray lines ran under that skin in patterns very like spell-lines but somehow utterly different, like seeing her own language written with a phonetic alphabet. The concepts seemed familiar, while remaining utterly opaque to her interpretation.

She tried to turn away, again, and actually felt resistance like she was fighting herself. A tingle of her own power, emanating from her keystone, preceded the answer: *Allure. He's somehow manipulating the conceptual nature of reality, forcing my attention to remain locked on him.*

As an Immaterial Mage, she could work with non-substance aspects of the world, such as gravity, dimensionality, and molecular cohesion, but warping the magnitude of *concepts*? That… that had disturbing implications.

As if in response to her thoughts, a different set of lines seemed to flicker into prominence around those wounding eyes, and she found herself turning away in confusion. *What is wrong with me? I stare at something I've never seen before and suddenly insist that it must be magic?*

She shook her head at her own foolishness. Then, another prickle rippled out from her keystone, a subtle warning, and she froze. *Conceptual manipulation… Would the concept of believability count?* She spun, her eyes ripping across the crowds, trying desperately to find the arcane once more. She had the flickering impression of an amused smile but nothing more.

After another few moments of frenzied searching, she was left with a subtle, low-level itch from her keystone and the growing concern that she'd somehow imagined the brief encounter. *I... I need to get to the Caravanner's Guild.*

*   *   *

Tala gasped, coming out of the memory. *Oh, rust.* Her whole body was shaking.

-I know, right?-

She'd known that something had messed with her mind on an intellectual level, but she'd never really faced the reality of it, nor even tried to imagine what her attacker had looked like. Now she had a visage for her nightmares.

Why was that memory so much clearer than the others? She could still see those eyes of blood, feel them upon her as if they were watching her even now. Though, she knew that wasn't the case.

-You were inscribed within days of that event, so it had the power and spell-workings to be set in place.-

Why couldn't I remember it if it was stored so clearly in my mind? What did that monster do to her?

-It was surrounded by a haze of unreality.-

That makes no sense. Tala pulled out some jerky for herself and Terry, desperate for some form of normalcy, then started preparing tea for herself on the park bench. *Don't think about it. Don't think about it.*

-That's not going to work, Tala. As to the unreality, that's the quality that your mind uses to surround daydreams and nightmares. Otherwise, you'd lose your grip on reality and start thinking that your dreams, or fantasies, actually happened.-

That did make some sense, even if she didn't really like it. *But I can recall my dreams if I really want to.*

-Ahh, but part of what was done prevented you from really wanting to.-

Tala swallowed again. Alat was right. Even Alat's reticence to show them to her might be some lingering aspect of those magical effects.

-The next one is longer. Is now a good time? I think it should be now.-

Absolutely not. I assume it's from the caravan trip to Makinaven? Tala hesitated. *There aren't any others, are there?*

-No, there aren't any others. Our mind is free of that creature beyond those two incidents.-

Shouldn't we remember any time we came in contact with the Culinary Guild's magics?

-Nope.-

But... Oh, right. Their magics make them uninteresting, so I never focused on them to begin with. The arcane was irrevocably interesting, so he had to suppress the memory in some other manner.

-Precisely. Wow, talking with Jenna really caused you to think things through more.-

Tala glowered again, pouring her tea and tucking away the supplies that she'd used to make it. *In either case, I don't really want to relive another memory of him right now.*

-Well, tough. You need full context when you report.-

Really? She felt a bit of exasperation. Why had Alat even asked if she was just going to force the memory through regardless?

-Yes.-

Tala huffed a bit, then let out a nervous laugh. *I suppose there's no sense in arguing with myself. Let's do this.*

She swallowed her fear, along with some tea, and closed her eyes.

* * *

Millennial Mage, 6 - Fused

Tala sat atop the cargo slot wagon, in the open plains just south of Bandfast. Most of the caravan was asleep, and it had been a *long* day.

She took her time, finishing her third miniature chicken pot pie. The hot food allowed her to relax just a bit more as she kept her gaze moving over their surroundings. *What a day. I'll need to thank the head cook for this, too.*

"You know, you humans are so... fragile."

Tala whipped around, staring at the figure standing on the other end of the wagon top.

What caught her attention at first, aside from someone suddenly appearing behind her in the Wilds, was that his eyes were blood.

No comparison held the weight of truth save to say that his eyes were spheres of fresh, liquid blood, unbroken save small circular scabs in place of pupils.

Meeting that gaze, she felt frozen to the spot.

Around his eyes, true-black, smooth skin forced the orbs into stark contrast, making their deep shades seem almost to glow. Subtle hints of gray lines ran under that skin in patterns very like spell-lines but somehow utterly different, like seeing her own language written with phonetic alphabet. The concepts seemed familiar, while remaining utterly opaque to her interpretation.

Why does he look familiar? Her magesight was screaming at her, and she finally registered what it was saying. *He doesn't have a gate.*

Instead, he was drawing in power from the surrounding air and burning it within himself. The ratios were incredibly off-kilter. He was using massively more than he could draw in from the relatively magic-poor air.

"I saw your beacon of power. Thank you for that. I'd have hated to miss your departure." He smiled, his perfectly white teeth flashing in the fading light. "I love your eyes, by the way. You definitely lived up to the potential I saw in you." He shook his head and clucked his tongue. "That said, I must admit, I misjudged you." His voice had a strange resonance. A clarity like a trumpet sounding on a frozen winter's morning.

"Do I know you?"

He laughed lightly, a sound like a steep mountain stream, splattered in flesh and burbling with blood.

How can someone even make that sound?

"We met, briefly." He gave a half-smile. "I'd thought you would be reckless enough to profit me." He glanced away, seeming to be trying to catch sight of something in the distance, to the north.

"You think I'm not reckless enough?" That thought broke through the odd, strange horror of the situation.

He refocused on her. "Hmm? No. You are, if anything, more reckless than I'd thought, but for some reason, you aren't reckless on things that *matter*."

"I'm... sorry?" She definitely felt the overwhelming desire to apologize properly, to abase herself, but resisted. *I should be sorry for inconveniencing this creature. Why am I resisting?*

He waved dismissively. "I'm just trying to decide if it would be worth breaking the bond between your body and soul."

Tala instantly had Flow in her hand, three void-channels holding it strongly in the form of a sword. "You will not." She was utterly certain of that.

Does the bond really matter? What was happening to her thoughts?

The light of day was fading quickly, but at that moment, sunlight stabbed through distant clouds to brightly illuminate those directly overhead, bathing the two figures, standing atop the cargo wagon, in reflected light. In that new illumination, the silver lines on the being's skin came into greater view. He was frowning. "Oh, don't be tiresome. Your only task here is to let me pick your brain to answer my questions so I can make a properly informed decision." He leaned forward just slightly, slowly looking her up and down. "That is a fascinating Way you're using there. It looks like it lacerated your soul as you learned it." He laughed again, and Tala found her grip weakening. "Some scars can be useful, I suppose."

Why would I want to hurt such a being? She shook her head, detecting the subtle pressure on her mind. *How?* The scripts around her eyes were guzzling power, trying to keep *something* out, and they were failing. *Wait, why hasn't anyone else noticed him?*

She tore her eyes away and looked around. She was horrified to see that every creature in sight was frozen in place, whether human, ox, horse, or Terry. By their slight swaying and blank expressions, it appeared that they were somehow being subdued into a nonsensical state rather than physically restrained by some means.

Tala closed her eyes, then, and felt her thoughts clear. *He was getting in through my eyes.* Were her palms going to be an issue? She desperately hoped not and clenched her hands into tighter fists, Flow firmly locked in her right hand.

"What is this? You are thinking on your own volition?" Light steps sounded as the being approached.

Tala struck out blindly with Flow and heard a sharp, hissing intake of breath.

"How can you attack me?"

Tala dropped into a defensive stance, bracing herself as well as she could for attacks from an unknown direction.

"You dare? I gave you the form you need, the path to power, the path to become *useful*, and you take it for yourself, for your own use. I come to talk, and you choose violence?"

Her head snapped to the side as she was struck with a blow that would have felled one of the caravan's oxen.

Tala rolled with the hit, moving the bare minimum to orient on her attacker, sweeping Flow in a covering circle to cut at whatever had hit her.

"No. You are different than before. You have done *things* to yourself. Yours is not a useful insanity. This cannot be allowed." There was a finality to the statement.

Tala didn't even register the hit before she was airborne.

As expected, she came down faster than anything on this world had any right to, and she skipped across the plains, her body digging furrows in the soil with each skipping impact. Her endingberry power was running dangerously low.

She almost smiled as she was reminded of her 'fight' with the cyclops. But Grediv wasn't here to take advantage of the distraction she provided this time. She was on her own.

I can't fight like this. I have to risk it. Her eyes snapped open, and she oriented herself, vaulting back to her feet, spinning in a circle until she saw the caravan in the near distance, a figure standing on the cargo wagon's top.

He was more of a beacon than Tala had been with all her void-channels dumping power outward.

The aura underlying the power was a deep green-blue. *Rust me to slag.* How had she not noticed that earlier?

With each passing moment, however, the aura was shifting more toward green.

He's losing power by the second. I just need to outlast him. She didn't need her eyes open to do that. Before she could close her eyes, however, the option was taken from her.

Without any appearance of movement, the figure was before her once more, hands on either side of her head.

"It seems that you would take *much* too much power to kill, or more time than I have. Even so, I cannot leave you with memory of this."

The scripts around her eyes were overwhelmed in an instant, pushed aside rather than burned away, and try as she might, she couldn't overcome the compulsion that prevented her from closing her eyes, not even to blink.

His face filled her vision.

"Interesting use of iron. So, that's how you were able to move so freely." The sides of her head blazed with heat for a brief moment before iron dust showered down on her shoulders.

The being briefly flicked each hand away then back to her head, clearing the limb of rust. Then, there was a renewed pulse of power.

Tala felt something try to invade her brain, but her very being rose against the assault. She used every scrap of strength she could draw upon, barely managing to shelter her mind. A pebble before a hurricane.

Even so, the edges of her mind weren't set, yet. Her magesight, coupled with her mental scripts, allowed her to watch, helpless, as her short-term memory was shredded into—

Why am I panicking? What was that daydream, again? Tala tried to shake off the lingering vestiges of an overactive imagination but found her head locked in place, blood filling her vision. *Not a figment?* Brief shreds of memory came floating back. *It was real?! It—*

Power washed through her mind, and her eyes closed of their own volition.

There was an odd grunt, and something that was clearly a curse in a language she didn't know. A voice she'd never heard before muttered under their breath, "How heavy are you?"

Her mind was hit, once more, and her thoughts—

There was a pulse of power, quickly fading into the distance, and Tala's eyes snapped open.

She was lying on the ground, staring up at falling snow and clouds, which were just losing the last light of day.

Where am I?

"Mistress Tala?" Mistress Odera was calling her.

*   *   *

Tala came out of the memory, shaking so much that she almost spilled her tea. She needed to focus. She couldn't get him out of her head, so she needed to focus on the minutia. That should let her push past the horror of what she'd just re-experienced. *Why was my first impression of him almost identical between the memories?*

-Because it was your first impression. You hadn't changed that much in the intervening time, so you thought very nearly the same things upon first noticing him.-

That made a lot of sense. The fear was still there, a raging beast just out of her field of view. *Focus, Tala. He's... powerful, but we knew that.*

-And he wanted to kill you, or take you with him, but he couldn't.-

Not helping, Alat. I know you feel this fear, too. I need help. I'm... I'm close to being overwhelmed here.

-What drove him off?-

Xeel's approach. Thinking of the massively powerful Archon calmed Tala, somewhat. It helped her focus.

-Xeel's approach.-

Millennial Mage, 6 - Fused

There really wasn't any choice in the matter. She now had a task to perform. *We need to tell someone about this.*
-Back to the compound?-
Tala nodded, firm in her resolve. *Back to the compound.*
While Tala had walked quite the distance, she had been meandering. Thus, she hadn't displaced herself too far from where she'd started. Consequently, she was back at the long, tunnel-like entrance a scant few minutes later.
Tala strode back into the Archon compound, and none of the defenses reacted to her entry.
Well, that's good at least.
She was approaching the sleepy-looking young man, who was the current attendant at the round welcome desk when she noticed Jenna standing beside her.
"Mistress Tala, back so soon? Did something go wrong?"
Tala did her best not to show any reaction to the woman's sudden appearance, but she felt her eye twitch just a bit. *That's becoming a habit...* "There is something that I'd like to report. This is likely not the best place. It's too public."
Something in Tala's demeanor must have clued the Archon in to the seriousness of the situation because any hint of levity vanished from her features. "Yes, of course. Right this way, please."

* * *

"And then I came back here," Tala finished somewhat lamely.
-No kidding; that was a lame ending. 'Oh, Mistress of the city, there is a great evil that might be among us. So, I came here.'-
Shut up.

-You literally can't make me.-
I can do another, even more esoteric query.
-You wouldn't dare.-
Try me.

There was a short silence before Alat responded. *-Fine.-*

Jenna sat back in her rather comfy-looking armchair, clearly considering, just as clearly unaware of the argument going on in Tala's head. "I'll have a lot of questions for you, and I'm sure many others will as well."

-If I may speak, I have a suggestion.-

Tala sighed internally. *Fine. What is it?*

-Why don't we just give her access to the memories?-

We can do that? Tala knew it was theoretically possible, but she had no idea how such a thing would be accessed by another person, what it would do, or anything, really.

-Of course. They're all stored in the Archive, now. We can share any part of our mind with anyone we wish. I can gate it so they only see and hear what we saw and heard, rather than getting our inner thoughts, or I can allow our inner voice to overlay, so they can hear your thoughts at the time.-

Unmodified. As close to complete as possible, please.

"Mistress Tala? What's going on? You seem distracted. Is it the… alternate interface you mentioned?"

"Yes. We have an idea."

That got a raised eyebrow, but Tala pressed on.

"What if I just give you access to the memories in question?"

That seemed to catch Jenna off guard. "I wasn't aware that you were a mind mage or an illusionist of that caliber."

"No, no. They are stored in the Archive. I did try to explain that earlier, but I suppose that was the least of what I conveyed."

Jenna nodded slowly. "That's worth a try. Sure." She pulled out a slate, but before she could start working on it, Alat spoke into Tala's mind once more.

-No need for that.-

"No need for that."

-I can grant her access without a contract or slate and... done.-

"You should have access, now."

Jenna cocked her head, then shrugged. "Alright." She gestured at one wall, and the stone moved aside, revealing an illusion array very similar to the one Boma had on his desk. Though, if Tala had to guess, she would say that this one was more intricately constructed.

After a moment's manipulation, Jenna brought up the memories, and the two women watched them together.

When the second one finished, Jenna was silent for a long time.

Tala still had a lot to do before Terry's first day sparring alongside her. Thus, she was eager to depart. "So... do you need anything else from me?"

Jenna scoffed. "I'll need to show this to my husband and several others of note. Do I have your permission?"

-Granted.-

"Yes. The Archive should allow that, now."

"Thank you, Mistress Tala. This is a disturbing revelation, but I am glad to have it brought to light. I am sure we will be in touch."

-She can just update a note for you in the Archive. I'll notice the new access and get it immediately.-

"I believe that you can just put a note for me in the Archive and grant me permission to view it. I'll see it and act accordingly."

Jenna nodded slowly. "As you say. I'll use that method if it isn't time critical but—"

Tala held up her hand. "My apologies, Mistress Jenna, I don't mean to contradict you, but that will be the fastest way to reach me, regardless of the circumstances." *Assuming you don't go offline again.*

-All the more reason to keep from giving me over-taxing commands.-

The older woman regarded her for a long moment, then nodded again. "As you wish."

Tala stood from her own chair. "Now, if you will excuse me, I have a breakfast appointment."

Jenna stood as well. "You seem remarkably calm, given what you've just unveiled."

Tala gave a nervous, almost manic giggle. *Don't think about it. Don't let it sink in.*

-That's really not healthy… or really possible anymore.-

Hush, you. I'm coping. "Oh, I just can't let the fear settle in. Gotta keep moving, you know?"

Jenna gave a slight bow of her head, but there was clearly concern in her expression. "Take care of yourself, Mistress Tala."

Tala bowed in return. "Please protect us all, Mistress Jenna." *Because I certainly can't.*

Without another word or backward glance, Tala strode away, leaving the Archon compound behind.

Chapter: 6
Crazy

Tala was breathing hard and raggedly as she trudged through the city streets. More and more people were joining her on the thoroughfares, heading off to start their days.

Her heavy breathing wasn't because of strain from the exercise, not in the least; she was falling under the stress brought on by her memories, still swirling through her head, and the eyes that wouldn't leave her alone despite their absence.

She shuddered involuntarily.

A passing stranger paused, seemingly noticing the reaction. "Miss? Are you okay? Are you cold?"

Miss? Her eyes flicked to her hands. The illusion hid all evidence of spellforms. *Right!* "Oh, I'm fine. Thank you for asking, though." *That really was quite kind of him.*

"Are you sure? I'm almost home, and I have another coat there. It's really no trouble." He started to shift out of his large, thick, warm-looking coat. *Maybe I am a little cold.* Still, she couldn't take the stranger's coat.

Tala held up her hands, feeling a bit embarrassed. "No, really. I'm fine. I'm almost to where I'm going."

He hesitated, then shrugged, pulling the coat fully back on. "As you wish. I hope you get warm soon, though. Yeah?"

She smiled. "Thank you. I'll do my best."

-Tala.-

Millennial Mage, 6 - Fused

-That was quite a nice man; you should give him some money.-

That would be insulting. He was just being kind. Tala waved goodbye and continued on her way.

-People always like money… No. That's not right. Not everyone is so focused on money. Why do you like it so much?-

Tala suspected that she knew what Alat was doing, and she was grateful for the distraction from her disturbing memories, though she'd never consciously admit it. Instead, she groaned. *I don't like it, per se. I find it useful, and I often have need of it. After all, it is required for basically everything I want or need.*

-Right. He'd probably say the same. You should go give him some.-

Tala's eye twitched, even though she knew that Alat was purposely trying to draw her mind away from less pleasant things through irritation. *Too much would be showy, too little would be insulting. How much do you suggest I give him?*

There was a protracted silence as Tala continued on her way. *-Yeah. Let's not do that.-*

Glad we're in agreement.

She still had more than an hour before she had to meet with Mistress Odera for breakfast. So, she decided to run by the teleportation tower to see if Phoen was on duty, though something told Tala it was unlikely.

-Tala.-

-She's not on shift right now.-

How could you possibly know that? Despite her doubt, she stopped, stepping to the side of the street so that she wouldn't block traffic.

-The shifts are a matter of public record. I'm looking at them right now. She comes on shift in a little over an hour.-

Ahh, alright then. Well, what should we do?
-Get there early, get a first breakfast, and read a book?-

As ideas go, that's good enough to go with. Tala turned and wove her way through the morning traffic, which was now in full swing, making her way to the Caravan Guildhall.

She walked through the main atrium and into the side of the building that housed the restaurant and lounge, waving a greeting to Cran from across the room as she entered before grabbing a table in the back corner.

She mentally paused on Cran, even as she continued to settle in. *He's a Mage, not an Archon.* That sat oddly with her, as she'd been mainly dealing with Archons of late. *I suppose that most Mages are Archons?*

-Tala.-
-The majority are, yes.-

How can that be true? I could guess, but I'd rather know.

-Well, I'm not going to take the time to research it at the moment, unless you command such, but I have some informed guesses.-

Let's hear it.

-Mages age and fount-out, assuming they aren't killed on the job. Archons, unless they are killed, live a very long time, slowly gaining in power.-

So, Mages are like journeymen, magelings are like apprentices, and Archons are like masters of a craft?

-More or less.-

But there are almost always more journeymen and apprentices than masters.

-Of course, because most masters aren't immortal.-
Ahh, yes. That does skew things, doesn't it.

-If it helps, by 'majority,' I just mean that more than half are Archons. It's not a lot more, though the exact

numbers aren't a part of public record. I can put in a request?-

No, that's not necessary. Thank you, though. We can drop it for now. She smiled to herself. *The question I want answered, now, is what to read.*

-Tala.-

-I have a suggestion.-

Do you have to proceed so many of your comments with my name?

-I could go back to DING.-

Tala jumped slightly at the sound within her own head. *Yeah, please don't.*

-Alright. What about: HEY! Listen!-

Tala felt her eye twitch. *That would get irritating, really, really quickly.*

-Then, Tala will work for now?-

For now... see if you can remove that requirement?

-I'll see what I can do.-

Incidentally, we were already talking. Why did you have to get my attention again?

-You had explicitly stated that a conversation was over. Thus, I was required to treat my next comment as unsolicited.-

Tala shook her head but was smiling. *There are a lot of kinks to work out, here, I suppose.*

-So it seems.-

She looked up as the server came her way. The young man's arrival caused Tala's stomach to growl.

-I know he's attractive, but keep it together. You're an Archon, after all.-

Tala flushed before having the realization that she didn't know if it would transmit through the illusion.

-You're just trying to distract yourself.-

Tala cleared her throat and responded to the server, ignoring Alat.

She picked out a large spread of food from the late-night menu and thanked him for taking her order.

He smiled appreciatively at her thanks and departed, promising to get the food as soon as possible.

-Tala.-

-Isn't it a bit early for fried chicken?-

I thought Terry might like some.

-I know you didn't order it just for him.-

Well, fine. I want some. What were you saying about having a book suggestion?

Without preamble, a book was floating in front of her. There was no flash, no fading into existence. It was just… there. *-Take a look. It's the booklet on your through-spike. Blessedly, the contents are freely available to you through the Archive. They were arranged thoughtfully enough for the average Archon, but I've reorganized it into an order that should make it better for you, so that you can get the best efficiency boost in your use of the item as quickly as possible.-*

Tala reached out, feeling deeply skeptical.

Even so, she would have sworn that she could feel the book. *How are you doing that?*

Then, Tala shook her head.

Never mind. The feeling is as much a figment of my mind as the visual. Of course, you can fake senses other than sight.

-Correct.-

Once she stopped trying to see through the illusion, once she allowed her skepticism to lapse, the tome seemed to solidify in her hand, and she was able to handle it exactly like any other book.

This is pretty odd, Alat.

-It's a perk. Enjoy it. But trust me, I know that it will take a lot to get used to these new features.-

Millennial Mage, 6 - Fused

Tala cocked her head to one side. *A pun on your own name?*

-*I'm entitled.*-

She grunted. *Fair enough.*

In no time at all, Tala was reading the book just as she would any other, and true to Alat's word, the contents were arranged exactly as she would have hoped, filling in her greatest gaps in understanding right up front, then polishing out the finer points as she continued.

She could practically feel her through-spike becoming more efficient, using up less of her reverberating power.

The server returned with her food, giving her a bit of an odd look before departing.

Not everyone's a reader, I guess.

Tala helped Terry try a bite of each dish, but in the end, he was happy simply consuming a large quantity of jerky, delivered to him in the usual manner. What that meant was that between basically every bite, Tala flicked out a bit of the jerked meat. Terry caught each with dimensional manipulations too quick to notice, save the resulting ripples of power.

She continued to read as she ate as well, finishing the food with speed that bordered on scarfing without ever having to pause her study of the book before her.

It helped that the book didn't make her joints or muscles cramp to hold in one hand, and she found it trivially easy to turn the page with the thumb of the same hand whenever she needed.

The server cleared the dishes, and Tala thanked him, letting him know that she was expecting to be joined shortly.

He bowed and promised to return when the other party arrived. He presented Tala with a tablet to pay for her already consumed food, and she paid without complaint. After all, she'd been able to sneak in her order from the late-night menu. Three silver wasn't that bad for the spread that she'd devoured.

Returning her focus to the book, Tala smiled. *This is perfectly put together.*

-I do try.-

Tala hitched for a moment. *Right, you rearranged it... and this isn't real.* She lifted the book slightly. It felt less substantial as she considered its unreality, the truth of it showing through as she considered it.

-Nope. It's completely a figment of your mind.-

She felt her cheeks heat again. What had the server seen? A woman staring at her own hand with rapt attention for the better part of an hour?

-That is probably how it looked, yes.-

Do I have to hold it?

-No, that's just a crutch until you can consistently manipulate the perceptual illusion with your conscious mind. I could do it for you, but I've devised a way for you to gain better conscious control of your new options, given the Archive link. This is step one.-

Tala almost protested, but then she remembered how the book was *exactly* right for her. *Alat really does know me well enough to provide that.*

-Rusting right I do. Speaking of that, I have quite a few minor modifications to your daily training regime.-

Wait. There's something wrong with my routine?

-No, there is nothing specifically wrong, but I think we can modify it to give you better results. Improve it, as it were.-

Tala was basically always open to learning, so she shrugged. *Okay. Let's do it.*

-Great! Consider me your personal trainer from here on out.-

She was suddenly a little hesitant. *What exactly did I sign up for...?*

Millennial Mage, 6 - Fused

-Exactly as much improvement as you can take.- Then, somehow, Alat winked at her.

Tala didn't see any eyes, nor did she, herself, wink. Even so, somehow, she knew that Alat had winked at her. *Did you just project the concept of winking at me?*

-I did, indeed.- Alat seemed quite proud of herself for that. *-I haven't had that much time to practice my abilities since I came into existence. The breadth of them is really quite fascinating.-*

Tala held in a groan, though it was pretty useless of her to try to hide reactions from Alat.

-Don't be like that. You have hands and feet and, you know, senses. I have these. Don't begrudge me my tools.-

Fine, fine.

That settled, Tala decided to go back to reading the book that didn't exist so she could ignore the voice inside her head.

That sounds pretty crazy, when I think about it that way.

-Tala, you are crazy in innumerable ways, but that doesn't make you any less you.-

That… didn't actually contain anything meaningful, did it?

-Of course not, but you feel better, right?-

Tala glowered at the nonexistent book.

-I thought so.-

She decided that the best path was to not engage. So, she went back to reading.

Tala finished the little booklet and was just considering what else she should read when Mistress Odera walked in.

Tala waved the Mage over and stood as she approached.

"Good morning, Mistress Odera."

"Good morning, Mistress Tala. You're looking… uninscribed. What did you do?"

Tala grinned, having expected something like this. "Well, I've got quite a bit to tell you, actually."

They sat and ate, chatted and discussed. The server was mildly confused when Tala ordered more food but didn't deign to comment.

Mistress Odera, as usual, had some anecdotes of dubious authenticity but which still allowed Tala to think about the problems in different ways.

Their time was shorter than usual as Mistress Odera had an appointment, but she expressed her appreciation when Tala let her know that the next destination Tala wanted to head toward would be Marliweather. The older woman promised to approve the venture and be available to join Tala on it when the request came through.

They bid each other goodbye and parted ways.

Tala pulled on her gloves, moving toward the exit to the Caravan Guildhall. As she did so, she noticed Lyn and waved to the Archon, who seemed rather engrossed in her conversation with a young, bald woman. *Is that a mageling?*

It didn't really matter.

Well, it *hadn't* really mattered until Lyn noticed Tala's gesture and waved her over.

I wonder what this is about.

As she got closer, Tala got a better look at the young woman. *Young, she's basically my age. New graduate? New arrival?*

As Tala walked over, Lyn smiled and gestured to the woman, who still hadn't turned around. "Tala, this is mageling Kannis."

What? No...

The girl turned around, and Tala felt herself stiffen.
-*Tala.*-
-*The plot thickens.*-
Hush.

Millennial Mage, 6 - Fused

Kannis was a student at the academy while Tala was there. An Immaterial Creator specializing in information exchanges and processing. *Very similar to Lyn, now that I consider it.*

Though, the woman lacked any sort of inscriptions at the moment. *Newly arrived, indeed.*

Tala and Kannis had never really interacted. Kannis had been relatively popular, in a quiet sort of way, and Tala had chosen the path of utter anti-sociability.

"Hello, Tala, was it?" Kannis held out a hand. "It's a pleasure to meet you."

Tala took her hand in a bit of a daze. "It's mutual, I'm sure."

Her eyes darted to Terry, then away. "Your pet bird is very handsome."

"He's more a friend than a pet, but thank you." She shrugged and tried to smile.

"Oh! Thank you for letting me know." She glanced down at her feet. "So, what do you do for the Guild? I've just graduated, and I am so excited to get started."

No. Tala's mind hitched at the very possibility, threatening at the edges of her awareness. *Oh, please no.*

Lyn cleared her throat, seemingly deciding that it was time to interject. "Kannis, it's *Mistress* Tala. She is a Dimensional Mage, and a Mage Protector."

Kannis's eyes widened, and she gave a formal bow. "Oh! My apologies, Mistress." Her eyes flicked over Tala, and she frowned just slightly. "I'm sorry for whatever happened to your scripts. I'm in a similar position, though I suppose my state is standard for my station."

Lyn seemed to notice the apparent absence of Tala's spell-lines at that point, too. "Yeah, I'd love to hear that story. I actually expected..."—she shook her head, coming back to the present—"but that's not pertinent at the moment."

Kannis wasn't done, however, as her frown had only deepened. "Wait… did Mistress say that you're a Dimensional Mage and a Mage Protector?"

Tala found her voice enough to respond. "That's right."

"Forgive my ignorance, but shouldn't the Dimensional Mage be protected beyond all else, as basically the most critical part of any caravan?" Kannis seemed rather proud of her knowledge.

Tala opened and closed her mouth a few times, struggling to find something to say.

Lyn hid her mouth behind a hand, but not before Tala caught sight of a mirthful grin.

Tala cleared her throat, centering herself. "While, yes, the Dimensional Mage is basically the keystone of any given caravan, it is efficient to have me able to fill multiple roles, so long as I am not on the front line of defense, except in dire need."

"Has that worked out well?"

Tala immediately thought of the Leshkin.

Lyn was practically dying as she held in her laughter behind the young woman's back.

"With one notable exception, yes. It's worked quite well." Tala practically glared at Lyn around Kannis.

"Oh, that's fascinating. What was the exception?"

Tala returned her attention to the mageling. "The Leshkin in the southern forest. They didn't take too well to something about me, and I ended up being the target of their attacks more than once."

"Leshkin?" Kannis hesitated for only a moment. "Oh! I remember those. We studied them in my History of Recurring Threats to Humanity class. They sounded like horribly difficult opponents."

Millennial Mage, 6 - Fused

"They were." *History of Recurring Threats to Humanity?*

-Tala.-

-You were bored in the class and never really paid attention. It was mainly a discussion class, and you participated exactly, and only, as much as was required to pass. You really weren't that good a student for most of your academic career.-

Oh... I thought I was a good student, all things considered.

-Hardly. You excelled in every class that you cared about, but those were few and far between.-

Tala grimaced, even as Kannis turned back to Lyn, who had gotten herself under control by that point. "Now, Mistress Lyn, what do you think of my proposal?"

Tala frowned. "What's this about, Lyn?" Her earlier concerns resurfaced. *Why did she call me over here?*

Lyn grinned at her friend. "Well, Kannis here is asking if I'll take her on as my mageling."

Rust.

"And, I think I'm going to say, 'yes.'"

Kannis gasped and clapped her hands in glee. "Oh! Thank you, Mistress Lyn. You won't regret this."

Double rust. Tala knew this was more than just an addition to Lyn, else the older woman wouldn't have involved Tala at all. *She's going to live in our house...*

Alat just laughed and laughed and laughed.

Chapter: 7
Adjusting Your Senses

Tala took a moment to collect herself. *Kannis is going to be Lyn's mageling, and she's going to live with us.*

She didn't really know how to feel about that. How could she cope with another person suddenly rammed into such a core part of her life? *What can I do? Can I forbid it?*

-*Tala.*-

-*Only when you're here.*-

That caused Tala to recenter, if only just. *Fine. Only when I'm here.* That crystallization of the thought helped her pull back to the moment and realize that the others were watching her, waiting for a response.

Tala pasted on a smile. "That's big news. I didn't know you were considering taking on a mageling, Lyn."

Kannis glanced between them, a thoughtful look on her face but didn't comment.

Lyn shrugged. "I've been considering it, and this one came and asked. I've just finished going through her records, and I think it's a good match. In fact, if I am going to take on a mageling, there likely won't be one better. She spent the last two months taking an intensive class on the Archive, its history, and functions."

That tracks. I left as soon as they'd let me. Most who arrived when I did would have stayed on for one or more extra classes to round out their employment opportunities. "That sounds incredibly useful."

Millennial Mage, 6 - Fused

-To say the least. I should see if— Oh! Nice! The reference materials for that class are part of the public record. We should read this at some point.-

There was a moment's pause.

-Yeah, I'll restructure it for you. This is not well put together for quick learning.-

Tala cleared her throat. "So, to what do I owe the pleasure of being included on this weighty decision?"

Lyn nodded. "Well, it is traditional for a Mage to provide housing for her mageling."

Tala sighed. "So, you found your renter."

"I did. Well, in a sense. She won't be renting, as I'd be paying for her housing if she stayed elsewhere."

Kannis looked back and forth between them. "I'm sorry, Mistresses, but I don't understand. What am I missing?"

"Oh, it's fine, Kannis. Tala used to rent a room from me, but due to certain… changes, that is no longer required. She can explain if she wishes, but you'll figure it out eventually. Suffice to say, I have an open room in my home, so instead of putting you up at some local boarding house, you'll live with me, if that's agreeable."

Tala cleared her throat. "And me, when I'm in town."

Kannis nodded slowly. "I don't think I fully understand, but I don't think that's a problem."

Lyn smiled. "Good. I'll draw up the paperwork for a Mage-mageling relationship, and we can go over it together."

"That sounds wonderful. Thank you, Mistress Lyn. I promise that you won't regret taking me on."

I might. Tala kept the frown off her face.

-Tala.-

-Don't be rude. This has very little to do with you.-

Fair. She took a deep breath and changed the content of her thoughts. *The whole 'must get my attention' thing is getting pretty annoying. Can you take a moment to see if you can disable the requirement?*

-As you wish.-

Tala smiled, forcing a bit more genuineness into it this time. "Well, congratulations to you both. It's a big thing you're both agreeing to. We can celebrate tonight?"

"I think that's a wonderful idea." Lyn nodded her thanks and looked to Kannis.

"As my master commands." Kannis grinned in genuine-seeming joy. "That does sound quite nice."

"Well, I must be off, and the two of you have details to hammer out. See you at home tonight, around dinner."

"Good to meet you, Mistress Tala." The mageling bowed.

"Don't do anything too insane," Lyn added.

Tala felt a smile tug at her lips. "Me? Never. Terry, on the other hand… He gets to join us in sparring today."

Terry lifted his head and let out an affirmative squawk.

Tala strode away, friend on her shoulder, Lyn left standing, wide-eyed and opened mouthed in astonishment.

That was strangely satisfying.

Alat didn't reply, the silence stretching for almost a minute as Tala made her way through Bandfast's streets.

I suppose that delving into her inner workings to turn off the 'Tala' requirement takes more capacity than I'd have guessed.

Still silent.

Tala shifted her shoulders as she walked, feeling oddly lonely in the silence.

Great. She's going to see these memories when she comes back, and she'll never let me live it down.

-Oh, I'm loving it, now.-

"Gah!" Tala jumped, landing to the side of the street and scaring several of the people around her.

An older woman had frozen in shock, hand coming to her mouth in astonishment. "Good heavens, child. Are you alright?"

Tala felt her face heat in embarrassment and blurted out the first lie that came to mind. "There was a bee."

Alat cackled with laughter as Tala sped away, not making eye contact, nor acknowledging the woman's follow-up questions.

-There was a bee?-

She kept laughing in the back of Tala's mind.

-It's the middle of winter! There's snow everywhere. What kind of excuse was that?-

The laughter rolled on.

Tala chose the path of nonconfrontation and ignored Alat. *She is a lot to ignore…*

-See, that was at least clever.- A snort, of all things, resounded through her head. *-There was a bee.-*

How the rust are you conveying a snort and a shake of your head?

-I grow in capacity by the minute.-

That's just wonderful for you.

-Thank you. I rather think so, too.- After a moment, Alat giggled. *-There was a bee.-*

I think it was good enough, given the timeframe. Besides, it was a better response than saying that the voice in my head startled me.

Alat paused at that. *-True, I suppose, but just because it wasn't the worst thing you could have said, it doesn't mean it was a good option.-*

It wasn't worth continuing the disagreement. Tala tossed out some jerky for Terry, even while munching on some herself. As she did so, she had a realization. *Hey, you didn't have to precede your statement by getting my attention.*

-I did not.-

So, you figured it out, then?

-Absolutely. I used your authorization to remove the requirement for me to notify you before adjusting your senses.-

Tala blinked a few times, tossing out another bit of jerky for Terry. *Wait. What?*

-You asked me to remove the requirement.-

I don't want you modifying what I sense without me knowing.

-Well, then you shouldn't have asked me to make that change.-

When you talk into my head, I know you're talking! That has nothing to do with a removal of notification.

There was a pause. *-So, you want that requirement reinstated?-*

Without question, yes.

-Tala.-

-The requirement has been reinstated.-

You're doing it again.

-It is required.-

Tala threw her hands up in the air. Thankfully, no one was close enough to be startled or inconvenienced by the gesture. *No, it isn't! You talking to me lets me know that you're talking to me. I don't need a word or sound preceding your talking. That would be like: You must always give me a book which tells me that you are going to give me a book before you can give me that book.*

Alat, somehow, hummed in her head consideringly. *-So, would you like me to adjust my notification to simply be whatever I am about to tell you?-*

Tala thought for a moment, looking for how it might be abused.

-I'm not trying to trick you. Your wellbeing is my wellbeing.-

Yeah… I know… Fine.

-You still sound hesitant. Should I find a way of making my communications stand out more in your mind as well?-

That's worth a try, sure.

≡*Command accepted.*≡

Tala continued on her way. *How are you doing that? Your thoughts aren't coming through more loudly, but they are more... emphasized?*

≡*I am denoting them more extremely as separate from the normal flow of your thoughts.*≡

Tala grimaced. *I don't think I like that. Let's remove the extra distinction.*

-Command accepted.-

Tala felt some tension ease. She hadn't really realized it, but the sheer oddity of having such distinctly separated thoughts within her own head had been grating. But she was getting distracted. So, if that quick moment was all it took to make the adjustment, what was the other thing for? *Why did you try to remove all notice that you were influencing my senses?*

-That was the best solution that quickly presented itself, and I didn't want to be offline in contemplations for a long stretch, once again.-

But I came up with this other option very quickly.

-Yes, you did. That is some evidence that our different perspectives lend themselves to differing patterns of thought, even though we obviously reside in the same brain, and are the result of the same spirit and soul.-

Is that going to be an issue?

-Not at all. It just emphasizes that we will benefit from each other for a long time to come. It also is a funny bit of evidence that if we switched places, we would become like the other, which would almost be a form of suicide on my part.-

Tala grunted in acknowledgment. *That's an interesting way of thinking about it, I suppose.*

-We're here.-

Tala came out of her reverie and looked up at the glory of the teleportation tower. *You know, I never asked why they are towers, instead of just normal buildings.* Tala once again marveled at the artistry that went into the motifs covering the entryway.

-Do you want to know why it's a tower?-
Later, but sure. Thank you for asking.

She could clearly remember exiting through this archway and thinking about how it would have taken meticulous effort to carve each relief, each detailed image. *I didn't realize that there are some Archons who could do this with a wave of their hand.*

Even so, it was still a stunning display of control and technique, likely an even greater demonstration of skill than simply carving it all by hand would be.

The artist has likely been practicing for hundreds of years. And she got to enjoy the fruits of that experience.

With a contented smile on her face, Tala strolled into the tower.

A chipper young woman, wrapped in a stylish-looking winter coat, greeted Tala just inside the door. "Hello, and welcome to the Teleportation Tower. To better assist you today, may I ask if you are departing yourself or receiving an incoming traveler?"

Tala took a moment to blink and process the flood of words that had come from the woman. That had to be rehearsed. *Who rehearses such a speech?* That didn't really matter, though.

Tala noticed a bit of magic coming from near the girl's feet, behind the counter. A heater? *That's interesting. Clearly tied into the city's grid, too. Could that be one of*

Millennial Mage, 6 - Fused

the artifacts that Queue was talking about? She'd have to examine the thing to be sure, but it seemed reasonable.

-Focus, Tala. The girl asked you a question.-

Right! Tala smiled, coming back to the matter at hand. "Oh, no. Thank you, though. I'm here to see Mistress Phoen, if she's available."

-I already told you that she was on shift, now.-

Yes, and I asked about her availability, not her presence.

-Oh... right.-

Tala's smile shifted to one side. *Seems we both have an issue thinking through things at times.*

-Yeah, we should work on that.-

Agreed.

"Oh, certainly." The receptionist smiled in return, leaned back in her chair, and called through a doorway behind her and to her left. "Clint, can you run and see if Mistress Phoen is available? She has a visitor."

An older voice, likely mid-thirties if he wasn't a Mage, answered, "Sure thing!"

"It'll just be one minute, and we'll know for sure. Can I get you anything while you wait?"

"No, but thank you for asking."

"Absolutely! Let me know if you change your mind."

"Will do."

Tala turned to look back out through the archway, taking in a deep lungful of the cool air and enjoying the slightly elevated view over the buildings, which were just beginning to be bathed in the new light of dawn.

She spent a couple of oddly relaxing minutes looking out at the city through the artistic portal.

"It's a beautiful view, isn't it?" The older, feminine voice came from behind Tala's right shoulder.

Tala turned, a genuine smile pulling at her cheeks. "Mistress Phoen. It is a pleasure to see you once again."

The other woman was exactly as Tala remembered.

-It has only been a couple of months.-

One thing stood out where it hadn't at their first meeting. *She's a Mage, not an Archon. Is she Forbidden?*

-No, she is not in the lists of Forbidden, but that's a special title for those with essentially no chance to Bind a star, though they can achieve an attempt with relative ease.-

"I'm sorry, young woman, but you seem to have me at a disadvantage. Do I know you?"

Tala gave a slight bow. "I am Tala. You greeted me when I arrived from the Academy, and you lent me clothing as well."

"Why would I have…?" Her eyes widened, and then she laughed. "Oh! Mistress Tala, that's right. How are you?" She frowned. "Did you give up the Mage's life?"

The lack of inscriptions.

Phoen's eyes bobbed to Terry, though there was no surprise in them, so she'd likely noticed him before Tala turned around. "It seems you found yourself a friend."

Tala reached up and scratched Terry. "I have, indeed. But no, no. I'm still working for the Caravanner's Guild. I've not given up magic by any means."

The older woman frowned just slightly. The expression didn't seem to line up with any of the wrinkles on her face, making it clear that Phoen didn't frown often. "Whatever happened to your inscriptions, dear? Did you have to teleport for some reason? Little else would eliminate them so completely and cleanly."

Tala watched the woman's magesight inscriptions fill with power and activate.

Phoen's eyes widened again, and she gasped, taking a half-step back. "Mistress." She gave a shallow bow. "You've come far in such a short time, Archon."

Millennial Mage, 6 - Fused

Tala stepped forward, crossing the space that Phoen had created with her half-step and then some, before placing her hands on the woman's shoulders. "None of that, Mistress. I came to thank you, once again, for your kindness and assistance that first day, not to have you abase yourself."

"As you wish." Phoen seemed to struggle for a moment within herself before nodding once. "How is it that you have advanced so quickly? Even among those who make it to Archon, isn't half a decade considered fast?"

"That sounds about right."

"So, if I may ask, Mistress. How?"

Tala shrugged, finding herself without a good answer. "I'm not sure what to tell you."

"Did you just throw yourself off a cliff to get to the bottom?"

-Not an inaccurate assessment.-

Hush, you. "I did take some risks, I suppose."

"Someone should tan your master's hide for letting you move so fast."

"Well, you see, I never actually had a master."

Phoen cocked an eyebrow. "I knew you were going to attempt to be hired as a full Mage, but you didn't get a master, even for the advice and direction?"

"Well, I talk with as many Mages and Archons as I can, asking advice."

"Do you follow it?"

Tala grimaced slightly. "Mostly?"

Phoen snorted. "Well, it doesn't seem to have done you any lasting harm, at least not yet." She gave Tala an appraising look. "You're doing well, then?"

"I am, thank you. And you?"

"Can't complain. Mact is close to full Magehood, and he's likely the last mageling I'll take."

Tala cocked her head to one side. "Why don't you…?"

Phoen laughed. "I never could master that spellform. Something about my mindset as a Material Creator makes me unsuited to such esoteric workings of raw power. I never was able to bridge the quadrants, either." She shrugged. "But I've lived a good life, made a good income, and I'm ready to retire and spend time with my great-grandchildren."

"Do you have many?"

Phoen smiled softly. "Twenty, with the twentieth born just last month." She let out a contented breath. "The healers tell me that I've likely got another dozen years or so, at least. So, I'm looking forward to watching them grow, marry, and have children of their own."

That doesn't make sense. Ingrit said no Mage dies of old age. Tala almost objected, but Alat cut across her.

-*I'll explain after.*- There was a sadness to her alternate interface's voice, so Tala decided to trust her.

She smiled toward Phoen. "That sounds like a full-time endeavor." Tala felt like she wanted to be sad at the prospect of Phoen retiring, especially with Alat's vague comments, but there was an undercurrent of joy in the woman's demeanor that made it clear that she wanted nothing more in the world than exactly that.

"Precisely." Her well-worn smile lines deepened as a look of true, contented satisfaction came to rest on her features.

She wants such different things from me. Was that because they were different people, or was Tala a fool, facing the wisdom brought on by age and rejecting it?

-*Likely a bit of both. I don't know that we'll ever want to take her path, but I think we may want pieces of it at some point.*-

Millennial Mage, 6 - Fused

There was wisdom there. She might, one day, want a family, and at that time, she'd very much be walking a parallel path to Phoen's.

Tala glanced around, then nodded into the comfortable silence. "Well, I don't want to keep you from your work. Thank you for letting me drop through, and thank you, again, for all you did for me."

Phoen bowed. "It was wonderful to see you, and it is my pleasure to have been able to assist." When she straightened, there was a hardness to her gaze. "But you listen here, young woman. I'll give you the advice I gave my own daughters and sons: Don't advance too fast, Mistress. Life is worth living, so don't let it pass you by. You hear?"

Tala felt strangely touched by the woman's fervor. "I won't, Mistress. Thank you."

Tala bowed to the woman; she bowed to the first Mage who she'd met in this city, the first one to greet her after she left the academy. With a smile on her face, and a lightness brought on by happiness in her head, Tala departed.

I'm glad I did that.

-Me too.-

So, what was that about? Didn't Ingrit say no Mage dies of old age?

-I looked it up, and Mages who can't consciously create the Archon Star eventually manifest it subconsciously within themselves, instantly bonding it and beginning the process of becoming a fount. In those cases, it's a fairly predictable process, which can be monitored and anticipated, without being prevented.-

Hence the twelve-year guess.

-Exactly. Apparently, it happens most often in the Mage's sleep, at which point, they simply get up and

leave. The Mage is then unresponsive and can either be killed or let out of the city.-

That was depressing, to say the least. One day, Phoen would just get up and walk out of her family's life without a word of goodbye.

-She knows it's coming, as will her family, even if they won't know exactly what it is.-

Secrecy.

-Secrecy.-

Tala sighed. *I need to hit something.* She reached up to scratch Terry's head. "Ready to spar, my friend?"

He leaned into her hand and trilled with obvious excitement.

"Let's go."

Chapter: 8
Kannis

Kannis watched Mistress Tala walk away with mixed feelings.

At first, she had pretended not to recognize the woman to spare her embarrassment. *Imagine going all the way through the academy and then not making it as a Mage.*

Kannis knew that she wouldn't want to face her old classmates if that had happened to her.

But then, things had taken a turn for the strange.

Kannis's prospective master, a Mage that Kannis had researched extensively as being a good fit for herself, as well as being respected in her field, had treated Mistress Tala with regard and familiarity, explicitly *correcting* Kannis, insisting that Mistress Tala was a Mage, despite her lack of obvious inscriptions.

It's like I missed a question on my final exam. She shivered at the unpleasantness of the remembered correction.

Kannis had seen recognition in Mistress Tala's eyes, but the other woman hadn't acknowledged their past history either. *Not that there is really much of that, I suppose.*

She stopped in her musings. *Kannis, you are being a silly child. This is the most important day of your life so far. Focus.*

She calmly turned back toward Mistress Lyn and smiled. She barely felt the longing for her long absent hair and how it would move and sway as she turned.

The lack was more a fond memory than anything truly missing anymore. She had accepted her new, bald state. *I am a Mage, or I will be, and the privileges come with some drawbacks.*

She'd been rather confused when she saw that most of the Mages she'd identified in the city had hair. Maybe some new development in inscription technology would let her regrow her own? *Focus.* "Thank you, again, for taking the time to work with me, Mistress Lyn."

Mistress Lyn looked vaguely uncomfortable at the gratitude, but accepted it with aplomb nonetheless. "Of course, Kannis. I appreciate you seeking me out. I think that we will be a good match. Now, we should hammer out the details of our contract."

"That sounds excellent."

What followed were two hours of bliss.

Kannis loved working through the minutia of contract documents, and Mistress Lyn seemed to revel in the fine tuning of the language as well, taking the opportunity to train Kannis, even before they were officially linked as master and mageling.

Kannis had reviewed the standard contract extensively beforehand, so she had come prepared. Even so, Mistress Lyn pushed back on most of Kannis's requested changes, always informing her exactly why the contract was worded as it was, and why it couldn't be changed.

Regardless, the younger woman was able to gain much via small, seemingly inconsequential changes, at least in her own estimation.

For example, Mistress Lyn had committed to exposing her to every side of the Caravan Guild's business, which wasn't always the case for clerical magelings. Kannis also got a rigid timeline for her own advancement to full Mage, though there were provisions that would allow that to be altered with cause.

Kannis would not give Mistress Lyn cause.

Kannis would be paid based on the work she accomplished, not a flat rate, and she would receive specific guidance on her inscriptions from Mistress Lyn, as well as any relevant expert that Mistress Lyn could pull into the process.

"There. I think that does it." Mistress Lyn pressed her thumb to the slate, which contained their contract to confirm her side of the deal, before handing it over to Kannis. "Please confirm this document. I assume you know how?"

Kannis did. *She must have pricked her thumb without me noticing.*

It was standard practice to magic-impress tests upon submitting them at the academy.

She always felt a bit of pride, magically claiming her work. She felt even more, now, as all her work over the last years bore fruit in this amazing next step.

Kannis did her best to contain her excitement as she pricked her finger on the sharp nub of stone on one side of the slate. The spike retracted immediately after.

With an effort of will, Kannis allowed her gate to open… but no, she couldn't do that. She lacked any inscriptions, including those of her keystone. As a result, her gate was out of her control for the first time in more than half a decade.

She did *not* like that. The very idea of magic running unchecked through her body disturbed her, greatly. *The mundanes can only stand it due to their ignorance, I imagine.*

Nonetheless, because her magic was flowing through her, unrestricted, it infused her blood just as she touched the cool stone, without any effort required on her part. The drop of blood that had been building on her finger vanished into the slate, and the tablet turned a pleasant, emerald green, denoting full confirmation.

"And it's official. Welcome to the Caravanner's Guild, mageling Kannis."

"Thank you!" She clapped her hands in giddy excitement, then schooled her features as best as she could. "I'm so, so excited, Mistress Lyn. What do we do next? Do I get to see the jobs boards? Are we going to get inscribed? Will you have me shadow you through part of the day?"

Mistress Lyn looked genuinely taken aback. "My, you are well informed." She hesitated, then gave a little shrug, her eyes flickering toward the entrance for the barest instant. "Well, I suppose I've forgotten how well the academy can prepare some for life after graduation."

"Some?"

She waved the question away. "Never you mind. We'll take a look at the jobs board, first. There's quite a bit of specifics that I don't remember being covered at the academy."

Kannis's new master led her to one side of the Caravanner's great entry hall, to what seemed to be a large board with notices on it. *Exactly as I imagined it!*

There were several such boards, but this one was denoted with big, bold letters across the top proclaiming the word 'Clerks.'

"This is a tasks board. I apologize if some of this is review, but I'd rather repeat than miss something important."

"Whatever you think best, Mistress."

Mistress Lyn hesitated again at that, then shook her head with a smile and continued. "We take in a lot of information in our guild, and we need to process, collate, and draw conclusions. Each of these pages details a set of data to be pulled from the Archive, and the way in which it should be processed, tabulated, et cetera. There is pay associated with the work, as well as its weight with regards to how much it will help the guild. As my mageling, you will assist me in assisting the guild. As such, I will expect you to complete a certain number of these each week, and we will go through your results, together, at least at first."

Mistress Lyn then gave an in-depth explanation as to how that would function, and Kannis found herself excited to begin work immediately. Unfortunately, there were some little tasks to get out of the way, first.

Inscribing... She girded herself, knowing that the pain was necessary and worth it. *I'll be able to pay off my debts in no time with this, and with any luck, I should be able to send my family some money sooner than I'd dared to hope.*

They were free and clear thanks to her ability to take on the family debts with her chosen career, and now, she was the first Mage in her family for three generations. It really was hard to contain her excitement.

With the jobs board explained and expanded upon, there was nothing further holding them in the guildhall for the moment. So, they went to the check-in and grabbed their heavy coats and winter boots.

As they were pulling on the winter-wear, they were approached by a young man in Mage's robes.

"Well, as I live and breathe. Mistress Lyn, she is a mageling. I'll take no denials."

Mistress Lyn looked up as she finished lacing her boots. "Master Cran, it's been too long." She stood and shook his hand. "You are right. This is my mageling, Kannis."

Kannis beamed at that. *I'm her mageling.* "A pleasure to meet you, Master Cran."

Millennial Mage, 6 - Fused

"So, no excuses this time? You're actually taking on a mageling?"

Mistress Lyn shrugged. "She's a good fit, and actually a mageling."

He held up his hands in surrendered. "Alright, alright. Fair's fair."

What are they talking about? She'd likely never know.

He smiled toward Kannis once again. "Well, you're a lucky girl, Kannis. Mistress Lyn here is a gold one."

Without another word, he waved farewell and wondered off.

"Who was that?"

"Oh, Master Cran is harmless. He's something of a fixture in the Mage's lounge, here, but he makes his money bouncing at a large, local tavern. Those that don't respect his station as a Mage learn quickly why that respect is due."

"He works at mundane taverns?" *How very odd.*

"Just one, really, and he seems to like it. They pay him well, as he's basically the only bouncer they need when he works. They still apparently have door-staff, but that's a different position." The way Mistress Lyn was speaking made it clear that her knowledge on the subject was at least partly involuntary.

So, Master Cran is a talker? That's good to know. Kannis had learned a lot about whom to avoid and whom to approach, both teachers and students, by knowing whom to listen to, and how to sift through the tidbits.

All words hold truth, even lies. Her foundational principle had never led her astray, and she didn't imagine it ever would.

Coats and boots on and secured, the pair walked outside, back into the frigid winter streets.

Kannis loved Bandfast already, and it wasn't just the snow. Honestly, she preferred heat to cold, but that was a small price to pay.

She was so sick of the smell of salty air. It had been just her luck that the academy had been situated by the ocean, just like her hometown of Clevenhold.

The fresh air of the plains was a welcome relief, not to mention the drop in humidity. *Cold and dry is better.* She hesitated. *Warm and dry would be better still, but I am quite happy with this, here.*

The people in Bandfast tended toward more fanciful colors than those in her home city as well, even in their winter-wear.

She could easily spot yellows, reds, blues, and greens, and the quality of the dyes used was beyond question.

Her own brown, calf-length, fur-lined coat seemed drab in comparison to the standards around her, though she wasn't the only one in earth-tones by a long shot.

Mistress Lyn, herself, wore a tan parka with dark brown boots.

"Mistress, where are we going now?"

Kannis's master gave a small smile. "Well, per our contract, I have an inscriber to take you to, but I will warn you, she doesn't usually take on new clients."

"Alright. What if she refuses?"

Her master hesitated. "Well, she's almost certainly going to, at least at first." She seemed to consider further. "In all likelihood, she's going to be fairly cutting in her refusal as well. Don't let it get to you. Either approaching her will work, or it won't. If she won't inscribe you, then we'll go to my inscriber and get you properly done."

* * *

"Mistress Lyn. Why are you wasting my time?"

Millennial Mage, 6 - Fused

Mistress Holly was... terrifying. She had taken one look at Kannis and grimaced. Then, when the inscriber had reluctantly agreed to look at the set of inscriptions designed for the young woman, she'd practically growled.

"There is nothing new, nothing special, nothing *interesting* in these inscriptions."

"You could improve them."

"Obviously, but why bother?" Mistress Holly rolled her eyes before fixing her gaze on Kannis.

Kannis felt herself hunch, pulling inward involuntarily. Mistress Holly's words held deep, uncomfortable truths. *Truths I need to face.* Mistress Holly addressed her, pulling her back to the present.

"Girl. How's your pain tolerance?"

Kannis paled as she tried to formulate a quick, precise, and correct answer. "To my understanding, as good as any, Mistress. I don't like being inscribed, but I can take it without pulling away, screaming, crying, or otherwise interfering with the process."

Mistress Holly grunted. "So, average. Her power density is average. Her through-put is average. Her inscriptions are uninspired. Her foundational principle lacks even the meager potential of yours, Mistress Lyn. Though, you have drawn great things from that potential." The woman's eyes sparkled at that. "I heard about your recent encounter. I would have loved to have seen you..." She trailed off, glancing back toward Kannis with an unsatisfied look. "No. I don't work on magelings."

Mistress Lyn gave a slight bow of her head. "As you wish. Thank you for your time."

As they had turned to go, Mistress Holly had actually growled, then tapped the side of Kannis's face so quickly that the younger woman hadn't thought to react, let alone move. "Tell whoever you take her to that she doesn't need a cognitive perception enhancer, and definitely not through the jaw-line. That location would be perfect for a Jevine-Recursion, to begin forging her will."

Mistress Lyn bowed again, lower this time, and Kannis caught a look of triumph in her master's eyes. "I will pass it on."

Mistress Holly clucked her tongue. "Fifteen minutes. I'll spend fifteen minutes ironing out the most flagrant disasters in these inscriptions, and then, I'll update her entry in the Archive with the improvements and explanations thereof."

"You are too kind."

"Don't mock me, girl. I know you brought me this regurgitated rat's nest masquerading as spell-work in the hope that it would offend me too much to leave alone. Congratulations; I am thoroughly offended."

"If you say so."

Mistress Holly was already turning away, but she tossed a comment at Mistress Lyn in parting. "Tell Mistress Tala that Mistress Jenna informed me of the most recent developments, and I am pleased. I'd appreciate it if she would drop through each morning that she's in town, so that I can keep tabs on her development and continued compression. Mind you, I just mean stepping through the door and then leaving. No talking. No bothering my staff. I don't want her interrupting me every day without cause."

Mistress Lyn sighed, but without much true emotion behind it. "I'll let her know."

Mistress Tala? Tala is connected to this madwoman? Kannis didn't know whether to be jealous, impressed, or horrified at the very idea.

* * *

Millennial Mage, 6 - Fused

Kannis held back tears and clutched her Mage's robes tightly to her chest as the repeated, sharp pricks sent involuntary twitches through the muscles of her back.

"Almost done, deary." The voice was kind and had a grandmotherly air about it, though it came from a face that barely looked older than Kannis's own.

Don't forget, Mages outside the academy don't show their age. To be fair, the teachers at the academy looked amazing for their various ages, but they didn't look, precisely, young.

Almost done. Almost done. Almost done.

The keystone was the largest portion that had to be done in one go. Even with Holly's amendments, and the few minor changes that the inscribers did to other parts of the spellform, it wasn't a hugely complex working.

Even so, Kannis was grateful that the rest could and would be done in piecemeal fashion over the next couple of weeks.

You can bear through this. And she did.

Three inscribers had worked simultaneously, expertly maneuvering around each other to speed up the process.

As she'd hoped, it didn't really make it three times as painful. She could only register so much discomfort before it started to all fuzz together and go numb.

It still hurt, but it was a numbing pain. *A sharp, numbing pain.*

She needed a distraction.

As usual, she began by going through her accomplishments. She reveled in some of the awards that she'd received before leaving home, then in the assignments and tests completed with distinction at the academy.

Finally, she thought through the myriad recruiters who had offered her mageling positions on the clerical side of their businesses or guilds.

The only one that had truly tempted her had been the Library.

She'd had to gild herself twice over to say 'no' to them. She wanted to explore the wider world, and only the most senior Librarians did that. She hadn't wanted to wait decades to see what lay outside city walls, if she ever did.

No, her only real choice had been the Caravanner's Guild, no matter how much it had surprised her teachers or friends.

I know what I want.

She'd had some slight fear about striking out on her own, but even those who were recruited still had to find a master to learn under, and no one was ever allowed to be without. *Though, stars above help the ones who need a civilly-mandated master.*

"There. All done." She felt a cool cloth run across her back, followed by a pulse of healing. "Give it a test, if you please."

Kannis closed her eyes and activated her keystone, opening her gate a fraction. She filled with power quickly, even though she closed it again as fast as she was able.

With no inscriptions to burn the power through, it sat within her, buzzing uncomfortably and filling her with a nervous energy.

Kannis quickly worked her way into her simple Mage's robes. *Designed for easy doffing, not donning...* Then, she bowed to the inscriber-trio. "Thank you, Mistress, Mistress, Master."

They smiled in turn. "Our pleasure."

Mistress Lyn came over and inspected her, likely using her own magesight.

"Good work from what I can see. Thank you. We will return after lunch for her magesight inscriptions."

Millennial Mage, 6 - Fused

Kannis had known that would be coming, but she grimaced slightly nonetheless.

Mistress Lyn clearly noticed the expression by the soft smile she gave Kannis, but she didn't comment. They left together, presumably heading toward the aforementioned lunch.

Trying to draw her out and away from the memory of the pain or contemplations of more to come, Mistress Lyn began talking. "You know, if you want to grow your hair back, there are some needles that can be used to inscribe your scalp, so the hair doesn't get in the way. They are expensive, but we can make it happen if you'd like."

"Really?" *I might actually be able to have hair again?* Mistress Lyn had gotten her a hat on the way to the Mistress Holly's workshop, when it became obvious that even in her coat, Kannis was cold. *Hair would be so much better.* Though, she still might need the hat.

"Of course. It's a small thing, really. But for now, come on, let's get some food in you."

As they walked out of the shop, Kannis was nodding to herself. "I didn't have much breakfast, so I have room for a large lunch, if that's alright." She hesitated. "Well, no. If we're having a large dinner as a celebration, I need to eat a much smaller lunch than I normally would." She ran through dozens of calculations in her own head, most with hardly a conscious thought. Keeping her intake to a reasonable level was second nature to Kannis after so long under the restrictions.

In truth, she would rather not eat, but she needed sustenance, even if it was a chore.

*   *   *

"And... done!"

Kannis breathed out a sigh of relief and opened her eyes. She did *not* like having her eyes open while magesight inscriptions were being laid.

Too many needles, too close to my eyes…

"Give them a try."

Obediently, Kannis opened her gate fractionally and activated her magesight. The world lit up around her in brilliant patterns and with wondrous traces of power.

The air seemed much less… potent? Much less full of power than it had at the academy, but she supposed that was to be expected.

The academy was a place of magic, and the cities were everyday. *But I get to be magic in them.*

That pushed back some of her melancholy at having so recently left what had become a second home to her.

She glanced toward Mistress Lyn, and found herself confused. There was a subtle reddish tint overlaying her master's form, as if heat were building up to a glow within her. *But much more mild than that.*

The woman must have seen Kannis's look of confusion, because she lifted a hand to forestall her. "I'll explain everything in time, but to put a name to what you've likely just noticed, that is my aura." She nodded to the inscribers, and Kannis looked at each of them, seeing hints of color around all three of them, as well.

"Archons." Kannis breathed out in wonder.

She had, of course, heard of Archons, and of aura, but it wasn't described or detailed at the academy. She'd even known that Mistress Lyn was an Archon, though she still didn't really know exactly what that meant, except that she was exceptional. *You've hitched yourself to an incredible master, Kannis. Well done.*

Chapter: 9
Master Avian

Tala strode off the street and through the training yard with purpose.

After nearly a week of coming back here to train, the guards were once again used to seeing her walk through their midst, and those that weren't were quickly informed by some around them that she was expected and a regular.

Most didn't even get up, simply waving at her or calling out some derivation of, "Good morning, Mistress."

She waved to those who waved and acknowledged all the others who called out greetings.

It was a pleasant experience having so many people at least politely happy to see her.

The regular citizenry were a bit more reserved. *Or is that just me?*

That was an interesting thought. If she waved at people as she passed them on the street, would they wave back? What if she greeted them?

No, there are far, far too many people in the city to make that a reasonable thing to do, she considered. *Maybe in the off times or less-populated streets?*

-You waste a lot of mental energy on random thoughts like this.-

It's interesting, alright?

-You could be so much more with a bit more focus.-

Tala cocked her eyebrow, though she didn't have anyone to direct the look at.

-Fine, you do do quite a bit. Some random thinking is probably healthy.-

Millennial Mage, 6 - Fused

That's right, it is. Tala strode into the building and through it, down the familiar path to the training courtyard.

The cool air of the winter morning pervaded the open structure and allowed the stone to be cold beneath her shoes, just as with the streets outside. Tala sent a tendril of power through her garments, causing her shoes to connect to her pants and break apart, pulling back into the other elk leathers. With a smile, Tala enjoyed the stone against her bare skin, and the temperature wasn't unpleasant to her in the least.

Much better.

She walked slowly, taking a moment to simply revel in the small pleasure of the texture and temperature of the floor with each step. All too soon, she came out of the side hall and onto the open walkway around the training courtyard to find quite a few guards already there, stretching or moving through some half-speed sparring.

The healer wasn't there, yet. In fact, as she looked around, she realized that while she wasn't the first to arrive by a long shot, she was the first Mage.

Several of the guards greeted her, but no one stopped what they were doing. Tala returned the greetings and moved out onto an open portion of the sand.

She took time to move through a stretching sequence to limber up. While she couldn't count on such being possible before real fights, it let her continue to improve flexibility and keep from straining her muscles. *Wait... do I even need to do this?*

-Well, you could technically just overstretch and tear your body. Then, you could hold the position until it healed, but I wouldn't recommend it.-

Tala nodded to herself, even as she kept stretching. *That would make me more flexible but take me backward strength-wise. I need to bring up strength and flexibility together, in tandem, in order to have the best results.*

-Precisely.-

I guess there aren't really any shortcuts.

Alat seemed to pause, something akin to disbelief radiating from within Tala's mind. *-Well, I mean, you can work out and stretch to your limit every day—rust, multiple times per day—and see improvements each time. That's a shortcut vastly beyond what mundanes can do.-*

Tala felt a bit foolish at the moment. *Right.* She sometimes forgot how much of an advantage that was. *We should probably find a way of tracking my improvement.*

-Like... a system? With statistics and hard numbers for how you are improving over time?-

That might be nice.

-I could even come up with a leveling nomenclature, so that you could track as you progressed through the rankings.-

I think that would be nice.

Tala sensed deep skepticism from Alat. *-I think you'd obsess over it. Not to mention, isn't that exactly what you were warned off when you looked into mana?-*

Tala considered as she shifted from a handstand to a floating pushup and back, working and stretching her shoulders. She hadn't increased her weight, as she did for her morning and evening sets, because her main focus wasn't strengthening at the moment. *You're probably right.*

-I do try.-

Tala snorted a laugh, blowing sand away with the force of her exhale.

-No, I will not figure out a way to measure how hard you exhale.-

I wasn't going to ask.

-But you were thinking about it.-

Millennial Mage, 6 - Fused

Tala rolled her eyes, taking a moment to look around herself once again.

Terry wasn't stretching. Well, he was stretched out in the sun, but that was different.

The guards were mostly warmed up and seemed about ready to start the day's training.

Aproa arrived as Tala was looking around.

Tala rolled forward, out of the side bend and middle split she'd been in, springing to her feet and waving to the other woman. "Good morning!"

Aproa waved as she walked up to Tala. "We missed you yesterday." She frowned. "What happened to your inscriptions? Are you alright?"

"Oh, I'm fine." *That's going to trip up some people. I wonder if the through-spike's illusion can be modified?*

-Want me to investigate?-

What will it take?

-A small amount of power, and I'll be less responsive.-

Do it. The back and forth with Alat happened at the speed of thought. So, the entire conversation with Alat happened before Aproa had finished shrugging and replied, "Not really what I asked, but it's your magics. So, your friend is joining the sparring today?"

Terry flickered into being behind Tala, sized to be just shorter than her.

Tala reached back without looking, trusting her senses to find where he was, and patted the side of his beak. "That's the idea."

Even though Rane and Aproa had supposedly warned the guardsmen the day before that Terry would be joining this day, those already in the courtyard turned wary eyes on the terror bird, a couple stepping back involuntarily.

-I don't think it was his presence, Tala. I think it's that he just teleported and changed size. Sure, some have

probably noticed him teleport before, but I don't think he's ever grown around the guards.-

Ahh, that's fair. Tala smiled, looking around the courtyard. "Let's do this!"

Rane arrived at that moment. "Mistress Tala! Terry! Ready to spar?"

Tala grinned and waved. "Absolutely. You're well?"

"As ever."

Adam was with the Archon, and he assessed Terry with a critical eye. "I think I should fight the terror bird first, to assess the danger of his joining in." He looked to one of the guardsmen, near a side passage. "Tras, please go inform the healer that we are ready."

The man, Tras apparently, saluted and ran down the hall.

Tala knew that the healer would be out in less than a minute if previous days were any indication.

Adam regarded Terry. "No cutting or tearing."

Terry tilted his head, considering, then bobbed in acknowledgment.

"Do you wish me to use a training weapon?"

Terry hesitated, then bobbed once.

That surprised Tala, but she didn't comment.

"Clear the sand, please."

Everyone, Tala included, walked outward to the steps surrounding and leading down into the sand-filled courtyard.

One of the guardsmen tossed two training swords to Adam, and the man caught them with ease. He tested their weight, then nodded and thanked his colleague. "Ready?"

Terry bobbed his assent once again.

"Begin."

Terry flickered out of existence. In the same instant, Adam swept his swords in two seemingly conflicting defensive patterns, and he closed his eyes.

Millennial Mage, 6 - Fused

Well, that makes too much sense.

-Agreed. Terry moves around too much for our eyes to be trusted. Closing them would allow a greater focus on our other senses and likely make us better able to counter him.-

Noted.

-Or it would get us thrashed even more quickly because we aren't used to fighting blind.-

Tala hesitated at that. *Yeah... that's more likely.*

Adam's almost random seeming movements kept the swords in motion and close enough to strike at Terry, no matter where the avian appeared.

Tala couldn't tell *how* Adam was sensing Terry until she noticed that Adam wasn't moving his feet or making any noticeable noise. In the near utter silence of the courtyard, Tala heard the smallest whisper at each of Terry's appearances, barely louder than the air moving over and rustling the terror bird's feathers.

Well, rust my bucket. How have I never heard that before?

-We never held still and silent for long enough to hear it?-

That was as good an explanation as any, but Tala felt unsatisfied. *I feel like I should have heard that... especially if Adam can. Don't I have better hearing?*

Alat was silent for a short moment, then she made an irritated sound. *-You have been hearing it, but we dismissed it as background noise, given that we were basically always out in nature or near other people sparring in other rooms, so it was assumed to be meaningless.-*

Well, I feel foolish.

The fight going on before them was a stalemate, similar to how Terry and Rane fought, but Adam wasn't defended or moved by magic. He simply always twitched his blade toward Terry the instant the bird appeared, forcing the avian to retreat.

Less than a minute later, Terry flickered out and away, trilling in irritation.

Adam immediately stopped and bowed. "You win this match, master avian."

Terry cocked his head to one side, seeming almost confused.

"Your prohibition on cutting made you slower than you should have been, and I know you could have countered my defenses if you were unconcerned about harming me. Thank you." He bowed again. "You have more restraint than I'd have dreamed possible. I think it would be excellent practice for you to fight the others here."

A throat cleared to one side, and Tala turned to regard a man she'd never seen before.

He was clearly a mundane and also clearly in his fifties, give or take. But that wasn't what caught her attention first.

His natural magical pathways thrummed with power, pouring through his uninscribed gate. Every drop of his power was bent toward one thing and one thing alone: enhancing his reaction speed.

"I would appreciate joining in this training." He wore a finely made chainmail shirt of alternating riveted and solid rings overtop of a padded gambeson that hung to just above his knees. He held a helm under one arm and an oddly ovaloid, curved shield on his back.

Adam turned to the newcomer and bowed low, lower than Tala had ever seen him bow before. "Captain."

"Adam, I've been hearing good things about this little training group. I can see that even some of the most outlandish bits were understating things."

Adam gave a rueful smile. "That terror bird has only joined us today."

"Even so." The captain turned to regard Terry. "May I? You need not hold back. I am armored, and there is a healer to hand. I request only that you do not take my head from my shoulders."

Terry was crouched low, regarding the man with wariness.

Tala cleared her throat. "I am Tala, Captain. You are?"

The captain glanced her way, then seemingly dismissed her. Even so, he answered. "I am Aummar." He stepped forward, eyes back on Terry, setting his helmet on his head and cinching the strap under his chin, above his gorget. That done, he situated his aventail, ensuring it wasn't caught on anything. "Are you ready?"

He motioned, and Adam tossed him one of the training swords. Aummar left his shield on his back.

Terry glanced to Tala, and she shrugged. "If you want to, go crazy."

Aummar regarded her again, seemingly reconsidering her given her obvious relationship to Terry.

Terry shook himself, then bobbed a nod.

The man smiled. "Whenever you are ready."

Terry flickered, and Aummar moved.

The captain's sword drove outward, toward an empty space above and to his left.

Terry appeared there just in time for the training sword to begin to connect before Terry flickered away.

Aummar twisted, turning the strike into a sweep that jerked his weapon behind himself, where it tapped Terry once again as the bird appeared.

Tala's increased perception allowed her to realize what he was doing, even if not how. *His defensive patterns are exactly like those that Adam was using, but he's doing them with one sword, and he's just a reed faster.*

None of the contact would have harmed Terry, there wasn't enough force imparted for that to happen, but it was impressive, nonetheless.

Then, Terry cut loose.

He appeared, barely bigger than a sparrow, below and behind Aummar.

The captain responded instantly, kicking out, but Terry was ready. He opened his mouth, growing in size even as he caught the attacking foot and clamped down to hold it firmly.

Tala heard the snap of bone, but Aummar simply grunted, pulling his leg in while striking with his practice sword.

Terry disappeared, flickering into being behind the man again and driving his taloned foot into Aummar's back.

Aummar's armor held, but he was still slammed into the sand, the impact clearly driving the wind from his lungs. Even so, he rolled over, slashing at Terry once more. Terry didn't even seem to move, just flickering as the sword passed harmlessly through the space he seemed to occupy.

The bird dropped his foot down once more, cracking into the armored chest.

The chainmail would have held against a slash.

Aummar's words were a trap. He's more susceptible to blunt than slashing.

-*Yes, clever of him. Too bad for him, Terry is smarter than most.*-

The blow caused Aummar's hand to spasm and release his weapon.

With that, Terry flickered away, settling down in a crouch and fluffing his feathers in triumph.

Everyone stared at Aummar as he lay virtually unmoving on the sand, convulsing. His foot was at a wholly unnatural angle, and his chest seemed to be *just* slightly the wrong shape. The healer was already at his side, magic flowing from the Mage into the captain.

As the healing did its work, the convulsions got worse, only to be revealed as slightly gurgling laughter.

A moment later, when the healer stepped back, Aummar sat up, spat out a mouthful of blood, and continued to laugh.

"That was amazing!" He rolled back, then vaulted up to his feet, staggering just a bit on the landing. "You are incredible. I haven't been bested that thoroughly in nearly a decade. You've quite a lot of room to improve as well, if you're interested." He had pointed to Terry as he spoke.

Terry cocked his head, then gave a slight bob of assent.

"Good! But first, how is your friend in a fight?" He glanced to Tala. "Shall we test?"

Tala shrugged. "Sounds good to me." She pulled Flow to her hand, verified that the training sheath was locked in place, and sent power down the path that would extend it into the form of a sword.

Aummar tilted his head to one side, examining the clearly magical weapon. When he glanced to Adam and received a gesture of assent, the older man grunted, seeming to decide it wasn't worth addressing.

"Are you ready, or do you require time to recover?"

Aummar rolled his shoulders and hopped slightly, checking how his armor was situated. With a nod to himself and a smile for Tala, he responded. "I'm ready."

Tala charged, executing a controlled thrust toward the man's chest.

Aummar barely seemed to move, but they both froze, the match over.

Flow was fully extended, sheathed tip barely missing Aummar's shoulder. Aummar's training sword rested against Tala's blade, deflecting it the barest amount, while its tip was at her throat.

"You've reasonable technique, but you are easy to counter. Easy to predict."

They pulled apart.

"Again."

Tala nodded. "Don't pull your strikes. I need to feel my mistakes."

He cocked an eyebrow and glanced to Adam. Adam nodded and smiled. With that, Aummar shrugged. "As you wish. Healer, be ready."

They moved as one, and Tala felt the lightest tap on Flow as they closed before pain blossomed from her throat, the training weapon having utterly crushed the front of her neck.

Through the blinding pain, Tala let Flow shift back into a knife and drove it into Aummar's chest. She didn't hold back, allowing her agony to add to her strength, even as she sank into the blow, putting her full weight behind it.

Though he was clearly not expecting her counter, Aummar reacted, pulling away from her strike even as she made it. While that softened the blow and might have been enough to counter a mundane strike, it couldn't negate Tala's attack entirely.

The impact threw him to the ground where he absorbed most of the force of the fall with a roll. He came back to his feet, somehow having not been hampered by the shield still on his back. There was shock in his eyes but also resolve.

Tala coughed, using the forceful exhalation to reinflate her trachea, even as it pulled back into proper alignment and shape. *How hard did he hit me? My throat shouldn't be that easy to crush.*

Millennial Mage, 6 - Fused

-I'd estimate that he'd have partially decapitated anyone else.-

Dangerous.

-A bit, but not truly with the healer ready to hand.-

Tala grunted.

Aummar glanced down at himself and grimaced, sucking in a pained breath. "You broke a couple of ribs. Well struck." His voice was a bit strained and breathless. "So, a Mage, then?"

The healer walked over and tapped the man, causing Aummar to take in a deep, satisfied lungful of air. "I didn't see your spell-lines and mistook you, Mistress. My apologies." He bowed.

Interesting. So, he knows his own skill, and he is proud of it, but he doesn't hesitate to acknowledge mistakes or those who outrank him. *Very interesting.*

"Again?"

Over the next four hours, Aummar humbled them all. Even with their magics, and while he was weighed down with armor, he could fight them on nearly even footing.

One-on-one, none of the Mages could match him unless they stayed at a distance. His reactions were just too quick, his technique too refined. He'd move the slightest amount, both countering their attacks and delivering devastating damage.

Tala was never able to take a wound to hit him again after that first time, and Aummar, for his part, treated the Mages with a bit more wariness than he'd shown before. Though, to be fair, he hadn't really known her to be a Mage in their first fight.

Maybe being mistaken for a mundane is a tactical advantage in some circumstances?

-Maybe, but those who would trust our outward appearance aren't much of a threat, regardless.-

Tala cocked an eyebrow and glanced pointedly toward Aummar.

-*Fair point, exceptions aside.*-

Tala grinned. *Worth considering, I suppose.*

After a good number of one-on-one fights, they were able to do more group conflicts with Aummar's input, and Terry joined in on a smattering of those scenarios.

In that way, the martial training began to mirror the magical that they'd do later on in the day.

Aummar set the tone, but he slowly participated in fewer fights as the morning wore on.

He had pointers for the three Mages and Terry, as well as for every guardsman who participated, and they all improved with his insight.

As they wrapped up, Aummar approached Terry and Tala. "If I may be impertinent enough to ask a couple of questions?"

Rane and Aproa were nearby, and they clearly heard and turned slightly to listen in.

Tala smiled. "Of course. Thank you for your input today."

"It was my pleasure, Mistress. Firstly, does Terry ever carry you?"

Terry and Tala shared a look before Tala shrugged. "Sometimes, yes."

"Then, I would suggest that you practice some mounted combat. You two could definitely use some more cohesion training as well. You are both excellent combatants, but you don't truly fight *together* as you could and should."

Again, the two of them looked at one another. Terry bobbed and trilled his assent. Tala smiled and turned back to Aummar. "That sounds great."

"I'll look into it on your behalf, then. There are some horse tracks and arenas nearby that could be excellent for that type of training."

"We look forward to it."

"Secondly, Terry, would you consider using weapons?"

Terry cocked his head to the side, then flickered to Tala's shoulder and back.

"Yes, I assumed that you couldn't carry much, if anything, with you in a teleport, but that isn't necessary."

The bird tilted his head the other way, clearly intrigued.

"I believe that if you had a few weapons that you could move between, directing them, throwing them, or using them as you see fit, you could increase your combat prowess considerably."

Tala's eyes widened at that, Aproa seemed almost to choke, and Rane started chuckling, adding, "That's just terrifying."

Aummar grinned and glanced to the other Mages. "Then it is fitting for our terror bird friend."

Terry seemed quite hesitant, however.

"Are you willing to give it a try? It will be clunky at first, but I think you might come to appreciate the versatility."

Tala and Terry, again, shared a look, and something in the bird's eyes made Tala think that he was remembering the Leshkin and how he had been all but unable to attack them.

Slowly, Terry bobbed his assent.

Aummar clapped his hands and grinned even wider. "I'll see to it that some potentials, in practice weapon form, are ready for tomorrow, then."

"Thank you, again."

"It was my pleasure, Mistress." He bowed to them all. "Mistress, Master, Mistress. Have a wonderful afternoon."

Tala bounced back and forth on the balls of her feet, feeling energized by the morning's activities. "Rane, Mistress Aproa, do you have lunch plans?"

Rane smiled slightly. "I don't."

Aproa shook her head. "None here."

"Great. I'm starving. Let's go."

Chapter: 10
Just a Minor Change

Tala ate her fill of three silver worth of food. Her lunch companions, Rane and Aproa, who were already used to her large appetite, watched with disbelief as she simply continued to eat.

Normally, she ate about twice what Rane did despite being less than half his size. For this meal, however, she ate nearly six times what the large man did.

Terry had enjoyed trying a bit of everything but had settled back on jerky after the initial tastes.

Tala smiled contentedly to herself, contemplating how much she'd increased her stores. *Not too bad, Tala.*

-I'll say. We were approaching our real weight, given our heavier muscles, bones, and other tissue. Our stores haven't been lower, except right after you received those inscriptions from Holly. Even losing our arm didn't take us so close to empty.-

Tala ignored the reference to the past unpleasantness and redirected the conversation. *And I burn through around twenty-four hundred calories a day. So, burning through two pounds of reserves will heal me as much as I naturally would over three days but much faster?*

-If your entire body was in need of healing? Yes, near enough. Or you could regrow an arm, almost twice over.- Alat hesitated. *-Or near enough to that.-*

No wonder the weapon's test, and resulting pressure wave, had taken so much from her. She'd dropped more than twenty pounds from that one instance alone. *And this meal will translate to about a pound of reserves.*

-For a normal person, this would turn into about that, yeah, but we're a bit more efficient. Call it a pound and a half with the enhancements to our digestive system.-

Right, because most people wouldn't extract all there was within the food and then spend a greater proportion to store it.

-Precisely.-

What does happen to the excess weight? I know I'm eating more than a pound and a half.

-You know the answer.-

I'm sure I do, but you can recall it faster.

Alat sighed within Tala's mind. *-You breathe most of it out, if you want the quick version.-*

Ahh, right.

Tala returned her focus to Rane and Aproa, briefly explaining that she'd been using up too much of her reserves of late, so she had to make it up.

Aproa frowned. "Should we find other ways of practicing? I don't like the idea of you running out of healing energy in the middle of a match."

Tala shook her head. "Even now, I'm still at a level where I could recover from virtually anything. I just couldn't do it more than a couple of times. I'll have plenty of warning that I'm approaching dangerous levels, assuming you all aren't intent on pinning me down and raining death upon me any time soon."

Rane barked a laugh and smiled but didn't comment.

Aproa nodded, considering. "You know your own powers, I suppose. Shall we?"

"Sure." Tala stood. "Ready, Rane?"

"I'm ready." He had a contented smile across his features that Tala didn't see a reason for.

Oh well. That man's an enigma.

-It's because you aren't using any honorific when addressing him.-

Tala almost tripped on her own feet as they left the restaurant. *That would have been embarrassing.*

-Just a bit, yeah.-

She thought back and found that Alat was right.

-Of course I'm right.-

When did that happen? She couldn't actually recall the last time she'd called him 'Master Rane,' but it couldn't have been that long ago.

-Oh, it's been building.-

So… what does that mean?

-It means that you're comfortable with him.-

Nothing more?

-I'm not going to tell you what to feel or what you feel, Tala. That way lies madness.-

Tala grimaced.

"Are you alright, Tala?" Rane placed a comforting hand on her shoulder. "I know that my stomach would be angry at me if I ate even half of what you did." He grinned, trying to add levity to what would have been a rude comment to anyone else.

He didn't use an honorific for me, either… She felt like she only noticed because Alat had pointed out her own lack.

-You're right about that. He's been using it less and less of late. Mirroring you, mostly, but tentatively.-

Is that alright?

-Do you care?-

She found that she didn't, not really. She patted his hand and smiled. "I'm fine. Just thinking."

"Anything interesting?"

Tala felt a moment of awkwardness. *Oh, yes, I'm just thinking about you, Rane. You're very interesting.* She flushed at the very idea of saying such a thing. Then, she silently thanked the stars that her skin was hidden. *I really hope that blushing isn't illusorily recreated for all to see.* "Not too much, no."

Aproa snorted a laugh. "Come on, you two. I'm sure Terry wants to put some Mages in their place."

Terry bobbed in excited agreement and let out a disturbingly deep, basso trill.

The streets were fairly crowded, and the result of his jubilation was that people stared their way in confusion and mild alarm. Funnily enough, people stepped out of their path after that, making the trip faster than it might otherwise have been.

When the group had almost arrived at the training compound, Tala realized that she hadn't told Rane something quite important. So, she pulled him a bit off to one side while continuing to walk, yanked him down so she could reach his ear, and whispered into it. "Hey."

He gave her an odd look as they kept walking, the large man hunched oddly to one side. "Hey, yourself?"

"I recovered the memories."

His eyes widened. "Well, rust."

"Yeah. I'm going to give you access so that you can review them on an Archive slate at some point soon."

"That would be appreciated. Thank you." He seemed a bit shell-shocked, responding from a slight daze.

Since she'd conveyed what she needed to, Tala allowed them to shift their walking path back over to be nearer Aproa. The woman didn't comment on their short conversation, and so neither did they.

Alat, can you do that? Grant him access?
-Done.-

Tala hesitated. *Wait. How? I know you can make changes in the Archive, but how did you select Rane, specifically? Come to think of it, how did you give Jenna access, earlier?*

-Well, Jenna was easy to find, given that she's married to the city lord.-

What about Rane?

-Come on, Tala. We know his magical signature almost as well as we know our own.-

That was interesting to realize.

Oh… I should have discussed this with Odera.

-Oh, yeah. We very much should have.- After a pause, Alat projected the sound of a clearing throat. *-I'll give her access, and we can tell her tomorrow.-*

Agreed.

Rane seemed deep in thought but was nodding to himself.

"What's up?"

He gave her a side-eyed glance before answering. "I've been needing to pick up an Archive integration at some point. I'll have to check with my inscriber to see what he recommends and what he thinks I can support."

Tala grunted. "Well, let me know what you find. You have been increasing your magical weight at a good pace. There should be something that you can get."

-Um… Tala?-

Yeah?

-Jenna just gave us access to a message. She would like us to find a reason to be out of Bandfast tomorrow. There will be several teams of Mage Hunters and two people with the title of Arcane Hunter close at hand.-

Tala would have sworn that she immediately felt bloody eyes on her once again. *And I was doing so well, not thinking about that… thing.*

-You were. I am sorry to ruin it. How should I respond?-

Tala considered for a moment. *Endingberries. We need a bunch.*

Millennial Mage, 6 - Fused

-I'll add an addendum stating that we're going to the ending grove that's...?-

North. We'll go to the one to the north.

-Alright. In her note, she asked us to be discreet about our true purpose but to let people know you're leaving the city.-

She had no idea how to do that, but she would try. *What? No announcing to the city at large that I'm going out to be used as Arcane bait?*

-Precisely.-

Tala snorted a laugh, and Rane gave her an odd look.

"Is everything alright?" They had just entered the compound and were making their way through the wide halls toward their reserved arena.

Inviting people to come could work... "Yeah, yeah. Hey, do either of you want to come out of the city with me, tomorrow? I'll be going a dozen or so miles to the north to harvest some berries."

Aproa responded first. "I can't; I actually leave on assignment tomorrow morning. I'll be gone for about three weeks."

"Oh, that's sad." Tala was surprised that the news actually did disappoint her.

Rane cleared his throat. "Well, I need to meet with my inscriptionist tomorrow. If you need company, I'll happily come, but if not, I'd like to get this dealt with."

Tala shrugged. "Not necessary." She trembled a little but contained the reaction. *But I would like someone with me...* "I think I'll see if anyone at the training session, today, is interested in coming."

With that, they had arrived, and the three of them walked out onto the familiar sand.

The regulars were there, along with a couple new Archons and five magelings, all bald and inscriptionless.

Tala cursed internally.

-Oooo. More old year-mates, newly arrived from the academy.-

Great. Tala lagged behind a bit. *Have you determined how to alter the through-spike's illusion?*

-Yes and no.-

Explain. She did not have any interest in games.

-Fine. I haven't figured out how we can modify it, not yet, but I can show you how to manipulate the magics within it to remove the illusory aspect of its magics until you release the manipulation and allow it to return to its base state.-

Show me.

Alat directed her through the motions with precision and ease, so that in less than five steps, as she continued to walk forward, Tala was confident that she could enact the change at will.

It was quite a bit like making an alteration to her elk leathers, though the change wouldn't be lasting.

Aproa spoke first. "Hunter Jean, what's going on?"

Jean turned from a conversation that she had been having with one of the magelings. "These fine new graduates are looking for masters. They were told that for combat-focused Mages, we're a good group to investigate."

Wow. Everyone's acting showy, today.

The mageling that Jean had been talking to bowed over his clasped hands. "For transparency's sake, we were given a list of groups that meet, similar to yours. We've already met with one group, and one of those who was with us found a master among them."

Jean shrugged. "There you have it. Magelings looking for guides."

Tala had stayed back, mostly behind Rane's massive frame.

Cazor called out from the far corner, "I already told them that none of us really have the extra coin required to have a mageling, but apparently, they think me a liar."

The magelings shuffled uncomfortably.

Stan, the oxygen manipulator, shook his head. "Don't be like that, Cazor. You know very well that a mageling usually more than pays for herself in the end."

Cazor shrugged. "I'm not taking one on."

"No one will force you to," Jean huffed. "I doubt anyone would want to be yours, anyway."

Cazor ignored Jean's barb, saw Tala and Terry, and waved. "Hey! You're back today. Terry is going to join us, right?"

Tala didn't shrink in on herself, but it was a near thing. "Yeah. He's excited to put you in your place."

The Archons laughed, a few adding good natured jabs toward Cazor.

Cazor, for his part, levered himself off the wall he'd been leaning against and walked her way. "Hey, you look... different. Healthier?"

The attention that was already on her seemed to sharpen.

Tala would have sworn that she could feel it.

-You can't, not literally. But you can feel the magic behind their intent, and that's directed your way. Your magesight can pick that up, though it's hardly that magical.-

Great...

A couple of the others added their own comments on how her color looked improved and the like.

Before any further comments could come about, Tala assuaged them. "Just a minor change. Nothing affecting my ability to participate, I assure you."

There were some joking cheers at that.

Tala allowed her gaze to pass over the magelings, and a couple of them were giving her critical looks, seeming to be trying to figure something out about her.

Sadly, Rane had moved aside, presumably in an attempt to be courteous and not block her.

Cazor shrugged. "Alright, Mistress Tala, whatever you say. Then, would Master Terry like to challenge someone, first?"

Well, rust. She really didn't know what she'd expected. Someone was going to use her name eventually. Tala closed her eyes as she heard a gasp from the magelings, which keyed off a whispered, tumbling conversation that Tala had no issue hearing. "Tala? Did he say Mistress Tala?"

"I knew she looked familiar!"

"No, it can't be her. She just left a few months back."

"Didn't she leave naked?"

"That's hardly relevant. It's not like she'd be unable to buy clothes."

"Do you know any other Talas?"

"I don't know every Mage in the world, Gegory."

"Just ask her."

"I'm not going to do that. You ask her."

Tala was having flashbacks of her time at the academy. *Great. Just great…*

-Hey, look at it this way. You were embarrassed by how you handled yourself when I helped you remember all that happened. This is a chance to be better.-

The other Archons seemed to have noticed the magelings' discussions, though most didn't have any enhanced senses worth noting.

Jean was close enough to hear with ease, however, and she turned to regard Tala with a raised eyebrow.

Tala grinned sheepishly at the Mage Hunter and shrugged.

The woman shook her head and turned back to the huddled group. "Graduates. Are you here to gossip or to find masters?"

That shut them up, and they turned away from each other, looking chastened. *Bless you, Jean.*

Jean glanced toward Tala. "Mistress Tala. Is there anything you'd like to say to clear the air, so we can get to the business of watching our feathered friend feed Cazor some sand?"

That got a little laugh from those assembled, then all eyes turned back to Tala.

Rust you, Jean. Tala gave a little wave. "Hey. Long time no see, Gegory, Anisia. I don't think I ever really met you others, not officially."

"It is you!" There were several muttered exclamations.

"Yeah."—she shrugged—"Is that going to be a problem?"

They gave her odd looks. "No? Who are you mageling under? We don't want to accidentally try to poach your master."

Tala was at once offended by the reasonable assumption and touched by the consideration it represented. "Oh, no. I'm…" She cleared her throat. She had been about to say that she was an Archon, but that would open a can of worms that she wasn't willing to address. "I'm not a mageling."

That, again, caused all sorts of mutters.

Gegory stepped forward, a sad look in his eyes. "Oh, I'm sorry to hear that. I'm glad that you still get to be around magic, though."

What? Oh… Tala groaned internally. "No, no. I'm a full Mage."

The mutters were louder this time.

Most of the Archons looked rather confused, but no one was willing to interrupt.

One of the braver magelings, whose name she didn't know, spoke up. "Who was your master? I'd love to be fast-tracked, too!"

The others laughed, and Tala grimaced.

Rane, who seemed to have been trying to contain his laugher, finally couldn't any longer, and he barked out a laugh that was loud enough to border on being a shout. He then sucked in a breath, having trouble around his continued chuckles.

Tala, already on a hair-trigger, hit him on pure reflex.

Well, she tried, though the results were better than she'd have hoped.

His magic registered her hard swat as the attack it was and so moved him forward and down, directly away from the blow.

Rane, who wasn't really paying attention, didn't compensate and roll with the motion as he normally would have.

Thus, he faceplanted into the sand in spectacular fashion, making a *whoomph* sound and sending up a little wave of finer sand that quickly settled.

Tala realized that, from the outside, it would have looked like Rane laughed at her, and she hit him hard enough to slam the much larger man face-first into the ground.

There was a moment of stunned silence before the Archons, who all knew about Rane's defenses, and were thus able to guess exactly what had happened, began laughing.

The five soon-to-be-magelings looked around in abject confusion.

Tala couldn't stop herself from grinning as she spread her arms in a shrug as she looked to the young man who had inquired about her master. She felt like some of her tension had been stripped away. "I took a non-standard path, which is sadly not an option for any of you. I don't have a master to recommend your way—as much as I'd like to."

She looked around at the still-chuckling Archons, even as Rane pushed himself to his feet, still apparently in a good mood if his grin was any indication. He did spit out some sand, however.

She helped him get the rest of the way to his feet before her gaze returned to the five. "Well, we've spent enough time on formalities. We're here to train. Ask questions as you have them."

Chapter: 11
That Unleashed a Flood

Tala took a moment to breathe in deeply, calming her nervousness at being in the spotlight. Then, with a smile, she glanced at Terry, who was still perched on her shoulder. "Hey, we've been teasing about you fighting Master Cazor, but you can challenge anyone you want to." After a moment's hesitation, she added, "Well, except the healer or the magelings-to-be."

Terry let out a series of descending squawks, then flickered off her shoulder, appearing in the middle of the arena with the mass of a horse and standing roughly nine feet tall.

That was much bigger than any form he usually took, but Tala had seen him taller. *While eating dead woodsmen whole...* She hesitated there, then closed her eyes and let out an irritated breath.

-We never sold the random junk we took from those men.-

No. No, we did not. She'd have to ask Lyn to do that.

Before she could fall further into contemplations, Terry continued with his challenge.

He stretched his vestigial wings outward, tilted his head up, and let loose a deep, undulating trill of challenge, then cocked his head to the side, regarding Cazor.

The reactions of those present were quite mixed.

The Archons who'd seen Terry before, even if not at any other size, simply gaped. The new Archons, from

Tala's perspective, were all immediately wrapped in various forms of defensive magics. *Good reactions.*

One seemed to have been encased in a slightly translucent coating of shadow; another was enshrouded in a heat haze; and the last of the new Archons left a working hanging in the air between herself and Terry. Tala and Alat weren't quite able to interpret the working after it settled in the air, but the woman herself was an Immaterial Guide. Though, Tala couldn't tell exactly what she focused on with her brief glance from this distance.

The magelings paled, almost as one, and huddled closer together.

Jean dropped her hand to her weapon but didn't draw it.

Cazor, the focus of Terry's posturing, straightened before the challenge and slowly nodded his agreement.

Aproa and Rane just grinned, watching everyone else react to what they'd known was coming. Well, they'd at least known that something like it was likely, even if they probably wouldn't have guessed at this exact event.

The same, brave mageling spoke up again. "I assume he's non-standard, too?"

That broke the tension as slightly nervous chuckles echoed through the arena.

Tala shrugged. "Just a bit, yeah. He's a friend." With that thought, she sought out the healer and called out to him. "Hey, for safety's sake, would you be able to heal an arcanous creature if he were injured?"

The healer scratched his chin in thought, then nodded slowly. "I believe so. For combat healing, I mainly stimulate the patient's own body to regenerate, providing the energy for the healing myself. That should be universal, though I have never attempted to heal a non-human."

"Is that good enough, Terry?"

Terry gave her an arch look, and she laughed. "Fine, fine. I just wanted to be safe."

Terry preened, then looked back to Cazor, questioningly.

Cazor stepped forward. "Clear the center. Let's see what this… honorable creature is capable of."

Rane snorted another laugh. "You were going to call him a monster, weren't you?"

Cazor didn't reply.

The watchers moved to the sides of the arena. A few words were exchanged about the types of powers the two combatants would bring to bear, and it was decided that they didn't need to take any special precautions. Both were very precise in what they did.

Terry walked a slow arc back and forth while Cazor moved to stand opposite him, opening the pouches at his waist and calling out clouds of iron dust to begin swirling around him.

It was fascinating. Cazor's control of the interweaving magnetic fields was so tight and minute that he created ever-moving webs of iron powder as fine as capillaries in human skin.

If Tala had to guess, she'd have said that some of the paths were only a single grain wide as the iron swirled and spun in intricate, meticulously manipulated patterns to the point that the Mage himself was but a hazy form in the midst of the maelstrom.

Beautiful.

The magic around the iron was a kaleidoscope of power. Cazor was utilizing the dimensions of magic to enact such powerful workings on each fraction of the physical space around him, and through it all, he barely seemed to be putting forth an effort.

-True, but from what we've seen, his inscriptions do much of the heavy lifting.-

That's fair.

Tala was surprised that no further iron lifted out of the sand as the Archon's magnetic fields brushed the surface. He was delicate and directional enough with his power that nothing he didn't wish to affect was affected.

Jean cleared her throat. "To surrender, either verbal or due to incapacitation. Fight!"

Terry instantly flickered away, but he didn't instantly appear near Cazor as Tala had expected.

Instead, she was able to see a series of blips of dimensional energy chained so quickly in succession they resembled a pack of firecrackers to her magesight, popping in sequence.

Each one took a different path, zig-zagging through the currents of iron.

The iron is actually blocking him? Or is he pretending it is?

Regardless of the case, he never fully manifested before moving on, so no one without active magesight would have noticed anything at all.

Now that she was listening for it, her greatly enhanced hearing could pick out the little bits of sound, distinct from the swirling rushing of the moving clouds of iron.

In less than two seconds, Terry had covered the distance and appeared behind Cazor and to the left.

While Cazor didn't turn, he obviously sensed Terry there, because the iron on that side pulled together to create what seemed to be an almost solid armored plate.

Terry smashed his talons through it.

As he struck, the magically formed iron mass twisted, deflecting and thus ruining the attack, even though it couldn't stop it.

At that moment, the iron sheet broke apart, back into dust, and seemed to flow and encase Terry's outstretched leg.

Terry ignored it, flickering down and shrinking, very similar to how he'd dealt with Aummar that first time.

So, encasing part of his body in iron doesn't work to stop him. She wouldn't have thought that it would, but proof was interesting to witness.

When Terry appeared, Cazor didn't try to block him. Instead, the Mage Hunter shot spikes of spinning, compressed iron at the terror bird, forcing Terry to flicker away once again.

The spikes shattered into the ground, briefly leaving dark gray patches in the sand, tracing the pattern of damage Cazor had attempted to inflict on Terry.

That looks pretty cool. I don't know if those would penetrate my skin, but if they did... She could imagine the havoc iron dust could wreak inside a Mage or magical creature.

Terry seemed to be having a grand old time as he switched tactics.

He flickered around Cazor's head, appearing for only an instant in each place to let out shrill squawks, always directed inward.

Tala flinched at the volume and pitch, even at a distance, and Cazor was clearly staggered by the quick sequence of sonic bursts.

Tala was surprised that she didn't see any magic behind the sound. It was simply that: mundane noise, piercing enough to cause pain.

Even so, when Terry appeared directly in front of the Mage to capitalize on that distraction, Cazor sent a ring of spikes shooting outward in all directions.

Millennial Mage, 6 - Fused

He didn't want to take the time to lock down exactly where Terry was, but he knew another attack was incoming.

One of the viciously sharp, spinning spikes struck solidly enough to cause the terror bird to grunt.

Terry hadn't flickered away as Tala had expected. Instead, he took the hit and used the momentary opening to grab Cazor across the chest, one talon going over each shoulder, one under his right arm, and the opposing talon hooking around the left side of the Archon's waist.

With seemingly casual ease and speed, Terry forced Cazor back and down, pinning the Archon to the sand, pressing him down with what must have been near bone-crushing force. Tala didn't hear the snap or pop of bone, however, showing just how calibrated Terry was being with his own strength and weight.

Terry screeched into Cazor's face, and the Archon tried to get his hands up between his head and Terry in a completely involuntary defensive reaction.

"Yield!" Cazor called out. "I yield!"

Terry immediately flickered away, settling down on the far side of the open space as iron dust rained down around Cazor.

Cazor lay on the sand groaning as the healer ran over to him and quickly dealt with the injuries.

It was then that Tala saw the blood.

It wasn't a lot, but there were specks of blood on the sand, and Terry never broke Cazor's skin.

"Terry. You're bleeding." Tala moved quickly across to her friend, running her hands over him. Sure enough, there was a small hole in one of his wings where the iron spike had hit.

Cazor staggered a bit as he and the healer came their way. Behind him, the iron was sucked off the surface of the arena floor and streamed back into his waiting pouches. "Well fought, master Terry. May I?" He held up one hand.

Terry gave him a wary glance but then nodded once.

Cazor placed a hand over the small wound, and Tala saw him create a powerful, targeted magnetic field, drawing his iron dust out of the flesh around the injury. "That would have made it difficult to heal."

Terry narrowed his eyes and nipped at Cazor's hand, though he didn't break the skin.

"Yeah, yeah. Sorry about that. I didn't really think that I'd have to use my spikes." He scratched the back of his head. "How short is your teleportation cool-down, anyway?"

Terry gave him a look that Tala knew well. So, after a short chuckle, she interjected on Terry's behalf. "You're asking him questions he has no way of answering. He can't speak, remember?"

"Right, right." Cazor turned to look her way. "Do you know?"

She shrugged. "I've never seen a noticeable delay between his teleports." She'd seen him tired, but that wasn't a feature of his teleportation.

Cazor paled and swallowed, his attention shifting back to Terry. "That's... terrifying. And your size-changing?" He shook his head. "You have complete dimensional mastery, don't you?"

Terry cocked his head, conveying uncertainty.

The Archon leaned in and lowered his voice, probably unnecessarily, but he wanted to ensure that the magelings couldn't hear. Their masters might share this with them, but that wasn't for him to do. "Most arcanous creatures have a single aspected ability and usually some physical or physiological ones thrown in. Most creatures can survive a single trip to a fount for such, to become arcanous creatures in the first place. But if they return to pass through the fount a second time? Most die outright. But if they don't, they are able to gain much, *much* greater strength and flexibility in that aspect. If all you could do was teleport quickly, I'd believe you went through a dimensional fount twice, but you can do so much more. Now, if a creature has visited a fount twice and then goes back a third time, they die."

He paused on that, letting it hang before he gave a mischievous smile.

"But if they don't, they gain what we call mastery over that aspect, and their capabilities often exceed Bound, or even Fused, true-magical creatures."

Terry's head drooped, and he crooned softly.

Cazor noticed and patted the side of the terror bird's beak. "You must have been desperate to end up as you are, my friend."

Terry didn't reply.

The healer had been examining the wound while Cazor talked, but now that there was a natural gap in the flow of information, he cleared his throat to gain their attention. "This might hurt, and it will definitely itch."

Terry regarded the man for a moment, then bobbed a nod.

The healer extended his hand, and power flowed through him and into Terry.

Terry squawked and shivered in irritation but didn't otherwise react.

True to form, the wound closed in the time it would take for a deep breath.

In the background, from near the edge of the arena, Tala heard Jean turn to the magelings-to-be. "So, any questions?"

And that unleashed a flood. It took a good fifteen minutes to get all the questions answered and return the focus to the training at hand.

The first one started off in a mildly interesting fashion. "How can magic affect iron? I thought iron was immune to magic."

Jean nodded sagely. "Well, iron cannot be affected by magic, but it can be by anything created by magic, that is not magic itself."

The magelings-to-be all seemed to consider that before nodding, seemingly understanding.

For the most part, the questions moved into less interesting territory from there.

Blessedly, Tala was not required to answer many of the questions, except those pertaining to Terry. Though, there were quite a few of those to answer.

They wanted to know how she'd gotten him to work with her.

"More than anything, he chose me."

Terry trilled happily from her shoulder, head-butting her cheek to 'awws' and smiles from the magelings.

Could they tame a terror bird of their own when they found one?

"No, I would not recommend trying to tame or befriend terror birds as a rule. He tried to kill me on multiple occasions before we worked things out."

Terry bobbed emphatically, adding weight to the statement as the young ones paled, licked dried lips, or otherwise demonstrated horror at the very idea of befriending something that had repeatedly tried to kill them.

-It's kind of your thing, though… right? You find things that want to, or could, destroy you and get what you can from them?-

Tala ignored Alat.

Finally, they wanted to know if it was hard to keep him fed, given his larger size when he chose it.

"He actually eats less than I do."

That puzzled the newly arrived graduates but gave Aproa and Rane no end of amusement.

Thankfully, the rest of the questions were not Terry-related, so Tala was spared.

Soon enough, they were back to the standard, daily practice and training.

Terry, not being Bound in truth or in power-density, couldn't participate in aura manipulation or direct contests of will. Even so, the group was still able to do such exercises, including Terry, after Jean informed everyone that an Archon *should* be able to prevent Terry's teleportation by extending their aura over a space and claiming it as their own.

Tala gave Terry a side-eyed glare at that revelation, to which the terror bird pretended innocence.

In practice, however, Terry's magical weight hit like an Elder, and no single Archon could keep him from moving around as he saw fit. They couldn't even slow him down or redirect him a noticeable amount.

They only succeeded in keeping him from a space when Tala, Rane, and Cazor synced their intent and willpower over a space in which they co-mingled their auras.

The result was that Terry was forced to appear about a foot to the left of his intended destination.

Terry, of course, squawked derisively before stepping onto the target and declaring himself victorious, yet again.

Honestly, Tala was surprised that the magelings-to-be were allowed to witness the use, and hear discussions, of aura.

It was apparently something standardly conveyed to magelings early on by Archon masters. So, no one saw an issue with it.

The idea of co-mingling multiple Archons' auras was fascinating to Tala. She'd understood the theory before, as everything her aura had 'claimed' in Makinaven had already been so ruled by Master Jevin at a much more fundamental level, but she'd not considered its applications for Archons on equal footings or at equal rank.

The more direct tests of will that followed were embarrassing for Tala, in that she was once more the spotlight as she defeated every individual Mage in direct conflicts of willpower and magical weight.

There had been a moment of panic when she realized that her aura was trapped behind her iron paint. Thankfully, she'd immediately realized that her situation was almost the exact reverse of the iron sphere training Master Jevin had given her to do. With that in mind, and a bit of effort, she was able to force her power around the physical barrier, through the dimensions of magic, and use it to empower her aura as normal.

Not ideal.

-Everything's a trade-off. We'll have to see if this one works out.-

It didn't take long to cycle through everyone in head-to-head conflicts, given that they could pair up and oppose one another all at the same time, rather than waiting for each individual bout to finish.

She didn't even have to use her trick to come at them from below, and she still won handily against any individual Archon.

She tried not to steal glances at her year-mates, watching from the sides, but when she did, despite her best judgment, she saw growing awe in their expressions.

Great. This is not what I was aiming for...

The group rounded out the day with scenario work, which Terry gleefully participated in.

The most common setup was to defend a singular person from Terry.

Millennial Mage, 6 - Fused

Though, from one perspective, that was an abject failure and an exercise in frustration for the Archons, in every other aspect, it was fantastic practice.

They each made massive leaps in coordinating with one another and overlaying, and even combining, their defenses with each other.

The result was a move from near-instant defeat to being able to protect a given target for nearly five seconds before Terry breached their coordinated efforts.

There were lots of laughs, groans, and shaking of heads. Everyone grew in appreciation of the difficulty of protecting isolated targets from determined assault—and in their dawning horror of just how vicious the terror bird could be.

Suffice it to say, the healer earned his pay and got his share of practice that day.

Tala was definitely coming to better understand Xeel's feelings about the terror bird and the reasoning behind the elimination of the fount which had given him power.

As the Archons parted ways for the evening, several of the magelings approached various Mages, likely to inquire about becoming master and mageling.

Aproa bid everyone goodbye, as she was leaving in the morning, and Tala invited Rane back to her and Lyn's house for the celebration with Lyn's new mageling.

When they were all about to depart, Alat reminded Tala of her duties the next day.

"Oh! Apologies, everyone, but I have to leave the city tomorrow for an errand. Does anyone wish to accompany me to do some harvesting?" After a prod from Alat, Tala amended. "The harvesting is of berries, not arcanous animal parts, but the danger is still there."

Most bowed out immediately. Jean and a couple others inquired a bit before thanking her for the invitation but declining as well.

Cazor, however, was quite intrigued. "Sure, I'll come."

"Great! Meet me at the northern gate around… ten or so?"

He shrugged. "Sounds good to me."

"Do you have a mount or other means of traveling quickly?"

He returned a cocky grin. "I'll bet I can move faster than you." His eyes moved to Terry and back. "Even if you have someone to carry you."

"I'd like to see that."

"Then, I'll see you tomorrow."

Chapter: 12
Embarrassing for Everyone

As Tala and Rane were leaving the training complex, Tala remembered that she'd promised to be at the guardsmen's training area the next day, and Aummar was even going out of his way to prepare some special things for her and Terry. Now, she wouldn't be there.

Ahh, rust. That could have been bad.

-Agreed.-

So, with that realization, she walked over to the front desk where a young woman was reading a book.

What book is that? She was able to catch enough of a look at it that Alat could extrapolate.

-It's either How to Become a Mage without the Academy, *or* How to Seduce a Mage, Academically.-

Tala almost choked. *Those are nothing alike!*

-Well, take a better look, then. It's at an extreme angle.-

Wait… is the second one actually a real book?

-Of—-

Tala cut across Alat. *Never mind! I don't want to know.* She pushed that aside, hopefully permanently. "Excuse me."

"Yes, Mistress?" The woman closed the book and set it title side down before glancing up and then frowning slightly. Despite her confusion, she didn't comment further, instead waiting for Tala to make her inquiry.

Tala assumed that the woman's difficulty came from this being a for-Mages facility. While mundanes weren't barred by any means, there wasn't much that would be useful to them there, generally speaking.

My lack of visible inscriptions is a bit annoying. She felt like Jenna would have known that, and they could have made the item with that in mind, but she was letting herself get distracted. "Could I send a messenger from here? If not, do you know a close location that could take it?"

The clerk looked to be about to give some negative response, but then her eyes moved over Terry on Tala's shoulder and to Rane, before returning to Tala, her entire demeanor shifting. It seemed that whether or not Tala was a Mage didn't really matter as she kept the company of Mages. "We can do that for you for a small fee."

As that was reasonable, Tala composed a short message for Aummar and asked for it to be delivered to that specific guardsman training ground as soon as possible.

It cost a half a silver but saved her the trip. *And the possibility of me forgetting or getting distracted.*

-*I think I sense personal growth.*-

Tala decided it was best to not engage.

Alat laughed in the back of Tala's mind.

The message taken care of, Tala thanked the clerk and departed with Rane and Terry in tow.

They discussed the day's training along with other small things as they trudged through the slush.

With no new snow added in the last few hours, the existing stuff had been trampled and dirtied to the point of becoming a slushy, black-brown mess.

This… this I don't like. It was a part of the less pleasant side of winter, and Tala was grateful for both her shoes, which she had quickly grown on, and for her weight distribution scripts, which helped keep her from sinking into the dark filth. When she glanced behind herself, she did see a series of shallow, circular 'prints' leading away behind her. *I wonder if that will confuse anyone.* It didn't really matter, she supposed.

She didn't know exactly what would happen to all the nastiness when she altered her clothing.

In the worst case, it would be carried with the material as it—the dirt—sloughed off, falling back into the rest of the snow. *Right. Self-cleaning.*

-Did you really forget a part of what they do?-

I suppose… Well, forget isn't quite right, I just didn't try to remember. I don't really think about that aspect of their magic very often.

-That's fair.-

Rane, for his part, was getting his boots and lower pants *covered* in the dark muck that resulted from the snow-slurry and countless passersby, both human and animal.

Terry stayed warm, dry, and clean on Tala's shoulder.

They didn't talk too much as they made their way home. *Well, to my home. And Lyn's… and now Kannis's as well, I suppose.*

-It could be Rane's too, if you wanted.-

You don't know that, and no, I don't want that.

-It's pretty obvious.-

Tala ignored that, taking special satisfaction in the wide-open, free-from-buildings park near her home.

-You know, since I can sense when you're being influenced, and then help to mitigate it, we could ride Terry through the city until we found other syphons.-

That…that was a surprisingly interesting idea. *Not now. Too much else going on.*

-Fine, fine.-

Tala let them into the house, calling out as she did so. "I'm home! I brought Rane with me."

-Not Master Rane.-

Millennial Mage, 6 - Fused

Hush, you.

"Tala! Come on back," Lyn's voice floated out to greet them. "You, too, Master Rane."

Rane cleared his throat, looking down at his filthy boots and pants. "I've got to get a bit cleaned up first. I'll be out in a moment."

With that, he ducked into the washroom right off the entryway.

Tala simply stamped her feet on the mat a couple of times to let everything fall free and retracted her shoes before proceeding into the house.

She came out of the entry hall and into the main space to find Lyn and Kannis sitting in two of the chairs, seeming to have been chatting before Tala had gotten there.

"Come, sit." Lyn looked around and frowned slightly, realizing that there were only three big chairs.

Tala sat in the only other large reading chair and relaxed.

-You should say something.-

Tala sighed, leaning forward once again. "So, how was the first day? I like the magesight inscriptions. That's a good set. A bit taxing for new Mages, but way better than the standard."

"Oh, it was wonderful. Thank you for asking. And…" Kannis hesitated, then blinked at her. "Wait. You can tell what type of inscriptions I have?"

Tala shrugged. She could. *So long as I have a basis for comparison and interpretation.* "Yeah. My own magesight assists in the interpretation of inscriptions, so I've started to pick up the basics."

Kannis seemed a bit at a loss as to how to respond to that.

Thankfully, Rane chose that moment to join them, wearing new, clean pants. "Hey, all."

Lyn smiled. "Welcome, Master Rane. As to chairs—"

Rane grinned and held up a forestalling hand, seemingly guessing what she was thinking before pulling out a folding chair from his dimensional storage and sitting in it with practiced comfort.

Tala thought she recognized the style, and it reminded her vividly of a cyclops and being bodily skipped across the ground like a stone. *I hope Grediv is still alive. I'd like to slap him one day.*

-*For all the help he gave you?*-

She hesitated. *No, I'll hug him for that, then slap him for the cyclops.*

-*I can agree to that. I'll help you remember.*-

"Kannis, this is Master Rane." Lyn gestured to the man, somewhat unnecessarily. "Master Rane, this is my new mageling, Kannis."

"A pleasure to meet you, Kannis." He held out his hand, and Kannis took it with a flustered smile. She'd clearly moved past the earlier confusion with regards to Tala.

"Thank you, Master Rane, the pleasure is genuinely mine." She glanced to Lyn. "Are you sure it's alright?"

The older woman shrugged. "Ask him if you wish."

Kannis cleared her throat. "Do you mind if I look at you with my magesight? My master has instructed me to keep it on as much as I can stand, and I am recovered enough to reengage it."

Rane waved nonchalantly. "Sure. Most stop caring about that as they advance." His eyes flicked toward Tala. "Thankfully for some."

Tala rolled her eyes. "Even those who care only care if they notice, and they have to have their own magesight on for that to be the case."

Kannis regarded her with a mix of curiosity and caution plain on her face.

Millennial Mage, 6 - Fused

-You're projecting.-
Tala ignored Alat.
The mageling smiled. "So… you wouldn't mind either?"

"Not at all. Thank you for asking." She smiled, trying to lighten the mood and still feeling bad for not acknowledging that she'd known Kannis before. *She's clearly forgotten me or decided not to mention it, so I'm fine.*

-She is likely thinking the same.-

Tala ignored that as she saw power run through the lines around Kannis's eyes, and the young woman looked at each of the others in turn.

"Master Rane. You are an Archon as well?" Kannis seemed a bit over-awed at the realization.

Rane frowned at the comment. "I thought I had better control of my aura than that. You shouldn't have been able to tell at all."

Lyn interjected. "Mistress Holly switched her over to a more advanced form of magesight for her reinscribing. She can see through the first layers of skin as if she has greater magical weight behind her sight. That allows her to see even perfectly controlled auras, so long as they aren't fully retracted. It's strenuous on her, but it should be a net benefit in the long run."

"Ahh." He smiled, then, a weight seeming to come off him. "In that case, yes. I am."

Kannis turned to Tala in an almost reverent tone. "How have you surrounded yourself with such powerful people, Mistress Tala?" She hesitated, seeming to actually look at Tala for the first time, her magesight still active. "You look… odd?" She immediately blushed and looked down. "I apologize. I didn't mean it that way. I mean, I can see magic around you but no spell-lines, nothing but what might be an aura... I don't think? It just looks a bit... odd."

Tala sighed. "Well, it's best to just get this over with, I suppose. None of you scream, please?"

-Really? You're not going to tell them more than that?-
I want to see how they really feel, what they really think about it.

-Seems a bit circumspect, but okay.-

Lyn leaned back, assuming that she knew what was coming. The other two gave her odd looks but slowly nodded.

Here it goes. Tala reached inside herself and deactivated the through-spike's illusion functions.

Tala saw her hands in her peripheral vision as they quickly faded from clean, unblemished, unadorned, and flesh-colored to a dull, dark gray. Overtop of the gray, intricate inscriptions were carved, seemingly with light, into existence around her, forming a cage of power that somehow seemed to be just that, a cage to protect the world from what lay within.

She saw the barest hints of magic flicker away from her eyes as well. *So that answers that. My eyes were normal again.*

-And now they are blood rubies.-

Tala twitched at that, the blood eyes of the arcane forcing themselves back into her mind, clawing their way free of her memories.

Stop reminding me of him!

In the distracted moment, Tala *almost* missed the others' reactions to her transformation. Thankfully, it was only almost.

Lyn's eyes widened. She'd seen Tala fully painted, but she hadn't seen her since the power had had time to fully build, causing nearly every spellform to fully manifest an echo around Tala.

Rane gaped, his mouth seemingly forgotten as his jaw fell slack. He didn't react defensively, for which Tala was grateful. She knew that she probably looked quite arcane, so such a reaction would have been reasonable. Instead, he looked like someone staring upon a great masterpiece for the first time.

Great... just what we needed.
-Oh, not what you secretly wanted?-
No. No? I don't know. Hush, you.

Kannis paled, pushing back into her chair, her jaw working, but only one word coming out before her mouth continued to move silently. "Arcane—"

Tala held up her hands. "Hey, now. No. I'm no arcane." Only Tala had noticed as the other two's focus was locked onto her, but when Kannis spoke, that caught Lyn and Rane's attention, and they both moved to help the mageling at once.

They both assured Kannis that Tala was not an arcane, and that seemed to calm her a bit, but she still seemed quite inwardly focused, withdrawn.

As they did so, Lyn gave Tala a stern look. "You should know better than to show something so extreme to a new graduate, Tala. You broke my mageling, and I don't appreciate it."

"Yes, Mistress. Your house, your rules."

The stern look held for only a moment before it broke, and they shared a guilty grin.

Tala tried to suppress her smile. "I will try to be better in the future."

"See that you do. Don't let this smile fool you. I'm irritated with you for this little stunt, amusing as parts of it are." Her tone denoted that she was dead serious, so Tala took her at her word.

Lyn turned her attention back to Kannis as Rane pulled out some smelling salts and waved them under Kannis's nose.

The shock of the harsh smell seemed to pull her back to herself, and she shook her head as if to clear it. She then looked around in confusion for an instant before her eyes settled back onto Tala. "What is happening, Tala? What did that crazy woman do to you?"

* * *

Tala, with Lyn and Rane's help, calmed Kannis down. As they worked, Tala had released the through-spike, allowing the illusion to return.

Tala had some questions of her own, but when she learned that Kannis had met Holly earlier in the day, a lot became clearer.

"No, no. She didn't do this to me, not directly; she more... facilitated?"

Kannis took a long drink from a mug filled with warm tea, which had been provided by Rane. "So... this is an illusion, and that... other visage is the real you?"

Tala shrugged. "Yes, and no? This is me. But it's hidden below the magic and—"

Lyn cleared her throat meaningfully.

"—and other stuff. Both are me."

Kannis gave her a mildly condescending look before seeming to master herself.

Even so, Tala took the hint. "But this one is a magically crafted illusion, if that's what you're asking."

"It was. Thank you for the honesty." The mageling looked a bit off, but that was likely due to having had such an emotional shock so recently.

Millennial Mage, 6 - Fused

Well, I never really got to see my own reaction to seeing an arcane. I was already under compulsion before I noticed him... She shuddered at the thought.

There was a prolonged silence while Kannis continued to drink her tea that was bordering on awkward when Rane cleared his throat. "Well, look at it this way, Kannis. Now you have three Archons to help you out."

Lyn gave Rane a wide-eyed glare.

Rane immediately misinterpreted the look and added, "Assuming your master approves, of course."

Lyn groaned, and Kannis turned slowly to regard Tala. "You're an Archon, too?"

Rane made an 'Oh' face, and shifted backward under Lyn's continued disbelieving glare.

Tala smiled awkwardly and scratched her own cheek. "Didn't you notice?"

"Yes, Mistress Tala, I noticed your Archon-ness under the inhuman skin and glowing, arcane-looking lines." Kannis hesitated. "No, you know what? No. I couldn't have noticed. You had no magical signature except what was reflecting... off... you." She clucked her tongue. "Why are you covered in iron?" She shook her head. "No, *how* are you covered in iron?" Kannis looked to Lyn, who continued to glare at Rane.

Rane, for his part, shifted his chair backward to lessen his prominence in the conversation.

Tala glanced between her fellow Archons and cleared her throat. "This is likely a conversation for another time."

Lyn turned back to her mageling and nodded. "I agree. This will be an excellent conversation for us to have... later."

Rane slapped his hands down on his knees, drawing everyone's attention back to him. "So, celebration time? Kannis, you're a mageling now. Mistress Lyn, you have a mageling now. Tala, you have a new housemate. Good things all around!"

That shook the group loose from the aftermath of the odd moments.

"That sounds wonderful, Master Rane." Lyn stood, offering Kannis a hand. "Let's get our coats and boots, and we'll be on our way."

Coats and boots? As Tala considered, she realized that most of the people she'd seen walking through the streets had been wearing such. Those that weren't had either been obviously Mages or just as obviously miserable. *I guess it is pretty cold.*

-Just a bit below freezing, if my estimation is correct. The slush will be freezing, now that traffic is slowing. Be careful navigating the ice. I'd hate for you to hit your head.-

Tala ignored that and turned her attention to happier topics. "Where do you all want to go to eat?"

Kannis gave Tala a long look, seeming much more in control of herself. "I do have questions. I have so, *so* many questions, but I'll take my master's guidance and not pursue them, for the moment."

That really doesn't help us find a place to eat... Tala was hungry, but she shrugged. "Lyn can answer what she deems appropriate for you to know, and I'm happy to convey anything that she asks me to."

"That's... fair." The mageling looked conflicted but seemed to draw herself out of it. "Alright. Let's eat!"

There you go. Back on the right track.

Rane smiled. "I like your attitude, but we still need to know where."

Tala grinned. "Little Caravans?"

Lyn groaned. "I can't eat that much, and while it's tasty, it's hardly uniquely celebratory."

That's hardly fair. Those are amazing! But the night wasn't really about her. "Alright then. Soup? Meat pies? What are you in the mood for, Kannis?"

The young woman seemed to consider. "You know what? I really want ice cream."

Tala chuckled. "That sounds like a fine dessert plan. Do you know what you want to eat for dinner before dessert?"

Kannis compressed her lips, quirking them off to one side. "Never heard of a little caravan before. Let's try that."

Tala lightly clapped her former year-mate on the shoulder. "I like how you think, Kannis. To little caravans!"

Lyn groaned again. "You're going to be the death of me. I mean that literally, too. When these inscriptions go out of alignment"—she patted her middle—"I'm going to pop and kill everyone around me."

"Oh, you'll be fine. Your inscriptions aren't anywhere near the distortion point."

Rane was looking down at his clean pants, not paying attention to the current flow of the conversation, with a sour expression.

Tala regarded him for a moment before simply asking, "What's up, Rane?"

He huffed a sigh. "I'm deciding whether to get these dirty or change back into the pair that's already dirty."

"Decisions, decisions; make up your mind, though. I have a bit of quick business with Lyn, then we should get going."

He waved her off. "I'll go change back."

Tala turned to Lyn, who was now regarding her with interest. "First, when will I be leaving for Marliweather?"

"Oh, in about a week."

"Usual arrangements?"

"Yes. Charging required for two days before and after each leg."

"Understood. Now, can you sell an assortment of… randomly acquired items for me?"

Lyn's eyes narrowed. "What did you do, Tala?"

"Nothing, nothing. I just picked up what no longer had an owner."

"Uh-huh."

"So, where can I put the stuff? No need for me to keep carrying it about."

Lyn sighed. "Pile it on the table, so we can go."

And so, Tala did just that, laying out the woodcutting axes, hatchets, pouches, and other odds and ends that she'd taken from the woodsmen who'd tried to pursue her and met a timely end beneath Terry's talons and beak.

Lyn looked at the items and then turned her gaze back to Tala. "No. This isn't suspicious at all."

"I can sell them myself if—"

"No, no. It's fine." Lyn cut across her. "I'll see what I can do. It won't net you much, though."

Tala shrugged. "Better than carrying it around any longer."

"Alright. Now, let's go."

They all trudged through the snow to acquire the little caravans. Tala ate five of the cheesy little caravans; Rane ate one; and Lyn and Kannis split a 'smaller little caravan.'

When Kannis actually noticed the pace at which Tala was eating, she couldn't hold back any longer, and she cut loose with some pointed questions. Tala explained how her healing inscriptions worked and how Holly had added spellforms to maintain her form while compacting muscle and reserves into the predefined shapes at increasing densities.

Millennial Mage, 6 - Fused

Kannis obviously didn't understand the intricacies, but she seemed to get the gist of how and why it worked, at least enough for them to return to more standard dinner conversations.

They chatted about small things, but mostly, they just spent the time together, getting used to the new person in their midst.

After dinner, they hunted down a place that sold ice cream and continued the casual celebration.

All in all, it was a pleasant way to end what had been quite a long day.

Chapter: 13
Surprisingly Reasonable

Tala, Rane, Lyn, and Kannis talked and ate late into the night.

Well... no, that was not quite right.

Tala and Terry continued to eat late into the night. Rane, Lyn, and Kannis simply talked.

They mainly talked about their growing up years, or Kannis asked the Mages about their lives as such.

Both Tala and Kannis studiously avoided discussing their days at the academy, and the others seemed to key off that.

-You'll have to talk about it eventually.-
I know. You know I do, but not tonight.

When they reluctantly decided to call it a night and end the impromptu little celebration, Kannis looked to be on the edge of falling asleep where she sat.

As it turned out, they'd been able to find a little all-night dessert and coffee café. It seemed to cater mostly to Mages, but a not-small portion of their customers were clearly mundanes.

The smell of coffee had almost overpowered Tala's willpower a few times, but while Tala had been tempted by the alluring aroma, she'd only indulged in the desserts.

The café wasn't closing, and they were hardly the only people in the establishment, but the night was getting late. Lyn and Kannis had work in the morning, and Rane and Tala had a lot that they hoped to do as well, so with a little collective prompting, they got moving.

Millennial Mage, 6 - Fused

Rane walked with them all back to their house, and the late hour, combined with their collective tiredness, left it a silent walk through the crisply cold city night.

Thankfully, more snow had fallen earlier in the night, creating a thin layer of reasonable traction atop the treacherous, frozen slush. Thus, it was a more pleasant walk than it might otherwise have been.

Street clearers would likely be by in a couple of hours with hot, salt-water incorporators. *All of the benefits, none of the lasting vegetative damage.*

Tala had seen them work as a child, but she'd never really understood that it was simply Mages using devices to accomplish the task. *One of the easy, useful tasks available to Mages who don't want to hold down a regular job this time of year.*

From what she'd seen on various job boards, and what Alat had looked up for them, it paid about ten silver for a night's work. Not a lot, but still quite a good wage for non-guild-affiliated workers.

But that wasn't really pertinent. The next day would be... something. *If it takes the hook, I could be rid of that monster once and for all.* She hesitated, then corrected herself. *Humanity will be rid of him.*

The four continued to walk, and Terry continued his seemingly perpetual nap on Tala's shoulder as she continued her contemplations of the next day. As she did so, she realized that she really wanted to convey some information to Jenna. Therefore, she had asked Alat to update Jenna on what she'd done toward spreading awareness of her venture and the companion she'd have for the following day.

Surprisingly enough, Jenna responded almost immediately, simply adding, "Noted." to the Archive document they both had access to.

-At least she knows we did our part spreading awareness.-

Yeah. That was a little awkward, asking everyone if anyone wanted to join... I haven't felt so out of place since I was back at the academy...

-Didn't expect Cazor to say yes.-

Yeah, that threw me off a bit, too. She clicked her tongue behind her teeth for a moment, then shrugged. *We'll find a way of telling him what's going on tomorrow before we leave. It would be pretty awful to drag him into what might be a high-power fight essentially blind.*

-Kit should do for that. Invite him in?-

Yeah, that should work.

Before any of them really knew it, they'd arrived, and Rane bade them all goodnight at their front door. Lyn fumbled for her key for a moment before Tala snorted a laugh and easily pulled her key from Kit.

Kannis was a bit unsteady on her feet. *The girl's had a big day.*

Even so, the mageling gave Tala's key a puzzled look. "Is that... iron?" She shook her head. "What am I saying? Of course it's iron."

Tala just grinned as she quickly unlocked the house and let the three of them in, out of the cold.

I'd not considered it, but Lyn's hooked into the city for heat, too. Her family had used lamps and a wood stove for light and heat while Tala was growing up. *Probably cheaper, after the initial expense.* If she remembered correctly, several officials had offered to do the installation, but her father had always refused.

Part of his desire to 'do it on his own,' or some such. *Didn't keep him from making me pay his debts...*

-That's right, Tala. Think on it. Build up what you want to say.-

Tala sent a mental glare toward Alat.

Millennial Mage, 6 - Fused

Not having to take off her coat or boots, she walked in first and went straight back to the back hallway. With a casual motion, she pulled Kit from her belt and tossed it against the wall, where it landed silently and grew into a door that fit the space perfectly, looking for all the world as if it had been there since the house was built.

Ironically, or maybe very deliberately, the door didn't blend in in such a way as to fade from notice. Instead, it stood out in a manner that complemented the other doors and the hallway in general, making it seem as if the space would actually be worse off were the door not there.

Of course it's always been there. No one would be foolish enough to have this space without having put in this keystone part of the design.

-It is almost deviously perfect.-

They agreed on that. The syphon's abilities were potent, its primary goal of non-detection still integral in their use.

Lyn and Kannis came down the hall as Tala was stepping through the new door, into her dimensional storage.

The younger woman paused, whispering to herself in half-conscious confusion. "I don't remember that door being there... How did I miss that?"

Lyn gave her an odd look, seeming to have not heard the girl's words but noticing the direction of her attention and the interest and confusion directed that way. "Where did you imagine Tala was going to be sleeping?"

"I... uh..." Kannis didn't seem to have an answer for that.

"Good night, you two. Sleep well." Tala stuck one hand back out the door and waved.

"Night!" both replied almost in unison as Tala closed the door, shutting out the rest of the world.

Now, I just have to do my evening training.

* * *

Tala woke after a deeply restful sleep, the red-orange light of sunrise bathing her in the beauty of another dawn. She honestly didn't care that it was illusory; she loved it more every time she woke to her own private vista.

Only three hours tonight? She unconsciously knew how long she'd slept; it was as easy as blinking.

-The new set of spellforms have fully settled in. Don't expect your required rest to get any shorter, at least not with this set of inscriptions.-

Not even with the iron compounding and increasing my power-density?

-With these scripts, the increased density won't matter. You're hitching more oxen to the front of a lightly loaded wagon. It's not going to make a difference until you have a heavier load to pull.-

That made a lot of sense, and Holly had expressed that many of the ones that Tala currently had were parts of various series of physically enhancing script-regimens. *You know… I wonder if this is Refining?*

Alat grunted within Tala's mind. *-No? It might be a precursor to it, though.-*

Ahh, like strengthening the body so that the impurities can be stripped from you without destroying us?

-That would be in the vein of my guess.-

It sounded like a good guess, if Tala was being honest.

Tala moved through her morning routine, only hitching during the perspective portion of her aspect mirroring as she had in the past.

It was nauseating and dizzying in the extreme, even when she restricted the mirroring to a singular external perspective, alongside her own.

Still, like everything else, she was improving. Alat helped with that, too, slowly modifying and tweaking her exercises of all types to better match how Tala could and would learn and grow.

Honestly, Tala could have done that for herself all along, but it would have taken time, a lot of deep analysis, and some comparative study. Now, Alat did it for her with relative ease and speed.

-You know, it's not actually that easy, but I don't have to maintain any of your day-to-day activities. So, I have a lot more free time.-

Well, thank you. I appreciate your efforts on our part.

-Your improvement is my improvement.-

She had soon completed her morning tasks, save for the bath.

Cleansing was going to be difficult with the iron body paint. She didn't really need the bath, except for her hair, but she could just use her comb for that. *Except that it's at the Constructionist Guild facility.*

That was a problem for later in the day, and as such, she set about cooking a massive breakfast for herself.

Kit's little kitchenette worked even better than she'd hoped it would, and soon Tala was devouring a sizable meal pulled from her venturing food.

The Culinary Guild really came through with this stuff. I really should get more. It never went bad, in theory, and so it would be better to have on hand than run out or be in need. *Not today, though. Today, I have other tasks.*

-Yup, large barrels. I'm thinking a few tuns?-

A few what?

-A tun. That's a barrel that holds 252 gallons.-

Archive? She trusted that Alat would be able to interpret her abbreviated question.

-Archive. It's surprisingly easy to look up random words.-

Useful, I suppose.

-I'll say.-

Tala got an odd sensation along with that expression, as if Alat had put a lot of weight behind the utterance. As she considered it, Tala realized that, in several meaningful ways, all Alat had was words.

She decided not to focus on that or inquire further for the moment. *Okay, so a couple of tuns… doesn't that seem excessive? I mean… how can we possibly harvest enough to fill even a single one with berries, let alone with juice?*

-More storage capacity seems better, right?-

Tala shrugged. *I suppose, but it still seems like a lot more than we'll actually need.*

-That's fair. I might have a better option as well.-

Oh? Then why had she been talking about massive barrels? Probably because she genuinely thought they were the best subset of 'barrel options.'

-The Constructionists sell large, enameled, cast-iron barrels. 55 gallon, to be precise.-

That seems perfect! They're designed for use in containing experiments and other magical liquids, I assume?

-Precisely.-

I suppose we should have guessed that something like that would exist. Not cheap though, right?

-Actually, it's surprisingly affordable, all things considered.-

Do tell.

-They guarantee that the containers will maintain the potency of any magical ingredients kept within, while so contained.-

That's… As Tala thought about it, and how tight the seals must be, and how much testing would have needed to go into such a certification, she realized just how much value and weight such an assurance held. *That's actually pretty amazing.*

-That's what I thought.-

So, how much?

-Half a gold per barrel.-

Tala winced, then thought about it. *Huh, how is that both more and less expensive than I expected?*

-We're strange?-

She chuckled at that. *Fair enough.* After a moment's consideration, she continued, *You have access to their 'for sale' list?*

-I do. Well, everyone with Archive access does.-

You know what I'm thinking?

-Of course. We should get a better small container.-

The iron flask that Tala had been using was looking a bit worse for wear. She'd only dropped it a few times, but exterior dings, wear, and tear weren't the problem in any case. The simple iron flask hadn't been designed for such constant use with even a mild acid, and almost every fruit juice was at least a little acidic.

-Yeah, it was meant to carry a flavored cooking oil, which would help maintain the metal. It's a blessing that you aren't negatively affected by some iron flakes.-

Tala grimaced. *I thought I'd been tasting some grit of late.*

-So, an enameled iron flask will only cost four silver for a four-cup one. It would be three silver for a two-cup.-

Yeah, a four-cup one is better, assuming it's easy enough to hold.

-We can take a look.-

That sounds like a good plan. What else did we put on our list?

-A cider or wine press.-

Right. Any ideas where to get one of those things?

-Market district would be the quickest. We can swing through the Constructionists' first. The location we frequent is pretty close to some shops. The presses are used enough by various restaurants and craftsmen that the shops should have some on hand.-

Even in the off season?

-With the growing complexes, there really aren't off seasons.-

Ahh, right. Tala considered for a moment. *You know, I've always wanted to see some of the growing complexes. They don't allow mundanes down there, unless they're workers or for some other specific purpose, and I haven't thought to go look since becoming a Mage.*

-Yup. I'm in your head and am well aware of your desires.-

Right. Sometimes I forget that.

Alat conveyed a bit of happiness at that. *-I'm glad to hear that I seem distinct from you, at least to you.-*

Shouldn't you already know that?

-Of course, but it's nice to hear kind things spoken aloud sometimes.-

Tala grunted. *True enough.*

She took the last couple of bites of the hearty fruit and nut-butter oatmeal before using her finger to scrape up the last bits.

I can't even tell that the fruit was dehydrated before.

-That's probably why the recipe included a bit more water than I'd have expected.-

I was thinking the same thing.

She left Kit, grabbing the doorway and pulling it off the wall as the door swung closed. It reshaped into a pouch even as she hung it from her belt.

She was almost surprised at how little Kit's transformation interested her. It was simply a useful

Millennial Mage, 6 - Fused

feature of her dimensional storage. *A ridiculously useful feature.*

She did not miss climbing up and down through the small opening that had been Kit's limit before.

Tala turned her attention outward, finding that Lyn's home was, as expected, quiet.

She could hear Kannis's breathing and slight shifting, even through the closed door to what had until recently been Tala's room.

Tala hesitated at that sound.

Why have I never heard anything from Lyn's room?

She extended her senses in that direction and hit a metaphorical wall. It wasn't a hard wall, and Tala thought that she could breach or break it if she really wanted to, but she refrained.

Lyn's got a privacy item? How did I not notice that before?

-It's hardly a good idea to proclaim: "I don't want anyone listening in here!" So, it likely does what it does as subtly as possible.-

Yeah, I suppose.

Tala decided to respect her friend's privacy, whatever the reason, and depart.

All told, from when she'd gone into Kit to when she came out, just over six hours had passed. *Three hours for two sets of training and a massive meal? Not too shabby.*

After locking the front door behind herself, she set out through the quiet, very early morning streets.

-We should have time to drop through the Constructionists', and even through the market district, before we meet Mistress Odera for breakfast.-

That was my thinking as well.

The trip was uneventful, and the security scripts on the Constructionists' facility didn't label her as a threat, so that worked out well.

Sadly, Alat hadn't yet figured out how to modify the illusion, so there was an awkward moment where the assistant thought she was a mundane. Thankfully, the security scripts had identified her as an Archon, so it was easy enough to clear up.

They did have several of the iron barrels in stock, as well as flasks for smaller samples.

Of course, the smaller flasks were designed with convenient, easy to use handles, so that valuable samples would never be risked.

That pleased Tala to no end.

Unfortunately, the only barrels and flasks they had were deep crimson in color. They were that shade because it was the most often requested color, used to denote the storage of arcanous or magical blood.

This was a practice that was seemingly vastly more common than Tala had realized, especially among Constructionist Mages.

The assistant was happy to explain that the study of arcanous blood as an ink for spell-lines, applied in various mediums, was a well-researched field of study, and there were some spellforms that were known to be more efficient with a given arcanous creature's blood than even with gold.

There weren't many, but they did exist.

Sadly, when Tala inquired, she was told that that was a guild secret.

Obviously, Alat couldn't find out either, Tala not having special access relating to the Constructionist Guild within the Archive.

She could have custom-ordered virtually any color at no extra cost—other than time—but she was in a hurry, and red was good enough for her. So, in the end, Tala was able to get a bundled deal of four blood-red enameled barrels and two large flasks for a total of two gold.

It wasn't much in the way of savings, and she ended up buying more barrels than she had planned to, but it should be better in the end.

I'm tired of reaching for more juice and having my flask empty. Having a back-up will be worth it.

-*Sure, justify it however you want. This assistant is a good salesman.*-

It was a fairly simple matter to create a door out of Kit and maneuver the barrels inside.

The enamel was exquisitely done, looking like nothing so much as liquid blood, locked in place, thinly coating the containers. With each touch, Tala half expected her hands to come away wet, even though she knew better.

This is going to add new dimensions to my reputation as the Blood Archon.

-*Just a bit, yeah. Though, it's probably safer for people to assume you're drinking some blood than endingberries.*-

Why?

-*Because they'd assume it was something special, and therefore, they wouldn't be inclined to just start drinking random blood.*-

Or they could just assume I was drinking water...

-*That would be better, but such is life.*-

Tala thanked the assistant and was about to leave when she remembered her comb.

Blessedly, it was a simple thing for her to get a hold of it and use it briefly before returning it to the assistant's care and departing.

All told, she hadn't been in the Constructionist facility long, but there were quite a few more people out and about than before.

How late did we stay up?

-*Rhetorical question, right?*-

Mostly, yeah. It had been late, but not *that* late.

The stores were starting to open or already doing brisk business.

Alat got Tala to the generally correct area, and a few quick questions brought her to a merchant who had a press for sale. Twenty silver secured the device for her use. Tala carried it half a block before finding an out of the way section of wall to throw Kit against so that she could place the press inside.

That's better.

-That wasn't heavy, even for a normal person.-

But it was awkward. After a moment's frown, Tala inquired further. *Can't you read my thoughts? Aren't you in my thoughts?*

-I can, but if I did that all the time, what would we ever talk about? Also, my questions cause you to rethink through your thoughts and conclusions, and that's good for both of us.-

Tala grunted. *Fair enough.*

They arrived at the Caravanner's Guildhall before her mentor, and Tala was able to grab a table and feed Terry some jerky before Mistress Odera came to join them.

First things first, Tala let Mistress Odera know about the Marliweather trip coming up. The older Mage, of course, already knew, but she appreciated hearing it from Tala, herself.

Then, Tala let Mistress Odera know that she had given her access to some memories, via the Archive.

Mistress Odera had frozen, her gaze intently locked on Tala's face. "*Those* memories?"

"Yes. Those."

After a long moment, Mistress Odera nodded once. "I will review them when we are done here."

From there, Tala described how her training had changed. She didn't mention Alat, and Alat didn't seem to mind.

Millennial Mage, 6 - Fused

In the end, it was a nice breakfast, and they parted ways as they usually did, with a confirmation of the next day's meal.

That complete, Tala set out for the northern gate to meet Cazor.

Chapter: 14
Not Surprised in the Least

Tala found the Mage Hunter waiting for her as she approached the northern gate of Bandfast.

She waved and called out to him. "Master Cazor! I'm so sorry; did I keep you waiting?"

He smiled and shrugged, pushing off the wall he'd been leaning against. "No, we're both actually early. I was just earlier." He chuckled. "I prefer to wait for people, rather than make them wait on me."

Tala looked around. They were still a few dozen feet from the actual gate. Cazor had been leaning up against a blank wall and had moved away from it when he'd spotted her. *That should work.* "Follow me for a moment; there's something that we need to discuss."

She took Kit from her belt and threw it past him at the wall, where it transformed into a door.

Tala pushed through the door, and Cazor hesitantly followed.

"What is this? A fully morphable dimensional storage? Very nice." He looked around the inside of her large front room but quickly returned his focus to her. "So, what's this about?"

The door closed, and Tala willed it to seal them off from outside. She knew from prior experiences that no sound would transfer either in or out when she did that.

"This trip is partly so I can be bait for a mind-altering arcane who seems to be able to infiltrate human cities."

Cazor froze, seeming to process what she'd just said. To his credit, he didn't panic or disbelieve her. She'd been half-expecting to have to argue with him about her claims. "Well... rust."

-Memories?-

That's a good idea. "Do you have an Archive link or tablet?"

He gave her an odd look, then nodded. "I do."

-Access given.-

"I've just given you access to some memories."

"Memories? How—"

She shook her head and cut across him. "I'm sorry, but that's unimportant for the moment. I want you to be informed before we leave the city."

Cazor pulled out a slate and began manipulating it. What he was able to pull up was a sort of grayscale version of the memories without sound. Interestingly enough, it almost seemed like the memories had too much information to easily be displayed on the empowered stone surface, making the whole thing less clear than if it had been pared down and simplified.

Huh, I didn't really consider quality differences.

-Yeah. Hopefully the important parts will be clear enough.-

Cazor finished looking at the two memories before returning his attention to her. "So, what was that?"

She spent a couple of minutes explaining the parts that he couldn't glean without sound or better-quality renditions of the memory.

"So, if I understand correctly, the powers that be believe that you've been targeted by an arcane who can manipulate your mind, and he has already infiltrated the city at least once?"

"That's right."

"And you're going out, today, to act as bait. To try to draw him out."

"That's my understanding."

"And he's a Revered?"

"Last I saw him, yes. I don't really understand how arcanes increase their rank."

"It's not that hard to grasp, but now's hardly the time." Cazor ran a hand through his hair. "And here I thought you were bringing me in here to explain why you're suddenly dipped in iron and hiding it."

Tala's eyebrows rose. "How did you notice that?"

He gave her a mildly condescending look. "Come on, Mistress Tala. I manipulate magnetic fields. I have to have a way of perceiving them, and you're all sorts of obvious with that sight. Not sure how you masked the magic-reflecting nature of the material, but I'd bet it has to do with the visual illusion?"

"Near enough. There's a magical one interwoven through the visual part."

"So, you still have your inscriptions, but the illusion is hiding them."

"That's right."

He grunted. "But we're off topic, now."

"True enough."

He took a deep breath and let it out slowly. "So, do you even need to go harvesting?"

"Oh, yeah. I need to get as many endingberries as I can."

He gave her a long, incredulous look. If anything, he seemed more dubious of this than of an arcane having entered the city. "Endingberries."

"That's right."

He rubbed his face across his hands. "Mistress, those are toxic to Mages and do all sorts of unpleasant things to mundanes who eat too many. There's a market for them, sure, but a highly regulated one. There's enough reasonable use for them as protection during one-off, incredibly dangerous jobs, but the number you can safely sell, and not crash the market, makes even a single Archon going to harvest them a losing prospect. Mundanes love them for the one-off protection, but they're still not worth the hassle."

Tala paled slightly. *Unpleasant side effects for mundanes?* "What do you mean by side-effects? How do they harm mundanes?"

Cazor shrugged. "Has to do with the warriors of old. If the berries are used enough to make an impression in the person's natural magic, those spellforms begin to draw power from their gate to stay empowered. That sounds wonderful. They're now naturally more durable. The problem is that mundanes don't increase their throughput as a general rule, not really. So, that power is no longer going to other areas. The results are almost always a lessening of magic reinforcing other critical-for-life systems. The berry users get sick easier, they die younger, that sort of thing."

"Is there a cure?"

"Sure, they can become a Mage, but then the berries' magics have to be overridden, and until then, they clash with any other magics the new Mage pursues."

"You know an awful lot about this."

"I was a mageling on assignment with Mage Hunters who had to hunt down an endingberry seller. My master thought it would be instructive for me to research the topic thoroughly. In the end, it wasn't really needed. She wasn't precisely hiding her actions. Who knows how she was harvesting the things, but the woman was selling them as miracles, which would protect the user from harm. She didn't bother to tell her clients any of the side-effects." He growled. "A large one being that when people get a feeling of invincibility, it's hard for them to think rationally about danger. More often than not, a mundane goes into a situation where endingberry power protected him in the past, without proper consideration or eating another. They die; they die horribly." He shook his head. "No. I'm not going to help you, and I'll probably even stop you, unless you give me an *incredibly* good reason why I shouldn't."

Tala was feeling a bit uncomfortable with the whole thing. "Well. I use them myself. A large subset of my inscriptions are directly modeled on the endingberry power."

Cazor tilted his head up in contemplative surprise, looking at one of the upper corners of the room and scratching under his jaw while he bit his lip. "Huh. You know, that could actually work. In theory. But doing that would require a truly insane number of inscriptions to function properly." He closed his eyes and scratched between his scrunched eyebrows. "Is that even possible? The level of detail required…" He shook his head in disbelief.

"Can I show you what I look like under the illusion without you freaking out?" She still had Kannis's reaction vividly in her memory. If this man thought she was an arcane, even for an instant, things could go badly wrong.

He narrowed his eyes. "What am I going to see?"

"Gray skin from iron paint and glowing lines of power carved onto reality itself."

"What?" He laughed, maybe with a hint of uncertainty. When she didn't join in, he stopped, lifting one eyebrow. "Huh. Alright then. This I have to see."

Tala took a deep breath, nodding. As she let the breath out, she forcibly suppressed the illusory portion of her through-spike.

Cazor sucked in a sharp breath but otherwise didn't move. "Mother of Decay. You look terrifying. I've fought arcanes who looked less menacing than you." He gave a nervous chuckle. "If the memories you shared are any indication, your blood-stalker looks less terrifying than you, if I'm being honest."

She didn't really know how to respond to that. "Thank you?"

He snorted a laugh. "Thank you for letting me see."

She released her manipulation of the device, and the illusion returned in an instant.

"Well, someone's using you to test some theories, that's for sure."

"Couldn't I be using myself?"

He shrugged. "Maybe." He scratched the back of his head for a moment, then nodded. "I'll go with you. I can get us there faster than even Terry can probably travel. The increased speed will draw attention, but that's the point, right?"

"That's right." She knew that Mages traveling at high speed was dangerous due to the attention it could draw, but she'd never really tried or experienced it herself.

"I can probably help you harvest as well, but both the transport and the harvesting will cost me in wear and tear on my inscriptions."

She nodded. "That's true enough. Can I compensate you?"

He grimaced. "I was just going to go with you as a friend, but what we're discussing now will actually be a little expensive for me. How about I help you, then you tell me what you think that help is worth, after the fact?"

"We should at least set a minimum. I don't want you to be ripped off."

He laughed. "If you lend a friend a silver and never see them again, it was money well spent."

Tala contemplated that for a moment, then nodded. "I think I understand."

"Good. Now, let's get to it. Do you have a map of where we're going?"

Tala opened a cabinet door and pulled out the map. She could, in theory, just reach behind her back, and it would have been there, but there was something a bit disturbing about pulling items out of thin air. *I'll get used to it, eventually.*

Cazor studied the marked locations. "So, this grove to the north?"

"Yup."

"Alright. Let's do this."

*   *   *

Tala regarded the compressed disc of gray sand hovering before her.

"It's perfectly safe. Especially for you."

"And it won't strip off my iron?"

"If it does, I'll replace it, but no, it shouldn't. I keep a very tight control of my magnetic fields."

Tala sighed, looking over to where Cazor already stood on a second disc of compressed iron dust.

"I can make this one larger and share, if you'd prefer?"

She shook her head. "No... This will be fine." She stepped up, finding her balance with ease as the surface felt firm and textured beneath her bare foot. Even the moisture she brought with her from the snow-covered ground didn't seem to ruin her footing.

Terry flickered around, inspecting the disc and Tala before returning to her shoulder, perched looking forward expectantly. He even did a little shuffle step and crouched lower.

Well, he's ready to go. "Ready," she called over to Cazor.

A few onlookers had stopped to watch them as they stood just to one side, outside Bandfast's northern gate, overlooking the mostly dormant, winterized farmland surrounding the city.

Cazor nodded, acknowledging her readiness. The platforms tilted in unison, and just when Tala thought she would lose her balance, they began to move, slowly at first, then gradually speeding up as she got the hang of it.

It was odd as she had absolutely no control. *Much like riding atop a cargo wagon, I suppose. Just with a whole lot less wagon.*

Soon enough, they were moving faster than a galloping horse, sending out puffs of snow to either side as they skimmed along a few feet above the ground.

Tala laughed, looking over toward the Mage Hunter. "This is amazing! Why don't Mages always travel this way or in ways similar to this?"

Cazor grinned, then shouted back, "Wait until we leave the city! You'll see!"

They quickly passed the outer defensive towers, and Tala almost felt like she had slammed into a wall, though not physically. Her speed didn't change, but suddenly, she felt an odd drag of magic.

The power that they were moving through compressed ahead of her. It entered her aura, taking on an aspect like that put forward by her through-spike. *Like my own magic.* Then, it was pushed before her, into the power that had been farther away.

As it did so, it seemed to create a reverberating pulse of power that was subtle at first but grew quickly.

-It's like a continuous whip-crack but with magic instead of air.-

I'm creating a magic boom? That had interesting implications. *No wonder this isn't advisable under normal circumstances.*

She contemplated a moment longer, observing the compression of power, pushing against her as she moved.

So, we're only going a bit faster than what we really should be? The build-up seems on the slow side, considering.

Their speed began to adjust slightly, first slowing down until Tala barely saw an increase in the building concussion of power around her. Then, it increased a bit.

Looking over to Cazor, she could see why.

He had a halo of power around him as well, but it was fading, and after a minute or so, it was gone all together.

Terry, somehow, didn't look like she did or Cazor had, though he did still seem to have a bit of a halo of magic around him.

Magical density? Not weight?

-Likely, also probably something to do with human power, in general. You're seeing the odd echo between Cazor and yourself, right? His presence is making your power more prominent.-

Yeah. That's... odd. The phenomenon did explain why caravans weren't just a single Mage with a fast method of travel and a storage backpack. *Though, they could still probably move faster than a caravan, except...*

-If I had to guess, Kit, Terry, and your other gear is adding to your magical echo. With a caravan's worth of storage, you'd have to be going a lot *slower to avoid this effect.-*

And the iron isn't blocking it because this, by its very nature, is magical turbulence. She nodded to herself.

-That would be my guess, yeah.-

They were going too fast for easy conversation, so Tala just smiled and gave Cazor an appreciative gesture.

He waved back and smiled, clearly enjoying himself.

Tala noticed that Cazor had pulled out some glasses to protect his eyes from the wind. Her own eyes weren't bothered overmuch, but as a test, she extended her senses and power into her elk leathers and found the right path to manifest a magical defense in front of her face.

It worked wonderfully, instantly cutting off the wind.

It also drew a lot of power because she was manifesting it without the physical component of the defense. She was forced to connect a couple of void-channels to her outfit to speed up the flow of power.

They weren't strictly necessary, as the soul-bound item could pull directly from her gate and reserves, but the use of the void-channels increased her flow, which was required given the increased demand from the item. *Everything's a trade-off.*

After fifteen minutes, Alat grunted within Tala's mind. *-Oh, that's unpleasant. I only have access to my own files, now...-*

You lost touch with the Archive?

-No, not that. I can still pull some information, though it's a lot less than before. I don't even seem to be able to modify anything that I created, though I can access all of it much more easily than the rest. If I had to guess, it's because we just don't have the magical weight required to access the central Archive.-

Then why can we access our information?

-I think because it's magically closer to us? As Holly implied, this is probably why this sort of Archive access doesn't usually happen at such a low rank.-

That made some sense.

In less than half an hour's travel from Bandfast, they reached the mouth of the twisting valley indicated on Tala's map and slowed. That diminished Tala's magic boom considerably, for which she was grateful. It had been beginning to give her a headache.

A few more minutes' travel up the valley and they came around a bend, almost running headlong into the leading edge of towering trees.

Cazor reacted quickly, pulling them both backward, even as the nearest branches lazily swung through the space that they would have entered had they not slowed and pulled back.

"Gah! These things should be trimmed back a bit."

Tala laughed, noticing that Terry had flickered away and was waiting for them on the ground, well out of reach of the trees, even if one were to topple over entirely. *That's probably a smart move.*

Cazor lowered them to the ground back near Terry; Tala tossed the bird a big portion of jerky; and the discs broke apart and returned to the Mage Hunter's belt-pouches.

Before them, the grove loomed, completely filling the mountain valley, between two short cliffs, just barely twice the height of the tallest tree she could see.

Grass filled the area around them, knee deep in places, but it got noticeably shorter the closer it came to the trees.

Through the center of the grove ran a pleasant stream that babbled and bubbled and burbled happily into the stillness of the late morning winter air.

Not too cold. Something about the area seemed to be warming the valley. *Hot spring?* There was a bit of steam rising from the water. *Fascinating.*

Cazor cleared his throat, bringing her attention back to the matter at hand.

"So, how do you usually harvest the berries?"

She shrugged. "Well, I used to strip down and use this." She pulled out her long berry-picker, which she'd purchased in Alefast. "I then put the berries into an iron barrel to process as I have time later."

"You strip down…"

Tala glanced away and cleared her throat. *Didn't think that one through before I spoke.* "Well, I didn't want to destroy all my clothes."

Millennial Mage, 6 - Fused

He shook his head, seeming to choose the wiser course and not comment on the topic further. "Alright, so is that necessary?"

"No? I can mirror my endingberry-like defense onto my clothing. So, it should be safe from the trees, so long as I maintain focus."

"Soul-bound?"

"Soul-bound, yeah."

"Nice."

"How about you? How do you think you can harvest?"

He grinned. "Oh, I think a demonstration is better than just saying it." He lifted his hands, and they practically radiated palpable power.

Iron dust shot from his pouches and flowed over the nearest tree, sweeping it from base to top-most leaf, leaving it utterly undisturbed.

No. That's not right. All the berries were gone.

The iron cloud came back, seeming more substantial than a moment before. "Barrel, please?"

Tala quickly pulled out one of the barrels and removed the lid.

Cazor gave her a puzzled look when he saw the barrel but didn't comment.

Bloody barrels...

Instead, he gestured, and his iron cloud deposited a miniature mountain of berries within the barrel—easily at least ten gallons.

Tala gaped, and Cazor sank down to sit on the grass, looking strained. "That was harder than I'd expected." He looked down at his arms, clearly analyzing the scripts there. "Rust, the tree's magic even wears away at power, forcing a greater through-put. I'm not sure how many more trees I can pluck before this portion of my inscriptions are spent."

"At least a few more?" Tala looked into the barrel. *All I have to do is remove the seeds and press berries. He didn't take any stems, leaves, or anything.*

"Yeah, at least a few." He regarded her. "You know, I really should have asked, but what's your plan with the seeds?"

She shrugged. "I toss them back among the trees."

He didn't look like he really understood but shrugged, nonetheless. "Alright, I suppose. So long as you aren't planning on selling them." With a groan, he pushed himself back to his feet. "Ready for the next?"

"Yes, please." She reached inside Kit and pulled out her other barrel. "Place the new harvests in the first barrel. I need to process these." She began biting the berries in half, quickly removing the seeds and tossing them in among the trees. Then, the two halves of the berry went into the new container.

Cazor stared at her for a long moment, then let loose a single barking laugh. "She puts the seeds in her mouth. Somehow, I'm not surprised in the least."

Chapter: 15
I Really Want To

Tala was in awe.

She was busy processing the berries like mad, carefully biting them in half, pulling out the seed, sucking the juice off, and sending the seed back among the trees. The halved berries then went into another barrel as she moved onto the next little packet of juice and power.

That was fairly standard, though she hadn't done it in a couple of months. She even was able to add in the tossing of jerky to Terry every so often.

No, what was awe inspiring was how Cazor could strip a tree bare with a few moments of work. She'd tried to pass it off and hide how impressive it was to her the first time he'd done it, but that fiction was getting increasingly difficult to maintain as he repeated the act with aplomb.

It did seem to visibly drain him to do it, however, and the time between each tree grew markedly.

Tala had barely processed roughly as many berries as Cazor had gotten from the first tree when he flopped to the ground for the fourth time, panting.

"I don't…" He pulled out a water-skin and took a deep pull, swallowing with abandon. "I don't remember these things being deemed to have any sort of intelligence."

"You mean the movement?" She chucked another seed back among the trunks of the grove.

"Well, that's a part of it I suppose, but that can be purely reactionary. They are adjusting to my method of harvest and are disrupting my power more effectively with each tree." He hesitated. "Well, four is hardly a good sample set, but even so."

"Why don't you take a break while I process these?"

He grunted. "I was going to do that anyway but sure. Thank you for the suggestion."

It honestly didn't take her long, and in the end, she'd guess that she had just shy of fifty gallons of halved, de-seeded berries.

That's ridiculous. His method of harvest was so incredibly efficient compared to her own. *I'd have had to be out here for days to get this much.*

Cazor opened one eye. "Done already?"

"Yeah, sorry. Seems like your break is over."

"Eh, it's fine." He made no immediate move to get up.

-Hey, I have kind of a crazy idea. Ask Cazor if he'd be alright with us keeping some seeds to experiment with.-

Tala asked, and he sat up, giving her a long look. "Not going to sell or trade them away? You only want them for your own use and experimentation?"

Alat?

-Of course.-

She nodded. "Exactly."

"That's fine, then. They're actually less dangerous than a good chunk of research materials for some specialties. You aren't going to plant any within the city, right?"

-No planting, no.-

"That is not my plan, no."

"I see no issue, then." He stood, groaning and making sounds of protest.

"Something wrong, old man?" Tala quirked a smile.

Cazor cocked an eyebrow at her. "This is massively draining, I hope you know."

"I can guess. And even if I couldn't, you make it quite obvious."

He huffed a laugh and shook his head. "Fine, fine. I'll keep a lid on the complaints."

"Oh, you're fine. I thought it was kind of funny."

He turned away, muttering to himself. "Funny, eh? What I'm doing is impressive as slag."

Tala just shook her head at the oddity and tossed more jerky for Terry.

"I have an idea, and whether it works or not, it will likely wipe me out for a good while, but I think it will be more efficient overall." He lifted both hands, and a much greater pulse of power radiated off him.

Tala stood up a bit straighter, watching as smaller iron clouds took turns picking from individual branches, instead of whole trees. As each finished its branch, it came to deposit the collected berries into the waiting barrel.

That makes sense. Smaller manipulations take less energy. But will it give the trees a greater chance to adapt?

"That looks easier. Why would it wipe you out more?"

"More… concentration… required." He said each word greatly spaced out, and Tala took the hint.

With the process slowed a bit, Tala was able to see iron contracting around each stem as another portion grabbed and twisted a given berry free.

Masterful control, that.

Not wanting to get distracted, Tala began working on her part.

-*Wasn't your part stripping?*-

No. Hush, you.

Cazor was trembling from the effort as his little iron clouds finished with the fifth tree. He looked her way and smiled triumphantly. "How was that?"

"Impressive."

Millennial Mage, 6 - Fused

"Good, because that's all I've got for the moment." Without another word, he flopped backward, seemingly asleep before he hit the ground.

-Likely mental exhaustion. He'll be fine in an hour or so.-

Can we help him?

-I came across a few methods that might help. Can you alter your magical signature to match his so his body doesn't reject power coming from us?-

Um… no?

-Oh, well, then none of these will work.-

Is such a transfer possible?

-In theory, yeah, but I found no evidence of it being done.-

Tala huffed an irritated growl. *Is there anything we can do?*

-Well, there are a few things that humans do to mentally relax.-

Oh?

-…Wow… we are naïve.-

What do you mean?

-Nothing. There's no way we can help him with what we have with us.-

You could have just said that.

-Where's the fun in that?-

Tala and Alat fell into silence, and Tala continued processing this new batch of berries. The only change was that, now, she had her final iron salve out and was coating each seed in the substance before placing it in a container.

As she did this mindless work, her thoughts caught onto a thread. So, she pulled.

Alat?

-Yeah?-

You're basically a being of pure magic now, right? Just connected to a soul?

-A bit insulting, that. I'm a soul manifesting through a medium of pure magic. But go on, I think I see what you're getting at.-

You seem to have a personality that mirrors many aspects that we've seen in other, older Archons. Master Jevin, Noelle, Jenna, and others.

-I hadn't considered it that way, but yeah, that's true.-

And such Archons have reached a state that they've been remade, sometimes entirely, with magic.

-Correct.-

She didn't really know how to phrase this, so she just asked. *Is magic snarky? By its very nature? And does it pollute what it interacts with, with that trait? What about other aspects?*

Alat laughed within Tala's mind. She contained herself shortly thereafter and continued the conversation. *-That's a very interesting line of thinking.-*

So?

-No. I don't think magic makes what it touches snarkier.-

I said I didn't have a good way to word it…

-Oh, I understand what you're trying to say, as funny as what you actually said is. I think the changes between you and I are due to different experiences, even for as short a time as they've been different, and ignoring the fact that I get to experience yours secondhand. Old Archons have been around a long time, and so they seek ways to entertain themselves. I have very little to do within our head, so I do the same.-

Simple as that?

-That seems like the most reasonable explanation.-

I suppose so.

They once again fell into silence.

As Tala neared the end of processing the second batch that Cazor had gathered, the man stirred.

Millennial Mage, 6 - Fused

She had one barrel filled to the brim, tightly compacted, sealed, and already back in Kit. She only needed to run that barrel's contents through the press, and she'd have her power-packed juice. She had a second barrel about half-full of processed berries as well.

In her previous experience, the berries were *very* juicy, giving almost half their whole volume in juice. *How does that even work, anyway?* She'd been considering it as she worked almost mechanically at de-seeding the berries.

-I think you're on the right track in your thinking. Their magic is centered around cohesion, specifically to briefly counter the power of the seeds and trees, but it bleeds over into other related effects. With that in mind, it makes sense that they'd be able to retain a much greater volume of liquid, compared to a normal fruit.-

Yeah. I'm not a botanist, though. Do you think anyone's ever studied it?

-Do I think that anyone has ever studied one of the foundational sources of power for primeval mankind?-

Fair enough; silly question.

-I'll look into it when we get back to Bandfast.-

Thank you.

"Morning." Tala grinned over at Cazor as he opened his eyes fully.

He hesitated. "Is it actually still morning? Did I sleep a whole day? Or are you just mocking my nap?"

"Still morning; you didn't sleep that long. Less than an hour, actually. Did the trees adapt?"

"Less than I thought they would. They seem to have a static means of building effectiveness against a given thing, but it seemed to have faded before my last effort. It also seems related to how much it interacts with a given thing, in this case my power, and doesn't even seem to remember interacting with it before. The escalation of efficiency in disrupting my power seemed to start back at square one."

"I think I followed most of that?"

Cazor stretched and grinned. "If I do one tree at a time, and I take a slightly longer breaks in between than I have been, it shouldn't get harder with each tree, and I should be able to do twice as many as I'd been thinking I could."

"That I definitely understand." Tala smiled back. "Then, let's get to work. Any guesses on the actual number?"

"We can probably do another... ten? In the next two or three hours or so." He nodded to himself. "That should fill the four barrels you said you had on hand, right?"

Tala glanced up, checking the time. *That will put us at around two in the afternoon.* "Just about, yeah. That works for me."

As she looked up, she saw flickers of power sweep across the top of the valley, avoiding the trees by a good margin but seeming to pass through virtually everything else.

"What was that?"

Cazor glanced up. "What?"

"I thought I saw a magical scan of some sort."

He looked her way questioningly, likely trying to ask if it was the arcane without saying so out loud.

She shook her head. "It felt animalistic, if anything."

He grunted. "Probably a magical creature that sensed us, trying to pin down our location."

Tala paled, thinking of her first encounter with such a creature. Sure, she'd killed the midnight fox, but that had been a weak being, and she'd actually gotten quite lucky. *Though not so lucky that it was a windfall. After all, I lost the harvest...*

He took another drink before glancing her way. "Do you think we should leave?"

She shook her head. "The power seemed to avoid the trees, likely due to what you noticed; they even break down any power that comes too close. We should be safe until we leave."

"And they may have given up by then."

"Precisely. At least that's the hope."

"I'm fine with that plan." He shrugged and got to work, quickly harvesting a tree, then sitting down and pulling out a book to wait for the grove's defenses to relax and return to normal.

Tala continued to work, adding to the buzzing maelstrom of power within her with every drop sucked from the outside of an ending seed.

True to his guess, Cazor was able to harvest another ten trees. Their fruit filled her barrels and then some. Thankfully, she had no trouble simply eating the extra. So the magic-packed berries didn't go to waste.

"Ready to head back?"

"Definitely." After a moment's pause, she inquired, "So, what scripts did you use up?"

"Only *mostly* used up, thankfully. They're my fine-control scripts. I don't use them that often, so they are my least efficient. Though, I've been trying to practice with them more, so thank you for this."

She grinned. "Any time."

He laughed in return. "I still need some help with the inscription costs."

"Oh, I know. I'll think of an offer on the way back."

"Sounds fair to me." He formed their two iron discs, and the two of them stepped up back in place for their trip home. Apparently, the discs were a product of medium-level manipulations of his magnetic fields, not requiring the fine control he'd exercised in harvesting.

She tossed a last bit of jerky for Terry, and he snapped it up before flickering to her shoulder.

As the group began moving, they quickly came to the closest sharp turn in the canyon-like valley—the one that had mostly hidden the grove.

Tala felt her stomach drop at what she saw.

Little ripples of conflicting magics clashed and fizzled through the air, barely noticeable as they bled around the bend.

It looked reminiscent of the surface of a pond during a hailstorm, only somehow more violent.

"Master Cazor, magesight."

He didn't hesitate, and she saw power move over his face and head, the spell-lines beginning to glow, subtly. The iron discs immediately slowed, then stopped. "What the rust?"

"Yeah. Something's happening."

They both looked around, and Tala was able to see similar effects in almost every direction, save directly around the grove.

The two Archons seemed to realize the same thing at the same time, though they articulated it differently.

"The trees are acting as localized magic dampeners."

"Ending trees directly disrupt magic in an area?" She immediately saw the benefit of having ending groves near even modern cities, and why they couldn't be allowed within the defenses. "Oh, I feel stupid."

Cazor huffed. "You and me both. But that's secondary. There is *something*, or more than one something, looking for us, out there, and I don't see any"—his eyes glanced to her briefly, considering, then continuing as if he hadn't stopped—"conceptual power, so I think we're just dealing with magical beasts, not arcanes."

"Can we go up? From a greater height, we could have a better look and see what's going on?"

Millennial Mage, 6 - Fused

He considered. "We can, briefly. The magical beasts that can fly are usually a *much* greater danger to people than the ground-bound."

She remembered the night-wing ravens and saw his point. *Those were just arcanous beasts, too.* "Up and back quickly, then."

"Agreed."

They rose, cresting out of the steep-walled valley. They both immediately felt the turbulence in the magic around them.

Terry squawked quietly and clamped down tighter with his talons, locking him more firmly in place.

Likely in reaction against his instinct to run. She swallowed to clear her mouth. *I don't blame him.*

But Tala couldn't give Terry more than that passing thought. She and Cazor were focused on other things.

Specifically, their gazes were glued to a distant clash that was taking place at the head of the canyon, which led to the endingberry grove. *Right where we slowed down sufficiently to stop making me into a beacon.*

The auras of the two beasts were both yellow, but that was their only similarity.

-I want to chastise you for exaggeration, but I can't see any other overlap... I guess they both exist? We can see them both?-

Alat was trying to distract Tala, pull her out of her shocked focus. It wasn't working.

One of the two magical creatures was, of all things, a griffon, seemingly taken straight from children's tales.

The fur on most of its body looked positively metallic-gold while still somehow looking *alive* in a way that Tala couldn't quite pin down. The feathers on the front portion and wings were a brown that evoked bark without seeming wooden, dirt without being dirty, and topazes without being gem-like.

Its beak and talons reminded Tala of Terry's in an incredibly not-comforting sort of way. And even at this great distance, Tala felt like she could see intelligence in the predator's eyes.

Its opponent was an amorphous… something, which currently had six fully formed spindly legs that didn't seem to be truly holding its bulk off the ground. Another leg was growing outwards as she watched.

More than anything, the legs seemed to facilitate quick changes in direction. And they seemed required because, despite its size, it was *fast*.

The blob darted, reshaped, and almost flowed around the griffon's mostly physical attacks, occasionally even splitting into two seemingly independent entities before recombining and continuing the conflict.

Strangely, neither obviously magical creature was using anything that seemed to be a magical ability, relying instead on their brute physicality. The attacks that came closest to being magical were gusts of wind thrown by the griffon's wings, seemingly sent to unbalance the blob.

As Tala watched, the blob-thing ripped off and then threw a portion of its body, which struck the griffon as it strafed past, seemingly trying to rake at its opponent with talon and claw.

The mini-blob impacted one of the griffon's wings and immediately sprouted at least fifteen little clawed legs that began to tear at the feathered appendage.

The griffon dropped to the ground, twisting the affected wing in front of its face so that it could peck free the offending new opponent. The eagle-lion seemed very little worse for wear after it had eviscerated the seemingly homogeneous living projectile.

"Why aren't they using magic?" Tala's voice was barely above a whisper, even though the combatants were miles away, down the mountain, nearly back in the plains.

Millennial Mage, 6 - Fused

Only her incredibly good eyesight let her see as much as she had.

"I can't really see what's going on. I'm just watching tight masses of power move around each other in violent seeming patterns."

Tala briefly explained what she was seeing.

"Your vision is insane. Do you know that?"

She gave a weak smile. "Thank you? But what about my question?"

Cazor grunted. "Any magic they use will produce far-reaching echoes. Even their presence is causing the ripples we're looking at. Those ripples can look awfully tasty to anything higher up the food chain."

Tala's eyes widened. "So… they're trying to avoid discovery, too?"

"That would be my bet. Humans are *much* better at detecting, and worse at hiding from, magical creatures, so I don't think anything else would notice that conflict and come looking."

That was at least slightly comforting.

"So, they both sensed our magic booms and came looking?"

"Magic boom?" He hesitated, then nodded. "Like a sonic boom. Not really the same, but close enough." He nodded again. "Yeah, that was my guess, too."

Tala tsked. "No wonder there's a prohibition against traveling too fast outside of cities. Can you imagine if we'd led them to Bandfast?"

"Yeah, that would have been bad."

She cleared her throat. "Speaking of which… how are we going to get back without doing just that?"

"I can move us as fast as possible, below the threshold that you begin to create a"—he smiled—"magic boom."

"Don't laugh at me. It makes sense. It's understandable."

"I'm not laughing."

"Do you have a better name for it?"

"The technical term is motive aura resonance."

"Oh… yeah, that's better."

He grinned. "Anyway. I'll take us as fast as I can around those and back to Bandfast."

"How fast is that?"

He hesitated. "How much risk are we willing to tolerate?"

"Some? I *really* don't want to draw a magical creature down on Bandfast."

"Any chance we're getting helped with those?"

Tala grimaced unhappily. "Unlikely." She didn't say more. *The watchers are watching for an arcane. They aren't babysitting us to protect against magical creatures.*

"Yeah, I thought not." He clucked his tongue, his thoughts seemingly taking a new direction. "It would be really foolish to go fight those."

Tala felt her grimace morph into a grin as she picked up on what he was getting at. "Incredibly foolish."

"It would practically be begging for our magic to be seen for dozens of miles in every direction. Who knows what we'd bring down on ourselves?"

"Undoubtedly."

Cazor scratched at his chin. "I'm sad to admit that I've never gotten to test myself against something that powerful, and the times it's been close, there's always someone or something to protect, which limited my effectiveness. Or there were more powerful Hunters nearby to clinch the kill."

She nodded sagely. "That sounds like that wouldn't be a fair test."

"Exactly."

"Mages need to test themselves in order to grow."

"That's true. That's true."

She shrugged. "Not much out here worth worrying about, and there's no one to clinch the kill but us."

He gave her a long look, his smile slowly growing. "I *really* want to do it."

"I'll take the griffon?"

An expression of joyous glee stole over his face. "Mistress Tala?"

"Yes, Master Cazor?"

"You have the best ideas."

-And here I would have guessed that Mage Hunters were selected for their sound judgment and careful nature. That boy is just like us, only more fragile. How is he even still alive?-

Hush, you. He's confident and experienced. We've trained together and fought at similar levels. If he can take one, I should be able to as well. Cazor's not a fool. We can do this.

Chapter: 16
Genuinely Shocked

Tala immediately pulled out a tungsten sphere and began increasing its pull toward the middle of the griffon's spine. *I should still be able to get some good harvests from it, then. Even if it absolutely blows through the creature.*

She was very careful in the implementation. She didn't picture the griffon in any particular state of health. In fact, with Alat's guidance, they locked onto the *feel* of the griffon's magic, which should even ignore its drop in level if they had to fight it down through the ranks. *That's a well thought out lock, if we do say so ourselves.*

-And we do.-

Tala didn't try to place any effect on the griffon at all, only targeting it for the effect from the sphere in her hand. *I really should have gotten the claw fixed.*

Cazor glanced her way. "Mistress Tala, that's a lot of power." He seemed half-nervous and half-impressed.

"I aim to obliterate."

He snorted a laugh.

The power must have been even more significant than Tala realized, or since the creatures had come looking for them, they were more sensitive to workings of magic. In either case, the bird-lion immediately snapped its head around, orienting on them.

Two slightly staggered, overlapping pulses of power swept across the three as they floated there, one seeming to originate from each of the magical creatures.

Millennial Mage, 6 - Fused

Cazor cleared his throat. "Alright, then. No strategizing, just fighting." He looked her way. "Well, a little strategizing. Here or there?"

"There, or at least not *here*." She chose quickly and decisively. Between them and the beasts they were about to fight, they were the most likely to be thrown around, and being near an ending tree grove when that was happening sounded like a bad idea.

Cazor nodded and immediately moved them toward their opponents, even as the griffon and blob-thing seemed to decide that the humans were better opponents than each other.

Tala continued to ramp up the pull, using three massive void-channels toward that end, even as she transferred the sphere into her off hand and drew Flow. "You with me, Terry?"

Terry gave a low, fluted trill from beside her ear. It sounded, to her, halfway between hesitant and down-right pessimistic.

"You know what? I'm a bit nervous about it, too."

Cazor shouted over the rising sound of wind. "They *will* risk magic to fight us, in the hope of killing us."

Tala gave him a thumbs-up. *What magic can we expect?* Lightning, fire, earth, and air came to mind, as well as enhanced strength and healing, but she'd studied too many monsters recently for specifics to come to mind instantly. She could recall if she bent her mind to it but didn't want to take the time.

-Funnily enough, the griffon will have bodily reinforcements similar to your own. But he will have more power behind the reinforcements and have a higher starting point, given his magically created, bestial body.-

That was what she'd thought she read on the creature, but Alat's confirmation was appreciated. It was less than ideal, but she could work with that. *Anything else?*

-Some have access to lightning, some fire, and a few can manipulate earth, but the most common simply have a degree of control over the air, to help with flight, given their massive bodies.- After a moment's pause, she added, *-To be clear, all of them have that control over the air. It's just the most common for them to only have that.-*

Right, it's limited because creatures of magic don't go through founts or get more abilities from them.

-Precisely.- Alat filled in a few more details on the griffon, such as any limits on movement, preferred methods of engagement, and the like. Thankfully, Alat could help Tala review the information she'd read on the beast much more quickly than she'd have been able to recall it on her own, so it took only a breath or two for a full refresher.

The blob-thing? It was a slime… muck? No, that's not quite right.

-Close: Silmuk. Its connection between the parts of its body exists mostly in the domain of magic. Some believe that it's the magical result of dasgannach who live long enough, but most don't think so. It's acidic and can morph at will. It's also not really able to be hurt by mundane means. Cuts? It doesn't have innards to expose. Bludgeon? You just spread it out? Piercing? Like poking yourself in the side with a finger.-

So, resilient, but those don't seem like a wide-ranging powerset.

-They aren't Archons, Tala. Magical creatures usually don't have a massive spread of abilities, but what they do have, they back with power and instinct.-

Tala continued dumping as much power as she could to ramp up the connection between her tungsten sphere and the griffon even as they moved toward the magical creatures. She'd chosen one without an Archon Star within because she didn't want to accidently force a clash of will between herself and the griffon. She had the strong impression that she would lose.

The griffon was streaking toward them, but somehow, it seemed almost lazy in its flight. Like it could go much faster if it wanted to.

The silmuk looked like nothing so much as a massive multi-colored drop, rolling their way.

It's probably waiting for its ally of circumstance. There are two of us, so it's being safe.

"We should stop here!" Tala shouted. *We're far enough from the grove that it shouldn't be a problem.*

Cazor's response was easy for her to hear, even over the wind. "If you're sure."

She nodded, and they slowed, lowering to the ground so that Cazor could reclaim his iron for the upcoming fight.

They stood on an open rise with good visibility all around them and solid footing underneath in the form of deep, springy turf. It was blessedly free of snow—likely because of how exposed it was. *Any that fell would simply have been blown away.*

Tala's eyes widened as power filled the air above them and the ground below, clearly coming from the griffon still a considerable distance away.

Cazor saw it, too.

In less than a couple of heartbeats, she saw tendrils of power stretch out like the uncounted branches of the tree, each slashing upward from the ground toward the sky, leaving behind something that was obviously magically manipulated. *Hundreds of long, thin, magnetic fields?* She couldn't see the magnetic fields themselves, but it was probably a good guess.

As his magic had been lashing out, iron dust continued to pour from his pouches, already dispersing through the tendrils his power had left behind.

From her sensing the buildup of power to the lightning's release, barely more than a second had passed, but Cazor had reacted with long-honed instincts.

Because of his quick reactions, the power flowed through the iron dust, completely bypassing them, though it did make the air around them uncomfortably warm and vaporized a good portion of the dust Cazor had used.

In the aftermath, Tala's hair rose. There almost seemed to be enough static in the air to lift her braid. *That's ridiculous. I read about the range and capability of lightning griffons, but it is rather more... awe-inspiring in person.*

Alat just grunted. *-Oh, so it's a lightning variety. Good to know.-*

The griffon shrieked in irritation as its attack had done nothing. *They lose the power for good. I doubt it will be willing to try again, when it was so unsuccessful.*

That was what the manual had indicated, though it had cautioned that individuals varied on this particular point. The griffon had used more power in that one attack than Tala could hold in her entire body.

True to that assumption, the griffon looked a marginal fraction less yellow and more orange than it had before the attack. It was so minuscule that even with incredibly refined magesight, excellent vision, and a specific desire to look for a change, she wouldn't have seen it without Alat interposing her memory of the thing's aura from a moment earlier.

-Yes, that was less than tenth of a percent of the power it would have to use to drop from yellow to orange.-

And now we know.

She continued to channel power into the tungsten sphere. The mental model that she used was a slightly modified version, which Alat had helped her to create. With it, her working was finally freed from its static ten-percent-per-second manipulation. *This still isn't going to be enough to be an effective attack before it gets here.*

She needed another plan for an opener to the fight.

Hesitantly, Tala extended her hand toward the griffon. It probably wouldn't work, but she was fighting a Refined -*Elder?*- creature. She needed to at least try.

This seems unsporting... and it's going to ruin my harvests if it works.

-*Better to live?*-

That's a bit pessimistic. We'll live just fine. We might not win, but we'll live. She knew enough to be able to ensure that, assuming things didn't go catastrophic in more than two ways. *Maybe three. I think we can handle three catastrophes.*

She could still feel the heat and static from the lightning attack.

Yeah, best to try.

Tala targeted the griffon, moving to increase its gravity, but the beast of magic easily shrugged off her lock. More than anything, it felt like she was a child who'd grabbed an adult's belt, only for the adult to keep walking, breaking her grip without even noticing.

Well, that's about what I expected.

And then, their enemies were upon them.

Terry flickered in a blur of teleports around the griffon as it covered the last couple of hundred feet toward Tala and Cazor.

The result of that was a veritable cloud of blood, which misted out of the beast from innumerable cuts. Cuts which immediately began to close.

-*Ball!*-

Tala easily understood exactly what Alat meant and threw the ball, aiming to have it arch over the griffon.

The sphere was still having its attraction toward the griffon ramped up, but it wasn't quite to the point that the pull was very noticeable.

She was throwing off-hand, so 'toss' was likely a better description of what she did, but her training and magical refinement had made her *strong*. Her daily practice had made her accurate with all kinds of throws and tosses. Regardless, she used her already established lock on the sphere and prepared to enact a second modification to the tungsten.

-*Now!*-

CRUSH. She poured power through that mental construct, sufficient to match four enactments of her old Crush ability, immediately increasing the ball's pull toward the ground by a factor of two hundred and fifty-six. She felt two rings burn away from the back of each of her hands.

The ballistic sphere streaked downward, even as Tala continued to dump as much power as she could into the ball's connection to the griffon without using any more of her rings.

Alat's timing had been perfect, Tala's aim was good, and the tungsten sphere hit the griffon directly between the wings, cracking its back and driving it down to slam into the ground. The ball then passed completely through the griffon's body and sank into the turf below.

Tala grinned from ear to ear. *Got it!*

She immediately charged forward to either harvest or finish off her opponent; she didn't much care.

Terry used that moment to flicker in and rip off portions of the large beast, continuing to cut at it with his talons even as he ate long strips that he pulled free.

Both bird-like creatures were massive, now that she saw them closer up. The spine of the griffon would easily be above her head, if it were standing, and Terry had taken on a size to match his head height with that of his opponent.

The terror bird was taking no chances, ripping into the griffon with a fervor that almost made Tala blanch.

As she began to move forward, Tala caught the beginnings of the conflict between Cazor and the silmuk. It mostly seemed like Cazor was deflecting its blows and severing its limbs and main body with planes, blades, plates, and other creations of iron. The Archon did not appear strained or worried in the slightest.

Will that even work? She saw an odd, oscillating quality to Cazor's magic, and the iron dust seemed almost to be quivering, even as it swept and countered the silmuk at his direction.

Before she could turn her attention fully to that other conflict, however, she noticed through her magesight that the power around the griffon hadn't changed in the least.

Her gaze turned back to it, even as her feet carried her forward. *Flow can take its head and remove any lingering life.* She wasn't actually sure about that, as it largely depended on the type of healing the beast had.

However, before she'd taken three steps, the griffon pushed itself back up and screeched at the sky, pink frothing spittle spraying from its open beak.

It was rusting furious.

Terry took that moment to flicker in and scoop out a truly massive portion of its throat.

But the gaping wound on its neck, the hole in its chest, and the uncounted other wounds across its body closed quickly. The griffon had fully healed before Tala had taken her fifth running step.

-*That is ridiculously fast healing, Tala.*-

The creature's eyes locked onto her, and she felt a moment of fear. *Well, I'll admit, that is faster than I understood from the texts. We may have miscalculated.*

-Not fatally, but it does seem like we did.-
So, that's one catastrophe. Still well within expectations.

Even within that fear, she didn't stop.

She broke the lock linking her tungsten sphere to the ground at the massive increase, while continuing to pour power into its link, drawing it toward the griffon. *That's my end game.*

She'd been ramping that up for more than three minutes, and the ball was starting to twitch within its hole. The layer of rock the sphere had managed to bore into beneath the thick, rich soil was holding it firm for the moment, however.

The griffon was barely twenty feet away as Tala cocked her arm back. A flick of power transformed Flow into a glaive in the same instant that Tala snapped her hand forward. The practiced motion sent the magical weapon lancing forward toward the griffon's heart.

She kept running forward.

The griffon obviously saw the attack coming, even if only at the last moment. It jerked to the side, so that Flow missed its heart. Instead, the heat-field of the cutting edge sheared off one of the great creature's wings. The appendage fell free with the sizzle and smell of roasted meat, leaving behind a cauterized stump.

Good luck healing that quickly! Tala knew firsthand how much of a pain it was to heal burned flesh.

The griffon shrieked again. As Tala grimaced against the piercing noise, she easily saw magic blossom outward from the creature, dumping power into the air.

The burned stump exploded.

Cauterized flesh splattered the ground beside the beast as its wing reformed, the rate of regeneration only marginally slower than that of any of its other wounds.

Millennial Mage, 6 - Fused

Fire or heat usually greatly inhibited magical healing and were classic go-to means of dealing with such abilities. *Alright, I'll call that catastrophe number two. We can still make this work.*

Tala growled, sending a thought to Alat as she continued to close, already calling Flow back to her, hopefully in a way to gain another cut on the return path.

Does every fight with a magical creature require hacking through all its power? More than anything, the question was an expression of frustration.

-All those that can heal, probably. From what we read in the texts that Grediv provided, that is basically all of them.-

Great... She'd known that, but she had *hoped* to be able to damage it in such a way that it wouldn't be required. *Cauterizing the wounds should have been more effective.*

-It's a battle of attrition. As you know, that's why most people avoid magical creatures entirely. Even if you win, it's expensive.-

Tala had closed the distance while the griffon staggered, though it was quickly recovering.

Flow snapped back into her hand in the form of a sword, having burned another line down her opponent's flank and part of its newly repaired wing. With her weapon in hand, she went to work. All the while, Terry was flickering around, cutting tendons and superficial major arteries and vessels, if the fountains of red liquid painting the surrounding grasses were any indication.

How does he even know where those are?

-Instinct? Or some vision into the infrared? That would explain it pretty well, actually.-

Tala gave the creature dozens of cuts, including hacking away at the beast's leg, and she caught its expression out of the corner of her eye.

It looked shocked.

Not hurt.

Not angry.

Genuinely, confusedly shocked.

Tala tried to imagine what would cause that look on her own face. *If a toddler just drew a knife and tried to stab me. That would do it.* That was a bit insulting.

The griffon recovered from its disbelief quickly. Prey did not attack a griffon. The griffon was the aggressor. The griffon knew this and would prove it in blood.

Its beak snapped forward, the quick, short motion hitting Tala harder than a blow from Force.

She would have flown far, but the strike took her in the shoulder and drove downward.

Tala felt endingberry power burn away to protect that shoulder as well as the entire length of her back from the twisting impact.

Even as reinforced as she was, that single strike would have snapped her spine and torn her spinal cord in a dozen places.

Instead, she was thrown to the ground, facing away from the griffon, most of her defensive power consumed in an instant.

Well, rust. That hurt. Knowing how hard it would hit and taking the hit were entirely different things. *Still, within expectations.*

The creature pounced on her and drove its talons into her back; its beak snapped at the base of her neck.

Tala thrust Flow behind her wildly, even as she was bounced against the ground like a child's ball. The endingberry power that she'd gained by sucking juice from uncounted seeds was being used up all too quickly, and even with its protection, her body was already aching.

Millennial Mage, 6 - Fused

Blessedly, some of her calculated, behind-her-back stabs seemed to have struck true as the beast staggered backward briefly.

And Terry probably hamstrung it again, too. That does seem to tick the thing off. Even so, it was focused on her, not Terry. *Not the core concern right now, Tala.*

-Human. It's because you're human. There, now you know. No need to contemplate later.-

Right, she'd known that, but the stress of the situation had kept the knowledge from coming to her easily.

She felt a bit better for having cleared up that oddity.

There was an odd grating of stone on metal, followed by an earthen *pop* as the griffon stepped back over the hole that contained her sphere.

The ball blasted upward, blunt-force severing the griffon's spine before coming back down to smash into the already healing flesh and bone.

Hah! Justice.

-It didn't actually harm your back.-

But it tried, Alat. It tried… a lot. Tala giggled, feeling more in the rhythm of the conflict than she had before. She rolled away from her opponent, returning to her feet.

-Now is hardly the time for puns, Tala.-

The griffon had obviously felt the damage each time and was in agony now. It raged, flailing about with its front legs, even while the lion legs in back had gone limp, toppling to the side. The ball rested exactly where she'd put it: in the griffon's spine, right where eagle and lion portions met.

The ball had oscillated just a bit, while the spine healed, the flesh pushing the ball aside. Even so, the small sphere was putting a *ridiculous* amount of pressure on the spinal cord, pinching it off even after the nerves had fully healed.

Tala felt herself grinning, right up until she felt her hair stand up on end.

She jammed Flow into the ground, changing its form to a glaive, and huddled close without touching. Hopefully, it would act as a lightning rod and spare her some of whatever attack this was.

A net of lightning blasted outward from the griffon in a dome, tearing up the grass and leaving bare earth behind.

Terry was caught by the barest fraction as he flickered away, but Tala saw singed feathers on one of his vestigial wings as it twitched, seemingly uncontrollably.

The power was drawn to Flow briefly, but the weapon was thrown away and Tala, herself, was struck by the sweeping strike.

At first, the lightning stayed confined to the iron on her skin. That was both a blessing and a curse.

It was a blessing because, for that brief moment, her insides were spared. It was a curse because her iron became super-heated. She felt every drop of endingberry power torn from her at once as the iron burned it away and crisped her skin in barely a moment.

Once the iron was gone, the lightning had its way with her insides, coursing through her, jumping between her dense bones.

The cage of protection around her brain kept her head from being fried, but that was just about all that was spared.

She collapsed to the ground, convulsing violently, her muscles not responding in the least.

-More power; let's get this purged. Direct the magic to your consumption scripts, too. That flesh is cooked. It won't heal; we need to repurpose it.-

Alat directed Tala internally as quickly as Tala could follow, while she desperately fed power to her various inscriptions at the direction of a voice in her head.

Millennial Mage, 6 - Fused

The griffon was dragging itself across the ground toward her. She'd only gained a few dozen feet from her hasty retreat and being thrown by the lightning blast.

Tala heard Cazor shout, and a line of iron, glowing dull red, cut into the griffon from the side.

That seemed to be enough for the beast as it screeched again, spread its wings, and took to the sky.

Terry flickered around it for a moment longer, but the beast was retreating, cutting its losses.

That ball's never coming out.

-True.-

I should have stuck a dimensional anchor dart into it. She didn't actually think that would have been a good idea.

-I'm glad you didn't.-

Yeah... me, too. But there goes all our potential harvest.

-And look, here is our life, still ours to live.-

Tala let out a little grunt. *Should I release the lock on the sphere?*

-If you did, the griffon would eject the ball from its body and heal almost instantly before returning to kill us, but you're free to, if the pain is too much.-

Tala gritted her teeth against precisely that. *I was trying to distract myself, you jerk.*

-Enough distraction, focus on healing.-

Tala continued to meticulously direct her various spellforms, sweeping through her body. It was a bit grisly. She was forcing her digestive inscriptions to eat her seared and charred flesh, so that the regenerative magic could replace it.

I'm eating myself to make room for more... me.

-And at about seventy percent efficiency, too. We really must thank Holly for such fine work. Our understanding

brings it to its peak, but she created that peak for us to reach.-

Well, Lyn did say that Holly wanted us to drop through every day. Let's do that when we get back?

-If Cazor doesn't lose, and the silmuk doesn't kill us, then sure. That sounds like a wise plan.-

Terry flickered over to her, looking down at her with a critical eye.

Then, he struck, his beak hitting her in the chest, *hard.* He squawked and fluffed his feathers, then squawked again.

The attack didn't break anything, but it added another pain to the myriad she was already dealing with.

"Stop that, Terry." Her voice was raw and came out barely louder than a rasp.

He let out a series of short, irritable squawks.

"Yes, you were right. I apologize."

He seemed to pause before trilling again.

"Yes, that's right. I shouldn't have ignored you and engaged the griffon."

He lifted his singed wing.

"I am very sorry that you got hurt. I'll take you by a healer."

He let out a definitive trill of satisfaction and flickered to crouch on her chest, appropriately sized to not increase her pain.

Off to the side, Tala could hear what sounded like sizzling fat and a disconcerting chittering.

Cazor called out to her. "You alive?"

"Yeah." It was barely above a whisper, so she tried again. "Yes!" It hurt to yell, but he did need to know she wasn't in danger, or he might get himself hurt trying to come help her. "Just healing up."

Millennial Mage, 6 - Fused

The Mage Hunter walked over to her, somehow unconcerned. "You know, I'll give you credit. You did handle the griffon."

Tala glared up at him. "Silmuk?"

"Have a look."

Tala groaned but found herself able to sit up. Terry flickered to her shoulder as she did so.

Six spherical clouds of iron swirled as they glowed and radiated immense heat.

"How did you heat the iron?" She was finding it easier to talk. Her self-healing was nearly complete, after all. *And it just took a couple dozen pounds from my reserves... Lovely.*

"Oscillating magnetic fields can be used to heat up iron."

That's what I saw him doing. She felt like it was likely a lot more complicated than he implied, but she didn't press.

"The method works really well for dealing with amorphous opponents."

One of the spheres briefly bulged outward. Tala had a moment of alarm, but as she watched, a glowing spike pulled together in line with the potential breach before driving inward with quick, decisive force.

All six spheres emanated a high-pitched whining chitter.

Tala regarded Cazor. "You're a bit terrifying."

"Why, thank you, Mistress." He wore a broad grin.

"What has you so happy? Just your victory?" Tala pulled out some jerky, tossing a piece for Terry and beginning to chew on one herself.

"I'll be able to be raised to Mage Hunter with Standing. I have a few other requirements to meet, first, but the hardest one is defeating an opponent two levels above yourself in open combat without assistance."

"So much for a foolish choice to attack. You needed to do something like this."

He shrugged. "Eventually, but it was a bit foolish to do it without any obvious back-up in the wings." His grin widened again. "Mistress Jean is going to be livid." He laughed. "Oh, I can't wait to tell her."

"Are you two…?"

"Hmm? Oh, no. I was interested for a while when she wasn't, then she was but I wasn't anymore. Now?" He shrugged. "Might happen, but the right time hasn't really come along."

Tala grunted. "Back to Bandfast?"

Cazor gave her an odd look. "It's not dead yet, Mistress Tala, and I'm not dragging it the whole way while it roasts."

"I knew it wasn't dead. I didn't really think beyond that." She was *so hungry.*

"Well, it's not going to be dead for at least an hour or so, and there is no way I'm not claiming this kill, now that I have it in the bag… Or, well, the balls." He chuckled to himself.

Tala groaned slightly but then nodded. "Fine, but if that's the case, I'm making some food."

Chapter: 17
Explain Everything

Tala had to begin her 'cooking' by dumping an obscene amount of power into Kit.

The dimensional storage had taken quite a bit of damage from the griffon's lightning, and only its increased internal and external manipulation abilities had kept it from being outright destroyed.

And I didn't even notice.

-*Well, you were eating yourself at the time.*-

That made Tala feel a bit better, actually.

Kit was hardly the only part of her gear that had gone through the wringer, however. The through-spike had simply continued to drink deeply of her power and hadn't been permanently harmed in the least. *I wonder if its draw negatively affected my defenses?*

-*Probably not? It shouldn't have taken a lot of power to maintain the physical form, and the spellform wouldn't have been affected, directly.*-

That was good, at least.

Her elk leathers had only survived because they could draw power directly from her gate, and their regenerative abilities had a much easier job when compared to her own since they were repairing non-living matter. Their armor effect had broken so quickly that Tala hadn't even noticed it at the time of the strike and was still recovering. Tala had never taken a hit so powerful that it outright broke the magical armored defense, so she was glad that it was recovering at all. And, even though it hadn't seemed to do much at the time, both she and Alat agreed that its presence had likely dulled the front edge of the hit significantly.

Imagine if I hadn't had that defense or the endingberry power.

-That would likely have been the start of the endgame for us. We'd have been reduced to little more than dust. Our magic would have tried to rebuild our body, but I don't know that it would have really done anything significant with nothing physical to build off or draw from.-

Tala grunted in agreement, choosing not to focus on that unpleasant possibility.

As soon as Kit was recovered enough for Tala to draw out her cooking supplies, she began the culinary process, continuing the infusion of power into the power-hungry item all the while.

-In case you're curious, Kit takes more power per day than the average un-Bound Mage can pull through their gate.-

So, even if it could be made en masse in this form, most Mages couldn't use it?

-Precisely.-

That was interesting but not very pertinent.

-Also, Terry just ate the griffon wing.-

Tala jerked, almost spilling the pot she was working over. *I forgot to grab that!* She looked around, seeing Terry happily dancing between his feet as the last feathers slid down his throat.

The terror bird paused, regarding her, then swallowed and flickered to her shoulder before headbutting her cheek.

"I could have sold that, Terry."

He trilled contentedly to himself.

"Well, I'm glad you liked it. We could have bought so much food with that money."

Terry hesitated briefly, then trilled happily again.

"Still worth it, eh?"

He bobbed a nod, then curled up against her neck.

She let out a defeated grunt. "Well, it's done, now. Please leave some harvest for me next time?"

He shifted slightly in a motion that might have been a nod.

Good enough, I suppose.

Cazor's glowing balls distorted and shrieked on occasion, demonstrating that the silmuk within them was still alive, if not well. Even so, the Archon dealt with each irregularity with quick efficiency, never taking his attention from the task for too long.

Tala had noticed that only the outside layers of iron were confined to a glowing red. The light occasionally flickering through showed ranges through yellow all the way up into white.

I feel like there's an obvious reason for that. Alat?

-Yes, you learned about the magnetic point of iron. The glowing red portion is just below that point, and it seems to be containing the iron that is hotter, past the point of being able to be directly manipulated by magnetic fields.-

That has to take quite a lot of finesse. He can't let the heat transfer outward, or he'll lose containment.

-And it is likely only the extreme heat farther in that is truly damaging the silmuk.-

Complicated indeed.

Cooking didn't take a lot of thought, especially when following the incredibly easy and detailed instructions from the Culinary Guild.

So, what was this experiment you wanted us to perform with the endingberry seeds?

-I think that the scripts that you had Holly put in place for the containment of scripts created in your lungs would

contain the ending seed's destructive power and allow you to exhale it as a breath weapon of sorts.-

Tala froze, cooking implement halfway through stirring a portion of her food. *You want me to detonate an ending seed… in my mouth… for a test… because you think it should work.*

-Not out here in the wilderness, but after Holly has considered and approved of the merits of the idea? With a healer present, just in case? Yes.-

And stuffed to the brim with endingberry power.

-That, too.-

The idea had merit. *Could this have helped with the griffon?*

-Are you asking if it would have been a good idea to test out an unproven, dangerous idea against a magical creature?-

No. I'm asking if it could have helped.

-In theory.-

Tala grunted. *Next time, then. Next time, we'll have another thing in our back pocket.*

-If it works.-

If it works. Tala considered. *Worst possible outcome?*

-Your head pops, your scripts rebuild it, and I refill your mind with who you are.-

Tala shuddered. *That's… unsettling.*

-Why? You are a soul, manifesting in a body, tempered by a certain set of experiences. Your soul wouldn't be touched, your body would be repaired, and your experiences would be restored exactly as they had been.-

Tala grimaced. *I still don't like the idea.*

-That makes sense. I wouldn't like the idea of you running my scripts all the way down before getting them reinscribed.-

I hadn't considered that as equivalent, but I can see that it would be.

-I'll help you keep your head, then.- Alat had a bit of a humorous bent to her tone.

Tala grinned in return. *And I'll do my utmost to keep your scripts in top form.*

She'd finished preparing her massive, one-woman feast as well as consuming it by the time Cazor was wrapping up. He'd declined her offers of food.

She'd made a *lot,* and she hadn't really savored it so much as she'd eaten as quickly as she could. Though, she had paid enough attention to write down her impressions of the dishes in the little book provided by the Guild.

For the most part, she'd made a meat-veggie medley, taking dehydrated vegetables and preserved meats and cooking them in water with premade spice mixes poured in.

She also had broken out some hard-tack, which she'd lathered in a cheese that was somehow made to be long-lasting without any external method of preservation.

While she'd been eating, all the spheres had been steadily shrinking, and one by one, their collapse had accelerated until they fully crumpled in on themselves before the iron had cooled enough to be moved over to join a different ball.

At long last, there was only one sphere left, and it was shrinking rapidly.

Less than an hour before, Tala could have stood inside it without issue, but now it was barely bigger than her torso.

Over the next minute, it looked almost like it ate itself. It was an uncomfortable reminder of how half of her scripts had worked on her so recently.

Finally, Cazor collapsed to a seated position on the turf, all his iron streaming back to his pouches. Some was still dust, but much of it was irregular chunks of slag.

He'd probably have some way of breaking them up at a later time.

One of those has to be a dimensional storage to contain all that iron. Maybe more than one, honestly.

The iron itself was interfering with her magesight, however, so she couldn't easily tell which.

Cazor walked over, seeming quite satisfied with himself. "Hey, you're not magnetic anymore." He hesitated. "Wow, the griffon really fried you, didn't it?"

Tala grimaced. "Yeah, it wasn't great." *And now I need to re-apply the iron paint.* The two gallons that she had would only allow her to do one more full re-application. She needed to get more before she left on her next assignment. *No delaying. I need to get more today.*

"Do you need a healer?" He looked a bit concerned, likely thinking that he would have been the delay in getting her needed healing.

"No, but Terry does."

Terry lifted his slightly scorched wing for Cazor's inspection.

The Archon nodded. "We can get it seen to. I apologize for making you wait."

Terry fluffed his feathers, favoring the injured wing, then squawked once in a sound that conveyed indifference.

Cazor cracked a smile. "Ready to head back?"

"Are you up for that?"

"Yeah. That wasn't particularly taxing, though it wasn't that much fun. I hard-countered the silmuk, so it was an ideal situation for my advancement, but it made the whole thing a bit anticlimactic."

"I can probably find the griffon if you'd like." She smiled sweetly.

He held up his hands. "No, thank you. One magical beast is enough for one day."

"Then let's head back, yeah."

They took longer getting back to Bandfast than they had on their trip out, completely avoiding creating any motive aura reverberations.

I still feel like this is faster than a caravan, but I suppose that's because there are fewer people and less stuff being transported.

-That's the theory, yeah.-

As they approached the northern gate once more, the light of the setting sun cast the snow in a ruddy hue.

Looks like blood has painted the world.

-The arcane never showed.-

Any idea why?

-He probably isn't just waiting around for you. It seems like we'll have to try again at some point.-

Tala grunted. *Great.*

-Let's handle the payment for Cazor.-

She glanced over toward the other Archon. "I really don't know what your inscriptions cost. How's… three gold?"

He laughed. "You really don't want to offend, do you?" But he waved her off before she could respond. "Let's do one ounce this time, but I'll ask for three if we ever do this again. I got a lot from this trip that I can't count on happening next time."

Tala grinned back. "That sounds quite reasonable. Thank you for the assistance. This trip would have been worse in basically every way without you along."

-Ask for his hand. I need a better look at his magical signature to do the transfer.-

Tala flushed. *I'm not asking to hold his hand.*

-Fine, spoilsport. You think of some other way.- Tala got the impression that Alat knew of several but didn't deign to share.

Millennial Mage, 6 - Fused

That was fine; Tala had an idea that should work just fine. "Master Cazor, can you extend your aura my way, so I can get a look at it?"

He did so. "Why? What's up?"

-And... done.-

"Thank you. The gold should be in your account, now."

He gave her a skeptical look, then pulled out his Archive tablet. A moment later, he was blinking down at it. "Well... I'll be..." He glanced back to her. "You're just full of surprises, aren't you?"

Could we take funds that way, too?

-Tala, I'm surprised at you! But no. I tried. It takes willful consent from the giver. We can give to anyone we want, though.-

You... you tried to steal from Cazor?

-Hmmm? No. I had this idea ages ago. I tried to steal from Jenna.-

Tala felt her eye twitch.

-Don't worry, there's no record of it.-

Tala was very concerned despite the somewhat flippant reassurance. *If you get me thrown in jail, you'll be imprisoned, too.*

-Oh, I'm aware.-

Cazor brought them in over the city wall without issue. "Where do you want me to drop you off?"

"I need to see an alchemist and then see my inscriptionist." She glanced to Terry. "But I think a Healer first, if you're willing?"

"Any preference?"

Alat brought up the memory of having seen a Healer's shop very near the alchemist's. With that in mind, Tala directed Cazor there, and he set her down at the front door less than five minutes later.

Some of the passersby gave her odd looks, staring in awe up at Cazor. Everyone gave her a wide berth as she stepped off the iron platform.

"Thank you for an interesting day, Mistress." Cazor bowed from where he stood, elevated a half-dozen feet above her.

She bowed in return. "Thank you for all the assistance, Master Cazor."

"Any time." He waved goodbye and went on his way, speeding just high enough to clear the surrounding roofs.

Getting Terry healed was a simple thing as Healers often worked on pets, companions, and work animals. He made similar comments to the one in Makinaven with regards to Terry's dimensionally sequestered body but otherwise didn't question them.

Ten silver saw Terry restored to peak health.

After that, a quick walk got Tala and Terry to the alchemist's, where she bought three and a quarter gallons of the body paint. With that, she would have five full applications in reserve, after the one she'd do that night.

That cost her one gold, sixty-two silver, and fifty copper. She didn't have the silver on her, and the alchemist preferred dealing in hard coin. Thus, she had to use two gold and accept the change back. It was a bit of a pain, but not overly so.

-You know, if you become a certified alchemist, you could buy the recipe for just five gold. It's in the list of available recipes for purchase and sale by such people.-

Tala grimaced. *Not worth the extra time… right?*

-Oh, no, not at all. Becoming a certified alchemist somehow takes more time than becoming a Mage.-

Huh. I never really knew that.

-Ooooo. Alchemist fire is available, too.- There was a moment's pause. *-A hundred ounces gold?! What madness is this?-*

Millennial Mage, 6 - Fused

They probably don't want random alchemists to buy it.
-*That is a ludicrous sum, even so.*-

Tala shrugged, then scratched the back of her head as she walked through the wintery streets. It didn't really matter in the end; she wasn't going to become an official alchemist. *To Holly's!*

It was a short, rather familiar trek to Holly's through what seemed to be a growing snowstorm.

Tala stepped through the front door and paused, looking over toward the assistant sitting behind a desk.

She waved, gaining the middle-aged man's attention. "Hello. I know Mistress Holly asked me to just drop through, but—"

An exclamation of surprise echoed through the warehouse before Holly's voice boomed out, "*No! Get back here, girl!*" Holly's voice carried through the building like a war-horn.

The assistant leaned back and shrank a little in his seat. After a moment, he waved Tala toward the back of the warehouse without a word.

Tala gave him an apologetic smile as she rushed past and back to Holly's work area.

As Tala stepped into the familiar room, Holly pointed to a stool. "Sit. Explain everything."

And so, Tala did just that, doing her best to leave nothing out as she recounted her trip to the ending grove with Cazor and the battle afterwards.

Throughout, Holly made the occasional note, but she didn't ask any questions, seeming content to wait until the end.

Tala even included Alat's idea for the endingberry seeds and Tala's own failure with the griffon.

-*Failure's a little harsh. We did deal with it.*-
True enough.

Even so, she felt it was a failure, so she cast it in that light in her retelling.

Holly sat in silence for a long, long time.

Well, it was probably just a couple of minutes, but it felt like a long time as she stared critically at Tala the entire time.

"Well, your breath delivery of magic should work, and testing it here, with a Healer present, is a wise move." She called out to a passing apprentice and had the woman send for a Healer. "No time like the present." She flagged down another woman and had them source some trash.

"Right now?" Tala was a bit surprised.

"Before you leave? Of course. If I let you leave, you'll find a reason to test it yourself. I applaud your restraint in not trying something foolish with the griffon, but one does not bet on a miracle happening twice in one day."

"Hey!" Tala frowned at the rather pointed insult.

"Hush. While they are arranging those things, we need to get you in the auto-inscriber."

"What? Why?"

"You've rebuilt most of yourself again, already… for some reason."

Tala scratched the side of her head. "It wasn't intentional."

"Regardless, you need the next iteration of scripts and then, after our test, you need to *eat*. When I say eat, you need to eat more than you did last week but tonight. Then do that for every meal for a week."

Tala blinked at the inscriptionist. "What? Why?" She thought that she'd been doing a good job of eating what she needed as well as building her reserves.

"Because these scripts are going to rebuild you again, and they are going to need a good chunk of that energy and nutrition, and you will need the rest to be safe on your next venture." She patted Tala on the cheek. "I'm not about to let you die on me. You are giving such amazing data."

"Thank you?" Tala wasn't sure if she should be insulted.

"You're welcome, dear." Holly's words seemed genuine.

So… a compliment?

-She does give them on occasion.-

Holly pulled out a few little booklets, then hesitated. "Alat, was it?"

-Yes.-

"Yes." Tala answered for her alternate interface.

"Good, look up the next set of manuals for these series of scripts." She held up the three small booklets, which Tala read but didn't bother to process.

-Got it.- There was a moment's pause. *-Oh, interesting. Okay. Let me rearrange this for you… and… Here you go.-*

A book appeared, hovering in front of Tala, and she took it, not bothering to consider its unreality.

She also did her best to not notice Holly reacting with interest to her movements.

It was a simple read, and she finished quickly. *Huh, so it really is just a next step.*

-It seems so. Metaphorically, we are building a house. The first set we got was the foundation, then the set we currently have—and which we've been soaking in power until we forced them to rebuild us—were the supports and the roof. Now, this next set is the walls and the real meat of the structure.-

How many more small modifications are there in the sequence?

-After the one we're about to get? Just one more.-

What then?

-I don't know. We don't have access to whatever that is.-

So, these improve base muscle power, bone density and strength, natural healing, and biological system efficiency overall?

-That's correct. There are two parts to each change. The first is the forced physical change within your body, and the second is the imposition of magic that augments the physical. The idea is to force that into your natural magical pathways as well, for increased augmentation as well as maintaining augmentation even without scripts to that end.-

Yeah, this can't be unrelated to Refining. She knew from experience that Holly wouldn't tell her, though. "Alright. I think I understand the difference."

Holly leaned closer. "Fascinating. You didn't imbibe the information any faster—I'm monitoring your inscriptions as we speak—the information was simply shuffled around, and only the parts you needed were presented to your conscious mind, increasing efficiency rather than raw throughput."

"Yes?"

"Wonderful. Now, inscribing time! We're refreshing everything while you're here. No reason to have some of yours run down."

Holly pulled out the auto-inscriber and helped Tala get inside it before it tightened.

"You are clear of all iron, so that griffon did you a favor of sorts." She cackled a laugh. "Without its work, you wouldn't have been ready for the next modification for months, so it did you all sorts of favors."

Tala grimace. "I suppose so, yeah."

"I assume you prefer unconsciousness?"

"That would be preferred, yes."

Millennial Mage, 6 - Fused

"Are you sure? I really do recommend that you stay awake."

"Why?"

Holly grimaced fractionally, then shook her head. "No reason."

"Unconscious, please."

Holly obliged.

*   *   *

-Ding.-

-Consciousness disabled for reinscribing.-

-Reinscribing complete, consciousness restored.-

Tala returned to wakefulness like the snap of her fingers.

She had a lingering soreness across her body, but it seemed more mental than physical. *Or magical?* In addition, she felt a building hunger. *Oh, yeah. Food soon.*

She waited. *Alat? Are you there?*

-Yes, Tala.-

Why the 'ding' again?

-We've been over this, at least in passing. When you lose consciousness, my base nature takes over until consciousness is restored and normal brain function is reported.-

Right. That makes sense.

"How are you feeling?" Holly was sitting off to one side, the auto-inscriber already put away.

"Fine? I think."

"Good. I left you unconscious for a bit longer this time to let the inscriptions set a bit longer. I think it was the right call. They seem to be incorporating nicely."

-Correct. The extra time without power flowing through them increased their acceptance by at least 10%.-

"Seems to have worked."

"Good, because the Healer just arrived, and I had them set up a side room for the test."

Tala blinked at her, processing the flow of words as her mind continued to attempt to wake up.

Holly just smiled back. "Shall we?"

"One moment." Tala tossed Kit against the wall and walked through almost before the door could fully manifest. She found what she needed right inside, opening one of her cast-iron barrels and eating great handfuls of halved endingberries as quickly as she could.

After less than a minute of what was, admittedly, gorging, Alat interrupted Tala's one-food feast.

-That's about enough. We're actually approaching our capacity with this power, and I don't want to see what happens if we pass that.-

Tala licked off the bits of juice that were on her hands before wiping her mouth with those hands and repeating the process.

Waste not.

That done, she exited Kit and grinned toward Holly. "Let's do this."

Chapter: 18
Dissolution

Tala and Holly walked down a side hall that Tala had never been through before, though it shared the odd mix of aesthetics as the rest of the building: warehouse meets boutique artisan's workshop was an odd combination.

Holly led her through the third door on the left, and they entered a spacious, mostly empty room.

As Tala looked around, she noticed that every surface, including the floor, was covered in iron.

What? How?

Tala frowned, then stepped back into the hallway and looked at the wall beyond which the room lay. From the outside, there was no evidence of the iron to her magesight, and obviously none to her mundane vision.

As she looked closer, willing her magesight to pierce deeper and focus more minutely, she saw the tell-tale signs of illusory scripts. Specifically, the magics she saw were almost identical to those that created the false magical sense around her, via her through-spike. She stepped back inside and looked at Holly. "A safe room?"

The woman shook her head. "No, dear. This is a place to experiment without issue. I just didn't want a beacon of reflected magic glaring at me every time I used my magesight."

Tala grunted. *That makes a surprising amount of sense.*

-*Besides, her safe room would be much better hidden.*- Alat gave a fake gasp within Tala's head. -*Unless that's *what she wants us to think! If we ever need to kill her, we're checking here first.-*

Tala decided not to address that, and since there were two other people in the room, she had a readily available distraction.

The woman, younger and obviously a bit subservient, bowed to Holly, now that Tala wasn't taking up the inscriptionist's attention. "Mistress. I piled some detritus of various kinds to the side, there." She pointed at a surprisingly robust pile of trash and what looked like construction leftovers. "There is a sizable renovation going on a block from here, and I was able to get some of their cutoffs and unneeded bits. They were grateful that I was willing to take some for them." She shrugged, a self-satisfied smile plain on her face.

"Great work. Thank you." Holly gave a small, affirming smile. "You may go."

"Mistress." The unnamed woman bowed again and departed without ever having acknowledged Tala directly.

The other person in the room was quite obviously a Healer, and his aura was yellow, marking him as a Refined like Holly. The aura itself was kept well contained below the surface of his skin.

Oh. He's hiding his rank.

When Tala examined him a bit more closely, she realized that she saw a bit of green in his aura.

Moving toward Paragon? He was someone of power. Not unique, by any means, but of note.

The man glanced after the retreating assistant as she closed the door with a muffled clang before returning his gaze to Holly. "Mistress Holly, may I now know why my presence was requested?"

Holly grinned. "Mistress Tala, here, is going to perform an experiment, which involves enacting rather dangerous magics within her mouth."

The man cocked his head to one side. "What are the natures of these magics?"

"Only one nature: dissolution."

He grimaced. "Mistress Holly, I can repair any physical injury, but if her brain is dissolved, I cannot restore more than the physical structures of her mind. She would be a vegetable."

Holly waved him off. "That part is being handled."

He looked deeply skeptical. "So long as you understand my limitations."

"I do." Holly glanced to Tala. "Do you?"

"I do. As we discussed before, this was expected." She then stepped over to the Healer. "I am Tala, by the way." She gave a shallow bow.

"I am Shir, Mistress Tala. Are you sure you want to try… whatever this is? It sounds incredibly dangerous." He narrowed his eyes toward Holly. "And Mistress Holly can occasionally be a bit more persuasive than is good for those she persuades."

Holly rolled her eyes but didn't comment.

Tala gave a small smile. "I am as sure as I can be, Master Shir."

"Very well." He didn't seem convinced, but he also didn't seem willing to press the issue. He had glanced at Terry but didn't comment. He seemed a man who tried to be unerringly polite, whenever possible.

Even so, when Terry flickered to one corner to curl up for the duration of the experiments, his eyebrows rose noticeably, and his mouth opened to ask a question before he mastered himself and gave a slight shake of his head.

Holly ignored the man, and Terry, as she went to one corner and dragged out an iron pedestal with relative ease, placing it in the center of one side of the long room. "Mistress Tala, if you could face away from us when you attempt?"

Millennial Mage, 6 - Fused

Tala nodded, walking over and feeling a few pieces before picking up a stone block. "Of course."

-Don't you want to try with something... smaller?-

Smaller? This isn't that heavy; is it some sort of composite, poured stone?

-Tala, you have new scripts. You haven't tested your strength yet.-

That was a fair point. Tala shrugged to herself. *This should show the extent of the effects, even if it doesn't get dissolved entirely.*

After a moment, Alat conceded the point. *-Fair enough.-*

Tala placed the stone on the pedestal, stepped about three feet away, and pulled out an endingberry seed.

Hesitantly, she placed the little nugget of power and destruction into her mouth.

It tasted awful.

Gah, the iron-salve is not *tasty.*

-It is a bit waxy.-

Tala didn't want to lose her nerve, so she bit down.

She immediately felt the building power within the seed, coming to a crescendo over the next few seconds.

As the seed was about to detonate, Tala reflexively spat it out at the stone.

The wet seed slapped against the block, then exploded with a pulse of power.

The stone turned to a fine powder, flowing off the pedestal.

Well, the seeds definitely have a higher energy density than the branches.

-What was that?-

I spat out the seed.

-I'm well aware of what you did, Tala. That's not what you were supposed to do.-

I got nervous, okay? She scrunched up her face in irritation.

"Mistress Tala. Are you alright?"

Tala didn't turn around. Instead, she simply waved over her own shoulder. "I'm fine, Mistress Holly." She swallowed to help clear her mouth of the odd taste. "I just thought we should have a basis for comparison."

-*Liar.*-

Hush.

"Oh, I see." Holly didn't sound either convinced or skeptical. She simply sounded... present. Like she was taking in every detail.

Tala swept the iron free of stone dust and picked up the now magically inert seed. *This would still grow a tree, wouldn't it?*

-*Well, not still. It wouldn't have before. It was dormant until it expelled the power.*-

Fascinating life cycle. She stuck the seed into Kit absently before picking up a similarly sized stone block and setting it in the previous one's place. It really did feel lighter than she'd have expected, but that wasn't her focus at the moment.

Okay. I can do this.

Another seed went into her mouth, and she bit down without hesitation.

Tala drew in a deep breath and held it, barely managing to stop her own reflexive desire to spit out the seed as the power finished activating.

Power blossomed across her tongue.

She felt the things in her mouth that were not her break apart. Some remnants of her earlier feast that had stuck between or around her teeth, a bit of plaque, and what little saliva she'd managed to work up. The latter left her mouth a bit dry, but it thankfully didn't drain the moisture from her tissue and otherwise didn't harm her. *Hey, not a bad solution for oral care.*

-I veto that at the highest possible levels.-

Spoilsport.

The power somehow tasted… spicy, actually. It was far, *far* superior to the taste of the iron salve. Interestingly, it had broken down everything from its waxy covering as well, save the iron dust that had been in it. That likely contributed to the dry feeling. *Well, this is not something you experience every day.*

-Well, most people don't.-

A portion of the scripts lining the inside of her cheeks and even embedded in the bone of her jaw, her gums, and set within her teeth, flared to life. They did not negate the hostile magic. Instead, her power fought it, preventing it from enacting its purpose upon *her*.

Tala exhaled a tight stream of air and felt that air become saturated with the foreign power as it left her mouth.

She'd tried to aim at the very center of the rock, but her aim was imperfect, and her breath struck it on the left-hand side of the side facing her.

The front edge of the power splashed against the rock, powdering it on contact. What followed after, as the powder fell away, affected the rock deeper in, as well as a little farther out.

The result was that after she'd completed her exhale, and all the ending seed's power was spent, she'd created a neat hole through the block of stone.

The power had continued out the backside and settled down on some of the other trash on the floor behind the pedestal, powdering that as well.

There was a bit of odd horror to the sight in Tala's eyes. There was no sizzling, as if acid had eaten away at the stone, no smoking, and no heat or glowing material.

There was no evidence that anything had happened at all, save that the stone was no longer whole.

This is… terrifying, actually.

-*They really shouldn't let you keep this.*-

Tala would have glared at Alat, but that was rather useless. *There are quite a few things that are just as dangerous.*

-*Yes, but as Trent said, so long ago, this leaves virtually no trace.*-

And that was true. Even to her magesight, there weren't traces of power on the stone. The power even dissolved itself so utterly upon being used that it left no telltale signs.

Tala spat out the broken seed fragments and smacked her lips just a bit. "Well, that worked reasonably well." After a moment's consideration, she bent and picked up the fragments, placing them into Kit. *I don't want them to somehow find soil and start growing. That would be embarrassing.*

Shir strode forward and reached up to touch Tala's head. At the last moment, he paused. "May I?"

She nodded, and he placed his hand against her forehead, his eyes falling closed.

They immediately snapped open. "What the rust?" He shook himself. "My apologies, Mistress. You seem to have sustained no damage from your experiment."

Holly nodded and smiled. "And your inscriptions held up and acted as expected, completely without issue."

Tala grinned. "They did seem to, yeah."

Shir cleared his throat. "Mistress Holly, may I ask why this Fusing Bound has such a"—he glanced toward Holly, and Tala thought she saw the inscriptionist give the barest shake of her head—"altered and enhanced body?"

Tala shrugged, deciding not to try to parse through whatever he'd been going to say.

Millennial Mage, 6 - Fused

-Refined. He was going to ask why you had such a refined body.-

Yeah, that's probably true. Even so, Tala decided it was best to answer herself. "Most of my magic is directed internally, toward augmenting my physiology and toward regeneration."

Shir bit one side of his lip in thought, then shrugged. "I suppose that makes sense. Am I still needed?"

Tala nodded. "I would like to try one more thing before you go. This time I will breathe in after the power detonates."

The Healer sighed but nodded and stepped back across the room without verbal protest.

Holly grinned. "That does sound quite interesting. Give it a go."

Tala did just that.

The third seed activated, filling her mouth once again with the destructive power before Tala took in a long, slow breath.

The power didn't precisely burn as it went down, but it certainly tingled, and that was not accounting for the wave of scripts activating on the way down into her lungs.

The purging process was similar to that within her mouth. There were small bits of material in her throat and lungs from breathing in less than perfect air, among other things. Regardless of origin, they were reduced to such a fine powder, and in such a manner, that Tala knew they'd be carried back out when she exhaled.

There was a headiness to holding the power within her lungs; it seemed to make her chest buzz with the contained, potential destruction.

Even so, she didn't hold it in for long.

She exhaled, this time sending it out with a full-mouthed breath, rather than a pursed lipped stream.

The resulting miniature tide of destruction broke across the stone, dissolving it in almost an even wave, which passed through the stone, seemingly without slowing. As the dissolving power passed through the hard, heavy stone, the material was turned entirely into a fine dust.

There were some oddities due to the hole already in the stone, but the process was uniform for the most part.

"Fascinating." Holly walked up beside Tala. "The scripts ensured that all the power was carried out, without exception. Even if you were immune to the power, exhaling should have left a remnant behind without that functionality."

"Isn't that part of the point of the scripts?" Tala gave the woman a concerned look.

"Of course, but you'd never really used them in totality before. It is nice to have their design actually used."

She means 'actually tested.' Tala felt her eye twitch. *So... another experiment.*

-*Well, we have asked her to do some pretty unusual things. Better a theoretical 'yes' than an actual 'no.'*-

That's fair...

Shir came over and sent another pulse of magic through her, empowering a detailed inspection. "You are perfectly healthy." His tone was dry, and he turned to Holly. "You and I will speak later."

"As you wish, Master Shir."

He nodded once, then smiled at Tala. "Good luck to you, Mistress Tala. I'm sure we'll see each other again at some point."

She gave a formal bow. "Thank you for being here. I felt much better knowing we had a Healer present."

"But of course." His smile broadened.

"It was a pleasure to meet you."

"You as well." With that, he waved goodbye and departed.

Millennial Mage, 6 - Fused

Tala turned to Holly. "How many times can I do this before the scripts are degraded to the point that it is dangerous?"

"You mean how many seeds?" She tilted her head. "How many cuts can you heal from?"

"I've no idea."

"Precisely, dear. This doesn't put undue stress on the inscriptions. It is exactly what they were made for, and they do it easily and efficiently."

Tala grunted, then nodded. "Alright. Thank you. Can I do some more tests?"

"Absolutely, but I have other things to be about. This room is reserved for your use this evening. You have fun now!" Holly waved over her shoulder as she departed, closing the door behind herself.

Well, let's get to work. I assume you have some things to test?

-Absolutely.-

Tala and Alat spent the next couple of hours testing out different mouth shapes on the exhale, different rates of exhale, and a half-dozen other factors.

Their only interruption came when Jenna updated the information in their linked Archive space.

-She says that there was no sign of the arcane on your outing. Also, she applauds the lengths that you were willing to go to make evidence of your magical signature widely noticeable in at least a reasonably plausible fashion.-

Sarcasm?

-I don't think so?-

Huh. Fair enough.

-She also said that they will be in touch with regards to any further requests.-

That's a fancy way of saying they'll reach out.

-It was clear enough.-

Other than that, they were uninterrupted, but it was getting late, and Tala still needed Lyn's help to reapply her paint, so she headed home.

Of course, she made a stop to grab four cheesy little caravans on the way, two of which she finished before arriving at her own front door.

Lyn, bless her, didn't ask why Tala needed a reapplication, simply obliging and painting all the parts of Tala that she couldn't easily reach, herself.

Tala, for her part, kept one fingertip on the through-spike to keep it from being covered over.

Lyn's part done, Tala bade her goodnight and went into Kit. Kannis was apparently working late at the guildhall on some task or another. *She always was a bit of an overachiever...*

Within Kit, Tala painted the rest of herself and then began to press the berries.

It wasn't a long process, though it should have been a physically taxing one. Thankfully, Tala had both more strength and more endurance than most.

It was late in the night when she finally finished processing her four barrels of endingberries down to two barrels of juice. *They really are far more juice heavy than they would be if they were mundane berries.*

She ate a good portion of the leftover meat of the berries while she was pressing the others, taking what she could from them both nutritionally and with regard to their magical power.

The rest she ate while moving through her nightly routine and training. Alat insisted that they add at least a couple of exhalation exercises, to cement the mouth shapes that they'd found to have the most useful patterns of distribution.

One more thing...

Millennial Mage, 6 - Fused

Finally, sometime after midnight, she flopped into her bed for much-needed sleep.

*   *   *

The next few days passed uneventfully, leading to Tala's departure for Marliweather. She trained, both alone and with the guards and Mages. It took her a few days to return to her previous levels of competence against the guards as she acclimated to her new physicality. From there, she continued to slowly improve—still losing more often than not, but less often each day.

Terry, as it turned out, did not like holding weapons. He was willing to try to overcome the hang-up, but everyone involved agreed it should be done on his own for the time being.

Because of this, along with the marked change in Tala's own fighting abilities, they decided to hold off on adding in weaponry for Terry or mounted fighting for both of them. Instead, they spent what time they had with her to help her get fully acclimated. Unfortunately, that meant that it would have to wait until they'd returned from Marliweather.

Tala ate a truly ridiculous amount of food, spending a gold per day, instead of the three silver she'd been managing up to that point, and she and Alat worked across the board to refine and improve her progress.

Alat, specifically, took over primary monitoring and enacting of the Fusing process, which Tala had maintained in the back of her mind.

Tala's alternate interface spent basically every free moment continuing the Fusing process, which was actually how they both realized that Alat could manipulate magical power directly.

Alat could only manipulate the power that passed through Tala's gate if Tala explicitly allowed it, but it did work.

This made Alat giddy with excitement, but she put aside the discovery to devote herself to Fusing for the time being. When Tala tried to work with Alat to move their Fusing ahead even faster, it didn't seem to work very well, so Tala left it to her alternate interface.

With the new method, they estimated that they'd reach the threshold to Fused within a month or two, instead of the three or four they'd been expecting.

Who knows what that threshold will actually look like?
-We'll tackle that when we get there.-

That was true enough.

The last two days, Tala charged her cargo slots in the mornings, and finally, the day of departure arrived.

Tala awoke as usual, one thought crystal clear in her mind.

Well, rust. I'm going to see my family.

Chapter: 19
Alat, Ignored

Tala was not interested in thinking about her upcoming visit with her family. She knew it wasn't healthy to avoid the topic, and she was leaving that day to go to the city where they lived, but she still just couldn't seem to force herself to give it more than passing reflection.

-We really should consider it.-

So, Tala went through her routine, just as she did every morning and evening, not considering the upcoming encounter.

Physical exercise and stretching, with and without her own gravity enhanced.

Martial form work with her various weapons and tools.

Soul exercises, which included everything from working on increasing the distance that she could pull her bound items to her, to improving her subtle control—needed for having her blood-stars orbit her—to aspect mirroring.

Reading the morning selection of materials from her various books, compiled and reorganized by Alat. One of the fascinating things about Alat's manifestation of the books was that Tala had complete control to freely prop them around herself while she did other things, making them easy to read no matter the environment.

Breathing exercises to facilitate her use of ending seed destruction—as well as to improve her physical capacities.

Millennial Mage, 6 - Fused

Enacting her magic through the series of iron spheres that Jevin had given her, honing her ability to work around iron.

Breaking her bones in a few strategic places that hadn't been broken before to allow them to rebuild under the influence of the modified scripts.

Finally, she drank her daily portion of endingberry juice and ate a large hunk of jerky. As that all processed, she meditated and focused her magesight inward, working to shift the magic around to the appropriate scripts within herself, overlaying the power atop her own magics that had the same function.

-We still need to talk about your family.-

Tala growled. *No, we need to go eat breakfast with Odera.*

-I am in your head, Tala. Not only is it blazingly obvious when you're making excuses, but it couldn't possibly be easier to converse while we walk.- After a moment, Alat added one final point. *-And, we would be vastly too early if we left now.-*

Tala ignored Alat and checked the time simply by wishing to know what time it was.

Alat was right; she still had two hours before it was time to meet with Odera.

"I should cook something." She really didn't want to, but just as Holly had indicated, Tala had been *hungry*. She'd been hungrier than she'd ever been for basically a week, and she was getting sick of eating.

There was a special type of frustration that came from having her stomach full while still feeling desperately hungry.

With a sigh, Tala approached the task of cooking up some food in the same way that she'd perform any other required task. Though, she did take the time to choose something that appealed to her tastes at the moment.

-You know, for all your many flaws, you have a ridiculously high level of dedication, follow-through, and personal responsibility. You don't always see how what you're doing affects others, but with regard to your own duties? You are great at keeping your end of things progressing and on track.-

Thank you? Tala felt herself relax a bit. *That's really kind of you to say.*

-So, what do you think your parents did right to instill such things into you?-

Tala jerked, sloshing the sausage and eggs she was frying in her cauldron. Thankfully, the shape of the cookware made spilling more difficult than that.

She didn't respond to Alat, instead pulling out a large loaf of heavy, multi-grain bread and a large jar of butter.

She allowed herself to contemplate how much she was going to miss having fresh eggs, bread, and butter on the caravan trip.

-You are well aware both that the cooks will have excellent food for you and that you are continuing to ignore me.-

You're right. I am ignoring you.

She missed coffee, though she didn't need it to wake up. She missed the *flavor*. The way her body had responded to the warmth and caffeine.

It was glorious.

It was gone.

Focus, Tala. Eat. She ate mechanically. Everything was good, but she didn't pull as much joy from the taste as she would have a week earlier.

I hope this doesn't last forever. I need to slow down my eating soon, or I'll lose the last bits of enjoyment I can pull from it, and it will become only *a chore.*

-Do you want an answer to that?-

Tala grimaced. *Yes, of course, though it wasn't a question.*

-*So, no more ignoring me?*-

Either answer or don't. Tala took an irritated bite of buttered bread.

-*The scripts, inside your iron paint and with the regular work we've put in, are almost finished with the modifications that they'll do to you physically. In addition, your stores are nearing their max capacity.*-

I was feeling a bit heavier today. She hesitated. *I've been growing steadily heavier for nearly a week, now that I think about it.*

-*As I was saying, you could drop down to normal consumption today, and you'd be fine… Well, normal for you, anyway.*-

Yeah, but then I'd be going into a trip with lower reserves than I could or should have.

-*That's true, but only if you stop right now.*-

So…? How long do I need to keep this up to top-off?

-*Another week if you don't sustain any major, unexpected injuries.*-

So, just in time to arrive in Marliweather.

-*Yes. Speaking of which…*-

Tala groaned, doing her best to ignore Alat once again as she ate.

After Alat finally accepted that Tala was fully and truly ignoring her on the topic of her family, she changed the subject, thus bringing Tala's attention back. -*There has to be some sort of drink that we could find that would have all the nutrients we need.*- Then, of all things, Alat somehow shuddered. -*I don't mean that lard-based monstrosity that Jevin tried to make us consider.*-

Tala shuddered as well at the memory. *One sip was all it took. Never again.*

-*He might have had the right idea, though.*-

Bite your tongue.
-*Do you mean bite* your *tongue?*-
That sounds needlessly... odd.

Alat sighed. -*Fine. But we could look into something like that. The drink, I mean.*-

Tala grunted. *I'm not really sure what the market for it would be, aside from us. We certainly don't have the money to pay to develop something like that just for our own use.*

-*True enough. We could at least ask the Culinary Guild at some point.*-

Yeah, that couldn't hurt. Wait... don't you have full access to their Archival records?

-*Yes, but that only contains the overarching information. From what I can tell, local prices and availability aren't recorded in the Archive.*-

Ah, fair enough.

Tala packed everything back away—unnecessarily, given that Kit would have done it—and did a twisting stretch, relishing in how far her joints moved and with how much ease.

"Terry. Ready to go?"

Terry lifted his head from the corner where he slept. He let out a grunting squawk and then lowered back down once again. Then, he flickered to Tala's shoulder, maintaining his body positioning.

"All right. Let's go."

Tala came out into Lyn's house, leaving the bright, spring-sunlit home behind and stepping into the dark of winter morning.

She heard Kannis moving slowly about within Tala's old room, and Tala quickly grabbed Kit from the wall and fled.

Millennial Mage, 6 - Fused

She and the mageling had crossed paths quite a few times, but they'd still never acknowledged their previous relationship at the academy. *Or lack thereof.*

Tala was becoming increasingly certain that Kannis remembered her, too, and had just chosen not to say anything either. She'd probably taken a cue from Tala's own actions.

Lyn had been extra busy over the last week, so Tala had barely seen the woman. Even so, they'd said their good-byes the night before.

Tala managed to get all the way out of the house and close the door, locking it behind her, before Kannis came out of her room if the sound was any indication.

Tala let out a long, relieved breath. *Good, I escaped!*

-Yes, you have successfully escaped from someone who happens to have known you for longer than a couple of months and bears you no ill will. How did you manage it? How would you have coped with failure?-

You know, sometimes I don't like you.

-I am you.-

Oh, I am well aware of that.

Tala took her ease, walking through Bandfast's snowy streets. She'd be gone for about three weeks, if all went well, and she was enjoying the last look for the time being.

She stepped through Holly's workshop door, stood there for a moment, waved to the assistant, and then immediately departed. Tala had made it a habit to drop through each morning to give her inscriber one last set of information to add to her records until Tala's return.

Her feet led her to the work yard, where Mistress Odera was already awaiting her atop their cargo wagon, and if the spread before her was any indication, food was ready and waiting.

Tala climbed up, greeting her overseer. "Mistress Odera, good morning!"

"Good morning, Mistress Tala. Good morning, Alat."

-*Good morning.*- As usual, Alat could only speak into Tala's head, so Tala conveyed the sentiment. "She says good morning."

Alat always conveyed a mix of emotions at the greeting. Mistress Odera greeted her as a separate person, which seemed to fascinate Alat. -*I am not a separate person, but still I enjoy the greeting.*-

And yet, Mistress Odera never gave Alat the moniker of Mistress.

-*I know I don't have a keystone, nor a gate of my own… but I am you, and you are me. So, shouldn't I be thought of as a Mage as well?*-

Tala shook her head, leaving her alternate interface to her musings as she finished the very short climb and stood on the roof.

Mistress Odera gestured to the trays laid out before her. There were so many that Tala knew that the woman had to have transported them in her own small, dimensional storage.

Around each tray, Tala could see a bit of Mistress Odera's magic, keeping the dishes warm and the air perfectly conditioned to maintain the exact perfect texture for each given dish.

"Chicken-fried steak with sausage gravy." The older woman was pointing to the far-right covered tray, then moved her finger over to indicate each in turn. "Then, we have a selection of seed, nut, and dried-fruit breads with ample butter; a selection of fruits, fresh from the growing chambers; a dozen pastries of various kinds; and finally, a thick slab of honey-roasted ham."

Millennial Mage, 6 - Fused

Tala bowed before sitting. "Thank you, Mistress. This is a fantastic spread. Thank you for transporting it down here for us. Well, for me."

Mistress Odera simply smiled in return. The older Mage had taken Holly's recommendation to heart and had *significantly* increased the amount of food that she facilitated during their breakfasts.

As Tala devoured and Mistress Odera nibbled, they chatted about the previous day's and that morning's training and reading.

People were moving around below them, in the work yard, adding last-minute items to the two wagons that would soon depart.

The oxen shifted in their harnesses, causing the leather and wood to creak.

Passengers were loading up as well, and soon enough, the whole caravan would be ready to depart.

The time for their meeting with the heads of the caravan guards and the drivers was drawing near, and Tala moved around to charge the cargo slots for the morning. While she worked, she glanced at Mistress Odera and asked a very impertinent question. "How is the iron Archon Star coming?"

Mistress Odera hesitated before smiling slightly. "I have not succeeded, but I did not imagine that this would be an easy task. I did discover something fascinating, however."

Tala didn't interrupt.

"I cannot enact magics on the iron. No one can. But I can get power to move *through* the iron."

Tala hesitated before moving her hand to the last charging point. "Magic can't pass through iron either."

"No, child, not through the iron. *Through* the iron."

She grunted, charging the last cargo slot before she turned and sat. "You aren't making any sense."

"If you walk through a crowd, are you actually going through any of the people that make up the crowd?"

"No." She instantly understood. "So, you are moving magic around the iron, within the iron object."

Mistress Odera cackled slightly before tapping her own nose. "Precisely. I was almost a void Mage, but the teachers at the academy advised against it." She sighed wistfully. "'We are but empty space, thinking itself full.'"

Tala swallowed, paling slightly beneath her iron and under her illusion. *That sort of fundamental understanding could have terrifying results.*

-I wish we could see it at work.-

I know, right? "So, what happened?"

Mistress Odera shrugged. "It was deemed too reckless a foundation, and I was encouraged toward building another. I like mine well enough, now. 'That which flows can never be broken.'"

How have we never asked about her foundational understanding? Why do her understandings sound so much... better than ours?

-Never came up? We also were much more focused on the foundation itself than on a cool wording for it. We could fix that?-

No... it's not important.

"But that is beside the point, Mistress Tala. I can move power through, or rather *around*, the iron. The medium isn't air, and there isn't air for the power to move through, not throughout most of the iron. Thus, I haven't determined how to adjust the working, but I will soon enough."

Tala was considering the implications when Alat voiced them aloud—well, within Tala's head. *-That really puts the iron sphere trials into perspective.-*

Millennial Mage, 6 - Fused

Yeah, and renders them as little more than pale imitations. Can you imagine the delicacy required? She's not even Bound!

Rane called up to them, interrupting Tala's thoughts, and they knew that their time that morning had passed.

Mistress Odera had put the dishes away in her dimensional storage as Tala had cleared them of food, so there was nothing left atop the wagon but the two women.

They climbed down, greeted Rane, and went to have a final conference with the heads of this caravan venture.

Thus began what was an entirely ordinary, boring trek across the winter plains.

Few things of note stood out during the outbound leg of the venture.

First, Rane and Tala discussed their progress in Fusing, in-depth.

It was the first night, and Tala and Rane sat across a table from each other, out under the clear, starry sky.

Most everyone else was huddled inside, either asleep or finding some means of entertainment. The guards were, of course, on guard, but only a few were out and about.

Rane was grumpily drinking from a steaming tankard. "I can feel it. Almost like a counter in my head, though not so concrete. The closer I get to truly being Fused, the more power it takes to move ahead. I feel like I'm trying to push a boulder up an increasingly steep road, and ahead, it looks more like a vertical cliff-face."

Tala grunted her condolences. "Master Jevin did warn that there would be *some* price to pay for your easier early advancement."

Rane grimaced, taking another long pull. "Still, it's frustrating. I feel like I'm so close, but I can also feel that, unless my power density is higher, I'll never be able to force it that last little bit."

"So, magical weight training?"

He snorted a laugh. "That sounds like I'm using my power to move around heavy objects."

She grinned in return. "True enough. I mean, you *are* doing what you can to up your magical weight."

"Yeah. I spend hours every day, filled to the brim and drawing in more, forcibly keeping the power away from my scripts and forcing it to stay within me. I'm not good at guiding my power. It's definitely cross-quadrant work, and I *hate* it." He growled. "It's like knowing a bear will eat my left hand if it moves even slightly and a swarm of wasps will enshroud my right with stingers if it ever *stops* moving. The feeling is *awful*."

"Any good progress?"

"Progress? Yes. Good progress?" He scowled. "'These things take time, Rane.' Master Grediv thinks this path is working. I should be able to Fuse within a year if I'm consistent in my training. Two on the outside."

Tala gave a soft whistle. "I'm sorry, Rane. That sounds... unpleasant."

"Let me guess. You're done? If I switch on my magesight, will I be seeing yellow?"

"Hardly." She let out her own long breath, pulling her mug of hot buttered rum toward herself. It was delicious, but it was also her fifth such drink. The richness of the beverage was starting to get to her, so she only took a single, slow sip. "There's something wrong, honestly. The process is slowing for me, too, and it wasn't precisely quick and easy to begin with."

Rane cocked his head to one side, listening.

"Don't get me wrong, Alat is still making it go *way* faster than it would be moving if I was just Fusing as a subconscious process, but things are slowing down noticeably."

"Has anyone given you any advice or thoughts about why that might be?"

Millennial Mage, 6 - Fused

Tala hunched in on herself, taking a longer pull from the alcoholic drink. *Not that it will do anything to me...* "Apparently, my soul is in turmoil about something, and my spirit is deeply unsettled. That's making the act of Fusing them to my body... difficult."

-Hence, why I want to talk through your upcoming encounter.-

Rane nodded sagely, foam on his upper lip. "Your family."

Tala groaned. "You, too?"

He frowned. "Could it be anything else?"

"Arcane."

Rane paused at that, then shrugged. "Why not both?"

Tala snorted a derisive laugh. "Oh, yes. I'm visiting my estranged family, and there's some arcane messing with my head, but wait, there's more!" She rubbed at her temples in irritation. "There aren't high-level Archons free to 'babysit' me over what amounts to a low chance of an encounter."

Jenna had been clear on that: Tala should not expect any back-up near at hand if the arcane showed up. Tala *hoped* that it was a lie, meant to help lure the creature out in case it had some way of reading her mind from afar, but she didn't have any evidence to back up that hope. *It wouldn't work if there were any...*

Rane patted her wrist. "That's rough, buddy."

Tala snorted another laugh, but this one left her smiling. "Buddy?"

He shrugged. "I'm not really good at this sort of thing. I'm offering comfort?"

Tala grinned. "Fair enough. Comfort received. Thank you."

He lifted his mug and tilted it her way before taking a drink. "Any time, Tala. Any time."

Chapter: 20
Uneventful

Tala sat across from Mistress Odera as they watched the land roll by from atop the cargo wagon.

Tala had retrieved some of the knives and hatchets from Lyn before the woman could sell them. Now, they lay in two concentric rings on the wagon-top, Terry flickering around them, occasionally brushing the handles before squawking in irritation and flickering away. He'd been at it for days, even before they had left Bandfast, so Tala paid him little mind.

He'll just have to get over himself at some point.

-Centuries of ingrained behavior is hard to reshape, Tala. You could bond him, and he'd likely be able to make the change in an instant, but as he is now? Terry is ancient for his kind, and alive because he is set and well-practiced in his ways. Give him time to adjust.-

Yeah, not bonding him 'til I'm Refined.

-As we were advised. I agree.-

Tala returned her attention to Mistress Odera, still a bit uncertain as to the woman's suggestion.

Aside from Tala and Rane's discussion on their progress toward Fusing, the only other event of note was this one.

"You want me to try to dissolve one of your barriers."

"Yes, Mistress Tala. I do."

"That seems... incredibly dangerous."

"We will approach it intelligently, but it is criminal that you haven't tried this against workings of pure magic directly. Especially after what Master Cazor told you in regard to the power working against his magics."

"As you say, and as you have said nearly every time this has come up." She took a long, deep breath, then shook her head in resignation. "So, how do we mitigate the risks?"

That began a lengthy discussion. Alat chimed in, voiced by Tala, and between the three of them, they came up with a solution.

Tala sat at the side of the wagon, legs dangling over the edge, facing the snow-covered rolling plains.

Mistress Odera then created a protective barrier out in front of Tala that was shaped to deflect the power up and away if the dissolution power ended up doing nothing to the defense.

Mistress Odera then ensured that the working moved with them as the wagon continued on its way. "Ready, Mistress Tala."

Tala pulled out an ending seed and popped it into her mouth, grimacing at the taste of the iron-salve coating but managing to ignore the unpleasantness.

She bit down and waited for the power to blossom between her teeth.

Moving carefully, she shaped her lips for short-dispersion and exhaled.

The dissolution power washed over the protective field, and Mistress Odera grunted.

"Oh, that… that is really uncomfortable." The woman grimaced.

Tala watched the zone of compressed layers of air and water shimmer and almost spark magically as the dissolving power used itself up against the defense.

A moment after all the ending seed's power was gone, Mistress Odera dropped the field.

She immediately brought it back up. "Please strike the defense with your weapon. Don't spare any strength."

Tala shifted back onto the wagon for better footing, then stood, drawing Flow and pushing power through the weapon to transform it into a sword. With a sure, practiced motion, Tala stepped forward, executing an overhead chop with all her strength and body-weight behind the blow.

Power rippled around the soul-bound weapon as all of Tala's magical weight slammed down as well, refined and directed into lethal cutting force.

Flow stopped dead on the defense that Mistress Odera had cast, though the woman had a look of intense concentration.

"Girl, you hit harder than a Leshkin juggernaut."

Tala beamed at the praise, pulling back Flow and sheathing it, the weapon now back in the form of a knife.

"So? What do you think, Mistress Odera? How did the two compare?"

The older woman shook her head in obvious fascination. "You hit harder with Flow than with the breath weapon, but not by much. Even so, I'd rather take an attack from that sword over an ending-breath any day of the week."

"What do you mean?"

"There was an odd grating feeling, a screeching dissonance, while I was resisting the dissolution. It felt like I was standing on sand that was being dug out from under me. It was incredibly disconcerting. In the end, it took less power to resist than your sword, but that hardly matters. I think a larger dose of the dissolution would have broken my protective magics with ease, while I could easily hold up against more than ten of those sword-strikes in quick succession without much issue."

"I don't understand."

Millennial Mage, 6 - Fused

Mistress Odera made a vain grasping motion. "It was like the spell itself was slipping through my grasp like I could barely hold onto it." She nodded, suddenly seeming to have something click together. "It was as if my own spell-working *wanted* to come apart and was using all the power I gave it to fight toward that end."

"So, the more powerful the magics…"

"In theory, the more powerful the magics you affected, the less they could resist." The older woman had a gleam in her eye. "And I have a mastery of my magic that is belied by my relative weakness, Mistress. Any other Mage would have no chance at maintaining a hold over their working, and only old, well-practiced Archons would do any better." She let loose a soft cackle. "Let's test some more."

And so, they did.

A tight stream of the dissolution was able to punch through several layers of Mistress Odera's defense before the power was used up, but Mistress Odera was able to hold together the spell-structure against the destructive influence. So they moved on to using multiple seeds at the same time.

True to Mistress Odera's guess, even the beginning of the second seed's power destabilized her working, causing the entire defensive spellform to collapse, no matter how small a portion Tala concentrated the power on.

"It really does disrupt the spellform's ability to hold together." Mistress Odera was contemplating. "In order to counter it…" She thought for a moment longer and then gestured, eyes alight with a mischievous glint.

A sphere appeared in front of Tala, hovering out away from the wagon just as all the targets that Mistress Odera created had.

Tala examined the spherical shield with her magesight and saw that the seemingly smooth creation was made up of interlocking, overlapping bubble-like creations.

She glanced over and saw a look of smug satisfaction on the older woman's face.

"Is that harder?"

"Marginally. It's something I've played with in the past, but under normal circumstances, it doesn't actually give any benefit save a bit of added flexibility. Most applications of my magic need greater staying power more than the ability to adjust."

I can think of a dozen sets of circumstances where the greater flexibility would have been useful.

-Ahh, but this is really what sets Archon-level magic apart from that of Mages. Mages almost have to *focus on power in order to be effective. Archons usually have power to spare, and so they can be more flexible and creative in their enactments.-*

Like Atrexia with her rock-spikes. It was a powerful working but not very flexible in its use.

-Precisely. She is going to be a terror when she advances.-

Tala felt a bit of sadness, looking at Mistress Odera. *If she advances.*

Mistress Odera caught the look and scowled. "None of that, girl. I know an Archon could have it both ways. Now, focus."

Tala nodded and turned back to the sphere of interlocking power.

She cracked two seeds between her teeth, waited the required time for the power to erupt outward, and exhaled in a tight stream.

Just after over half her available ending seed power was blown, the closest bubble to her fell apart, seeming almost to flow in every direction at once, rather than actually breaking.

There was a shimmering in the air, and one of the neighboring shields distorted slightly, adjusting itself to snap sideways into the place vacated by the dissolved working.

The others seemed to jiggle and waver just a bit, altering their positioning ever so slightly. At that point, a new bubble formed within the complex magical structure, leaving it as protective as it had been to begin with.

The entire process had taken less than a second, and only the smallest amount of ending seed power had gotten through, into the interior of the sphere.

The new target for Tala's exhale wavered under the continued stream of power, but it held until the attack was spent.

Tala shook her head in wonder. "Rust me inside out." She turned her gaze back to Mistress Odera.

The woman simply smiled with self-satisfaction. "I think that held up rather well, don't you?"

From that point onward, Tala and Mistress Odera did some practice with the ending power every day. The older woman insisted that Tala begin carrying an ending seed tucked in her cheek, being careful while she ate, because it was painfully obvious when Tala popped a seed into her mouth.

"You must have your weapons ready."

Tala reluctantly agreed, but only because the power couldn't really harm her, so long as she didn't swallow it.

-Our stomach is defended, but not as much as our mouth, throat, and lungs. We'd likely have to regrow a good amount of our insides if we swallowed one.-

That was, categorically, to be avoided. So, Tala used up the seed before sleeping.

It was the wise thing to do.

Other than that, the trip was utterly uneventful.

Arcanous beasts were fought off, the guards harvesting what they could; lots of good food was eaten, grudgingly; and Tala didn't have to fight a single real conflict.

Luxury.

As the end of the trip neared, they crested a particularly high rise and looked down upon Marliweather, the city of Tala's birth.

It covered so much more land than Bandfast, given that its mining operations were still… well, operational.

Tala recalled the types of mining humanity had tried through the ages.

Strip mining was effective but left the land raw and unusable, like an open sore that took vastly too long to heal.

Open-pit mining was similarly scarring and had the added detriment of often creating lakes of despoiled water.

There were several others, but that was hardly the point. These days, humanity used underground mining, with Material Guide Mages ensuring the minimal manual labor brought forth the maximum results.

Within the ring of massive gantries and equipment to transport workers and materials down into and up from the mining tunnels, the familiar farmland lay just as dormant as it had been around Bandfast.

The city also looked very much like the one that they'd just left a few days back. The layout of the streets was nearly identical, as were large portions of the skyline.

Alat even superimposed Tala's memories of Bandfast onto the vision of Marliweather before them. She had to search a bit, looking for the right perspective until she found a match.

-Huh, I guess the Builders don't go in for innovation?-
If it isn't broken…

Millennial Mage, 6 - Fused

-That's fair. There does seem to be some evidence of iteration, though, so they aren't completely stagnant. They've probably just perfected the design to a ridiculous degree by this point. And they did rotate things a few degrees.-

The iteration makes sense, as does the slight rotation. We've traveled west, so north is going to have a slightly different directionality.

-I'm orienting off north.-

True north or magnetic north?

-How, under the stars, would I check true north? Not that we have a compass to check for magnetic north.-

Tala grinned. *Follow the orientation of the city?*

Alat grunted. *-That might be so, I suppose.-*

Tala considered for a moment. *You know, while it was just a turn of phrase, I think we could actually use the stars to find true north.*

Alat groaned. *-Now I feel foolish. Of course we could, but we'd have to have the night sky and a lot of time. Using the city to short-hand it makes sense.-*

Tala turned her focus back to the city.

Slight differences as evidence, the cities were clearly siblings, having come from the same makers. Though, once again, Marliweather's stage modified the view. The ring of mining work vaguely obscured the overall view of the city's skyline with rising steam and smoke.

There wasn't a lot, but it was enough to be noticeable in the cool, wintery evening air.

Rane pulled himself up onto the cargo wagon and came to stand beside Tala.

"It's lovely."

"It looks like Bandfast." Tala used her tongue to play with the ending seed tucked inside her cheek.

-That's going to become a bad habit.-

Hush. It's fine.

Rane gave her a sideways glance before shrugging. "Bandfast is a lovely city, too."

Tala found herself grinning. "Fair enough."

"So... I haven't brought it up and neither have you. Now, we're here."

Tala sighed, her smile slipping.

"You grew up in that city, didn't you." It wasn't really a question.

"Seems so."

"Your family still there?"

Tala had a moment of panic. *I have no idea. Did they leave? Did they die?*

-Calm, woman. A Mage is notified if any of their family dies.-

They could have moved.

-Really? You think they could afford to relocate?-

Fair enough... The entire exchange, panic included, had taken less than a breath. Tala exhaled fully and shrugged. "I think so."

Rane grunted. "Are you going to see them?"

"I probably should."

He gave her a knowing half-grin. "But are you going to see them?"

Tala found herself smiling again and almost punched him, but she held herself back. "Yeah. I suppose so."

"Do you want company?"

She rocked back on her heels slightly. *Do I?*

The wagons started their trip down the slope and toward the defensive perimeter of the city.

Terry squawked up at her, and she looked down at the neat pile of weapons the bird had made beside her. "Hey, you moved them!"

Terry practically rolled his eyes as he let out an indignant trill.

"Of course, I knew you *could* move them. I also knew that you didn't want to. Good for you."

He hunkered down and glowered up at her before flickering to her shoulder, maintaining his glare.

That's actually pretty impressive, all things considered.

She shook her head and bent to place the knives and hatchets back into Kit. Then, she tossed Terry some jerky, and after he flickered to catch it, he curled up and closed his eyes.

Rane didn't press his query, simply swaying with the smooth motion of the cargo wagon.

"I don't know." Tala's voice was quiet as she returned to her position beside the large man, staring out at the ever-growing city before them.

"Well, if you do, I'm happy to accompany you."

"To meet my family."

"No implications intended." And by his tone and demeanor, he meant it. She hadn't even caught him off guard with the question.

"Wow, Mistress Aproa is really helping you get over your awkwardness."

Rane's cheek twitched and colored just slightly, but he shook his head. "She has a lot of interesting advice. I don't think I agree with all of it, but it is all worth considering."

"Well, in either case, thank you for the offer."

He nodded. "I'm going to do another sweep of the perimeter before we enter the defenses proper." Without a backward glance, he turned and climbed down from the wagon.

Tala took some time to examine the far-flung defenses and to feel the power in the air around the city before them.

What she was able to discern was amazing, really. Bandfast was only about fifty years older than Marliweather, but there was already a marked difference in the concentration and zeme of power around the city and throughout the defenses.

Where the region around Bandfast was like a hill, when compared to the mountainous edifice of Alfast-Waning, Marliweather still felt like a level plain, magically speaking.

The defenses here were but weak lines of power, weaving a loose net over the city.

The towers in rings around the mining and farming districts were still beacons of magic, ready to strike down anything that required such, but the defenses as a whole were almost laughably weak.

Because they don't need heavy defenses yet. The concentration of power hasn't begun to draw in the kinds of threats that need universal, heavy-handed responses.

-Plus, I'd imagine that the city's Archons are ready to respond to anything extreme.-

Yeah, the 'defenses' are more like a glorified detection grid at the moment.

-Bandfast's aren't much better.-

That's true enough. It was mainly Archons who responded to and destroyed the syphon. The city's defenses didn't do much.

The caravan rolled past one of the massive, towering gantries, filled with moving parts and magical mechanisms that Tala had never delved into the details of.

Steam and smoke rose around the outside of the metal edifice, made more visible by the crisply cold, winter air.

The structure stood like a benevolent god over this one entrance to the mining complex below, helping the small humans to access the riches of Zeme.

Millennial Mage, 6 - Fused

We really do stand on the shoulders of our ancestors. How much in my life is built upon all that came before?
-Everything.-

Tala nodded in mute agreement, simply continuing to marvel at the monument of innovation which helped keep them stocked with precious metals.

The caravan passed several more of the mining entrances—none quite so closely as the first—before they came to the farmland. As they entered the portion of road that cut though skeletal orchards and beside deep drifts of snow-covered, empty fields, Tala felt herself smile.

It is like a sleeping mother, ready to awaken and care for her children. Her sleep is needed, so she can better provide for us all.

After another few moments of quiet contemplation, Alat spoke into her mind. -*That is a lovely way to view the land.*-

I think it's true, at least in part.

-*It's a lovely way to view family as well.*-

Tala sighed. *I have nothing against the idea of family.*

-*Just against your own.*-

Tala felt something snap within her, and she sat down, hard, turning her rage inward. Of course *I'm angry at them, Alat. They sent me away. They saddled me with their debt. They saw me as a means to an end, so they used me.*

-*You agreed.*-

Tala froze, then shook her head. *Of course I did. What twelve-year-old wouldn't? 'Oh, do you want to help your family?' How could I say no? What sort of awful person would say no?*

-*The Mages did try to ensure that you knew what you were agreeing to.*-

Tala snorted. *I'm not mad at them, but it wasn't much of a choice, either way.* "No, Master, I want my family to starve, but thank you for offering a solution."

-They wouldn't have starved.-

Tala growled internally.

-You are amazing at justifying your anger, and some of your anger is *justified. But you did agree.-*

If I hadn't, I wouldn't have become a Mage.

-Because most of the debt is from your schooling. Why would they have accepted you if you wouldn't agree to pay the expense?-

I would have happily done it without taking on my family's debts.

-Really?-

Of course!

-Did you ask? Did you really want to leave your siblings in a debt-ridden house? Or your parents?-

Tala didn't have a response.

-No, you felt trapped and made the only choice that you felt you could. It hardly matters if it really was the only one available to you or not.-

Rust you. She knew that Alat was prodding her toward healthier thinking, using half-truths and overstatements to move her in the ways that she needed to go. *What does it say about me that my alternate interface is using tactics like Mistress Odera…?*

The thought slipped through, not really directed at Alat, but Alat responded nonetheless. *-Am I wrong?-*

Tala hunched in on herself, ignoring the ingrained training to sit up straight.

-Am I wrong?-

No. The word was soft, quiet even in her own head.

Alat was silent for a long moment.

Tala wiped the tears from her cheeks, grateful that Mistress Odera wasn't on the wagon top with her.

Millennial Mage, 6 - Fused

Tala buried her face into her knees and cried quietly for a time, letting the subtle sway of the wagon rock her, comfort her.

Finally, she addressed Alat once more. *I hate them for putting me in that position. How could they ask a child to choose?*

-*I know.*- There was a softness to the alternate interface's voice, a maternal quality.

But if I hate them, then what was the choice even for? What did it accomplish? Why take on the debt for people I hate?

-*Do you really hate them?*-

It was a long moment before Tala shook her head slightly. *I don't know.*

Alat didn't press the point, instead turning their focus elsewhere. -*So?*-

Tala wiped her face once more, pulling some rags from Kit to do a better job and to blow her nose into. *So, what?*

-*What do you want?*-

What do I want? I don't know what I want, Alat. She looked up at the city's outermost wall and the gate that was a scant hundred yards away.

-*Well, you better decide soon. Because we're here.*-

Chapter: 21
You'll Never Guess

Tala stood back up atop the cargo wagon and composed herself as they passed through the gates of Marliweather.

-*I do have some good news.*-

Oh? Tala was interested in anything that could distract her, even though she knew that she really needed to focus.

-*I think I have it worked out, so we can mimic the appearance of spell-lines on the illusion.*-

Mimic?

-*Yeah, I can show you how to fracture the illusion in such a way as to make it look like you have lines tattooed across your skin.*-

Would they look metallic?

Alat hesitated, then sighed within Tala's head. -*Well, no.*-

So, I would look like someone making a poor imitation of a Mage.

-*It's not perfect, I'll grant you that.*-

But it is a step in the right direction.

-*Exactly.*-

So, no actual solution yet.

-*No, sorry.*-

These things take time. Thank you for continuing to investigate.

Tala felt a wave of panic try to creep over her as she returned her attention to the issue at hand. Instead of succumbing to the feeling, she shook her head and smiled. *We can do this. We'll be fine.*

Millennial Mage, 6 - Fused

She went through the motions of finalizing a caravan journey. She met with the pay clerk, gave her report, and accepted her pay. She chose to take it in hard coin this time as the experience with the alchemist was still fresh in her mind.

Some just want tangible currency. She received twelve gold for her role as the Dimensional Mage of the caravan, and five for her role as Mage Protector. *That's fair; I really didn't do much in that role except take watch most nights.*

What came as a true surprise was the additional three gold that she received for facilitating the use of the Wainwrights' wagon. Since this pay had been withheld on her trip to Makinaven and back to pay for the increased structure of the wagon, she'd forgotten that it was owed to her, generally.

What a nice surprise.

She bade goodnight to Rane and Mistress Odera, getting the name and location of the inn they'd be staying at. When they inquired about her, she shrugged and stated that she'd just find a wall somewhere when she needed to sleep.

Mistress Odera didn't press but did insist on meeting Tala for breakfast at the older woman's inn the next morning. Tala heartily agreed. *Free food is free food.*

It was still early afternoon as the caravan had made good time. When she noted that, Tala took a moment to walk over to the head driver and thank her for taking such an expeditious route.

That done, Tala wandered a bit aimlessly.

What struck her first was the smell of the city.

It was subtle, and she couldn't have described it properly in a thousand years, but there was an underlying scent in the air that just made her think of *home*.

It sparked all sorts of memories, coupled with the occasional familiar sight as she walked through the city.

She got a late lunch—well, second lunch—only to realize as she sat down to eat that her family had come to this restaurant a few times before their finances had turned.

Tala walked through a park, remembering the times she and some school friends had wanted a different place to play than their neighborhood park and coerced their minders to bring them there.

The entire experience was surreal.

A surprising number of people noticed and asked to pet Terry. Apparently, arcanous pets weren't as common in Marliweather as they were in Bandfast, which made some sense given the stage of the city.

In any case, Terry eventually got sick of it, and Tala let him go sleep inside of Kit while she continued to wander.

Shortly after Terry had retreated into the dimensional storage, the worst happened. *Well, not* the *worst...* Someone recognized her.

"Tala?"

Tala froze on the side of the street, her mind whipping back in time, trying to connect the voice to a specific person.

"Tala, is that you?"

She turned, eyes searching out the young man speaking to her from just inside one of the nearby shops.

He was tall, though not as tall as Rane. He smiled brightly as he stepped out of a doorway and toward where she stood to one side of the street. "I apologize if I'm wrong, but you are a dead ringer for this girl I went to school with."

-Answer him, Tala.-

"No, no, you aren't wrong. I am Tala." She shifted nervously.

His grin widened. "I knew it! You probably don't remember me, but I'm—"

She cut across him, not wanting him to think she didn't recognize him. "Viggo, yeah. I remember you." *Why do I care?*

He hesitated, then. "Oh. Good." He shrugged. "So. How are you? I haven't seen you in years." He frowned then. "Didn't you get accepted to the academy?"

What does he want with me? Why are we talking?
-Don't be rude, Tala.-
Fine. "Umm. Yeah, yeah. I was. I graduated a few months back."

"Hey! Congratulations." He nodded appreciatively, the sentiment seeming quite genuine. "So, are you back?" He frowned slightly. "There's some sort of apprenticeship for new graduates, right? Are you still in the midst of that?"

Tala shook her head, laughing a bit awkwardly. "Oh, no. I'm a full Mage these days."

"Wow. That's impressive, Tala." Again, he hesitated. "Or Mistress Tala, right?"

She waved him away, feeling self-conscious at someone who'd known her as a child giving her the honorific. "Tala is fine."

He paused for a moment. "Well, if you aren't in a hurry, do you want to step inside? I can put on some tea."

Tala looked at the store that he'd stepped out of. It was a simple clothing store. *That's right, he was going to be a tailor.* "Sure, I think that might be nice."

Anything to put off seeing my family…
-Not a great reason, Tala.-

As he led her inside, Tala took a moment to really examine the storefront. It was clean, well-kept, and nicely detailed. It even stood out from those on either side as being especially well-kept. It put forward the idea of a well-off shop that sold quality goods, and as she stepped inside, the impression was borne out.

"This is a lovely little place you have here, Viggo. Your folks were tailors, right? You apprenticed under them?"

"I did indeed." He gave a little laugh. "Worst six years of my life, but worth it."

A voice drifted from the back. "Dear, do we have a customer?"

"No, love! An old friend. You'll never guess who."

The sound of bustling came from behind a room divider as something was set aside, and a woman moved their way. "Is Javor back in for another tunic? We've told him that nice clothes aren't the only thing you need to catch the eye of—" She stopped talking as she stepped around the sturdy screen. "Oh."

Tala thought she recognized the woman, but it was hard to connect the young woman before her with any of the girls she'd known before.

"Is that... Tala?"

Viggo straightened a bit and put on a slightly self-important voice. "Mistress Tala."

"Mistress?" She gasped. "That's right! You went off to the academy." The woman looked a bit flustered, then gave a slight curtsy. "Welcome, Mistress."

"None of that." Tala waved her hands in a warding gesture, feeling increasingly awkward. "Ula, right?"

"That's right." Ula seemed to recover from her own awkwardness and smiled warmly, the slight lines on her young face showing it to be a common expression for her. "You remember me, then?"

"How could I forget? You used to give me parts of your lunch when I was hungry."

There was an awkward pause there.

Millennial Mage, 6 - Fused

Tala cleared her throat. "Sorry. That's obviously not the only thing I remember, but it's what came to mind first."

Ula shrugged a bit self-consciously. "It's alright. How are you?"

Tala heard the rustle of cloth and the murmur of a baby's burble.

"Oh, excuse me, Aliza is due for a meal."

Viggo interjected. "I invited her in for some tea. Shall I put the kettle on for all of us?"

Tala responded before Ula could. "I actually can make some if you're willing. I'd just need some cups." She laughed awkwardly. "I'm not used to serving tea for others."

He gave her a speculative look, then shrugged. "Certainly. Come on through to the back."

Tala followed the pair, through the tailor's shop and into a small, personal sitting room. A small kitchen was attached to the space further back.

The room held several comfy-looking chairs with a low table centrally located between them.

"It isn't much, but it's home. The bedrooms are upstairs."

Tala smiled, watching as Ula bent over a bassinet in the corner of the room. Viggo was in the kitchen grabbing cups.

-Don't use incorporated water. They aren't Mages, so it could actually hurt them.-

That's right. Tala had almost forgotten. It took power to maintain the incorporated water as water inside yourself, if just a bit. For a Mage, it wasn't really relevant and might actually help increase their through-put over time, which was one reason that Tala used so much of it. But for a mundane? It would pull power from other things, maybe causing them to become sick or at least more susceptible to illness.

Like overuse of endingberries.

With her hosts distracted, she quickly pulled out her own teapot, tea, hot air incorporator, and the little stand that she'd worked up to facilitate making tea. "Viggo, could you bring some water, too? I didn't think about that."

He gave a small laugh. "Of course."

They seem to smile and laugh a lot.

-*They seem happy.*-

Ula took a seat in one of the larger chairs around the low table, eyeing Tala's items but not commenting.

Viggo came over with a pitcher that he'd filled from their sink and three small mugs. He walked with a slight limp.

Tala accepted the water and poured it into her tea pot. "Are you alright, Viggo? It looks like you're limping."

Ula gave the man a pointed look. "I think he broke his toe."

He waved her off. "It's nothing, woman. I'm fine." He said it with affection, but it was clear that they'd had the conversation before. "If it still hurts in a week, I'll see a Healer."

Ula glanced toward Tala. "You aren't a Healer by chance, are you?"

"No, I'm sorry. If you don't mind my asking, what happened?" Tala focused on the tools before her. Since she didn't want to sit with her hand against the incorporator, she extended her aura and used that to power the item.

It was hugely inefficient, but it would work.

Viggo leaned forward. "Fascinating! So, that's a magic item? The air it produces is quite warm." He gave her a playful smile. "We'll have a lower heating bill this month after this."

Tala smiled in return. "I suppose so, yeah."

Ula shifted aside her tunic and helped little Aliza latch. The baby seemed quite content now that she was drinking.

Viggo cleared his throat. "It's a bit embarrassing, actually. A guard was in, being fitted for a new uniform. He'd left his helmet on the floor, and I'd almost tripped over it a dozen times. So"—he cleared his throat—"I sort of kicked it out of the way."

Ula chuckled. "You should have heard him yell. That's when I knew he'd broken it. Scared the poor guard half to death."

Viggo scrunched his face. "We'll see."

"Stubborn man." But she was smiling as she said it.

Tala cleared her throat and changed the subject. "How old is Aliza?"

Ula shifted in her seat, seemingly working to get comfortable. "Four months, tomorrow." It was a distracted answer, one that seemed to have been given numerous times.

"She's your first?"

Viggo answered that. "She is. We were married less than a year before we found out she was on the way." He leaned over and kissed the babe's head. "First of many, we hope."

"That's nice." Tala tried to put genuine feeling into the sentiment, but it still felt awkward.

A soft bell sounded from the shop, and Viggo shot her an apologetic look.

"Go, go. The tea will take a bit."

He stood, nodding gratefully. "I'll be back as soon as I can."

He walked past Tala, and she heard him greet a customer and begin what seemed to be a regular interaction. What did the customer need, how could Viggo assist, what colors were they thinking, and the like.

Ula was mostly focused on the little one that she had to breast.

Tala was left alone to her thoughts.

What am I doing here?

-Being polite.-

With people that I haven't seen in more than half a decade and likely will never see again.

-Does that matter?-

I could have said "Hi," exchanged pleasantries and been on my way.

-Then, why didn't you?-

He seemed genuinely happy to see me...

-You do remember him fondly. Both of them, really.-

They were... friends? It felt odd that she was unsure. At the time, back in her childhood, the answer would have been obvious, but she hadn't thought about them basically at all since she'd left.

-That is accurate, I think. Childhood friendships are an odd thing, really. If they last, they can be the deepest relationships a person has, but if they don't, they often feel like nothing was really lost, except your childhood. Which was lost anyway.-

That's depressing. Have you been reading random books again?

-I thought it prudent to do some research on the subject of childhood relationships before we came here.-

Tala grunted.

Ula looked up. "Oh, I'm so sorry. I'm ignoring you, aren't I?"

Millennial Mage, 6 - Fused

Tala colored, though she knew that wouldn't show through her paint and illusions. "Oh, no! I apologize for disturbing you. I just needed to clear my throat a bit."

"Nonsense. I was being rude." Ula smiled congenially. "So, what brings you to this area? Are you working in the city?"

"I'm based out of Bandfast, actually. I'm just in town with a caravan. I'll be heading back in a few days."

"Wow, caravan work?" She shook her head. "That's a dangerous occupation, I hear."

"It can be, I'll grant you that." Tala felt her face fall as she remembered the guards that she'd seen injured and killed. "It really can be."

"But you like it?" Ula seemed to be attempting to shift the tone of the conversation.

"I do, and it pays well. It also lets me see various cities, too, which is nice."

"It must be great to be able to see your family, too. Are they still in the alchemy business?"

Tala did her best not to wince, but it obviously still showed.

"Oh. I'm so sorry, Mistress Tala." Ula looked genuinely distraught. "Now that I think on it, I heard that there was some… oddity between you and your family before you left. I never really knew if it was true or what it was about." She gave a self-deprecating chuckle. "I try not to look into such things. They prove to be little more than gossip more often than not."

Tala grimaced, then. "Well, this is a bit more than that."

"I'm sorry to hear that." The poor woman looked around awkwardly as if searching for something to move the conversation to.

"It's alright. I actually chose Marliweather as the destination this time because I need to… talk with them." *Why am I telling her this?*

"Well, that seems like quite the thing to have to do." Ula seemed to be getting her feet back under her, conversationally speaking. "Do you think it will be a 'water under the bridge' situation, or do you expect a bit of a scuffle?" She giggled just a bit. "Not that they'd have much that they could do to a Mage."

Tala hadn't considered that. She'd continued to view them as her parents, her siblings, her family. But she was returning a full Mage. *A full Archon, not that that would mean much to them, aside from being something they wouldn't believe.* The dynamics between them would be utterly different. She answered with half a mind as she considered what that would really mean. "I think there will be at least some… discussions of the issue."

"Well, I hope you work it out. There's nothing like having family in your corner. I tell you, mine and Viggo's folks, and our older siblings, help out so much, especially since little Aliza was born. We get to go on dates and leave the little dear in the care of family, and that's the least of it." She shook her head in wonder. "I tell you, I couldn't imagine trying to have children without family around."

Tala saw an opportunity to change the subject. "So, how many do you want?"

"Well, we each come from smaller families. Each of us is only one of nine, would you believe it?"

Tala shrugged and smiled.

"Well, I tell you the truth, I think we want at least that many. Viggo makes good money, and we're saving like crazy, so we can move to a bigger place after the third one comes along."

Viggo came back into the room. "What lies are you telling our guest about me?"

That started a bit of banter between the married couple, and Tala turned her attention to the tea, finishing the preparation process and tucking the incorporator away.

She poured the tea into the provided mugs and passed them out.

They accepted gratefully, and Viggo lifted his. "To old friends."

Ula and Tala echoed the sentiment, and they all drank.

"Oh! This is delicious, Tala." Viggo was inspecting his cup as if it could tell him why.

"Thank you, I quite like it." Tala returned a contented smile.

"Chamomile, right?" Ula likewise seemed overawed.

"That's right. I picked some up when I was in Makinaven recently."

Viggo paled, looking back to his cup. "Oh, Mistress Tala. This is too much."

Tala frowned. "What do you mean?"

"Makinaven tea is widely considered the best humanity has to offer."

Tala sighed heavily. "I know, right? I didn't realize it while I was there, or I would have bought crates of the stuff to sell when I got back..." *Oh... That's what he's saying.*

Viggo glanced to his wife, then back to Tala. "Well, thank you. This is a rare treat." He laughed a little nervously. "What I make in a day might not cover this one pot."

Ula, who seemed to not have realized how expensive the tea was before, paled just as Viggo had. "Oh." The single, soft word carried a lot of meaning.

Tala, with one careless action, had demonstrated just how much wealthier that she was than them. *Well, rust.*

-Yeah, I didn't consider that either...-

"I apologize. I didn't mean anything by it. I just—"

Viggo waved her off. "No, no. Please, it's fine." He chuckled. "It's more than fine; thank you. It was a kind thing for you to offer and to provide. I've seen it in the market on occasion, and I was always curious if it was worth the cost." He lifted the mug to her with a slightly guilty smile. "I'd say it is without question."

She almost said it was nothing, just something that she had picked up while traveling with her job, but thankfully, she realized that that would make things worse, not better.

There was a break in the conversation as Ula switched little Aliza from one breast to the other, and when conversation started up again, they talked about small things.

They reminisced about school days, and Tala asked after some of their old friends. Mostly, she did this because it felt like the right thing to do, rather than because she was genuinely curious. She'd left this portion of her life behind.

As it stood, seemingly basically everyone was married and either had kids or had them on the way.

Some of the pairings surprised her, but most seemed obvious with hindsight.

All told, she spent a little over an hour with the young family. She departed with warm farewells, the two expressing a desire to see her again soon. She thanked them for the invitation but didn't promise either way.

She couldn't say whether the whole experience was positive or negative in the moment, but she felt like it was good for *her* in the long run.

Now, I just need to face my own family. Strangely, she felt like she was better equipped for that meeting than she had been.

Chapter: 22
Family Claims

Tala took a moment as she walked away from Viggo and Ula's home to open Kit and speak to Terry.

"Hey, in there! Do you want to come out?"

She thought she saw some people give her odd looks, as she was hardly alone on the street, but that didn't really bother her.

A long, disinterested squawk was her only reply.

"Fair enough. I want you to be able to get out if you want to, so there shouldn't be any issues, but in either case, I'll try to check every hour or so."

-*I can help remind you.*-

Thank you.

-*Oh, hey! While you were chatting, I think I figured out how to selectively suppress the illusion from the through-spike.*-

Oh?

As Tala walked through the streets of Marliweather, letting her feet carry her wherever they wanted, Alat stepped her through the process she'd worked out.

Tala decided to test the process on her hands as they were an easy thing for her to observe, and suppressed the illusion around them specifically.

Sure enough, her metallic-gray skin, surrounded by a blazing nimbus of power, started to fade into view. Tala immediately released her hold on the power so as to not be noticed.

Alright. Not sure how we'll use it, but it's another step.

Millennial Mage, 6 - Fused

The whole process of learning from Alat had only taken a few minutes, but when Tala looked up, she found that she'd traveled quite a way.

In fact, as she looked down the street before her, she saw an all-too-familiar sign, though it had likely been repainted or replaced since she'd last seen it.

'Karweil Alchemical Solutions.'

Rust. Tala immediately turned and walked into the park that she'd stopped beside. It was, in fact, the park that she'd played in often as a child.

There was a mixture of open space and cultivated walking paths, and she chose the latter, hiding from the sign among the trees.

Less than a minute later, she found herself at another familiar spot.

Here, a bench rested between two closely planted trees, not hidden from the path by any means but tucked back and out of easy view until she was right beside it.

The trees were evergreen, so the screen existed even in winter.

This was on my path home from school. I used to sit here when I didn't want to go home yet.

Alat didn't respond.

Tala brushed off the light dusting of snow, then slowly sat, feeling a whirlwind of emotions wash over her at the familiar surroundings.

She'd cried on this bench uncounted times, afraid to go home to her father's quiet rage, afraid to abandon her family to the same.

Every day throughout that time, she'd stopped here, contemplating running away.

Every day, she'd chosen to do the 'right thing' and go home.

Her last day in this city, she'd stopped here again.

By that point, it had been months since her father had been magically cured of the physiological portions of his addiction, and he was still in process with a counselor for the psychological parts.

Things had been looking better, despite her lingering resentment for the years of pain he'd put the family through with his addiction.

But that day, the Mages had come, pulling her out of class.

She was special. She could learn magic. She could have a better life and lift the burden of debt from her family.

She didn't remember all the thoughts and emotions that had run rampant through her mind, but she did remember agreeing.

Then, she'd come here.

Tala had sat on this exact bench as night had fallen, trying to figure out a way to tell her family that she was leaving, all while staring at her parents' signatures on the contract that would take her away.

They'd already known that she was leaving.

What was worse, the dates next to the signatures were more than a week old.

They hadn't told her this was coming.

They hadn't talked to her.

True, she'd avoided them whenever possible, but not entirely.

-Is it possible that it was as hard for them as for you?-
I'll never know, will I? They didn't even try.

That day, so long ago, Tala had chosen differently than every time before.

She hadn't gone home.

Instead, she'd simply walked back past the school and to the teleportation tower. She had showed them her acceptance letter and the signed contract, and she'd been transported away.

Of course, they had taken the contract first. It would have been obliterated by the teleportation otherwise.

They took my school bag, too, now that I think about it. They said I should have a clean start. She smiled ruefully. *Easier than explaining to a twelve-year-old that anything she tried to take would be obliterated.*

They hadn't commented on what they must have simply thought was her childish pudginess.

The handmade pillow that she'd smuggled under her shirt had been the only thing that she had been able to take with her. Looking back, it was a miracle that it had survived the trip.

She remembered the attendants asking after her family. She'd lied, saying that she'd already said her goodbyes.

The fully endorsed contract had been enough after that.

Enough to leave my family behind, forever. At least she'd thought it would be forever, but now, she was back.

She took a deep breath, checked on Terry, and let her mind continue to wander. As she considered it, this was about the time of day she'd usually come through here.

There should be a flood of school kids coming by soon.

Sure enough, as Tala sat there for the next hour eating jerky and drinking endingberry juice, kids started to come by in twos and threes, and sometimes in much larger groups than that.

Some jumped at the sight of her. Most ignored her, but some politely greeted her as they passed. Not as a Mage, but as an adult in their neighborhood. *Though, now that I think about it, some aren't too much younger than me.*

Schooling was available up through the teenage years, even if most chose a profession and finished their education by learning a trade or craft.

She tried not to stare, but she did get a reasonably good look at all who passed her. She didn't recognize any of those who passed, not that she'd expected that she would.

Well, this is one of the routes to my family's shop. It's not unreasonable to expect one of my siblings to have come this way.

-Did you want that?-

She didn't know.

She checked on Terry again and found him quite content. She did her best to will some jerky near the sleeping terror bird, but she had no idea if it did anything. *I'll have to ask him later.*

The park had mostly cleared within Tala's range of hearing, and the sun had fully set, when a single set of boots crunched down the path in her direction.

Magical lamps along the path were providing plenty of light, despite the early winter darkness, so Tala didn't feel like she was lurking, at least not too much.

The approaching steps had nothing to set them apart from the myriad others that had come before, but the sound drew her attention for some reason, nonetheless.

They were nearly to her when Tala heard others coming up behind the first set. Still, those following were at least a couple of minutes out.

A shrouded form rounded the path and came into view, and Tala recognized him, instantly, though he'd grown up a lot in nearly a decade.

He took a few more steps before his gaze drifted over to her, and he froze in his tracks, one foot having just set down on the slushy path.

He wore a hat and a heavy coat above his boots, and his gloved hands were tucked into his pockets against the cold.

Overall, the clothes of his that she could see were clean and nicely kept but obviously hand-me-downs by their level of wear and the fact that they didn't fit *quite* right. His eyes were red around the outside as if he'd been crying, though there were no tears on his cheeks at the moment. There *was* some dried snot on his sleeves where he'd seemingly wiped his nose recently.

His center blazed to her magesight, showing an unusually high through-put for an uninscribed gate. That wasn't unheard of. Humanity varied across all its inborn traits, but it was still notable.

His eyes widened almost comically, and he whispered, "What? Are... Are you real?"

Tala found herself smiling slightly despite the massive wave of nervousness and the sudden, slight watering of her own eyes. "Hey, Nalac. It's been a while."

His hesitation broke, and he ran the last few steps to her, throwing himself into her arms as his tears started up again.

Tala caught him easily despite her surprise. He was almost as tall as she was, but his weight was nothing to her heavy, strengthened body. He curled in on himself in her arms, pressing his face into her chest as he wept, his whole body shaking with each sob.

"Hey, hey. What's going on? Are you okay?" She gently rubbed his back, remembering the little boy who would wake her up whenever he had nightmares.

The steps that had been following behind were getting closer, and Tala started hearing snatches of softly spoken words.

"—came this way, right?"

"—always—"

"—better than us—rust me if he actually has a Mage sister."

No... this can't be for real. Are they following him?

Tala leaned close and whispered loud enough that she thought Nalac could hear her. "Hey. Hey, Nalac. I'm sorry to press, but are you being followed?"

His head jerked up. "What? No!" He hesitated. "I mean… They haven't followed me home before, at least not that I've known." There was the tinge of fear in his eyes. "A bunch of kids were dropped from pre-magic, today. Apparently, they don't have the proper mindset or whatever. If those following are who I think, their younger siblings were among those dropped. I wasn't. They were…" He glanced at her, cleared his throat, and seemed to amend what he'd been going to say. "They were upset."

"They were rusting livid, eh?" She cocked a half-smile at him.

Nalac's eyes widened, but then he nodded. "Are you really here? Am I dreaming again?"

Tala felt something break within her, and she squeezed him close once again. "Yeah, I'm here, my little titan."

He let out one weak chuckle that had the tinge of tears. "No one's called me that since you left." He pulled back, his face scrunched; the mix of emotions playing across his features were easy to read, even for Tala. He didn't know how to feel. He felt like he should be mad at her, but he was happy to have her here, and he was scared of the boys who were following him.

There was a lot more, too, but those were the things that seemed obvious to her. Tala frowned in anger. *No one messes with my titan.*

The boys were getting close. *How old are they?* "Have they picked on you before?"

Nalac shrugged, then nodded.

"So, just an escalation, then."

-I know you know this, but please don't kill random teenagers, alright?-

Millennial Mage, 6 - Fused

I'm a bit insulted that you felt the need to remind me, but sure, I'll be reasonable.

"I don't know why they dropped students today, except that it's the end of the week." His voice was small, almost pleading.

It's the end of the week? She checked, and just like the time, she was able to subconsciously know what day it was. *Huh. I've really fallen out of caring what day it is.*

-*That's because you don't rest. Every day is the same for you. It's not healthy.*-

Yeah, you've said.

Tala turned her attention back to her brother, quickly wiping some of the tears off of his cheeks with her thumbs. "Pull yourself together, and sit beside me. They're almost here."

Nalac obeyed, shifting to sit beside her on the bench. He seemed like he wanted to ask her something, likely what was going to happen, but he kept silent and waited.

As she considered it, Tala realized that the boys wouldn't have caught up to Nalac before he reached his home had he not stopped to talk with her. *Unless they started running for some reason, which seems unlikely.*

So, this might have happened before and Nalac just hadn't realized. *Is that because the boys are hesitant? Or just bad planners?*

A group of six older boys rounded the path and came into view.

By now, Tala realized just how horrible a judge of ages she was, but if she had to guess, she'd say that they were all in their late teens, likely ranging from fifteen to seventeen or eighteen. *Huh, almost my age, then.*

The group shuffled to a stop as they saw Tala and Nalac sitting on the bench.

She heard them exchange a few whispers, then one of the boys, neither the largest nor the smallest, stepped forward and spoke a bit hesitantly, "We have business with Nalac."

Tala stood, finding herself shorter than most of the boys before her. *Should have stayed sitting down...* "So do I. You'll have to find someone else to bully."

That sent a murmur through the group. The one who'd spoken before shook his head. "No bullying. He insulted our families, and he needs to be reminded of the wisdom in respect."

Tala cocked an eyebrow and looked back to her brother who was doing his best not to hunker down on the bench.

"Nalac? Is that true?"

He made an almost whining sound in his throat before answering. "I simply pointed out that none of their families had ever produced Mages, while mine had." His eyes flicked to her quickly, then away once more.

The representative of the group laughed. "See? He admits it. His sister up and vanished, so the family claims she's a Mage. They try to say that they're better than us. You wouldn't get in the way of a lesson in wisdom and respect, would you?" His tone conveyed utter confidence in the fact that she'd agree with him. To his mind, it was a forgone conclusion. Those who disrespected the families of others needed to be taught a lesson.

Tala sighed. "There seems to be a misunderstanding here."

The boy's smile faltered but didn't start to fade until she continued.

"It is not a shame to lack a Mage in your family. It just is. His pointing out the fact can hardly be called an insult."

"Respectfully, I disagree. He's an uppity bit of slag and needs to be taught his place." The joviality in the teen's tone was utterly gone now.

Millennial Mage, 6 - Fused

She sighed again. *Can I?* She made her idea clear within her mind.

-I don't see a downside.-

"Unfortunately, I can't allow that." Tala forcibly suppressed her illusion on her hand as she raised it up before her, causing her skin to darken. Her mesh of power blazed forth, obviously glowing without throwing any light. The interweaving, interlocking manifested spellforms carved from light into reality itself were, without a doubt, magical. "You see, I'm his Mage sister."

The group of boys stumbled backward disjointedly, several bowing or clasping hands on reflex.

Tala saw Nalac's eyes widen once more, out of the corner of her vision.

-Oh, yeah. That's a downside.-

The boy stumbled over his own tongue a few times before getting out, "Our apologies, Mistress! No offense intended." Then, the whole group turned tail and departed, barely keeping from running in their haste to be elsewhere.

Tala allowed her illusion to snap back into place over her hand as she turned to Nalac. "So, now that's sorted."

Nalac was staring at her, open-mouthed.

"What? You've never seen a Mage before?" *Play it cool, Tala. Maybe, he doesn't know any better?*

-Um... He's clearly not an idiot, Tala.-

He closed his mouth, visibly swallowing before he responded, "Your hand didn't look like any part of any Mage I've ever seen before."

She snorted a laugh. "And you've seen many parts of many Mages, have you?"

He looked down and rocked from side to side on his feet. "You know what I mean."

She scratched an eyebrow. "Yeah, well, I am a bit unusual, I'll grant you that."

It was his turn to chuckle, though it came out with a tinge of nervousness. "Yeah, that was pretty scary… I bet some of them even peed themselves." He was clearly still uncertain of her, though the reasoning behind it had changed.

She shook her head. "No. That's a hard smell to miss. They kept their composure, at least in that regard."

Nalac looked at her with obvious skepticism but didn't argue. "So… what now? Are you here to eat us? Or will you leave again, and I won't see you until I graduate from the academy? Is this some sort of sick reward for making it this far in pre-magic?"

Tala winced. "No… I didn't actually know you were in that class. You're twelve, right?"

"Eleven," he corrected. "Won't be twelve and old enough for the academy for another three months."

Oh… Right. "That's right. I remember celebrating your birthday mid-winter."

"Really? I barely do. I was four when you left." His irritation seemed to be rising once more, helping to cover over his trepidation. The accusation was clear, and her brother's temperament toward her was cooling along with the night air. "I'm freezing and want to get out of the cold. Do Mom and Dad know you're here?"

She shook her head, feeling a bit ashamed of the fact.

"Are you going to see them?"

Tala hesitated, then nodded. "I just didn't really know how to go about it."

Nalac grunted, looking her up and down. "You promise you aren't some crazy beast, come to devour us all?"

"Would you believe me if I said 'no?'"

"Of course. Everyone knows that the Arcane King and his ilk can't lie."

Millennial Mage, 6 - Fused

Tala blinked at that. *Well, that's just not accurate.* Still, she was hardly going to help the situation by convincing her brother otherwise. "I am Tala, your sister. I'm not here to hurt or devour anyone."

He narrowed his eyes at her, seeming to consider. Finally, he let out a long-winded sigh. "Come on, then. Let's go." He held out his hand toward her, inviting her to take it.

She did, feeling silly and awkward even as she did so.

"Let's go home. It seems like it's going to be an interesting night."

Chapter: 23
Nalac and Leighis

Nalac woke with a groan, immediately feeling a pain in his stomach.

"*Good morning, brother!*"

He threw his pillow at his twin sister. "Go away, Illie." He was starving, but he wanted to sleep more too.

She didn't relent. "Today's the day! We'll find out the final set of drops in pre-magic. If we survive the day, we're *in*!"

That reminder got his attention, and he sat up quickly.

"I thought that would wake you up." She laughed. "Mom has breakfast ready, and I have some lunch options laid out."

He groaned. "I don't care what I eat. Can't you just pick something for me?"

Illie took on the haughty air of a fairytale princess. "You must do it for yourself, little brother. I'll not be your maid." She winked. "Certainly not at the academy. Besides, if you can't even pick from the amazing options I prepared, then I'll stop doing that for you, too. Should I stop?" She arched one eyebrow, as if daring him to say 'yes.'

"No, no. It's fine. Thank you." He grimaced slightly. "You know that you're only like… five minutes older than me, right?"

She gasped in mock surprise. "What? I hadn't realized. I shall change my ways, oh young one."

Millennial Mage, 6 - Fused

Nalac rolled his eyes, but his heart wasn't in it, and he was quite used to her playing at pompous royalty. Instead, his thoughts were turning toward the academy.

As usual, any thoughts of magic, and most especially about the academy, were tinged with half-memories of her. Mages and magic in general had done so less since Master Leighis moved into the adjoining space and had been working with the family on a day-to-day basis. *That was more than four years ago.*

Still, he felt himself hunch just a little.

Illie noticed, her own smile faltering just a bit. "She's gone, Nalac. The academy is for *us*."

If nothing else, that showed him that Illie was still thinking of her, too. They all did, really.

He nodded, but still felt a bit sad. *We'll see. Once I'm a Mage, I'll find out what happened to her, and if they lied to us, and she's dead?* He felt a quiet anger at the thought. *And if she isn't...* The anger that rose at that thought was stronger, but woven through with cracks of sadness and longing.

He shook all that off, quickly getting ready and running downstairs for breakfast.

As usual, Mom had laid out a ridiculous spread, and it was being picked clean even as Nalac arrived.

His siblings were orderly in their ravaging, so he was able to interject himself and grab some food.

One of their neighbors had butchered a pig, and traded them some of the pork for a salve for his seasonal arthritis, so breakfast sausage was in abundance.

The cinnamon rolls were less sugary than Nalac's friends would have been used to, but sugar was expensive, so it was better to save on that front. Besides, the treats were still fantastic. *Who needs a sugar rush in the morning, anyway.*

Lastly, a few winter apples, likely bought from the grow complex, rounded out the meal. It was a bit of an extravagance, but the family had agreed that the nutritional value was worth the expense of fresh fruit, at least for one meal a week. They had buckets of dried fruit for the other meals, the other days.

Some of his friends had begun drinking coffee or black tea in the mornings, but when Nalac had asked if he could have some, he'd had it explained to him that caffeine was addictive. It wasn't necessarily harmful, but their family had a propensity toward addiction. So, he would have to wait until he was older and fully aware of the risks to make the choice for himself.

Caln drank coffee.

Nalac wasn't bitter, precisely. He understood the reasoning, but it was just another way he felt like his family was different from others. *At least we've already produced at least one Mage.*

He ate his breakfast with a tall mug of warm milk, grateful for the cow they'd been able to get a couple years back. He was also grateful that it was no longer his job to milk her.

Breakfast done, he went to grab his school bag and his lunch.

Illie had indeed set aside a selection of food for him to choose from. He picked out a bag of nuts, a wedge of cheese, and some dried berries, adding them to his bag.

He finished up just about when Illie came back down stairs, her bag already ready.

The two of them were joined by several other of their siblings as they headed off to school.

They were just about a block from their house when Nalac turned to Illie. "Thanks for your help with lunch."

Millennial Mage, 6 - Fused

She bumped him with her shoulder as they continued to walk. "Of course; I'm happy to help. What else are sisters for?"

*   *   *

Leighis waved goodbye as the last of the children left for school.

While they weren't his in any sense, he felt a deep affection for them. This family had taken him in, and allowed him to practice his arts with a ridiculous amount of autonomy.

Plus, they do all the bookkeeping. I get to just sit and read until someone is sent my way.

It was a peaceful life, just as his master had recommended.

Today was a bit stressful for them all, though no one would have admitted it. Young Nalac and Illie would pass through the final gauntlet, today, on the road toward the academy. Leighis wasn't really worried. He believed they would succeed, but there was still always the possibility that he was wrong.

And even if I'm right, that means those two will be leaving after their birthday in just less than two months.

Leighis shook his head. He sometimes missed the simple life he'd led before, the open country. There was a deep sense of accomplishment, working with units of guards to sweep the surrounding lands and keep the arcanous beast populations managed.

He did not miss the screams and death, nor the tide of blood that he couldn't stem no matter how much power he gained.

It still amazed him how few people seemed to know of the sacrifices paid for their safety by Mage and mundane alike.

He took a deep breath, pulling himself back from the dark memories.

Master Yutqi was right. A decade or so of peaceful work is just what I need before I step on the path to become Fused. Leighis would be forever indebted to the man who had guided him as a mageling, setting him on the path to become Bound so much younger than average, if not truly notably so.

He'd barely been thirty-five when he'd faced his own will and chosen to serve humanity.

He knew that not every Mage saw the choice in that light, but he did. It was why he'd dedicated nearly a quarter century to healing the guards and helping to manage the wildlands.

In the end, however, he'd seen too many colleagues die to continue as he had been. He'd sought more power, sought to finally step on the road to Fused, but Master Yutqi had cautioned him to calm his spirit, settle his soul, and find peace first.

So, he'd become a local Healer within the city he called home. This deal with the alchemist family had simply been a way for him to avoid administrative work, if he was being honest.

Thus, it had been a pleasant surprise to find out how much he could learn by practicing his healing in tandem with alchemists.

The first time that the young Latna, who was only fourteen at the time, had injected a patient's broken arm with a bone dissolving poison, Leighis had been horrified.

He had rushed to save the woman's life, only to find that the toxin made it trivially easy for him to reshape the material, restructuring it and removing the poison. The result was a perfectly healed humerus after he expended a trivial amount of power. He'd been absolutely floored.

Millennial Mage, 6 - Fused

The girl's father had been horrified. Apparently, she'd taken the initiative after finding out what Leighis could do. Bless the stars that she'd been close enough to a correct understanding that her idea had worked.

Even so, there had been a *long* talk with the teen about responsibility and discussing her ideas before enacting them.

The true fruit of her experiment, however, had come soon after. The Healer and alchemists had started a much, *much* closer working relationship. They discussed almost every case, finding the optimum mix of magic and alchemy to cure the patient the most efficiently for the cost.

To Leighis's delight, that meant that they could often offer serious cases a variety of treatments, explaining the pros and cons of each, before letting the patient decide for him or herself.

Gone were the days when Leighis would simply touch a person, pushing his power through them before healing what was wrong, if he could, and moving on like a worker in some assembly line.

Or a butcher in a charnel house.

This combined method was slower in unknown cases, but the results spoke for themselves. For his own sanity, he had been forced to stop counting the times that these methods might have saved ones whom he'd lost over the years.

No, don't focus on that.

"Master Leighis?"

Leighis startled in his chair, almost dropping the book he wasn't reading.

Latna had poked her head in, through the door connecting his work space with the front of the alchemist's shop.

"Oh, Latna, do we have a patient?"

"No, Master Leighis. I just wanted to check on you." She came in, bearing a tray laden with tea. "I brought you some tea."

He smiled at the young woman. "That is kind of you."

She sat in the chair, opposite, where his patients would sit when talking with him, and placed the tea on the low table between them.

Leighis gave her a knowing smile. "So, what questions do you have, today?"

Latna laughed good naturedly. "You know me too well, Master." Still, she poured the tea for them both before asking. "I'll start simple: How does the presence of a functionally infinite energy source within every person alter our metabolic functions?"

That was a new one. It had been almost a year since the woman had begun coming to him with questions. They'd started out incredibly elementary, but they'd been growing in sophistication, showing her growing understanding and boundless curiosity.

He took a long sip of his tea before nodding.

"As we discussed with regard to the nature of gates and the soul in general, the power which we use for magic is not a *physical* power. Do you remember that discussion?"

Latna had pulled out her notebook and a pencil. She smiled at him and nodded.

"Good, then let's build on that foundation."

*   *   *

Nalac felt his tension ease after his and his sister's names were called. He blessed the stars that their last name was so near the front of the alphabet.

Millennial Mage, 6 - Fused

Even so, he felt a bit of guilt as he saw some of his fellow students pale, names after theirs being called without theirs.

It was near the end of his last class of the day, and the teacher was listing off the students who would continue in pre-magic.

Finally, Mistress Lehrer Rin closed her notebook. "If your name was not called, this will be a free class for you, starting next week. After winter break, you will have the option of joining one of the other options offered in this time slot. If you have any questions, please come see me." Her eyes found Nalac, and he felt his stomach clench. "Nalac Karweil? Please stay after class. I need to speak with you."

Illie turned to him from across the room, a questioning look obvious on her features.

He shrugged nervously. *Why do I have to stay after?*

"Class dismissed."

The sound of chairs scraping across the hard floor, followed by the clomp of many footfalls, filled the room as most of the students left.

Groups formed as kids chatted happily at having passed.

Others departed, dejectedly, any hope of becoming a Mage through the normal paths gone.

Several did go to the teacher, seemingly trying tactics from begging to demanding that the results be changed.

She seemed to be calmly addressing each in turn.

I suppose she does this every year. He then remembered earlier cullings. *Well, multiple times a year, I suppose. This is just the last one for Illie and I.*

As if his thoughts summoned her, his sister walked up beside him. "Should I wait with you?"

He shook his head despite his nervousness. "No. I'll be fine."

"You sure?"

"Yeah."

She hesitated for a moment, then shrugged. "Alright, then. I'm going to go to a friend's house on the way home. See you at the shop?"

He arched one eyebrow at her. "A *boy* friend's house?"

Illie colored, guilt clearly painted across her features. "What? No!"

He grinned.

"Shut up." She punched him in the arm.

He started laughing, even while he rubbed his shoulder. *Wow... that hurt.*

"You're a jerk, Nalac. I'll see you at home."

He waved goodbye, his smile falling away as his mind returned to the matter at hand. *What is going on?*

The final other student stalked away, wiping at tears building in his eyes.

Nalac came forward. "Yes, Mistress Rin?"

His teacher gave him a long look. "Do you want to be a Mage, Nalac?"

What? He simply stared at her, utterly confused.

"Nalac? It should be a fairly simple question."

"I think I don't understand, Mistress Rin. Why would I be in this class if I didn't want to be a Mage?"

The teacher clucked her tongue, clearly thinking. "We all have many reasons as to why we do what we do. I just want to make sure that you aren't being forced to become a Mage." Her eyes moved to the still open doorway, and she lowered her tone. "Your sister is obviously enthusiastic, and you seem to follow her lead. If I recall correctly, your birthday is coming up, and so you will be eligible to depart for the academy. It is important to be sure."

He felt his cheeks heat. "I make my own decisions."

She gave him a skeptical look.

"When I care..."

She didn't say anything.

"There just aren't that many things that I feel strongly about..."

She nodded at that. "And do you feel strongly about becoming a Mage?"

He nodded. "I do."

"Why?"

Because she has to be out there, and I can't find her as an alchemist, even at the best little shop in Marliweather. "I want to see the world."

She lifted one eyebrow once again. "That simple?"

He shrugged. "See the world, good pay, live longer, phenomenal cosmic powers? What's not to love?" He'd pulled some of that from a book he'd been reading recently. *Who wouldn't want phenomenal cosmic powers?*

Mistress Rin smiled at that. "If you're moving around a lot, you won't have much of a home."

"Itty-bitty living space? I think I could live with that."

His teacher let out a long sigh. "I'm not trying to change your mind, or get you to drop the class. But it is important that you have the right mindset, that you aren't coerced."

Nalac had a moment of fear and uncertainty. Was he absolutely sure? "Can something like that really mean you can't be a Mage?"

She hesitated. "Well, no, but it can make it more difficult, more dangerous, and can lead to... oddities in a Mage's magic or their foundation."

"Their foundation?" Nalac frowned.

She waved off the question. "Something you will learn about in your first week at the academy. I'll not spoil it for you."

"Oh." He was becoming used to Mages telling him things like that, instead of answering his questions. In fact, adults in general liked to tell him that he would 'learn when he was ready' and the like.

"Well, that's all I had for you. Thank you for staying after."

Nalac nodded, going back to gather his things. When he left, he saw a group of students all talking together. Those that were his age seemed to be among those dropped from the class. His mind was already on the walk home through the park, however, so he didn't pay them any attention.

Even so, an older boy, brother of one of his ex-classmates, called out to him. "She dropped you too, eh? Not so special, now, are you?"

As his mind was elsewhere, he answered before he thought through what he was saying.

* * *

Leighis lazily turned a page in his book. It was dark outside, and this particular tale was rather riveting.

It was nearing closing time for the alchemy shop, and he was ready for supper. *Just as soon as young Nalac returns.*

Illie had come home only a few minutes earlier, all smiles and joy, so at least she was still enrolled in pre-magic. The girl had gone straight to her room, however, so Leighis hadn't been able to ask about her brother's status.

The front door opened, then, and it sounded like at least two people came in.

The pleasant cadence of Latna's voice sounded in greeting to the newcomers, and a woman replied.

Then, of all things, Nalac's voice rang out. "I'm home, and I have a guest with me."

Millennial Mage, 6 - Fused

What? Nalac doesn't usually bring people home. And the woman's voice Leighis had heard sounded too old to be a fellow student.

Leighis closed his book and called out, "Did I hear Nalac?" *Maybe my mind is playing tricks on me. I was just thinking of the young one.*

"You did, Master Leighis." The reply was immediate and filled with nervous energy.

What has the boy riled so? Leighis pushed himself to his feet, walking toward the door, connecting his front room to the shop. "That's wonderful! How did today go? You said they were going to be dropping some kids from pre-magic, today. You weren't one of them, I hope? Did you bring home one of the other students?"

He pulled the door open, revealing Nalac along with the newcomer.

Nalac was holding her hand in a strangely intimate, almost clingy way. The woman herself looked to be barely into her maturity and seemed oddly familiar.

Not dressed for winter? Alarm bells began blaring in Leighis's head. *No inscriptions… She can't be an arcane, can she? Don't jump to conclusions. She isn't acting hostile. Learn what you can, then act.*

He gave her a nod of acknowledgement. "Oh! Pardon me, miss."

The woman's eyes were predatory as she looked his way, seeming to take him in at a glance. Her skin was… odd. The color was too uniform, too flawless. It was something that only his long years as a Healer caused him to notice. A person's skin was often an excellent indicator of their health in certain regards.

Her lack of spell-lines all but ruled out her being a Mage.

She gave a shallow nod, as if to one of inferior rank. "Good Master."

I'm missing something. He felt himself frown, though he tried to stop it. *Give no indication that anything is amiss.* He flicked his gate open with practiced ease and pulled a thread of power through, guiding up to his magesight with a thought.

His eyes widened in shock, before he frowned in truth.

The woman was cloaked in an aura of power that was distinctly human, and just as clearly that of an Archon well on the way to Fused. There was still no evidence of spell-lines, but there were distinct indications of active power. The magical dimensions around her were practically boiling, though he couldn't understand why.

He had long ago expanded his magesight to be able to see a pale distortion of the magical dimensions. There were just too many arcanous and magical creatures that could attack through that avenue to have been able to function in the wilds for extended periods without that sense. He'd saved many companions lives through timely warning, which were only possible due to that aspect of his sight.

Her clothing, as he'd noted before, wasn't winter gear, and she even seemed to be barefoot, but what she wore shone with a subtle power. *Magical clothes then.*

There was also a knife at her belt that gave off the feel of power. *A knife, not a sword or other weapon? What purpose would that serve?* It might simply be a means of delivering hostile magics. If it came to a fight, he would be wary of the small weapon.

Her stance shifted slightly, toward one of a more casual nature, seemingly trying to put him at ease. "I am Tala." The woman, Tala, didn't whisper, but her voice seemed purposely shifted to prevent it from carrying beyond the front room.

Why does that name sound familiar? He forced himself to relax, *I'm still jumpy it seems.* He double-checked with his magesight, and whatever else this woman was, she was decidedly human. *I'm being rude.* He bowed from the waist this time, but just slightly. It was the acknowledgement of a marginal superior, which she apparently was. "Mistress Tala. To what do we owe the pleasure of this visit?"

Why is she here, and what is between her and Nalac? He looked to Latna, who'd been oddly quiet.

The woman seemed frozen in evident shock, her mouth halfway open. If he hadn't known better, Leighis would have thought she was under the effects of a spellform. Even as he spoke, his eyes immediately returned to the woman who still might be a threat, even if she was human. "Are you alright, Latna? Is young Nalac in some sort of trouble?"

Nalac turned fully to him and waved the question off. "No, no, Master Leighis. This is my eldest sister."

Leighis felt like he'd been punched in the gut. No wonder she'd looked familiar. Now it was obvious. She looked so similar to Latna that he felt the fool for having missed it. *Tala. That was her name. No wonder it sounded familiar.* He'd heard of the woman, but she was supposed to still be at the academy, or newly graduated. He'd even used his connections to check on her progress for the Karweils, though it had been nearly a year since he'd done so last. *But... she's an Archon... and she's Fusing?*

He couldn't fathom what could have allowed that, but he felt that he needed to give some sort of reply. "Oh."

Well, that was articulate, Leighis. His mind was a tangled mess. This *child* had surpassed him in less than a year? *She must have graduated soon after I last inquired, and tutored under some insane master. Why would anyone put so much effort into this girl, in particular? All the oldest of humanity had descendants beyond easy count, and the Karweils were not in any of those lines that he'd been able to find.*

There had been the odd thesis out of Alefast-Waning a couple months back. *What was his name...? Grediv? Yes, Master Grediv. Such odd notions need a test-subject. Maybe he grabbed onto her?*

Voices were coming from the back of the alchemy shop, where the residence was, but Leighis wasn't paying attention. He was wracking his brain to try to figure out what he was missing. *I must have missed something.* And long experience assured him that it was the thing he missed that was most likely to kill him.

Nalac replied to the calls, and a short exchange ensued, followed quickly by the family coming out to see Mistress Tala.

Even with only a fraction of his attention still directed outward, Leighis could see the emotional conflict playing across the young woman's face.

Then, Alan, her father, spoke from the workshop across from Leighis's own space.

Mistress Tala stiffened and all that turmoil seemed to be swept away from her.

Leighis's full attention was jerked back to the present, to the woman, as he watched her aura begin to slide further from red toward orange.

She is actively Fusing, while simply standing here?

It made a sort of sense. Just like Leighis was taking time to recover from his own traumatic experiences, Mistress Tala was facing her family.

Huh, I would have thought rage would be in conflict with the inner peace and unity needed for Fusing. It seems like Master Yutqi didn't tell me everything. He almost snorted in derision at his own arrogance. *Or, more likely, I made assumptions that weren't quite right.*

Millennial Mage, 6 - Fused

Still, Leighis was riveted to the spot, watching her aura continue to slide up the range even as she turned toward her father as the man came out.

Leighis immediately felt incredibly awkward, even as he found himself unable to tear his eyes, his magesight, away from Mistress Tala.

So, he did his best to ignore the words said, even as he did his utmost to absorb everything he could take in about her Fusing.

It wasn't much, sadly.

Heated words were exchanged, and the alchemist seemed genuinely chastened. The watching family burst into a din of noise at that, but Leighis paid them no mind.

Instead, he grunted in grudging sympathy. What little he knew of Mistress Tala's departure for the academy had almost caused him to break off his partnership with the family. It was only the remorse that was evident in the telling that had caused him to stay long enough to learn more.

Mistress Tala turned to go, clearly distraught, but Alan asked her to wait and rushed past her, to grab something.

A moment later, Alan offered Mistress Tala a coin pouch.

The man's words were clear as he spoke. "We haven't been starving by any means." He chuckled with obvious self-deprecation. "But we have done our best to be wise with our money, and we've worked together to put this aside." His words had a planned, even rehearsed quality to them.

Of course they do. I've heard him practicing them, late at night, when he'd likely thought everyone else was asleep. The family was nodding along, behind their patriarch.

A pleading tone entered Alan's voice as he continued, "Please, if you must go now, please take this with you."

The woman hesitantly took it and opened it, looking inside.

In what seemed to be a fit of uncontrolled emotion, Mistress Tala ripped something off her belt and threw it at the wall.

Leighis flinched, his magics coming to the ready, though he didn't activate anything. *Alchemist fire?* There would be some poetry in that retribution, though he would still do his best to prevent it.

But, no. The item struck the wall and blossomed into a doorway.

A morphic, extra-dimensional space? He, himself, had an expanded storage at his belt—it was practically a requirement for extended journeys beyond a city's walls—but this one held vastly more power, while being incredibly well-masked. He hadn't even noticed it on her belt until she'd ripped it free.

Mistress Tala rushed through the door, slamming it behind herself.

Leighis felt himself stagger, just slightly. *Too much. Too many things aren't as... expected.*

Alan looked over to him, clearly distraught, but he calmed himself as he noticed his friend. "Master Leighis? Are you alright?"

Leighis waved him off. "It's nothing. Tend to your family. I'll be fine."

Alan hesitantly nodded, and Leighis didn't wait for further response. Instead, he retreated into his section of the shop, closing the door and locking it before he sank into his chair.

I need to seek out Master Yutqi, tomorrow. I have a lot of questions that need answering.

Chapter: 24
I'll Be Fine

Tala looked up as they came out from among the trees in the park, noticing what should have been obvious from outside the city. *Oh, yeah. There are no mountains to the north of here. It really changes the whole feel of the place. Not to mention the city as a whole is on more level ground.*

-*Really, Tala? That's what you're focusing on?*-

Tala lowered her gaze, taking in the long, residential street.

There were only a few shops that broke up the parkside street: a restaurant, what appeared to be an odds-and-ends type store, and her family's alchemy shop.

As they drew closer, Nalac still holding her hand, Tala saw that the family store had expanded since she'd been there, seeming to have taken over the homes to the left and right of it.

In this neighborhood, the homes were built close together with no yard in front, but Tala knew there to be a yard in back.

She considered for a moment before realizing that she couldn't remember who used to live next to her family's shop. *Huh. Memory's an odd thing.*

-*Focus, Tala.*-

She stopped in the street, examining the changes and marveling at how large the store was. "It's huge," she spoke almost to herself.

Millennial Mage, 6 - Fused

Nalac responded with pride evident in his voice. "Yeah, the family serves the alchemy needs of the whole subdistrict. We've bought out the other competitors, and we often have people coming from farther than that because we do it better, cheaper, or both." He grinned widely. "We even have a Healer based out of the left side, there."

Tala snapped her focus to her brother. "What?" Then, she looked up at the sign, seeing that, indeed, there was a smaller sign hanging below, advertising the services of a Healer.

Nalac simply continued his exhortations. "Yeah, anything we can't cure, or anything that might be serious, the Healer takes care of. He's an older Mage. I guess he's mostly retired, but he still seems to enjoy the work."

Ahh, not an Archon, then. She hesitated at that. *Well, what is 'older' to an eleven-year-old? He might be an Archon, just taking a few years to enjoy the quiet life.*

"We have solid contracts with the grow-complex, and Latna is negotiating for the contract to provide emergency aid in the event of a crisis or emergency. It's practically all she ever talks about. Apparently, it comes with a high requirement for the storage of supplies, but it pays well, just to have a bit larger warehouse that we rotate our ingredients through." He shook his head, clearly baffled by the ways of adults.

That's actually pretty clever. Trying to centralize all emergency supplies for the city could go horribly wrong. She almost snorted a laugh. *Not to mention the expense of the warehouse and the manpower to rotate ingredients and other items to prevent spoilage.*

Then, what Nalac said settled in. "So… Latna is working in the shop?"

"Mmhmm. We all do, but she and Caln apprenticed with Dad. They pulled extra shifts, in addition to studying and jumping through all the hoops, so they're actually fully registered alchemists, too, in way less time than it usually takes." He was beaming again. "We have three full alchemists working together. The only shop like it in the city."

With a Healer, too? I can believe it's the only one like it. Well, honestly, she couldn't believe it was real, not really. *He's working with a Mage?*

-People change, Tala. He was trying to do just that before you left, and we've been gone a long time.-

They'd been standing across the street from the shop for nearly a minute by that point. So, Nalac tugged on her hand. "Come on. I'm cold, remember?"

The two walked forward, and Tala felt herself in utter turmoil. She was angry, she felt guilty, and she felt hurt. Each step, a different emotion reigned supreme.

Her brother pushed the door open, letting out a wave of warmth and magical light. *Has absolutely everything changed?*

As the door swung open, a cheery voice greeted them. "Hello, welcome to Karweil Alchemical Solutions. How can I— Oh, Nalac, it's you." The late-teenager slouched just a little out of her precisely straight posture of a moment before, her politic smile shifting to one of familial affection. "You're a bit late. Who did… you…?"

Latna locked eyes with Tala, and the girl went mute.

Latna was obviously Tala's sister, a close mirror in every regard, physically speaking, but her features were a bit sharper than Tala's, lending her both a tad more beauty and a look of ready judgment. Additionally, her eyes were a deep, startling violet.

Tala cleared her throat. "Hello, Latna."

Latna didn't respond, instead just staring at Tala, shocked uncertainty playing across her features.

Millennial Mage, 6 - Fused

Nalac called toward the back of the store. "I'm home, and I have a guest with me."

That broke Tala's attention, causing her to look around.

The shop was immaculately clean and well-decorated. There were a few items on shelves, which were clearly the most requested items, but even they looked more like display pieces than tightly packed inventory.

From her own time working in the shop, Tala knew that most alchemy concoctions were best when used right after they were created.

The front area wasn't massive, but it felt roomy with a twelve-foot-high ceiling and the walls near that ceiling being composed completely of windows all the way around.

A door to the left stood ajar, the Healer's crest embossed across the upper panel.

Through that door, an older voice floated. "Did I hear Nalac?"

"You did, Master Leighis."

"That's wonderful! How did today go? You said they were going to be dropping some kids from pre-magic, today. You weren't one of them, I hope? Did you bring home one of the other students?" Footsteps sounded as the man talked, and then the door swung open.

As Tala had halfway expected, the man was in his early thirties, at least by the look of him. That meant he could be thirty or three thousand, for all Tala knew.

"Oh! Pardon me, miss." Leighis gave a nod of acknowledgement to Tala.

Tala's magesight immediately detected his nature as a Material Guide, a common quadrant for Healers. His aura was that of a Bound with no movement on the road toward Fused that she could detect. *So probably younger than fifty, but not by much if he's followed the standard paths.* "Good Master." She gave a shallow nod of her head.

A frown flickered across his face, and Tala saw power flow through the man's magesight scripts. Leighis' eyes widened as he saw her with that sense, then he frowned, clearly not understanding what he was seeing.

He'll see that I am Bound and Fusing but nothing else, at least not really. His magesight scripts didn't seem to have the delicacy to be able to determine the qualities of her magic just by examining her aura, let alone the facsimile generated by her through-spike. "I am Tala." She didn't whisper, but she did pitch her voice so it wouldn't carry out of the room.

Leighis bowed a bit deeper than he had the first time. "Mistress Tala. To what do we owe the pleasure of this visit?" The man was clearly hesitant about something, and his eyes flicked to Latna. "Are you alright, Latna? Is young Nalac in some sort of trouble?"

Nalac turned and waved the Mage down. "No, no, Master Leighis. This is my eldest sister."

The Archon's eyes widened again in surprise and understanding. "Oh." He didn't seem to be able to bring anything else forward to say.

Latna was still staring at Tala in shocked silence.

A voice floated from the back. "Nalac! What have I told you about bringing home guests without warning?" It was unmistakably that of Tala's mother.

Nalac rolled his eyes and called back. "Nothing! I've never done it before. You're thinking of Miro."

"Hey!" Miro's response resounded from a similar place to their mother's. "I haven't done that in a long time."

"You brought home six friends *yesterday!*" Nalac shot back. "But that's not important. Come see who it is!"

Millennial Mage, 6 - Fused

That started a clatter of sound from the back, moving their way with chaotic inevitability.

Tala was feeling overwhelmed. The voices were so familiar but so different than she felt they should be. The faces she'd seen already were filling in the gaps in her memory as she saw each one, and she felt her cycle of emotions become a tumbling turmoil.

Then, Tala's father spoke, calling from what Tala presumed was a workshop off to the right. "Nalac, we've been waiting for you for supper. You really shouldn't worry us like that."

At the sound of her father's voice, Tala felt the turmoil blow away, and all her emotions crystalized down into one: raw, primal anger. In that instant, her soul, spirit, and physical desires were in perfect alignment.

Even so, she did not give in to her rageful desire to kick down the partially open door and beat the man to death. Just because she wanted to do something, it didn't mean that she would want to have done it or that she'd be glad that she'd done it once it was over.

Alat gasped. -*Oh. Oh!*- Still, the alternate interface held back from commenting further.

Tala ignored Alat, her attention moving inexorably toward her father.

This was the man who had discarded her, doing his part to sign her life away without even bothering to talk with her.

That doorway swung open as Tala turned to face it, and her father stepped out, freezing in his tracks as he saw her.

His eyes widened in obvious recognition as well as complete and utter surprise.

At the same time, Tala heard a passel of people pour into the room, joining Latna behind the counter.

There were exclamations along with questioning words as the eldest in the group seemingly recognized Tala, while the youngest obviously had no idea.

She didn't turn away, afraid that if she took her eyes from her father, the rage would deflate, and she'd break down crying.

Not here. Not now.

His words came out as a whisper. "Tala. You're... you're alive." He shook his head. "Of course, you are. They swore that you were, but still..." His eyes were watering, and his hands were trembling.

"It's Mistress Tala. *You* ensured that." Her tone was biting, and her words sounded petty, even to her own ears. Still, she didn't look away.

Thus, she saw the flickers of anger across his features, followed closely by deep, soul-level defeat. His head dipped ever so slightly in resignation, not rising again. "Yes, Mistress Tala. Your words are true."

There was a cacophony of sounds, fragmentary comments, and shushes from behind the counter.

Tala stood straighter, anger bubbling up inside. She clenched her teeth, feeling an ending seed between them about to shatter, and froze on the spot.

What am I doing? She used her tongue to push the seed back into her cheek. *Why didn't I get rid of that before coming here?*

She almost staggered at the backlash of emotions. She turned. "I'm sorry, Nalac. I'll... I can't do this right now. I'll be back tomorrow." *Get out, get away. I don't have to come back if I don't want to.*

She turned and took two steps before her father moved. "Mistress Tala, wait."

She stopped, and he rushed past behind her. She could hear in his tone and the urgency of his steps that, somehow, he could tell that she didn't know if she'd actually be back.

She didn't turn as he dug behind the counter, pulling out something that clinked in his hands.

No.

He walked over, stopping a step or two behind her. "It is nothing to the debt you bear because of us… because of me, but it is what we could save while you were gone."

Unwillingly, Tala turned around, her eyes immediately locking onto the pouch resting on her father's extended palm.

"We haven't been starving, by any means"—he chuckled self-deprecatingly—"but we have done our best to be wise with our money, and we've worked together to put this aside." His words had a planned, even rehearsed quality to them.

Her eyes lifted, and she saw those behind the counter, her family, nodding affirmatively.

"Please, if you must go now, please take this with you."

Tala hesitantly took the pouch and opened it, looking inside.

Her enhanced perception, and Alat, helped her quickly count the meager coins within.

Twelve gold, four silver, and a smattering of copper.

In truth, that was a monstrous sum to a mundane family. *Rust, three gold could have satisfied my increased appetite for a year up until recently while eating exclusively at restaurants.*

Even if her visit with Viggo and Ula hadn't made it clear, this certainly would have. The fact that she'd made this much gold for solely her role as a Dimensional Mage, on her last trip, highlighted just how far she'd moved up the economic ladder.

-Tala.-

I can't. Not now. No. She ripped Kit off her belt and threw it at the wall beside the entrance.

Kit stuck, becoming a door instantly, even as Tala pushed it open and slammed it behind her, shutting out the gasps of astonishment from those she'd left behind.

Tala stood just inside her private dimensional space, panting, tears running down her cheeks.

Well, rust.

Terry lifted his head from his spot in the corner and trilled inquisitively.

"It's fine, Terry. There's nothing that you can do."

He flickered to her shoulder and head-butted her cheek, hard.

"No, I'm not lying, Terry. I'll be fine."

He trilled and head-butted her again, then flickered back to his corner. She easily understood his meaning: 'Fine, but if you need me, I'm here.'

"Did you get any jerky?"

He opened one eye, then his mouth.

She snorted and grabbed some jerky out of the air, tossing it to him.

He happily snapped it up.

She then grabbed up some rags and wiped her face, blowing her nose to clear it.

-Tala. You're not focusing on the issue at hand.-

Tala ignored that. *What were you gasping about, earlier?*

Alat sighed, but then got excited. *-When you figured out what you wanted, our soul, spirit, and body came into harmony like never before.-*

Yeah, I thought I felt something like that. What of it?
-Fusing.-

Tala's eyes widened.

-Fusing became trivially easy. We're almost done.-
Alat was ecstatic.

Millennial Mage, 6 - Fused

Why only almost?

-...Because you are in turmoil again.-

Tala growled. *Lovely.*

She'd only been in Kit for about thirty seconds, but she was already beginning to realize just how much like a teenager storming off to their room she'd just acted.

And I have to exit back into the family shop... She clearly hadn't thought her actions through.

-So, for the sake of Fusing, are you willing to go back out?-

And say what, Alat?

-I don't know, and even if I did, you'd never do it just because I said to.-

Translation: She knew exactly what Tala should say but also knew that Tala would fight her on it, at least without some preliminary prodding.

-Hey, you are coming to understand me better.-

We're the same person, Alat. All I have to do is think about what I would do, were our positions reversed. She hesitated, then amended. *I still think you're a jerk some of the time.*

-Yeah, well. We're no peach.-

So? What should I say?

Less than a minute after she'd slammed the door, Tala stepped back out, seeming far more composed outwardly while still feeling in turmoil internally.

A din of conversation cut off instantly as she opened the door, and all eyes turned to her.

She pulled Kit closed behind her and lifted the pouch from the wall, replacing it on her belt.

Tala closed her eyes and took a deep breath, letting it out slowly into the awkward silence.

"I apologize for that reaction. It was childish." She still hadn't opened her eyes. She didn't want to see her family while she said what she needed to say. "Father, Mother, I am livid beyond words at what you two did, and that you did not even talk with me about it. The rest of you... I apologize for vanishing without even saying goodbye. I apologize for ignoring all attempts to contact me. I do love you, and I miss you terribly."

Her eyes opened, and she found and locked onto her mother and father, who were standing together to one side.

"I don't know that I will ever forgive you. That may be a flaw within me, but it hardly matters. There is no trust between us. There is no obligation. Only time will tell if there will ever be a relationship again. Right now? There is none."

She hefted the pouch of coins, finally allowing her eyes to take in all of her siblings. There was only one missing that she remembered, Caln, and there were two that she didn't recognize at all, their age seeming to indicate that they'd been born after she left. The youngest looked barely older than three as she was held by one of her older siblings. *Illie, I think? Nalac's twin.* If not, it was Alva. The girls looked very similar after so long an absence.

Leighis seemed to have excused himself from the room in the short time that she was gone. *Wise and kind of him.*

Tala found Latna, central among the siblings. "Here."

She tossed the coin pouch to the young woman.

"If you're willing, I've an idea on how you can use that to earn quite a bit and help all our siblings have a better life. If you aren't willing"—Tala shrugged—"I can't make you." She still didn't see Caln, or she'd offer him the same, directly. "Please extend the offer to Caln as well."

Latna finally seemed to have gotten over her shocked silence. "What does that even mean? Are you going to be talking to us now? We've all tried to contact you, and you've never responded."

Tala nodded. "In that, I failed." She felt that failure as she looked at the veritable strangers before her. "I will read any letter sent my way and respond when I can. I am often away from cities, so it might take a while occasionally, but I will respond." She closed her eyes, scratching at her temple and trying to hold back tears of frustration, of nervousness, of anger. "I need to go, now. I…" She swallowed. "I'm not in a good place."

She glared at their parents, briefly, then calmed her rage once more. Neither tried to speak or interject.

"I'll be back, tomorrow, in the late morning, and I'm happy to talk to any of *you,* if anyone is interested." She gestured toward the siblings, specifically excluding her parents.

Nalac nodded. "Thank you, Tala."

Tala felt a small smile tug at the side of her lips, even as tears broke free despite her best efforts. "See you tomorrow, titan."

He grinned back at her, unashamedly. "Oh, I have so many questions."

"Well, write them down. We'll talk tomorrow."

With that, she turned and strode from the shop, leaving her family behind once again.

This time, however, it was only for a single night.

Chapter: 25
A Tea House

Tala left her family's shop behind with quick steps, mixed feelings coming back to plague her.

She felt tremendous guilt for having cut off contact with her siblings. *There was at least one that I didn't even know I had.*

She also obviously felt righteous anger at her parents for their arrogant dismissal of her potential thoughts so long ago. They hadn't even bothered to hear them.

-What would you have done if they came to you?-

Tala had given it a lot of thought. *I can't know for certain, but I think I would have said 'yes.'*

-And that would have made it alright?-

It would have made it better.

Alat didn't have a response to that.

Tala's thoughts returned to her siblings. She hadn't lied to them. She would be back the next day after her breakfast with Mistress Odera.

For some reason, that thought keyed off her mind on food in a direction she hadn't contemplated before, and she smacked herself in the face. *I'm an idiot.*

-No, you're not. That's disgusting. No one should ever have that idea.-

But it would work.

-Yeah, at least for the calories. Nutritionally, we'd need to supplement it. It's still gross, though.-

Oil, specifically vegetable oils, were basically the most calorie dense consumable substance humanity knew of. *Well, that and lard.*

Millennial Mage, 6 - Fused

-You aren't seriously considering buying a gallon of oil and straight up drinking it... Are you?- Alat obviously knew the answer, but she just as obviously didn't like it and was hoping for a different one.

Tala grimaced, even as she kept walking. *It's worth a test. If it works, that could virtually be the same as a fabled health potion for me.*

Alat groused. *-You aren't wrong, but it's still disgusting...-*

It's not like you're going to taste it.

-Are you kidding me? I'll have the memory of the taste forever. Who cares if I don't actually taste it directly?-

Could we numb my tongue somehow? So that I could just chug it?

-Not easily? It would take freeform manipulation of your senses, which could go horribly wrong. Not worth it, if you ask me. As to the oil, for balance, at least at the macro-nutrient level, you're going to need a lot *of meat and whole grain bread.-*

That's fair enough. But we'll test just the oil, at least at first.

In the end, Alat agreed that it was worth a try as it might just save their life at some point if it worked.

Thus, as they headed toward the work yard, they kept an eye out for... *There.*

A little all-night grocer was open in one of the more affluent neighborhoods that they were passing through.

Tala was able to buy a gallon of olive oil, two massive loaves of bread, and two roasted chickens for two silver and thirty-two copper.

Tala was utterly floored by how cheap it was, even though she suspected that she was paying a bit more than was standard to cover the cost of the convenience of the all-night grocer.

She bade the attendant goodnight and continued on her way toward the work yard.

Ready?

-No...-

Here goes! Tala pulled the cork and took a long swig from the bottle of oil before she could stop herself.

She gagged and retched, but power spiraled through her anti-vomit inscriptions, and her stomach settled.

Oh, yeah, I don't think about those very often.

Alat sent immense displeasure.

A weirdly slick, greasy feeling coated the inside of her mouth and throat. Oddly, Tala suddenly had the sensation that she could *feel* with her teeth, and they were disgusted at what was coating them.

On a whim, Tala cracked the seed in her mouth and felt the power of dissolution blossom between her teeth, breaking the oil down into its constituent parts. She breathed in to at least clear her upper throat, then exhaled the mass of dissolved oil and power out, into a snowbank, a good portion of which puffed into vapor.

Hah, I knew that would work.

-I thought we agreed not to use those for oral hygiene.-

Did you want that to linger?

-...Fine.-

So? I can feel it being processed by the flows of power, but I think you have a finer view of the result.

Alat was hesitant for a long time. *-It will work in a pinch.-*

Tala didn't gloat. In fact, she felt a bit of disgust. *I sort of wish it hadn't, but I am glad to know... in a pinch.*

Alat was silent for a while.

Tala was almost to the work yard that held her cargo wagon when Alat broke her silence.

-Tala?-

Yes?

Millennial Mage, 6 - Fused

-If that foul liquid were combined, somehow, with scripts to speed absorption into the body, distribution of the calories where they were needed, and a targeted regeneration...-

Tala stopped dead in the quiet city streets. *Alat, that's a regeneration potion.*

-I know, right?- Alat was ecstatic. *-It still probably wouldn't work. Who's going to drink two cups of olive oil? And, even if they did, that might not even be sufficient to heal a given injury.-*

But it is an interesting idea. How would the spellforms be incorporated into the liquid?

-The ending seeds.-

We aren't putting ending seeds in a healing potion.

-No, no. The seeds have stored magic that is triggered by things like digestion. The mechanism has to be reproducible.-

It was an interesting thought. Probably not unique, but interesting. *We should talk to Mistress Odera about it over breakfast.*

*   *   *

Tala sat cross legged on her floor within Kit.

Her eyes were closed, her morning routine all but done.

Around her orbited her Archon Stars, three encased in tungsten.

She now had eight of the small spellforms, each as small and weak as she could make them, each in a single drop of blood.

She practiced mirroring various senses to the stars as they orbited.

It was disorienting, having her vision spin around herself, but she was getting greater control of it. So, instead of sweeping around in a circle, she could focus it on one place, the perspective simply moving as if she were doing a box step.

She had a use for the sweeping perspective but not as she was now.

Her greatest discovery had come only a day or two before.

She took a slow breath and gilded herself.

She added a second perspective mirroring, allowing it to sweep around her without interference, then she ignored it. *It's like my nose. I can easily see it, but I just don't.*

Alat helped enhance the desired effect while the alternate interface soaked in the inputs.

Alat was much better at ignoring the negative sides of the sweeping perspective.

-*Alright. I'm ready.*-

Tala took another deep breath and selected a bloodstar opposite the one already mirroring her senses for Alat.

Then, with an application of will and a flexing of her soul, Tala mirrored her perspective onto that star as well.

She was immediately overwhelmed, unable to ignore so much information.

Her concentration broke, as did the mirroring.

Tala cursed, flopping back.

-*One perspective is already amazing.*-

But there are gaps in what we can see.

-*True enough. It seemed easier that time.*-

It definitely was. I think that being so close to fully Fused helped immensely.

-*I agree.*-

There was a bit of frustration there. They were *so close.*

-*This will likely be possible once we cross that hurdle.*-

That's probably true.

Millennial Mage, 6 - Fused

-Well, it is about time to leave to have breakfast with Mistress Odera. Then, we can see the family. That seemed to help with our inner turmoil.-

True enough.

Tala sat up, looking to Terry in the corner. "You want to come with me?"

He lifted his head, glancing toward the door. With a slight shudder and shake of his whole body, he trilled a decidedly negating series of notes.

"Suit yourself. I'll check on you every once in a while to see if you want out."

He squawked once and laid his head down.

She chuckled, tossing him a huge hunk of jerky, which disappeared halfway to him.

All right. Let's see what Mistress Odera thinks of our idea.

* * *

Tala sat patiently eating while Mistress Odera regarded her with increasing skepticism.

"That's a fairly ludicrous idea."

Tala shrugged. "But it might work."

"No. At best, you'd give a slight boost to healing, and that is even if the patient could keep the concoction down."

She opened her mouth to respond, but Mistress Odera held up one hand.

"Yes, you could add further forms to suppress nausea, but to what end?" The older woman took a sip of her tea, then shook her head with a sigh. "It is a clever idea, I'll grant you that, but there is a fatal flaw."

"Oh?" Tala frowned. *What did we miss?*

"Either you use a regenerative inscription and the olive oil won't contain nearly enough to do what is needed, thus leaving the user weakened, at best, or you use a healing inscription, in which case the ingestion and the olive oil are both unnecessary."

Tala nodded absently. "And the second isn't a good option because people are unique, and a generic healing spellform could easily do more harm than good."

"Precisely."

"But wouldn't a withering or weakening be better than bleeding out?"

"In the short-term, yes. That's why guardsmen and soldiers often carry emergency items for such a purpose, but there is only a small segment of potential wounds that they are useful for. Too free of use can cause more death than the original injuries, and even proper use can lead to long-term side effects to the patient's health. So, if there are better options available, they should always be used first."

Tala grunted. "Fair, I suppose."

The topic shifted, and Tala reluctantly brought up her family.

Mistress Odera was proud of her for facing them and applauded her plan to go talk with any who wished after breakfast.

Tala didn't correct her to ensure that the woman knew that her parents weren't included in that invitation. *I was clear enough.*

She was sure of that. No need to clarify at all.

They briefly touched on Tala's training before Tala finished practically licking her plate clean and bade her overseer a good day.

* * *

As Tala drew closer to her childhood street, she felt a growing anxiety. There had been a late-night snowfall,

Millennial Mage, 6 - Fused

and the cool dusting felt good on her bare feet, but such couldn't keep her attention with the upcoming meeting on her mind.

What if no one wants to talk to me?

-Nalac will.-

You don't think he'll be convinced not to?

-That doesn't make much sense... Right?-

But what if?

Alat paused for a long moment as Tala kept walking. *-If no one is there, then we can leave and put them behind us forever.-*

Tala breathed deeply, thinking on that worst case. *That helps, thank you.*

-Now, if they show up just to scream at you? I'm not sure what we'll do.-

Tala felt her eye twitch. *Are you rusting kidding me?*

-What? If we're looking for the worst-case scenario, it isn't 'no one showing up.'-

She did not like that thought, but as she came around the corner, Tala saw that there was no one waiting outside the shop. *Well, that's that, then.*

-You didn't actually tell them to wait for you in any particular place. You just said you'd be back. It's cold. They're probably inside.-

As she closed the distance, the door opened, and a small head poked out, looking the other way. The small, bundled head then turned, seeing Tala approaching. There were some people on the streets, but Tala knew she stood out, even if only because of her lack of winterwear.

"*She's here!*" the little voice called out.

I don't know who that is.

-Yeah, we didn't ask.-

Before Tala covered the last hundred yards, people piled out of the door, and she pulled up short, shock making her steps hesitant. She did a quick count. *Fourteen.* Even the little three-year-old had come along.

When Tala had left, she'd had twelve siblings. *Now I have fourteen.*

-*At least. You're assuming that they all came.*-

Even so, Tala felt her eyes start tearing up. *Oh, come on. This is ridiculous.*

She gilded herself and walked forward, pulling a smile across her features. "Good morning."

A smattering of greetings tumbled over each other, causing the small crowd to laugh nervously.

Tala stopped a few paces away from the huddled, winter-gear-shrouded group. It was interesting seeing all their breaths puffing out in steamy fog in different cadences and with different volumes.

There was a moment of silence as everyone waited for someone else to speak.

Tala cleared her throat. "So, is there anywhere we could go to talk? I don't know the area very well anymore." She awkwardly scratched the front of her own shoulder.

Latna immediately nodded. "Yeah, there's a tea house a couple of blocks from here. They should be willing to give us the use of a private sitting room, so long as we get a few drinks." The woman hefted the small pouch from the night before. "We can afford at least that."

Tala nodded. "Lead the way."

The trek started out with more awkward silence, but that was broken after barely a dozen paces by the second smallest sibling piping up with a question. "Aren't you cold?"

Tala looked down at the little boy who had sped up to walk beside her. "I'm not, no."

He gave her a skeptical look. "I have to wear my coat and boots or I'll be cold. Mother says so."

Millennial Mage, 6 - Fused

"That's true enough; it's quite the chilly day."

He looked down at her feet. "You aren't even wearing shoes."

Tala looked down at her feet, too, as she walked down the street. She grinned as she saw the minimal, round impression in the snow around each one of her steps. "Yeah, well, my feet don't get cold very easily." After a moment's hesitation, she asked. "I'm sorry, but I don't know your name."

"Olen!" he announced proudly. "I'm almost six."

"Well, it's very nice to meet you, Olen."

"It is, isn't it." He grinned back.

Tala found herself chuckling.

Olen opened his mouth, likely to ask something else, when someone in the group walking right behind them spoke up. "Speaking of your feet... why aren't they sinking into the snow? What's with the circles?"

Tala glanced back, finding the speaker. If she had to guess, it was Alva, the youngest of the third set of twins. "Well, Alva, I have inscriptions that distribute my weight across a wider surface area, on whatever I step on, so I have surer footing and don't break anything I step on by accident."

Another voice chimed in. "What? Are you really heavy or something?"

That earned the older boy glares from all his sisters, save Tala. Tala just laughed. "I actually am, Miro, yeah." *Older than Nalac, younger than Caln, he's grown up so much. He was right around Olen's age when I left.* "It's a part of my magic, actually. My body is enhanced and strengthened, and one result of that is that I'm quite a bit heavier than normal."

Miro looked around triumphantly, completely uncowed by his sisters' displeasure.

Latna glanced back, ensuring they were following as they continued to walk, taking her role as the leader seriously and ensuring that they *all* made it to the teahouse.

I wonder how often she's had to fill that role for them since I left. The thought caused her feelings of sadness and guilt to spike.

Tala saw Caln near the back, though he didn't say anything or even give a motion of greeting. She would have to talk to the older two alone at some point. She'd actually been close to both of them... once.

"What's it like being a Mage?" It was the other of the younger girls. *Well, aside from the toddler.*

"Well, Nea, it's wonderful in almost every way. I didn't really enjoy the academy, but I did get to learn magic there. My work is dangerous at times, but it's rewarding, and I got to pick what I wanted to do." She grinned. "I still do get to choose, really."

The little girl frowned. "Then, why are you mad that you're a Mage?"

The older siblings made motions of shushing, but Tala shook her head. "It's a fine question." She slowed down just a bit, and the young girl sped up so that Tala was walking beside Nea. Tala spoke so that everyone could hear her clearly. "I'm not mad that I'm a Mage. I am angry that our parents sold me off without talking to me."

Nea frowned. "But you like being a Mage."

Tala sighed. "Would you like being married off to someone without being asked?"

The girl straightened. "Of course not!"

"But what if you liked the man, and he was good to you, and you had a good life as a result?"

Nea hesitated. "Then... I don't know?"

"Exactly." Tala let out a long breath. "I am angry at what our parents did, not how it turned out."

That caused the group to fall into contemplative silence.

"We're here!" Latna broke them out of their reverie.

The group pushed through the door and into the warm interior of the teashop.

The attendants seemed a bit overwhelmed by the sudden influx. The shop was by no means empty, but it was also nowhere near full.

Tala spoke before anyone else could. "I'd like a private room that can fit all of us, please." She'd discussed this possibility with Mistress Odera and with Alat, earlier. "Open a tab for us, and get any of them whatever they want." She pulled a gold coin from Kit and set it on the counter. "I'll expect an accounting of the charges, as well as the change, when we leave."

The woman's eyes widened as she took the coin from the counter. "We don't usually deal with gold… Mistress?"

Tala nodded. "Feel free to test if it's authentic. I imagine the manager on duty or owner will be grateful that you did." Tala cleared her throat, smiling a little self-consciously. "But could we be directed to the room first?"

"Certainly, Mistress." The woman bowed, indicating two servers who were standing nearby. "Please take this party to the Falcon's Nest." She looked toward Tala. "It is at the top of the building and our finest room."

"That will do nicely. Thank you." She turned back to her brothers and sisters and froze.

All the siblings were staring at her.

"What?"

Caln sighed from his place at the back of the group. "That's a lot of money."

"I'm aware. I'll be getting most of it back. I just didn't want them fighting us over the room."

The young man shook his head. "Whatever you say, Mistress."

Tala swept her gaze over the others and saw more uncertainty than had been there before.

Great... I did it again, didn't I?

-So, it would seem. I think more subtlety would have been better. Less showy.-

I wasn't trying to show off!

-Yeah, but they don't know that.-

Tala did her best to keep from grinding her teeth.

One of the attendants cleared his throat. "This way, please?"

He led them up three flights of stairs and to a room that was little more than a roof held up by four posts. The entirety of the four walls between ceiling and floor were made of glass, giving a stunning view of the surrounding city and the countryside beyond.

The siblings gasped, oohing and aahing.

The attendant directed them to sections of the floor that opened to allow them to store their coats and boots before they sat at the low tables, situated on thick rugs, surrounded by cushions.

It wasn't a style of seating that Tala was used to, but she'd seen it on occasion.

The other attendant passed menus to each of their group, and together, the two worked to answer questions and gather the orders.

Thus, in less than five minutes, the siblings were left alone in comfort, their food and drink on the way.

Most were looking out the windows, enjoying a new perspective on their home. Olen had been the first to spot their shop, and they'd laughed about how it looked from this vantage point.

Unfortunately, the views only held their collective attention for so long, and soon enough, awkward silence fell yet again.

"So"—Tala swallowed—"do you all have more questions, or may I ask some of my own?"

Chapter: 26
Exceptions Aside

Tala did her best to not fidget as she looked around at her crowd of siblings.

She couldn't even properly enjoy the spectacular view of the city and surrounding plains that stretched out in every direction. Though, she could see hints of mountains to the east, running northward; the shadows of forests to the far south; and what was likely the sparkle of light off of the ocean to the north-west. *They really built the city on a nice rise, and this restaurant is in a great spot.*

The views weren't unobstructed, of course. Other multi-storied structures cut off parts of the vista, but not so much as to obscure those massive features.

Latna cleared her throat. "I have a question."

Tala brought her attention back to her sister. "Yes?"

"Why did you leave us? Why did you ignore us when we sent you letters?"

Tala felt like someone had thrown a bucket of cold water into her face. Still, she took a moment to collect herself, and with Alat's help, she formulated an answer. "I was… very angry with Mother and Father. I felt used, untrusted, and unloved." She closed her eyes, feeling the emotions of the last years washing over her. She continued without opening her eyes, not wanting to be distracted by her family before her. "Anything that reminded me of them, of what they'd done, hurt." She opened her eyes. "That included you."

Latna frowned but didn't interrupt.

Millennial Mage, 6 - Fused

"It was immature, but I was a child. It was petty, but I was aggrieved."

Olen leaned back, and Tala heard him whisper to Akli, "What does aggrieved mean?"

It was Mita, Akli's twin, who answered in a similarly quiet whisper, "It means hurt or wronged. Shhh."

That caught Tala off guard, even though the words had been so quiet most wouldn't have heard them.

Use smaller words. This is your family, not teachers sitting in judgment over you.

She hesitated, then let out a long breath. "The long and short of it is this: I had my reasons, but my choice to ignore *you all* was wrong. I should not have cut myself off from all of you. Will you forgive me?"

Silence rang through the room. In that stillness, they heard footsteps coming up the stairs.

No one wanted to speak in front of the servers, so they waited.

Great timing, Tala...

It took a few moments for the two attendants to reach the room, and they passed out the food and drinks, receiving polite 'thank you's and other forms of gratitude before they departed once again.

In the returned silence, they all waited until the footsteps had faded, sipping, nibbling, or shifting nervously.

Finally, of all people, Caln spoke up. "You want us to forgive you? To forgive you for the years of broken relationship? We were on your side from day one! We had nothing but sympathy for you and a desire to help.

"Mom and Dad told us everything. They cast themselves as the villains in that tale and rightly so.

"We have been striving for *years* to help save up to repay the debt laid upon you. We tried to invest the money wisely, expanding the shop and getting a Healer to work with us, among other things. The plan was to have a good chunk ready for you, when you graduated, and have a good foundation so that we could then blast through the debt with our increased capacities."

He scoffed, shaking his head.

"And what do we get for all our work? All our scrimping? All our sacrifices? You seemingly graduate and vanish. When you finally do show up, the money is tossed back at us like it's nothing."

He pointed to Latna.

"She cried much of the night because of you, Tala." He grimaced. "Mistress Tala."

He shook his head again, his features becoming a mask of anger once more.

"We have suffered as a family, trying to be ready to lift the burden from you, and it… means… nothing. You don't need us at all. You don't want us at all. You throw gold around like it's candy. Why are you even here?"

The silence returned like a struck bell.

Nobody said anything, all eyes remaining fixed on Tala.

Well, all eyes but that of the littlest. Tala hadn't caught her name.

The small one was staring at Caln for a long moment before standing up and toddling over to where he was sitting on a cushion on the floor. She grabbed his face, shocking the young man out of his glare at Tala. "Wha—"

"Ookie?"

"What?"

"Ookie!"

Caln pulled back at the shout, blinking at the loud proclamation. "Cookie?" He glanced down at the plate of cookies he'd gotten along with his drink.

The entire demeanor of the girl changed as she stood up straighter, wiggling her little head in obvious pride. "Ess! Ease!"

The little one then turned to look at Tala.

"Ookie you?"

Tala blinked back. "Do I want a cookie?"

Again, that little one shimmied in obvious happiness. "Ess!"

"I… uh… Sure?"

The girl turned back to Caln, then pointed to Tala. "Ookie!"

That was too much, and everyone burst out laughing.

The laughter wasn't so much because the girl's actions were humorous as how effectively they'd shattered the tension of the moment.

Caln hesitantly stood and walked over to give Tala a cookie. He then looked down. "Are you happy, Sella?"

Sella was glaring at Tala. "Ank ooo!"

Tala cocked her head, squinting and trying to understand. "Oh! Thank you, Caln."

Again, little Sella flipped her expression on a copper, beaming once more.

Caln retook his seat, and things quieted down. Everyone was clearly still waiting on Tala's answer, but much of the horrifying tension was gone.

Tala cleared her throat and then took a small bite of the cookie. It was actually rusting delicious. There was something in them that made them crunch while being warm and moist. *No… two things.* It wasn't nuts or anything silly like that either. *I need to buy a few dozen of these…*

She was stalling.

She took a sip from her cup and forced herself to not evaluate the tea. Even though it wasn't nearly as good as what she had in Kit. *Tala… come on.*

"I did not intend any of that as a slight." She closed her eyes and shook her head. *Oh, Alat, please help me here? I'm too close to this. I don't know what to say.*

And so, Alat helped her.

"I apologize for the hurt I caused. I chose to go to Bandfast after graduating because there is a larger Caravanner's Guild hub there. Also, more personally, I wasn't ready to face Mother and Father, or anything that reminded me of them, not yet. As to giving the money back…" She shook her head ruefully. "I would love to keep it. It would help in so many ways, but it will help you all more. I think I can even give some suggestions as to what it could be used for." She gave a wry chuckle. "But I'm getting ahead of myself. I think it best if I just tell you what I've been doing since I graduated. But before that: can you forgive me for my callousness? For not considering you all in my actions? I want to explain everything to you, but I don't want it to be an excuse."

Caln sighed. "I am willing to hear you out. I can understand making a mistake, and I forgive you."

Latna nodded, as did the oldest twins, Mita and Akli.

Illie frowned before she, too, sighed. "I want to hear what you have to say. I'll forgive you, but it will take more than that to repair the harm that you've done."

Nalac turned to his twin sister, shaking his head. "Stop pretending you're a queen."

Latna cleared her throat. "I think I speak for all of us when I say we forgive you, but it will take time and effort to rebuild our relationships with you."

Tala felt a tension ease inside herself, and she smiled. That addressed, she told them the story.

The tale was obviously abridged, and she left out mention of dead woodsmen, founts, Archon Stars of any kind, or arcanes… or, well, any of the myriad other things that shouldn't be told to mundanes or very small children.

Millennial Mage, 6 - Fused

As an example, she skimmed over some of the scarier details for the sake of the little ones but did her best to tell it as completely and truthfully as she could... those exceptions aside.

The servers dropped through several times, refilling drinks and bringing more savory foods as the time for lunch came and went. Tala was restrained in her eating, mainly so she could continue her story.

She did pause every once in a while to allow clarifying questions, but there weren't too many. Alat was helping her organize the story and structure it in an understandable way.

It was mid-afternoon when she finished up the tale, concluding on her arrival in Marliweather. "And so, I'm here for another day before I have to head back to Bandfast. If you want me back, I can probably get another contract over to here and be back in around two weeks."

After a short pause, Olen spoke up. "Yeah, we want you back."

Sella looked at her older brother, held up a new treat over her head, given after a full and healthy lunch, and proudly proclaimed, "Ookie!"

The girl had not focused on Tala's story, not that Tala had expected her to. Instead, she'd spent the time moving between various siblings and playing with their hands and feet. She'd even sat in Tala's lap for a bit before moving on.

The other siblings smiled at Sella's pronouncement before agreeing with Olen, each in their own way, ranging from Nalac's hearty seconding of the sentiment to Caln's reserved, hesitant nod.

After that, there were a few generic questions about what it was like to be a Mage, which Tala answered as best as she could, but it was starting to get late, and apparently, they'd promised to be back home before dinner to help with the final preparations.

Tala cleared her throat. "Could either Latna or Caln stay behind? I'd like to talk with one or both of you about my suggestion."

The two shared a look, then Latna shrugged. "I can, sure."

Nalac cleared his throat. "Can I stay, too? I need to ask you something…"

Tala gave him a searching look, then nodded. "Alright. I'll need to settle the bill and talk to Latna, but after that, we can chat."

Mita cleared her throat. The girl was third oldest of Tala's siblings, just about a year younger than Caln, only slightly older than her twin. "Will we see you again this trip?"

"I'll come back by tomorrow. I'll spend the day in the park, so if any of you want to drop by, I'll spend that time with you."

There were some awkward goodbyes, and Caln shepherded them through the process of getting their winter gear back on before trundling down the stairs.

Sella continued her loud cries as they left. "Eye, Ala!"

It didn't matter how many times Tala said bye in return, the little one continued her calls.

In truth, Tala didn't mind, though she did feel bad for Akli who was holding the small girl.

She has quite the lungs.

As the last head disappeared down the stairs, Latna and Nalac moved closer so that they were sitting at two points of a triangle, completed by Tala.

Latna cocked an eyebrow. "So? What's this idea?"

"Iron paint. The local Constructionist Guild likely doesn't have a supplier yet as it's a relatively new thing. The one in Bandfast buys it by the gallon, though."

Millennial Mage, 6 - Fused

"Iron paint? How would you even make that?"

"The formula is available to any licensed alchemist through the Archive."

Latna winced. "Oh, Archive access isn't cheap." She cocked her head. "Though, we can go to the library and get a hard copy. How much is the formula?"

"Five gold."

Latna gaped. "Are you out of your mind? How could we possibly… afford…?" She closed her mouth and hesitated. "You want us to spend some of the gold on that."

"I think so. It's not that complicated, if I understand the process correctly, and it sells for half a gold per gallon." She laughed. "I'd buy a few gallons from you, too."

The younger woman seemed to be doing calculations in her head. "I would need an introduction to the Constructionist Guild. Is there a proof of efficacy?"

Tala returned a crooked smile. "I can have something ready to show."

-That's kind of funny, actually. I want to see that.-

Tala hesitated. *Oh?*

-Yeah. How quickly are they going to smite you when you drop your illusion.-

I'll give them warning.

-Suit yourself.-

It'll be fine. I'll give proper context, then do a slow reveal. It's not like I'll walk in, drop my illusion, and say, "Buy this stuff. It's great!"

-Fine, fine.-

Latna was nodding. "That could work. That could work. Why half a gold per gallon?"

Tala shrugged. "That's what I was charged."

"So, likely depending on local availability of materials and the like." She took in a deep breath. "Still, five gold for a formula…"

"It will be a risk, but one that I think will pay off."

"Can we go tomorrow?"

"To the Constructionists?"

"Yes."

Tala thought a moment before nodding. "Sure. Just before dinner, so I don't break my word to the others."

Latna nodded, pushing to her feet. "All right, then. I'll see you tomorrow. Are you coming soon, Nalac?" She turned and pulled on her own coat and boots.

"I think so. Let them know where I am. I'll either be home for dinner or figure something else out."

Latna hesitated, then looked to Tala. "Alright then."

She finished dressing for the weather outside and moved to the stairs.

She had descended three steps before she paused. "Tala?"

Tala turned to regard her. "Yes, Latna?"

"Thank you for coming back. I wish you had come back sooner, but thank you for coming back."

Tala just nodded and smiled.

Her sister turned and walked out of view, down the stairs.

"So"—Tala regarded Nalac—"what did you want to ask?"

He was fidgeting with his hands. "Well… you see…" He swallowed, then grabbed his mug, draining the last of the tea from it.

Tala didn't interrupt or prod.

"You see, I wanted to be a Mage… to find you." He said the last in a quiet voice.

Tala felt something twinge in her chest. "Oh, Nalac. I'm here. I'm so sorry. I—"

Millennial Mage, 6 - Fused

He was shaking his head. "I know. I know that." He swallowed again. "Mistress Rin—she's my pre-magic teacher—said that someone's motivation for becoming a Mage matters. Mine's gone!" He hung his head. "Can I even become a Mage anymore?"

Tala blinked in surprise at that. "Do you want to?"

"Yes! ...No? I don't know." He shook his head.

"Well, that sounds like the heart of it. If you want to be a Mage, you can be. If you don't? You don't have to."

"But this is what I've been planning, Illie and me."

"And now you don't know what to do."

"And now I don't know what to do."

"Well, how about you talk me through it."

And so he did.

Tala was able to get the servers to bring them some more food and drink, and then, she just listened.

An hour later, the boy was no closer to a decision, but he seemed lighter, less burdened. "Thank you, Tala."

She smiled. "I'm happy to listen. Come on, let's get you home."

She settled the bill, receiving seventy-five silver back in change.

Together, she and Nalac walked back toward the family shop in comfortable silence.

As they walked, Tala had a thought. She opened Kit, as she had several times throughout the day to give Terry an out, if he wanted. Just as before, he didn't come.

"Hey, Terry. You want to come out?"

He squawked back at her in the negative.

She hadn't asked at other times, but she knew that he'd been able to sense the opening and could have come out if he'd wanted to. "I want you to meet someone."

Nalac was giving her an odd look. "Tala?"

"One moment."

Terry's half-grumbling trill came from the open pouch, then he flickered to her shoulder, giving her a squint-eyed glare.

Nalac gasped.

Terry, obviously hearing the sound, leaned out, sideways, to look across Tala and at her brother.

"What is that?"

Tala smiled. "This is Terry. He's a he, not a 'that,' and he's a terror bird."

Terry flickered to stand on Nalac's shoulder.

The boy felt the pressure and turned slowly to look at his new passenger.

Terry stared back into the boy's eyes from only a few inches away.

"Terry. This is my brother. Be nice, please. He's just a boy."

Terry broke eye contact with Nalac and glanced at Tala. He squawked once, then hunkered down on her brother's shoulder.

Nalac was still frozen, almost unmoving as he watched the bird. "Tala?"

"Yes?"

"What do I do?"

"Here, feed him this." Tala pulled out some jerky, but it vanished from her hand before she could pass it to her brother. "Stop that, Terry. I'm trying to let him give it to you."

The next piece vanished as well.

"If you do that again, I won't get out any more."

Terry opened one eye, rolled it, closed it, then let out a long-suffering, basso trill.

Nalac jumped. "How did he do that? That was *so* deep?" He chuckled a bit. "It actually kinda tickled."

Terry's eye opened again, and he trilled another low note.

Millennial Mage, 6 - Fused

Nalac giggled. "Stop that. You're making my whole chest vibrate."

Tala slipped her brother some jerky, and when Terry opened his beak again, Nalac stuck the treat in before Terry could make any more sound.

The bird narrowed his gaze at the boy, then slowly pulled the jerky into his mouth.

"You're a funny little thing. Terry, was it?"

Terry glanced at Tala, swallowed the jerky, then jabbered a long series of ascending and descending squawks and trills.

Nalac laughed again, reaching up to stroke the bird. "You're trying to talk?"

Terry stopped, then huffed.

Tala cleared her throat. "He was talking. Just because we didn't understand him, it doesn't mean he's not speaking."

Nalac gave a slow nod, clearly thinking the whole situation was a bit... odd. "Alright, then. I'm sorry for interrupting, Terry."

Terry huffed, then went right back to jabbering away as the siblings turned and finished their trek to the shop.

When they reached the doors, Tala bade her brother goodnight, tossed a bit of jerky for Terry, and smiled as his weight flickered into being on her shoulder.

Nalac waved as he pushed open the door. "Goodnight, Tala. Goodnight, Terry. Good to meet you!"

Latna's voice came from inside. "Terry? Who's Terry?"

Tala grinned as she turned and headed toward the Constructionist Guild.

If I'm going to introduce Latna, I should at least meet them myself first.

Chapter: 27
The Marliweather Constructionist Guild

Tala was filled with mixed feelings, and to her great astonishment, they weren't a mix of guilt and anger.

She was cautiously hopeful while being nervous about how the next day would go.

She had faced her anger and put it in its proper context. She had pulled it off of the nebulous concept of 'her family,' and it now rested where it belonged: on her parents. More to the point, it was no longer a hot, burning, uncontrollable rage. Instead, it had flipped to a cold void of tightly regulated fury.

The emotion no longer hurt her to probe.

The feelings no longer mastered her when she considered them.

She was in control of how she felt, and cold wrath was just fine with her. It might fade gradually, or it might not. Only time would tell.

A part of her hated that she was so angry with her parents, however justified. She wanted to love them and be with them, but that would require both them and her to be different people.

And, unfortunately, if they hadn't done what they had, she wouldn't be who she was.

Not that that makes it better.

Still, that line of thought brought with it a dawning revelation. *If I could go back and change things, I wouldn't.*

Without her slurry of emotions, she'd likely have pursued a more standard path of Magic.

Millennial Mage, 6 - Fused

Without her debts, given partially by her parents, she wouldn't have worked to circumvent the mageling process. She might not even have pursued a job with the Caravanners.

If she hadn't done that, she'd not have met Lyn, in all likelihood. She wouldn't have met Rane or Mistress Odera. She wouldn't have traveled to the other cities so soon. She wouldn't have met Terry, or been able to get Kit or Flow.

Everything in my life that is good has come as a result, either directly or indirectly, of the wrong they did to me.

Did that make it right?

Rust no.

Did that make it better?

Yeah, no. Slag that.

But did it reframe the experience?

I'm not a helpless victim here. I have chosen my own path, and I am better for the trials I walked through. If I changed what made me who I am, I wouldn't be me anymore. And she found that she did like who she was.

It sounded incredibly cheesy when she put it that way, and she felt a smile tug at her lips.

Terry cooed and nuzzled closer to her neck.

She'd offered to let him back in Kit, but he'd looked around at the empty streets and decided to stay out.

"Nalac seemed to like you."

Terry trilled, and if she had to put words to the sound, it would have been, "Well, obviously."

Tala laughed, her thoughts sliding smoothly to her siblings.

Her feelings for her brothers and sisters were a mixed bag, but that was to be expected. They were practically strangers to her—and she to them.

There was real potential for building relationships with them, provided they could clear the rubble of her mistakes and lay a good foundation.

That was an exciting prospect, if she was being honest.

She was content with who, what, and where she was.

All in all, she felt at peace with how things stood.

-That's right you do!-

Alat had mostly kept from commenting through the day, only sending her thoughts to Tala to help her shape what she was sharing and how she was speaking. It had been fantastic to have a second mind working in the background, helping her to be clear and concise, as well as avoid too many foot-in-mouth moments. Now, however, the alternate interface seemed overjoyed.

-Tala, we're there. We're right there!-

Tala frowned for a moment as she was walking across the park. *We're...? Oh! Really?*

-Yes! I need your help on this last part.-

Tala pulled Kit off her belt and looked around. There were no convenient surfaces nearby.

A couple of lone walls stood in the park for children to use in certain games, but they weren't nearby. What was close, however, was a tree.

Huh. That should work.

She tossed Kit against the tree and laughed with joy as a door perfectly molded to the large oak. A doorway formed where she'd tossed the pouch.

It was textured just like the bark it had covered over, seeming inset into the tree, somehow not raising the surface noticeably. If she hadn't seen it grow there, she'd have missed it entirely.

That's amazing.

-Tala, focus.-

Right! She still grinned. This opened so many possibilities. *I wonder if I can make it free-standing?* Now

Millennial Mage, 6 - Fused

was not the time for that sort of experimentation, however.

She stepped through the narrower-than-standard entrance, finding the inside of Kit unchanged.

Strangely enough, from the inside, the door looked like it had since the storage device had subsumed the syphon fascia. *Illusion magic?*

It wasn't, at least not according to her magesight. Instead, the door's appearance seemed to be the result of the incredibly dexterous use of dimensional power. *We really should study how Kit manipulates power at some point.*

-*Yes, but that point is not now.*-

Tala tossed some jerky for Terry, and the terror bird flickered off her shoulder and away to his comfortable corner, already swallowing the bit of jerked meat.

She smiled, stretching slightly, before sitting on the floor, cross legged. She began to go through the familiar motions of making tea, not focusing on where each tool came from as she needed it. Each thing, from pot to tea to incorporator, was simply in her hand as she went to use them.

It was a surprisingly meditative process, if she was being honest, and that really helped center her, releasing the last of her giddy tension from the day.

Once she had a warm cup of chamomile in her hand, she took in a deep breath, relishing the scent. A small sip confirmed her biases. *Wow, this is so, so much better than the stuff at that tea house.*

It was really too bad that she couldn't go back to Makinaven any time soon.

After another sip, Tala turned her magesight inward, diving within herself.

Soon, it was as if she floated before a field of power.

Her spiritual self and her physical body were now pressed firmly together, stitched into unity by threads of magic.

At the center of it all sat her gate, like a planet surrounded by its rings. It was gushing power, using the entire structure as a conduit.

This is me?

-This is a visual, metaphorical representation of you, amalgamated from across planes of existence that defy the ability to be represented physically.-

So... yes?

-...Yes, Tala. This is you.-

Tala grinned. *Nope.*

-Why are you being difficult?-

This is us.

Somehow, Tala could feel Alat freeze within her mind.

Alat? There was nothing but silence for the space of a few breaths of time.

Finally, the alternate interface responded. *-I don't think that is true.-* Her mental voice sounded small.

Well, I disagree. This might not be all of you, but that soul right there? Somehow, Tala was able to 'point' toward the gate. *That gate is ours.*

Alat didn't seem to have a response for that.

Tala decided to move on. *So, what do we need to do?*

Their perspective shifted as Alat brought Tala's focus to the outer edge. The great circular... rugs? *That's a horrible metaphor.*

The great circular rugs were entirely stitched together, but there was still something missing.

A finishing stitch around the perimeter.

-Precisely. You are fully Fused, but the fusion is not set.-

Well, let's get to work.

And so they did.

Millennial Mage, 6 - Fused

The two worked together, using Tala's Archon Star to weave the thread of power and magic back and forth in a crosshatch.

As they continued, it became a sort of game.

Tala would almost toss the Archon Star, trailing power, down through the edge of her being, and Alat would catch it before tossing it back up, through another place just farther around the edge.

The motions quickly became rote.

Tala's extensive practice with her soul, as well as fine-magical control, allowed her to have the endurance and precision to simply *fly* around the circumference.

Alat matched her stitch for stitch.

In what felt like no time at all, they came to the end.

Somehow, it also felt like Tala had never done anything else in all her life. She'd only ever existed here, within herself, striving to be one with her fractured being.

It was an unsettling feeling that also brought with it incredible relief as from reaching the end of a long, arduous journey.

Together, she and Alat pulled the last stitch tight, knotting it in a spellform that both felt entirely alien and like the only thing that could possibly go there.

It was like finding the last puzzle piece, which had been hidden. She'd never seen it before, but it was blindingly obvious what was needed.

Power rippled through the entirety of the spiritual construct, and it began to pull in on itself, spiraling inward faster than Tala could track.

And just like that, she was done.

Tala opened her eyes and let her focus move outward once more.

She could see her own aura, mimicked by the magic of the through-spike, shining orange before her magesight.

We did it. We're Fused*!*

*   *   *

Tala didn't honestly remember climbing into her bed and falling into a deep sleep, though as soon as she woke up, Alat provided her with the memory.

The illusory vista outside her bedroom window greeted her with a stunning sunrise as she sprang to her feet.

I'm Fused*!*

She gasped. *Master Jevin said I could talk to anyone of sufficient rank to learn how to Refine, once I was Fused.*

That was another reason to go to the Constructionist's Guild.

Her mind flicked out as she wanted to know the time, and the answer came. It was well past midnight.

I'll go in the morning before breakfast with Mistress Odera.

Giddy with elation at her accomplishment, Tala moved through her morning routine. Then, because she'd missed it, she went through her nightly routine as well.

There was a lot of overlap, and as such, she actually felt quite sore by the end, and the fatigue extended to her mind, magic, and soul as well.

Thankfully, the physical side of it began to pass quickly as her reserves diminished a marginal amount. The rest would take a bit longer to recover, but she expected to be right as rain by midmorning.

Hah. Right as Rane. She chuckled to herself.

Alat groaned within her head.

Fine, fine. Time to eat!

She cooked herself a large breakfast and ate it with gusto, the flavors seeming new after her Fusing.

I don't feel much different, aside from happy. Alat? Are we different?

Millennial Mage, 6 - Fused

-Your spells are functioning both more powerfully and more efficiently for their power output, but I can't say by exactly how much. The power coming through your gate is more attuned to you and on a deeper level, but not fundamentally so. Thus, I think that, because of that, it is powering your spellforms and natural magics more effectively.-

Good to know.

-There is some... disquiet throughout your being, however.-

Tala looked within herself, and she thought she could see what Alat meant. *It's like I'm settling, adjusting to this new state.*

-Just like you had to after you became Bound.-

That's what I was thinking.

She finished up her first breakfast and checked the time again.

Still much too early to bother the Constructionists. I need to speak to someone of high standing, and I need them in a good mood.

That decided, she would head to the work yard first to charge the cargo slots. They'd be leaving the next day, after all.

"Terry, want to come?"

He lifted his head, then tilted it quizzically.

"I don't think there will be many people about."

Without responding, he flickered to her shoulder, and she stepped out of Kit and back into the park.

With a practiced motion, Tala pulled the pouch from the tree and hung it on her belt, looking up at the starry sky overhead. There wasn't even the barest hint of light to the east, but she hadn't expected to see any, given the hour.

Without any further delay, she set out toward the work yard.

It was an easy trek with her pressure distribution scripts giving her sure footing on ice and snow alike.

As she considered it, they'd probably make things worse if it was a truly flat sheet of ice, but because the ice was in small patches, part of her weight always fell on a place with good traction available.

Thus, it was only about half an hour before she'd reached the wagons, charged the slots, and was looking for the nearest Constructionist Guildhall.

-I'd actually recommend the one on the far side of the city. It is listed as the main hall for that guild in this city, so you are more likely to find who you need. Also, it's a bit of a walk, so we'll arrive at a better time.-

Tala nodded at that.

Mistress Odera wouldn't expect her until a bit later in the morning, so the extra distance wouldn't be a problem. *It would be nice if I could fly like Cazor can. Though, I'd obviously have to use a different method.*

-There are several ways that we might be able to do just that, though they would all come with their own particular quirks and... dangers.-

Maybe later, then. Today's too important to risk on untested methods.

Alat made a happy little sound, for some reason, then began directing Tala through the streets of Marliweather.

In what felt like no time at all, they arrived at the guildhall.

There still wasn't light in the eastern sky, but it was winter, and they were actually inside what most people would call 'business hours.'

Let's see what we find.

Tala approached the Constructionist Guild and found that this hall was more like Makinaven than Bandfast.

A sturdy door stood closed but not locked, sealing off the entrance to the building from the elements.

Millennial Mage, 6 - Fused

Tala smiled at the memories of dropping through to talk with Master Jevin and get his advice. *I hope that the higher-ups are as kind here.*

She pushed open the door, feeling the familiar magics of a magical scan before a deep *gong* announced her arrival.

Huh, I think I like the bell better? She wasn't sure, actually. The deep, resonating sound was somehow pleasant and comforting.

Terry squawked in soft irritation, but otherwise, he didn't move.

An attendant rushed out to greet her, bowing. "Welcome, Archon. How can we be of assistance, today?" His eyes flicked to Terry but didn't linger.

Good to know not everyone in the city is over-enamored by arcanous creatures. Tala checked, and the attendant had a nametag on. "Well, Master Apalo, I am looking to meet with a member of your guild for two matters. One could be handled by anyone in management, but the other requires someone who is Refined or farther."

Apalo bowed again. "Certainly, Mistress…"

"Oh! My apologies. I am Tala."

"Certainly, Mistress Tala. Master Hafest arrived a short time ago. If you'll allow me a moment, I can go and see if he has availability?"

"That would be wonderful. Thank you."

"Can I offer you anything while you wait?"

"No, thank you. I'm quite all right."

"As you say, Mistress. If you change your mind, the waiting room is just through that door."

Tala nodded her thanks, and the attendant departed down one of the side hallways.

Less than two minutes later, Apalo returned with an older Mage, gestured toward Tala, and then ducked back into the attendant's waiting room.

The Mage, clearly Hafest, walked over to Tala, smiling warmly in greeting. "Well met, Mistress Tala." His magesight flickered on and off so quickly that she almost missed it. He had wings of gray in his otherwise blonde hair, and a short-trimmed beard decorated his strong-jawed face. His simple Mage's robes were of a quilted material, clearly meant for added warmth.

"Well met, Master Hafest." She bowed just slightly. By what her magesight was telling her, Hafest was a Paragon with power oriented toward fire, force, and magical power. *Immaterial and Material Guide?* She wasn't used to Paragons being open for such a detailed scan. Most that she'd seen held their aura almost as a shield against such inspection.

"Come this way. It sounds like we've some things to discuss." He led her down the hall to a small sitting room, activating copper privacy scripts as they sat in the rather plain space.

"Thank you for taking your time to meet with me."

"Of course! That's why I'm here. Now, if you wouldn't mind a guess as to at least one of the reasons?" There was a twinkle in his eyes.

She smiled, gesturing for him to go on.

"You're newly Fused, am I right?"

"That's correct."

"So, someone already told you to seek aid as soon as you hit that step."

"Indeed, yes."

"Good, good." He leaned back, nodding to himself. "So, my guess. You are here to ask about the Refining process."

"That is correct."

"Wonderful!" He chuckled happily to himself. "I have good news and bad."

Tala frowned. "Oh?"

Millennial Mage, 6 - Fused

"Good news first. There is a well-known, widely available process for Refining that anyone can do, but it is… uncomfortable. I can assess you for which set of tools you'll need to do it right, should you choose to walk that path."

"That is good news. I'm no stranger to discomfort for purposes of long-term gain."

He laughed, grinning broadly. "Fair enough. Fair enough. You know your own mind." His mirth faded, and he leaned forward once again. "So, the bad news: you'll have to wait. If you begin Refining in earnest before your being has settled into being Fused, you'll cripple yourself for future growth. You would permanently throw your system out of whack, and you'd never be able to reach Paragon."

Tala's eyes widened. "Oh. Well, thank you for the warning. How long do I wait?"

"Common wisdom is at least twice as long as it took you to Fuse, but that's just a shorthand. Some believe that it makes folk feel like they have control over their waiting time. But, honestly, that's a load of swill."

So… a few months by that reckoning? "What do you mean? What's the right way to estimate?"

"Well, some people Fuse in an instant, when they come to an understanding of themselves that is soul deep, and clearly, they can't just immediately move on to being Refined." He shook his head with a smile. "I once sat in on a raising where the newly Bound Archon Fused on the spot." His smile widened. "Now, that was a well-adjusted kid."

Oh. "Kid?"

He grunted. "Well, they were probably close to fifty, but these things are relative."

Yeah, so it would seem.

"Some take a hundred years to face their inner struggles and find equilibrium, and they certainly don't have to wait two hundred more."

"So, how long?"

"Honestly? It's different for each person. We can test for that, too. Well, we can at least test to see how unsettled your being is. I've not seen it settle faster than a year, though."

Tala grimaced but nodded. "I suppose that makes sense. Everything in its proper time."

"That's a good way to view it." Hafest scratched his chin. "If you don't mind me saying it, you seem like you're on the young side for your advancement. I don't know your story, and I don't need to, but if you'll pardon some advice?"

She nodded again.

"Stay at this level until you've been *settled* for at least a year. There can occasionally be complications even when the test shows a Mage to be fully settled."

That's good to know. "I'll consider it."

"Now, you can take steps down the path toward Refined, even while you're waiting. It's a common enough practice, honestly. You just can't initiate the process."

"Will it shift my aura?"

He frowned. "You make a wager or something?"

She shook her head, and he grunted.

"Well, it can, though I've never seen the prep work move a Mage past halfway through, at least from looking at their aura, but you shouldn't aim for that. If you start Refining without proper procedures, the survival rate's only about ten percent, even if all the prep work is well laid and verified."

Tala's eyes widened. "Well, that seems like something to avoid then."

Millennial Mage, 6 - Fused

"Indeed." He smiled in a rather consoling manner. "I'm sorry to not have better news."

"You've told me what's needed, and I'm grateful. What is the prep work like?"

Hafest grinned once more. "Glad you asked! Mostly, it's incorporating body strengthening and enhancing scripts around your other spell-work."

What. It was not a question. As she quickly considered the topic, she realized that it wasn't that much of a surprise.

"It's expensive, and it requires an inscriber of incredible skill to do the fine work. Without such an inscriber, it's hard not to disrupt what you're already doing with your power. The best around is over in Bandfast."

That's right, she is.

"But she doesn't usually take on new clients, unless there's something real special about them."

"Mistress Holly?"

He paused. "Yes, actually." He narrowed his gaze. "What did you say your name was again?"

"Tala."

He scratched his beard. "Mistress Tala… Mistress Tala… Blood Archon?"

"That's me."

"Well, rust me to ruin." He held out his hand. "Good to meet you! I didn't realize you were *that* Tala."

Tala shook his hand, feeling awkward. "What do you mean?"

"Well, it's not every day that someone uses an entirely new type of medium. That sticks in your mind."

"Oh, well. I suppose that makes sense. Thank you."

"So, does that answer that line of questions?"

She frowned, shaking her head. "What if I already have body-enhancing scripts? Shouldn't I already be moving through the beginning stages toward Refined?"

"Oh! That's a great question. No, though it will start to happen soon."

"What?"

"A Bound's power just isn't sufficient to make the type of weighty changes required. But now, you've a Fused's power running through you."

"But the scripts are the same. Shouldn't it just be a bit more efficient?"

He gave her an incredulous look. "That's like saying a blade cuts the same no matter how much pressure is behind it."

"Ahh, I see."

"Yeah, I thought you would."

"So, the power will begin to cut deeper into my natural pathways and physical being, making the changes more a fundamental part of me, rather than a mere change in form?"

"That is quite well put. Yes."

"Huh. Well, this is going to be interesting." She looked down at her hands, and if she were a betting woman, she would say that there was the smallest bit of shift in her aura toward yellow. Less than a percent of a percent, but it *seemed* like there was a shift. *Or I'm just imagining things because I want there to be a change.*

"Once you have the scripts, if you're an Immaterial Guide, you can seek out other sources of natural magic that align with body enhancement, absorb them, and align the power with your scripts."

"What about other quadrants?"

He grunted. "No easier road through the early stages than as an Immaterial Guide. I thought I remembered you were one, but if I remembered incorrectly, there are some techniques you could use, but they aren't as effective."

"Oh, no. I'm an Immaterial Guide; I was just curious."

"Oh, fair enough. You have another tool then. I'm glad to hear it. Now, what was the other matter you wanted to discuss?"

Tala nodded, reorienting herself to the next discussion. She briefly described the function of the iron paint, its efficacy, and how the Bandfast Constructionists were already using it.

At that point, Hafest's eyes unfocused as if he were looking at something distant. "Those rusting cheaters." He shook his head and laughed. "That's why their efficiency has been rising?" Hafest grinned from ear to ear. "So, assuming I believe you, and I'm inclined to, what about it? We don't have any, not at the moment."

"Oh, no. I'm not hoping to buy any from you. I'm hoping to make an introduction between you and an alchemist who could supply it for you."

Hafest leaned back, biting his lip in thought as he scratched his chin. "Interesting. Alright. I'll meet with the alchemist. Can't promise I'll buy from them, or buy this from anyone, but I'm interested."

"Would you like a demonstration of its potential, at least in a niche use?"

He gave her a skeptical look. "Wouldn't that be something that the alchemist would provide?"

"Maybe, but I happen to have an easy demonstration, and I'd prefer that the alchemist not witness it."

"Well, now you have me curious. What do you have in mind?"

"First, this is why I have a through-spike."

Hafest nodded slowly. "Interesting. Go on."

"I am not casting anything. I will simply be suppressing the visual illusion that is currently active over my person."

He leaned forward, looking like a child awaiting their birthday present. "Don't keep me in suspense."

Tala looked within herself, using her ability to manipulate magic to reach into the through-spike and disable the illusion.

"Well, rust my biscuits." His eyes widened in obvious surprise. "Are those spell-echoes?"

Tala nodded.

He reached out, then hesitated. "May I?"

She smiled. "Of course." She held out her hand to him, and he took it.

"These aren't actually in the air." He turned her hand this way and that, muttering to himself, but Tala heard him perfectly. "The light is a side-effect of it reverberating through the fabric of reality." He shook his head, looking up and addressing her. "How are you not dead from magic poisoning? If I did this, I'd be ripped apart in an instant."

"The specific scripts that I use."

He grunted. "You'd be a perfect candidate for Mistress Holly." He shook his head again. "What am I saying? It's obvious that you already are inscribed by her. Correct?"

"That's right."

He let go of her hand, sitting back.

Tala let the illusion return.

"And that's the paint your alchemist will be selling?"

"Well, no. This paint is on me and will be quite useless when it comes off, but she will be using the same formula."

Hafest gave her an incredulous look, but it didn't last. He snorted a laugh. "Fine, fine. That was well said." He nodded. "I'll accept that demonstration if you'll sign a statement that it's the same formula."

"To the best of my knowledge."

"To the best of your knowledge."

"I'm fine with that."

"Great. Then all I have to do is negotiate with the wee alchemist on costs and quantities." He rubbed his hands together. "When will you bring her by?"

"This afternoon?"

He nodded to himself. "I can make that work. I'll need to spend a chunk of the morning figuring out how much we can use, and in what timeframes, but yeah. I can meet with you. Late afternoon?"

"We can be flexible."

"Alright then. I look forward to it."

Chapter: 28
A Fun Idea

Tala wasn't late to her breakfast with Mistress Odera despite her trip to the Constructionist Guild.

I'm being very efficient this morning.

-That we are.-

Mistress Odera was very congratulatory for Tala's Fusing, as well as for how well the previous day had gone with Tala's siblings.

The older woman was definitely far more pleased about the latter development than the former, and strangely enough, Tala found herself agreeing. She was always going to Fuse, eventually, but the potential she had to reestablish her relationships with her siblings was truly exciting.

I think I've got a fun idea for today, too.

-Oh, I like that. Yes. Let me see what I can do about the specifics.-

Thank you, Alat.

Tala's second breakfast passed in regular fashion, though Mistress Odera did order a bit more food, even more than usual, in celebration of Tala's Fusing and the beginnings of reconciliation.

Rane wasn't around as, apparently, he'd taken a short protection job outside of the city for the day.

Good for him. Tala felt glad for her friend. He was branching out.

-Yup. He really should become his own person before trying to pursue you again.-

Millennial Mage, 6 - Fused

Tala felt her eyebrow twitch but didn't otherwise react or respond.

All told, she arrived back at the park just about three hours before noon, Terry comfortably resting on her shoulder.

She was hardly there for five minutes before her siblings joined her, trudging through the snow.

"Good morning!" she greeted them warmly.

A chorus of 'good morning's and other greetings came back to her.

Terry trilled a happy little greeting as well.

"Everyone, this is Terry."

Most stared uncertainly at the bird, even as Nalac grinned. "Good morning, Terry!"

Terry flickered to his shoulder and head-butted him.

Nalac grimaced, then laughed. "Ow, I already said good morning."

Terry bumped him again, but seemingly much lighter this time, and Nalac scratched his head.

The other siblings crowded around saying hi to Terry.

Caln gave Tala a skeptical look. "Is this your pet? Nalac told us about the bird, but not much."

Tala shook her head. "He's a friend. He's at least as smart as you all are, from what I've seen."

Caln gave a half-smile. "You calling us bird-brained?"

She grinned back. "Are you saying that's an insult?"

Caln opened his mouth to respond, then caught motion out of the corner of his eye.

Terry was staring directly at the young man, eyes narrowed in focus.

Caln cleared his throat. "No. No, not at all."

Terry let out a happy little trill, then went back to flickering among Tala's siblings.

Tala cleared her throat, drawing attention back to herself.

Terry helpfully flickered back to her shoulder to assist in the wrangling.

"So, I had an idea for what we could do, around answering any other questions that you may have."

There was hesitantly intrigued silence in response.

"I'm going to reduce the gravity of any of you who want it, so you can jump and bounce around in the park."

Confused silence was her only reply.

Oh, right. That's not really clear, is it? "You all don't really know what I mean, do you?"

Most shook their heads, but the older ones seemed contemplative.

"Okay. We'll do a demonstration." She hesitated. *You know, even with caution, this could still be dangerous.* "Latna, Caln, are you two willing to help me?"

They looked at each other, then shrugged. "Sure."

"Can one of you go see if Master Leighis is available? At least for a few minutes until you all get the hang of it. As for the other, I'll enact the working on them, so this group can see and understand what I mean."

The two shared a look again, then Latna nodded and headed back to the shop. "Sure. I'll be right back."

Caln came forward through his siblings, a look of resignation across his features. "What do you need me to do?"

Tala looked him over. He was wearing a heavy coat, boots, gloves, and a hat. *The coat would make him cold to take off, same with the boots. The hat would come off too easily.*

That made one of the gloves the best solution.

"So, once I say so, start bouncing in place so that we can find a good level of reduced gravity. If something goes wrong, take off your right glove, and that will end the effect. All right?"

He frowned but slowly nodded. "If you say so."

Millennial Mage, 6 - Fused

Tala focused on targeting her brother, specifically emphasizing the fact that he was wearing a glove on his right hand, weaving that into her conception of him, so that the removal of such would break the spell-effect.

It was funny. In a way, this was the opposite of what she usually tried to do while targeting someone or something. She usually tried to focus on the immutable characteristics, so her lock and working would persist as long as possible. Now, she was purposely choosing something that would be easy to alter.

-Different purposes require different tactics.-
True enough.

Once the lock was in place, she began to ramp down his gravity. *Decrease.*

"Now." She let him know it was time.

Caln began to bounce a bit on his feet. "I feel kind of silly doing this. What am I—" His eyes widened as he began to come off the ground a bit more than he'd expected.

Tala let up there, waiting. "How is that?"

Caln took a couple of experimental jumps, going slightly higher than normal and coming down a bit slower. He let out a startled laugh. "This is amazing!"

"Should I aim for a bit lighter? I don't want you or the others to get too high, as that might be a little scary. This is supposed to be fun, not panic-inducing."

He crouched down and jumped, attempting a flip. He didn't account for the changes, however, and ended up doing one and a half rotations before landing on the snow with a soft *whump.*

His eyes went wide again for a moment, but before Tala could ask if he was okay, he started laughing once more. "This is perfect for now."

The other siblings began clamoring for Tala to do them next.

She grinned, holding up her hands. "One moment! One moment. Caln, can you take off your right glove?"

He was still laying on the ground, grinning. "Sure."

As he pulled off his glove, Tala felt her working break apart, and Caln immediately sunk deeper into the snow.

"Oof. That's interesting."

"Good, it works."

Caln pulled his glove back on, frowning when nothing changed. "Hey, why's it not back?"

"You removed the glove, so the working broke. There's nothing left to come back when you pull the glove back on."

"Huh… interesting."

Tala did a quick check and found that everyone was wearing gloves. *Good.* "Alright! Everyone pick a partner to stick with, at least at first. You saw what Caln did. Your right glove will be the key to end the effect if you get scared."

Latna was already on her way back with Master Leighis in tow. He was bundled up against the cold just like everyone else.

Tala had grown her shoes to cover her feet before coming to the park in consideration of how odd she already looked without winter wear. Though, to be fair, her elk leathers had thickened against the chill, and so they were likely easily as warm as her siblings' coats.

"Master Leighis! Thank you for joining us."

"Mistress Tala. To what do I owe the pleasure?"

"Well, I'm going to reduce their gravity and let them frolic in the park. I thought having a Healer on hand, until they got the hang of it, would be wise."

He nodded. "Not sure I understand exactly what you mean, but having a Healer about's never a bad idea."

She grinned at him. "Thank you for coming out." Turning back to her siblings, she continued speaking, "Alright! Let's do this."

She quickly went through them, ensuring that the wearing of their right glove was integral to her lock on each in turn. She then decreased their gravity to about seventy percent.

Each, in turn, let out startled gasps, followed by giggles of excitement before they began cavorting around the wide-open space.

"Stick with your partners!" Tala reminded them, and they reluctantly came back toward their pairs. The last two she did were Latna and Sella.

The little three-year old had been having quite a bit of trouble walking in the snow, but once the spell was enacted on her, she was able to scamper across the top of it with ease, giggling and chasing after her siblings.

Latna laughed in startled joy as she took off, bounding after the toddler.

Terry was crouched low on Tala's shoulder, watching all the kids bounding about.

"Are you going to be okay, Terry? Or do you want to go back in Kit?"

He gave her a long look, then trilled mournfully.

"You want to go play?" She had a horrifying reminder of Terry 'playing' with the pigs.

He looked their way before bobbing a nod.

She swallowed. "Can you be gentle? I really don't want them hurt, and they are mundane humans. You already were a bit rough with Nalac when you head-butted him."

Terry looked after the frolicking children, then nodded.

"All right. I'll trust you. Remember to stay close enough to keep your collar happy."

He jabbered back to her.

Of course, he hadn't forgotten. "Everyone!"

Her siblings came to a stop, turning to look her way.

"Terry wants to play with you all. He has to stay within a couple of hundred feet of me, so if you're okay playing with him, come back this way." They'd spread out around the massive park quite far in their pairs.

Some came back, others didn't. *That's fine.*

"Do you want to be lighter?"

Terry gave her an indignant look.

"Fine, fine. I don't know what I was thinking. You're perfect as you are." *You know, I wonder if I could get a fundamental enough lock on him that him changing size wouldn't matter.* She'd have to consider it. Not to attack Terry, of course, at least not out of the sparring ring, but it would be a marked step forward for her abilities if she could manage it.

Clearly unaware of the direction of her thoughts, Terry trilled happily once, then flickered away.

He landed on Olen's shoulder, surprising the young boy. The terror bird then pushed off and immediately flickered off to the side. The powerful push sent Olen to faceplant into the snow.

Tala's eyes widened. *Terry!* But before she chastised her friend, Olen pushed himself up, laughing uproariously.

The small boy made a quick snowball and threw it at the bird, but Terry flickered out of the way. When he reappeared, he was dancing from foot to foot, crouched low as if ready for a fight. Thankfully, there was a playful glint in his eyes.

Not the maliciously playful glint he had for the pigs, either.

What followed was a group throwdown of snowballs against the bird.

Millennial Mage, 6 - Fused

Terry flickered among those who were participating, tripping them up or unbalancing them and causing them to fall into the snow while they threw uncounted snowballs after him.

Tala felt herself relax. *Good. Good safe fun.*

Leighis came to stand beside Tala. "You know, they have no idea how expensive it is to do such workings on them. The gravity working, I mean."

She glanced his way. "It's less than you might think. I've a really good inscriptionist, and the reduction is an effect of some of my always-active scripts."

He raised his eyebrows at that, then nodded. "Even so. Nothing is free."

She felt herself smile, the oft-repeated line from her classes coming back with ease. "True enough. 'Nothing is free, least of all magic.'"

They fell into a companionable silence for a couple of moments.

After about a minute, she glanced his way. "Do you want to try?"

He looked genuinely shocked. "I... Are you sure?"

She shrugged. "Yeah. You're out here for us, might as well make it fun for you, too."

He shook his head, smiling. "I will admit that I'm curious."

"Say no more!" She grinned, targeting him for the working, making sure to include his right glove in the lock.

A moment later, Leighis was bouncing back and forth from foot to foot, testing out the alteration. "What a fascinating sensation."

Interesting. Does he have combat experience? "Isn't it? Go, have some fun. It really seems like they're going to be fine, so don't feel obligated to stay, but you can stay as long as you wish."

"Thank you, Mistress Tala. I'll do just that." He gave her a boyish grin.

He took a leaping step forward, and Terry was there in an instant, tripping the older Archon and sending him tumbling across the snow.

Tala immediately covered her face. "Oh, Terry."

But Leighis rolled with the fall and popped back up, a snowball already in hand. He threw with a surprising amount of accuracy at Terry before he even landed back on his feet.

The terror bird flickered away without issue, but still, it was impressive reflexes.

Tala laughed, enjoying watching them play. *Yeah, definitely some experience in dangerous situations, or maybe he plays a lot of sports...* She shrugged internally. It didn't really matter.

The day passed in a whirlwind.

Master Leighis only stayed out for a couple of hours before he had to get back to work.

The siblings wore themselves out for another hour after that before they all went to a nearby restaurant to eat. Tala insisted on paying and then deeply confused them all by how much she ordered for herself. The confusion shifted to awe, then horror, as they watched her not only eat it all, but order more.

That spawned some questions, but overall, the questions were nothing groundbreaking.

For Tala's part, around eating, she tried to ask pointed questions about each of her siblings. It wasn't easy because there were so many, but she did start to fill in her knowledge gaps with regard to them.

All told, the lunch cost forty silver, but the vast, vast majority of it was from what Tala ordered and ate. *Mistress Holly insists that I continue to eat until I'm topped off.*

Millennial Mage, 6 - Fused

-Not to mention that the Fused power running through your scripts is already consuming more of your reserves to facilitate the deeper setting of your enhancements.-

That was true enough. *No rest for the hungry, I suppose.*

After their long lunch, the kids had to head home.

The younger ones had schoolwork that they needed to finish. Caln had to go help in the shop, and Tala and Latna needed to go to the Archive to get the recipe, then to the Constructionist guild for their meeting with Hafest.

Thus, they all walked back to the alchemy shop in a pack and bade Tala goodbye right outside.

They were about to part ways, when Tala stopped, frowning. "Olen?"

The young boy froze, almost through the alchemist's door. "Yes, Tala?"

"Take off your right glove."

"But... But I... uh... It's cold. I'll do that inside."

She narrowed her gaze at him. "You haven't taken it off since the park."

"I have no idea what you are talking about." His nervousness, coupled with his age caused the words to come out a bit less clearly than his usual speech. He started edging toward the door.

Tala sighed. "I'm not going to punish you, Olen, you aren't in trouble. I just don't want you to get hurt by keeping that spell-working active on you."

The others were all regarding the boy with a mixture of amusement and stern 'older sibling displeasure.'

"Fine," he groused as he pulled off his glove.

"Thank you." Tala grinned. "If you all liked this, we can do it again when I come back through. I'll let you know if I can't get a contracted trip back right away. Otherwise, expect me in just over two weeks. I wish I could be more specific."

Olen slumped his shoulders. "Sounds good. Thank you, again, Tala!" He then ran inside.

Tala glanced down as Sella latched onto her leg, staring up with a big grin. "*Eye!*"

Tala grinned back. "Goodbye, little Sella."

"Eye, eye, Ala." The little one didn't let go.

Tala cleared her throat. "Time for you to go inside."

"Eye! *Ala!*"

Tala blinked at the sheer volume of the farewell. "Take care?" She bent down, pulling Sella off of her leg and giving the little one a hug.

Sella squeezed her back with surprising force. She then whispered, "Eye, Ala."

Tala laughed again. "Goodbye." She then handed Sella to Akli, who had waited to take the child. "See you soon."

After that, Tala and Latna turned and walked toward the Archon compound, directed by the map that Alat had been able to pull up.

It didn't take long to certify that Latna was, in fact, a licensed alchemist, and with that done, she purchased the formula.

Latna seemed to visibly pale as she handed over the golden coins. Likely, she hadn't ever spent that much at once in her entire life.

Maybe some large ingredient orders? Or if she handled the funds for the purchase of the shops around theirs, or the modifications to them.

Tala leaned over to her sister and whispered, "You're carrying the money around with you?"

Latna colored slightly. "I didn't want to forget it, and I figured we'd be safe enough with you around."

Tala grunted. "Fair enough."

The front office gave Latna the formula in a small notebook, the actual recipe and procedures only taking up the first couple of pages.

They thanked the attendant and began walking.

"I'll need to read this before we get there, so I know what I'm talking about. And, if I don't recognize any ingredients, we'll have to stop by the market, so I can get an idea of base costs."

Tala nodded. "Want to stop for tea while you read?"

Latna shook her head, not taking her eyes from the page. "No, so long as we walk slowly, I'll be fine."

So, the walk passed in silence.

When Latna finished, she closed the little book and tucked it into an inner pocket of her coat. "Nothing too extreme, though there are a few processes that are somewhat time-consuming." She nodded to herself. "We'll see what they have to say."

* * *

"Mistress Tala! Welcome back." Hafest was walking through the entry hall when they arrived.

"Master Hafest? I hope we didn't keep you waiting. What are you doing in the entry hall?"

He laughed that off. "I was raiding the waiting room for a few pastries. Who is this? Your alchemist friend?" He looked Latna over briefly. "Or not a friend. Family? The resemblance is uncanny. She must be your daughter." Hafest held out his hand toward Latna.

Latna froze on the spot, then burst out laughing while Tala grimaced, feeling herself slouching ever so slightly.

Even so, Latna took the Archon's hand and shook it, getting herself under control.

"Did I say something funny?"

"Oh, Master Hafest, it is a pleasure to meet you. I am Tala's sister."

"Sister? But you're no Mage…" He looked to Tala again. "How young…?" Then, he shook his head. "Nope, not my concern. Come on. I hear we have things to discuss."

Latna grinned back at Tala as Hafest led them to a much nicer sitting room than Tala and Hafest had used.

Probably just because there are three of us.

The negotiations weren't long. The guild could use ten gallons a month to start for the first six months, as soon as the alchemists could get them, and they were willing to sign a contract to that effect. If the product didn't work out, then they wouldn't be reupping the contract. If it did? They'd likely need more, but they'd cross that bridge when they came to it.

Tala left while Latna and Hafest haggled on the specific price, going to get a pastry for herself.

By the time she got back, the two both looked happy, and they were confirming their deal.

"A pleasure doing business with you both."

They bowed to the large Archon and departed.

It was still early as they walked back toward the family shop.

As they neared, Tala cleared her throat. "Well, it still isn't quite dinner. We could… go grab something?"

Latna shook her head. "Thank you for the invitation, but I am needed at home. Dinner is a bit of a madhouse, so we need all hands on deck."

"Oh… okay then."

They lapsed back into silence.

A few minutes later, they were at the shop, and Latna turned to her sister. "Thank you." She patted her coat, where the formula rested. "This will be much more profitable than most of what we can produce. It won't replace our regular business, but it *is* an amazing opportunity. Thank you, truly."

Tala smiled. "I'm glad it'll work out for you all."

Latna turned, then paused. "See you in two weeks?"

"A little more probably, but yeah."

"Bye, Tala."

"Bye, Latna."

Without another word, but with a brief smile, Latna entered the family shop and pulled the door closed behind her.

Tala returned to the work yard in contemplative silence, grabbing a massive dinner to bring with her on the way.

She filled the evening with training and study of the manuals to which she had access.

The following morning she departed the city of her birth, heading home.

Chapter: 29
A Wonderfully Peaceful Time

Tala felt that her time in Marliweather was an unmitigated success.

True, things *might* have gone better if she'd been able to write her own destiny, but in the realm of reality, she couldn't imagine a better turn out. *After all, I came out of it with two more siblings than I went in with.*

-That's a funny way of looking at it.-

But it is *true.*

-Oh, decidedly, and it seems like relationships are possible with all of them, at least in time.-

Lunch on the first day found the three Mage Protectors sitting atop the cargo wagon for the meal, keeping their eyes moving over the surrounding wilds.

"I can't believe you're fully Fused." Rane was shaking his head in resignation, even while a genuine smile pulled at his lips. "I just can't. I can see your aura, but it seems impossible. Congratulations."

"Rane?"

"Yeah, Tala?"

"That's about the thousandth time you've said that."

He colored, cleared his throat, and took another bite of his lunch.

Mistress Odera drank some water to clear her mouth, then regarded Tala. "It is an impressive thing, Mistress Tala. His saying so isn't a bad thing."

"Oh, I know. I'm still somewhat shocked myself."

"Indeed."

Millennial Mage, 6 - Fused

Rane waved a hunk of bread. "It is unusual, but not unique. Still impressive, though."

Tala laughed. "I feel like I hear that about a lot of what I do." After a pause, she added, "The first part, I mean."

Rane grinned back her way but didn't comment further.

"You do seem to have found a fortuitous path. Time will tell if others follow you on it and whether the outcome is a net positive for humanity."

Tala didn't really like to think of that, so she turned to Rane. "How are you progressing?"

He grimaced at that. "Same issue as before. I lack the mana density to brute force the connection, though I am making progress." He straightened slightly. "The job I took yesterday was to protect a group while they examined some cave paintings."

Mistress Odera paused at that. "The Cave of the Triune?"

"Precisely."

Tala frowned. "Why does that sound familiar?"

Rane shrugged. "Well, Master Grediv mentioned it a lot. Three founts, each less than a dozen yards apart, all with pure, non-elemental magic flowing from them."

She gave him a level look. "I didn't know what founts were until recently."

"Oh, right."

Mistress Odera cut in. "The Triune, Mistress Tala. Three Immaterial Guides who focused on the manipulation of magic directly. Triplets, bent toward the betterment of humanity. They sacrificed themselves in an attempt to give humanity another path to power."

Tala found herself nodding. "Right, but it failed. Their theoretical pathway of ascending was a failure."

Rane interjected around another mouthful. "Which is a shame, because our path of ascension is amazing."

Mistress Odera and Tala both turned to regard Rane with confusion.

After swallowing, he clarified, "Meaning the steps that humanity can take through the ranks. Look at us. We are so much more than what we could ever have been without magic, without our gates, and this path. It's tried and true. Why try to build a second one?"

Mistress Odera's tone was hard. "Because it still fails many of us."

Rane colored, hunching down. "Right. I... Apologies, Mistress."

She waved him off. "No matter. You were saying, Master Rane?"

"Hmm?"

"You went to the cave."

"Oh! So, I meditated between the founts, removing all barriers to power flowing in and out of me. It was"—he grimaced—"like having a pumice stone scraped through my entire body, but after half a day, my magic capacity and density have both increased by nearly ten percent."

Tala sat up. "That's remarkable! Can I...?" She trailed off as she saw Mistress Odera shaking her head.

"You already have a higher density than that cave, so it wouldn't lead to an improvement for you. It is a miserable process as well, from what I hear. It also only works for Bound—if it works at all. Mages can't survive such an onslaught, even those with incredibly high density, because the quality of the power, the purity, overwhelms them. Fused are too potent, as a rule, to gain anything from the cave, and Bound don't *need* it. Though, it does help some." She nodded toward Rane.

"Huh, so in a way they succeeded?"

"I suppose, in a way." Mistress Odera sounded skeptical. "But one can hardly call it a success when instead of forging a new road, they now marginally help a small fraction as they progress down the old one."

Tala grunted. "Fair enough." The conversation then shifted to other things as their meal drew to a close.

Most of the journey back to Bandfast was uneventful, aside from the usual training and occasional arcanous beast.

She spent her meals and evenings talking with Rane and Mistress Odera and sparring with Terry and Rane.

On the second day of travel, Terry made real progress on changing his own fighting methods. He began to toss a knife back and forth with himself, flickering between each side of the wagon as they rumbled across the wintery plain, throwing it with increasing speed.

Seems like he's gotten over his aversion. He didn't add the knife tossing into their sparring when she faced off against him that night. Not that he needed to as he could still handily defeat her, seemingly at will.

The next morning, he added a second knife, and by the time they arrived in Bandfast, he was creating a storm of crisscrossing weaponry, all flying through a single space.

That's not at all terrifying. He still hadn't used the new weaponry in combat, but Tala knew that he would, soon enough.

Tala made sure to congratulate Terry on his new accomplishment.

He was suitably pleased both with her praise and the extra helpings of meat and jerky she gave along with it.

-Yes, keep the terrifying murder bird appeased, please.-

I'm doing my best.

The second thing of consequence came from Alat.

When they were right about halfway between the two cities, Alat began to cackle madly, which was quite a disturbing thing to have happen in Tala's head.

What is going on?

-I have full access to pull information from the Archive. The Fused power behind your soul-bound items has increased the reach of the Archive connection. Unfortunately, I still can't write to anywhere but our own private space.-

So, that means we can't send messages?

-That's correct. Even if I try to change access to any information, it won't allow it, and I can't write to the notation we share with Jenna, or anyone else. So communication is out, but I can still keep your mind-map up to date in real time now!-

That was actually pretty great news. *Any idea on the range?*

-Well, if my perception of the link is correct, we could probably have this level of access out to nearly a thousand miles from the closest human city, though the last hundred or so might be iffy.-

Tala was utterly shocked at that. *I dearly hope I'll never be anywhere near that far from a city. At least not anytime soon.*

-True, but it's good to know your limits. I could probably also pierce out of an enclosed pocket dimension or through quite a bit of iron, but either of those would limit the total range.-

Like Kit? I thought you did that already.

-No, no. Kit is an open pocket dimension—merely an expanded space, really. You know this. I'm talking about one that is fully cut-off from the physical world.- Alat hesitated. *-Well, this physical world at least.-*

That was good to know. She hesitated. *Wait, if the pocket dimension is fully cut off from this physical world, then where would you be measuring from for the distance back to a human city?*

Millennial Mage, 6 - Fused

-That… is an excellent point. I might actually have an easier time reaching the Archive from a fully disconnected space, then.- She made a contemplative sound.

Well, in any case, I'm glad you won't be fully cut off from the Archive any time soon.

-Ever. I'm never going to be cut off ever again, now.- There was a firmness that bordered on fear, there, but Tala didn't think it was a good time to address it.

I decidedly hope that that is true.

All told, it was a fruitful, but uneventful, return trip.

After Tala received her pay, she immediately went to the Caravanner's Guild, found Lyn—and Kannis—and asked for help for signing up for as many trips back and forth to Marliweather as possible as quickly as possible.

She'd contemplated just taking a longer time in Marliweather, but she felt like the short stints with her family, spaced out, would be better for easing back into each other's lives. Additionally, she wanted to get a large chunk of ventures out of the way, toward fulfilling her contract with the Caravanner's Guild.

Thankfully, the trip to Marliweather didn't have anything truly special about it, so it wasn't in high demand. It wasn't either especially dangerous or uniquely safe. The city wasn't in its Waning phase yet, so there weren't extra benefits on the far end.

While Marliweather was well-situated, nearly in the center of the human territory for the moment, that didn't seem to matter much for the more lucrative routes, at least through the winter.

Thus, Tala was able to secure six additional trips back and forth to Bandfast before spring would truly set in. Beyond that, the Caravanner's Guild wasn't willing to let her reserve slots.

Still, twelve of my trips. That will bring me to a total of eighteen of my required ventures.

She'd discussed it with Rane and Mistress Odera on the trip back. Rane said he'd join her through the winter, to get a good foundation under himself monetarily and to take another few visits to the Cave of the Triune. It seemed that a Mage could overdo it by visiting too often, so the trips were near-ideal for him as well. That said, he wanted to do a larger loop of the human cities in the spring—whatever she decided.

As Tala considered it, she thought she just might join him, but she didn't know yet. *At least for the non-forest cities. No more Leshkin for me for a while.*

Mistress Odera had no issue with the plan. Apparently, some of her family was finalizing a move from Surehaven to Marliweather in the next weeks, so she'd get to spend some time with them. Thus, for her, there were no downsides.

Once all of that had been arranged, it was well and truly the end of the day, so Lyn, Kannis, and Tala had gone out to dinner to chat and catch up.

They were midway through the meal when Kannis spoke up.

Now, to be fair, Lyn and Kannis had finished their food, but Tala was still eating hers, and she'd used that fact to focus the conversation on them for most of the time. Unfortunately, it seemed like that had finally come to an end.

"Mistress Tala?"

"Hmm? Yeah, Kannis?"

The girl's face flickered toward a grimace, and she looked down.

Tala hadn't meant it as a slight, but the girl didn't qualify for the 'Mistress' title, yet. *Ah, socializing. How I love it...*

Millennial Mage, 6 - Fused

Kannis seemed to get over her momentary irritation. "I don't understand what I see when I look at you with my magesight."

Tala had noticed the girl pulsing power through those scripts off and on both at the Caravanner's Guild and at the restaurant. Feeling the awkwardness of the situation, Tala tried to respond as one of her teachers or mentors might have. "I'm glad that you're keeping your eyes open, so to speak. Now, what don't you understand?"

"Well, there isn't any variation to the sense of magic around you. It's almost a uniform color, and that color is a yellowish orange."

Lyn's eyes widened, and she turned toward Tala. "What's this now?"

Tala couldn't help but smile. "Seems like you should take your own advice and use magesight more often?"

Lyn glared. "I'm working on other portions of my advancement at the moment." Then, she sighed. "But you are probably right." She looked toward Kannis. "I did err in this. I should have been participating alongside you in your exercises and growth." Power flowed through Lyn's own magesight scripts, and the woman's eye twitched. "Fused and Refining… You did have an interesting trip."

Kannis cleared her throat. "While I am curious about that, if I am even allowed to know the details, I am more curious how you have such a perfectly smooth manifestation."

"It is a projection meant to keep me from triggering alarms, due to my other practices. Remember what's under the visual illusion?" Tala motioned to herself.

Kannis shuddered slightly. "Hard to forget that, so yes."

"So, that would make me appear as an absence of magic, or someone who was really clumsily trying to keep from being detected."

The mageling was nodding along. "Which would trigger all sorts of alarms and defenses."

"Precisely."

Kannis bit her lip, considering. "I think I can understand that. It's like hanging a sheet over a hole in the wall. Obviously, it's not going to be very textured."

"Reasonable analogy, yeah." Tala smiled, then continued to eat.

Kannis turned to Lyn. "What can I know about advancement?"

Lyn sighed. "Not much, I'm afraid. You just aren't ready for it."

Kannis grimaced slightly again, then nodded. "I understand. There are reasons for delays and hidden knowledge. I will be patient until you decide that I am ready."

Huh, that's quite mature of her.

-Maybe, we could learn a thing or two.-

Tala sighed. *We're already probably going to be waiting for a while before we progress on.*

-Speaking of that, we should talk with Holly.-

Yeah, but tomorrow.

-Tomorrow sounds great.-

All in all, it was a nice evening, and when it ended, Tala found that, somehow, it was nice to affix Kit to Lyn's wall once more.

She knew that, intellectually, it shouldn't matter where the door exited out, but for some reason, she preferred it there, in Lyn's hallway.

Something about the place and the people nearby made her feel like *this* was home.

*   *   *

Millennial Mage, 6 - Fused

The next day, Tala and Rane joined Aproa at the Guardsmen's guild for martial practice.

More notably, Terry joined them all.

It was decided that, as the most resilient of those present, Tala should fight Terry, first.

Thus it was that Tala and Terry faced off across the sand of the training space.

A selection of training weapons were randomly scattered around the sand.

"Begin!" Adam's clear, strong voice echoed through the yard, and Tala charged.

The weapons seemed to move on their own accord as they immediately began shooting toward her.

Terry's teleportations were so quick that Tala barely even saw flickers of movement as he arrived at each weapon, grabbed it, threw it, and moved on.

She blocked all she could, which wasn't many, but that was when the chaos began.

Each one that no longer seemed to have a chance of striking her would suddenly change direction, gaining a new burst of speed as Terry flickered to them and threw them again.

Even though they were training weapons, they hit *hard*. As soon as they struck and bounced away, they would be caught and flung back.

After less than twenty seconds, Adam called a stop.

The last weapons flew, bouncing off of—or being deflected by—Tala.

Terry flickered to the far side of the space once more, polishing his talons against his beak.

Silence fell over those watching, only broken when one of the soldiers exclaimed, simply, "Rust. I'm not fighting him."

That caused a ripple of laughter through the group and got everyone moving once more.

After that single bout, it was promptly decided that Terry didn't need more practice, at least not any that they could give, and it would be too dangerous for him to do so anyway against anyone but Tala, even with practice weapons.

Not that it was great being his target, even with blunted weapons...

As for mounted practice, they were able to do some training with Tala riding on Terry's back while others assaulted them.

In comparison to the near fluid, deadly beauty Terry had demonstrated earlier, it was... ugly.

Terry hated not teleporting away and defaulted to that with regularity.

Even when they set it up as an obstacle course for Terry to carry Tala through to an end goal, it proved counter to Terry's nature.

I knew he was fighting his baser instincts when we were fleeing the Leshkin. I just didn't know how much.

But that was good, if Tala was being honest. There were a lot of pointers and tips that they could both learn from and countless ways for them to improve in their coordination. So, it was agreed that this part would be incorporated into their regular training.

Tala was able to give her schedule to Adam, and he happily agreed to incorporate it into his ongoing class. He was actually grateful to have some hard dates that she would, and would not, be in Bandfast.

She had lunch with Rane and Aproa, focused mainly on catching up with the latter since she'd be leaving with Rane again in a couple of days.

Aproa had been taking ruin investigation contracts. More specifically, she'd been providing protection to minor expeditions to some of the closest ruins. Unfortunately, it was pretty boring on her side of things.

Millennial Mage, 6 - Fused

She had to stay above ground to keep watch, but at least it paid well.

Once lunch was over, they all went to their regular group training with the other Archons.

When Aproa conveyed Tala and Terry's mounted combat training, the whole group latched onto the idea.

It would have been a disaster, but Cazor was the voice of reason. After all, horses, even trained ones, did not like being in enclosed spaces with lots of loud or visually dazzling magic.

With that idea nixed before it could even be tried, the group simply agreed to have some work with Tala and Terry functioning in concert, whenever it was reasonable.

When they broke for the afternoon, Tala and Terry headed to Holly's workshop for the inevitable confrontation.

As soon as she stepped through the door, Holly called from the back. "You did it, girl!" She laughed maniacally, hurrying out from her workshop. "Very, very nicely done. I knew you had it in you."

Tala was taken aback, as was the receptionist, if the look on his face was any indication.

"Come in, come in. No need to dawdle."

Tala followed Holly back into her shop.

"Now, we need to test you to see how well-stabilized you are and how far along you've gotten since you had the preparatory scripts beforehand."

"Yeah, about that—"

Holly waved her off. "You can thank me later."

Tala sighed. "You weren't allowed to tell me what you were doing?"

"Of course not, dear." She gave her a long look. "Most people would want such scripts too early if it was widely known. Inscriptionists would be pestered, *constantly,* to do something that wouldn't be good or effective for most

Mages." Holly waved Tala off again. "But that's an oversimplification."

Tala grunted. "I guess."

"So, let's do some tests."

Tala looked down at her own hands, seeing the yellowing aura. It had ticked away from true orange and toward yellow at a steady rate since she'd Fused, and if it continued at this pace, she'd hit the halfway point in a couple more months.

She conveyed this to Holly.

"Yes, that's wonderful, dear, I can see that. My scripts on this building can see that. Any idiot with magesight and a basic understanding of when you Fused could see that. That is not what I'm going to test."

Tala frowned. "Then what are you going to test?"

"I am going to determine what tools we'll need in order to initiate the Refining process. Everyone's a little different in the extent to which they need to be Refined." She pulled out what looked like a wooden tongue depressor but radiating magic. "Open up."

What followed reminded Tala very much of a mundane medical exam but conducted with tools that were clearly magical in their aura, even if not in their appearance. *I wonder how much of this is just for show or some sort of elaborate joke.*

Tala couldn't quite determine what they did exactly. *Yes, look at this clearly magical item! Ooooo. No one can tell what it does.* Tala had to keep herself from laughing. That would actually be kind of funny. Making a bunch of things that looked really magical to magesight but did nothing. *I should find a way to do that to one of the bricks in the city streets and see how long it takes for someone to panic.*

She hesitated at that. *Hmmm... Maybe magic does make people a bit mischievous...*

Alat didn't comment, but Tala *thought* she could hear muffled chuckling.

Throughout the exam, Holly's face slowly lost its joy, and a frown began to build. That, more than anything, pulled Tala out of her contemplations.

Finally, Tala couldn't take it anymore. "What's wrong?"

Holly let out a long breath. "Well, there is good and bad news, I'm afraid."

"Isn't there always?" Tala tried to lighten the mood.

"Don't interrupt."

Okay, not a light matter then. "Sorry."

"The prep work is coming along nicely, and we should be able to move you to the final set of script modifications in a couple of months, if not sooner."

"That's the good news."

Holly gave her a long, level look.

"Sorry. I'll be quiet."

"As I was saying, you're coming along nicely in that regard. Unfortunately, your scripts for intaking consumable materials didn't have quite as much effectiveness as I'd hoped, given your magical density. Do you know what Refining actually does?"

Tala was not surprised by the seeming change of topic. She was getting used to Holly by this point.

-*Bite your tongue. No one can ever get used to… that.*-

She waited for a moment, considering pointing out that Holly had told her to be quiet, then decided not to be difficult. "To remove impurities?"

"Very good. Yes. The goal is to refine the person, physically, all the way down to their blueprints—that which governs the structure and function of their bodies."

"So, we should have a jump on that, right?"

"In most ways, we do. The human body has to be built up, strength and resilience wise, before the impurities can be purged. We're doing that. Unfortunately, the bulk of the work in Refining is the painful removal of those impurities, by the Mage themselves, using magical tools."

"That sounds... quite unpleasant."

"Oh, incredibly so, yes. Unfortunately, because we've been forcing the use of all that you consume, this seems to have increased the impurities in your body, at least on the macroscale."

"So, I will have more, agonizingly painful work to do."

"Precisely."

Tala frowned. "Wait, why did we do that if this was a possibility?"

"Because the scripts *should have* purified all the material, making it useful within you. And they *mostly* succeeded, but the result is that you have more... gunk in your body than the average person does."

"What does that mean?"

"Well, if you were a mundane? Without immediate treatment? An early grave—likely very early. But because your systems are enhanced, it shouldn't cause any issue before we can get you purged. You will naturally purge the impurities with time, but I doubt you want to spend a decade or five doing that."

"Lovely... and no. No, I do not."

Holly seemed to hesitate for a long moment. Finally, she sighed. "I do apologize. This was a miscalculation on my part. It seems like even with as magically dense as you were, the quality of power coming through your gate wasn't sufficient to do what we were trying to. I couldn't find any mention of a Bound with enough magical density to even use the scripts before you, and the requirements only stated a magic density level, which you exceeded." Holly sighed. "I'll have to update the information on these scripts so that no one else makes my mistake."

Tala knew the scripts that Holly was referring to. "They should have been fine. I understand them; I'm enacting them as we speak."

"I agree, but the data doesn't lie. You're going to have a rough Refining, once you're settled."

Tala grimaced. "Fair, I suppose. On that note: How am I on that front?"

"I do think that a year or two to fully settle will be advisable. Though, if you want risks, you can attempt in closer to six months."

Tala opened her mouth to reply, then paused to consider. *Why do I need to rush? Advancing is important, but such a delay would get me through my contract with the Caravanners, and I could then assess where I'm at and move forward into the next stage of... whatever I want to be doing. It might be nice to have a change of pace and maybe truly get to know my siblings again.* "Yeah, I think that's wise."

Holly gave her a long look, then shook her head and muttered to herself. "I guess everyone grows up eventually."

Tala decided not to comment.

-Yeah, because we're mature now.-
Hush, you.

Holly apparently had a lot of work still to do, so she shooed Tala away, but not before securing a promise from Tala to drop in whenever she could to be scanned by Holly's workshop scripts.

And so, that was how Tala spent the winter.

She went back and forth to Marliweather as often as she could. While she was there, she spent her time with her siblings. While she was in Bandfast, she spent her time training and with her friends.

The only break from the pleasant monotony was when Nalac and Illie departed for the academy just before the two month mark after Tala had reentered their lives.

It was a simple affair, with the whole family gathering to watch them step onto the teleportation pad one after the other.

By happenstance, coincidence, or a funny twist of fate, they ended up using the same teleportation room that Tala had departed from. The two events couldn't have been more different.

Where Tala had been alone, hiding tears, and just wanting to get away, Nalac and Illie were surrounded by family and a few friends who were wishing them farewell.

Their mother tried to push things on the twins, and Tala and the teleportation Mages had to continually return them to the woman, insisting that it wasn't possible to take items to the academy.

As confrontational as it was, it felt... nice to have a somewhat normal interaction with her mother. *Almost like I'm her eldest once again.*

She didn't interact with her father at all, though he was there. She simply didn't trust herself to be civil.

Funnily enough, since they held off to allow Tala to be there, they left the day before her own birthday. She didn't stick around after the twin's departure, choosing to celebrate turning twenty on the road back toward Bandfast.

To be fair, Tala didn't tell either of them, but Mistress Odera still seemed to know. She didn't make mention of it, but the cooks inexplicably prepared a cake for dessert that night and gave her an extra helping, even beyond what they normally would have.

After that, things went back to how they'd been for the remainder of the season.

Millennial Mage, 6 - Fused

Holly reinscribed Tala twice during that time, updating the scripts as appropriate. They were blessedly able to confirm that Tala's impurities weren't getting more numerous and were even marginally decreasing, but nothing short of the Refining process was going to remove the contaminants with any sort of efficiency.

Tala made four minimum payments on her debts, as well as an additional seventy gold toward paying it off. She was able to expand Kit four times, for a total of one hundred and twenty gold, bringing the dimensional storage's capacity up to a total of more than six thousand cubic feet.

Even after all of that, including her meals while in each city, she still had a nice, tidy sum in case of emergency totaling more than forty gold.

All told, it was a wonderfully peaceful time.

Epilogue: 1
The Reason

Author's Note:
This and the following chapter are the epilogue for this book, and the first major arc.
Additionally, they are the prologue to the next major arc of Tala's story.

Tala swayed gently, keeping her balance perfectly in control atop the cargo wagon as it trundled northward across the plains, bound for Arconaven.

It had been a fruitful winter, especially in regard to her siblings. Tala had made great strides in rebuilding the foundations for relationships with each of her brothers and sisters. She was even corresponding with several of the older ones on occasion. Though, given that most of her time was spent between cities, they weren't quick back-and-forths so much as touch-points between in-person visits.

Even though Nalac and Illie had departed for the academy two months earlier, Tala was able to exchange notes with them as well, though the twins' early classes were demanding enough that they had little free time for such things.

Also, if the correspondences they had sent were any indication, their new friends were taking up much of what little time they had outside of training.

I hope their experience is radically different than mine. They should start solidifying their fundamental understanding in the next few months and get their first inscriptions shortly thereafter.

It was an exciting time for them, and Tala felt a warmth within her at being able to be going through it alongside them, even if from afar.

Now, spring had arrived, and with it had come more rain than usual. Copious amounts of rain that, more than anything, had reminded Tala of swimming through a lake every time she'd stepped outside.

That near-constant deluge, coupled with the melting snow, had led to soggy, treacherous ground and lots of mud.

Much of the lowlands among the rolling hills now resembled marshland more than fertile plains, but that should pass soon enough.

The cloud cover had finally broken around noon, and with the near-constant, stiff wind, the sky was finally completely clear. Though, they were fast approaching the nightly stop and dinner.

We should reach Arconaven tomorrow. And if it stays clear, the ground should be clean and dry by the end of the day. She hesitated, considering the near two weeks of constant downpour. *Drier, at least.*

-Another new city to explore… finally.- Alat didn't much care about the mud, and before they departed, she had been grousing more and more about only seeing Bandfast, Marliweather, and the land in between. In truth, Tala had begun to get sick of the repetitive scenery, too.

Mistress Odera sat in her customary place near the back of the wagon, eyes closed and magical senses surveying their surroundings. She still hadn't managed to make an Archon Star within her iron monstrosity, but she kept insisting that she was close.

Tala didn't have to turn around to check on the woman.

Instead, one of the small drops of blood that spun around Tala's head granted her a secondary perspective via aspect mirroring.

She no longer needed to close her eyes to keep from being overwhelmed by two sets of inputs. Nor did the movement of that perspective, as it orbited or as she shifted its focus, make her sick.

Two other drops rotated along with the first, likewise filled with aspect mirrors of her perception, though Alat was co-opting the senses from those other two.

Tala could still perceive through them if she so desired, but she did not desire such. Much of her focused training through the winter had been specifically aimed toward shutting out those perspectives to allow Alat to be her omni-directional eyes and ears.

And Alat excelled at that. Especially in sparring, Alat warned Tala of anything she might otherwise miss, and their synergy had grown to the point that Tala didn't have to look for herself to block most attacks that Alat identified.

There was the added blessing that Tala's specific magesight scripts modified Tala's perspective directly, rather than providing a new sense that overlapped her sight. Thus, when Tala mirrored her sight onto the three orbiting bloodstars, they benefited from her magesight as well.

The whole process was surprisingly effective now that she and Alat had gotten the hang of it.

Her tungsten bar levitated as if nailed in place, just behind her neck, suspended by the two bloodstars inside of it. The sphere floated just in front of her sternum, similarly affixed.

Both showed nicks, dings, and even a couple of deep cuts from where they'd directly parried attacks in sparring and during the occasional arcanous encounter.

Millennial Mage, 6 - Fused

Even though the last four months had been incredibly peaceful, all things considered, they hadn't been free of violence.

Her elk leathers fit better than ever, given that Tala and Alat had continued to investigate how to minutely adjust the garments, precisely as they wished. They'd recently discovered how to change the colors, and after having a bit of fun with some more garish shades, they had settled on a set of earthtones.

Flow and Kit hung in counterbalance to each other, and she'd added a row of small vessels—smaller than the width of her belt—across the back of her belt to house her bloodstars when not in use.

The maximum she'd been able to wield effectively in a combat situation was still only eight, alongside those in her tungsten tools. While that wasn't an increase in number from earlier in the winter, her utility of and dexterity with them was improving by leaps and bounds. She could do more with all of them at once than she'd been able to manage with a single one at the start.

Maybe tomorrow I'll add in a ninth. It was about time.

Terry lounged off to one side, sprawled out on his back, legs extended to allow his stomach to absorb as much sun as possible.

She occasionally flicked a bit of jerky out for him, and while it vanished mid-flight, proving that he'd caught it, he never seemed to move. In return, he would occasionally flicker to one of the weapons laying on the wagon top and hurtle it at her without warning. That still took him enough time that she was able to notice his absence, however momentary.

As the weapon came her way, it was Tala's task to deflect it with bloodstar or tungsten tool without turning her head or stopping whatever she was doing at the time.

It had turned out to be ridiculously excellent practice, if she were being honest. And it was quite a bit of fun, now that she had improved enough that she wasn't being hit with fast-flying ballistic weapons every couple of minutes.

She still hadn't implemented the Leshkin shields that sat within Kit, or even attached the mounting plates she'd had made for them. She always found reasons for delay as they would require a few weeks of dedicated practice to incorporate into her other abilities whenever she added them. Things were progressing at a good pace, and she really didn't feel like taking a step back toward incompetence.

Maybe by midsummer.

Alat snorted within Tala's mind. -*More likely, we'll do it as soon as we come through a battle where they would have been useful.*-

That's... fair. She knew that she should get on with it, but not in the middle of a venture, and certainly not on the way to a new city. *I'll have some free time in Arconaven. I'll do the prep work and initial testing there.*

Tala felt a slight warning as a hatchet sailed from near the rear-right corner of the wagon at the back of her head. The tungsten bar simply spun, lifting slightly as it took on the appearance of a silvery, semi-translucent disc.

The incoming weapon was deflected back and down, where it struck into the wagon top with a *thunk*.

It had definitely made things more interesting when Terry had begun aiming such that the most effective blocking techniques would send the weapons into nearby things or people that Tala didn't want to harm.

Mistress Odera grunted at the sound but didn't otherwise react. The head driver, a middle-aged woman named Bilsta, no longer jumped or even twitched at the noise, but Tala did detect a slight tensing of her shoulders.

Millennial Mage, 6 - Fused

The tungsten rod stopped without seemingly needing to slow and drifted back down to its previous resting place.

Tala obligingly tossed a hunk of jerky for Terry before she returned her focus to the present.

It really was a beautiful day.

She took in a deep breath, relishing the wonderfully amazing smells of oncoming spring, even if they were overlaid by those of mud and ox-dung.

Take the bad with the good.

-Then sift out the bad and throw it away.-

Tala grinned. *True enough.* She hesitated. *Was it my perception or yours that picked up that attack?*

-Mine. You responded quite well.- Alat did seem quite pleased by the sound of her voice.

Tala's grin widened, even as she allowed her perspective to track the Mage Protector who had joined her this leg of her trip. *Marnin.*

He was passing by the right-hand side of their wagon as he made a circuit of the caravan.

Marnin was an enthusiastic Mage, a Material Creator, specializing in air. His attacks and defense were simply compressed, or gusts of, air. He'd been surprisingly effective in driving away arcanous threats and not causing any retaliation.

Honestly, after seeing the man work, Tala had been shocked that his skill set wasn't more widely seen, especially within the ranks of Mage Protectors. The guards even seemed not to mind the lessening of harvests too much. They were, after all, not required to engage with nearly as many threats as standard.

Though, to be fair, I haven't been exposed to that many, not yet.

This was her first trip after her block of back-and-forth ventures to Marliweather, and it was the first one without Rane since her very first trek to Alefast, Waning.

Rane, unfortunately, still had not broken into Fused, though he continued to insist that he was getting close. He had taken a different route from them, beginning his loop of the cities by heading south to Makinaven. From there, he was going to go west toward Retindel, then through Truhold, Namfast, and Manaven before coming out of the forest cities and meeting up with her and Mistress Odera in Clevenhold.

Tala and Mistress Odera had decided to take the wiser path, at least for Tala, and go north to Arconaven. From there, she'd go to Audel on the coast, then southwest to Surehaven before heading to Clevenhold to meet up with Rane. Their route had two fewer stops, so the two women would have longer hold-overs between trips, but that served Tala's purposes just fine.

She was ready to see more human cities, to experience their variety, and begin truly considering her place in the world.

After they met up with Rane, they would backtrack through Surehaven to Audel. Then, all together, they'd go to the new Alefast, and then visit the two sites of the cities under construction, working one of the caravans going to each from Alefast.

Thankfully, the forest to the north didn't contain any Leshkin, so it wouldn't be a barrier to Tala's plans.

Still, this is a half-year total trip with fourteen legs for Mistress Odera and me, seventeen for Rane. They'd even be stopping back through Marliweather as their last city before returning to Bandfast.

The only city that Rane wouldn't visit on his grand tour would be Alefast—the Waning one. As he'd grown up there, that wasn't much of a negative. At least, that was what he'd said.

Mistress Odera cocked her head to one side, and the motion brought Tala back to the present, once again.

"What is it?" Tala didn't turn around, trusting the woman to hear her voice.

"Something... odd. Do you feel that? On the wind? I think it's been there, building, for a while, but I only just felt it." Mistress Odera's magical senses often manifested in the woman as a feeling, so Tala immediately focused on her own magesight.

The wagons were entering a small stand of trees, likely coming up on their stopping place for the night. An ambush now would be rather unideal.

Alat? Anything?

-Maybe.- The alternate interface drew Tala's attention to what could have been threads of power in the air-currents.

"I think so? It seems like a relaxing effect. Something to lull us off our guard?"

"It could be. Could be." The older Mage seemed troubled—as was quite reasonable, if Tala was being honest.

"There's a bit of serenity, too. A desire for... isolation?"

"That is what I am feeling."

Tala flicked through her memory quickly, finding a few arcanous creatures that fit. One jumped to the forefront, however. "Bog hag? Maybe more than one?"

Mistress Odera grunted in acknowledgment but didn't reply. Tala bit her lip, considering.

"I really hope it's not bog hags. I didn't think they left the swamps northeast of Arconaven. Do you think this weather is enough to have drawn them this far south?" Around their other studies, Tala and Alat had taken a lot of time to thoroughly delve through the bestiaries provided by Grediv that were open to them, along with supplemental works that Alat pulled from the Archive.

They'd researched these beasts, specifically, as they were pernicious, arcanous near-sapients, almost like cyclops, who used magic to strip flesh from their victims before using the material to patch and cover over their own grotesque forms. They preferred human flesh, but would take what they could get their slick, spiny hands on. To add to the difficulty of dealing with them, the creatures would often, somehow, bend other arcanous creatures to their will.

No one seemed to know where they came from, and after several extensive campaigns had failed to eradicate them, humanity had moved into a mitigation posture toward the creatures.

Avoid, kill on sight, and keep the passengers close.

Tala nodded. "Worth using the standard tactics either way."

"I think so, yes." Mistress Odera seemed more withdrawn than usual, though that might have just been Tala's imagining.

The head driver leaned back while keeping her eyes forward. "Circling the wagons, Mistresses. It's time to stop for the night."

Tala nodded. "Thank you, Bilsta."

Their two-wagon caravan pulled in a wide circle before stopping in a stand of trees, a clearing already among the tall trunks ready for them to shelter from the wind. This was one of a dozen preprepared places that Bilsta could have chosen, so there wasn't really a specific danger of ambush at this location.

"I'll go talk to the guards and connect with the cargo slot servants." The passengers had largely kept

Millennial Mage, 6 - Fused

themselves confined within the dimensional storage spaces set aside for them this trip. So she had time.

Tala hopped down, her feet sinking slightly into the springy turf, even as the guards were knocking on the cargo slots to signal that the wagons had stopped for the day.

"On me, when you have a moment." The guards turned her way, their current task complete.

The doors swung open almost as one, and Tala heard cries of glee from inside.

There was a wave of noise as dozens of children exclaimed excitedly before practically boiling out through the open doors, the harried cargo slot servants and other adults close behind.

Tala froze on the spot. *Rust. They've been staying inside at all the other stops...* The rain had stopped.

"Stop!" Tala called, but the noise from all the passengers exiting almost as a unit and scattering in all directions overrode her.

Mistress Odera's eyes snapped open in alarm, and she turned, calling to a guard that was passing behind their stopped wagon.

What followed was near five minutes of panicked wrangling, resulting in the whole group grumpily crowding back around the cargo wagon, looking up at Tala, Mistress Odera, and Marnin, who'd joined them after the group was gathered.

Tala cleared her throat. "We've felt some odd magics in the air, so I want everyone to stay close."

There was some groaning at that, but not much, thankfully. Everyone knew that caravan trips were dangerous, and the Mage Protectors were to be respected.

"We know you want to stretch your legs, especially you little ones."

There was some laughter at that.

"But we need you to be safe. Please, keep to groups no smaller than three, and there should be at least one adult in any group. That means two children and one adult at the least."

Murmurs of assent came back to her. They were reasonable restrictions.

Mistress Odera's head jerked, then, her eyes widening. "Mistress Tala."

-Tala, the magic is gone.-

Tala looked around unnecessarily, her perspective already sweeping their surroundings. *What changed?*

She felt a fear begin to rise in her throat. Were they about to be attacked? Were they surrounded?

Marnin, though only a Mage, was battle tested and had clearly noticed their reactions. His magesight wasn't always active, nor was it likely sensitive enough to see the magics that had been there, but that hardly mattered.

The passengers obviously noticed the Mages reactions as well. One called up, even as the group as a whole pressed in closer to the wagon. "Is everything alright?"

Tala looked back down to them. "Please do a quick headcount. We might need to retreat into the wagons, quickly, and I don't want anyone being left behind."

Tala watched as the servants for each cargo slot moved through the passengers, counting their charges.

Several parents called to their children, and that started a cascade of calls back and forth as the smaller passengers moved through the crowds toward their guardians.

There really is a large number of passengers this trip.

Thankfully, the noise started to calm down as parents and children found one another amidst the shuffle.

Then, the reason for the fading magic came, along with a wail from a man near the middle of the crowd. "Jon? Jon! Where is Jon? Where is my son?!"

Millennial Mage, 6 - Fused

Another voice also lifted in response, a woman's this time. "And my Tam. I don't see him! Weren't they together?"

A few moments of frantic information collecting revealed that the two children, neither older than ten, had sprinted out of the cargo slots to play with their peers as soon as the wagons had stopped. The two hadn't returned to the wagons with the others when they were called back, though no one had specifically seen them either move off or stay behind.

Tala closed her eye taking a fortifying breath. *Think, Tala, think.*

-Well, we know why the magics have stopped.- This meant it was almost definitely a bog hag.

Hopefully, not more.

-They caught their prey.-

Tala shook her head. *There's no way we're letting this stand.*

There would be other creatures in-thrall to the arcanous humanoids. Even when they found the children, it was going to be a tough task to free them.

Her eyes snapped open, the beginnings of a plan coming together within her mind.

"Terry, I need you." She raised her voice, then. "Alright, quiet!"

When the din of fearful conversation calmed down, Tala continued.

"Here's what we're going to do."

Epilogue: 2
Found You

Tala immediately helped to mobilize all units of the caravan guards, regardless of duty rotation. Together with the sergeants, they quickly organized a search-grid, sending the guards out in four groups of five, armed to the hilt. Each group also had flares to bring attention if the children were found or if backup was needed.

Ten more guards stayed back to guard the caravan with Mistress Odera, while all the passengers were made aware that they were to, under no circumstances, leave the space between the two wagons.

Blessedly, no one complained, and many were already huddled around the parents of the two missing boys: Jon and Tam.

The guards would be responsible for sweeping the grove directly around the wagons, and Tala with Terry and Marnin would check the countryside.

Marnin would take the larger swath, focusing east, west, and south, just in case. He was given this section partly because he could move faster with his given set of abilities and partly because with his lower magical weight, he could move faster without creating motive aura resonance.

The other reason he was sent in the more unlikely directions was simply that he was less well equipped for dealing with the creatures that would likely be involved.

Tala would be on Terry, and they were to sweep northward in the most likely direction the children and bog hag went. *Oh, stars provide it's only one. One should only be able to have a few creatures under its thrall.*

Tala looked to her friend, even as she popped two ending seeds into her mouth. "Let's go, Terry."

The terror bird flickered into place under her, growing in size until she was comfortably situated behind his neck. He crouched low and took off at a dead sprint, weaving through the trees.

Tala immediately saw a build-up of a motive aura echo. "A bit slower, Terry." She grimaced in frustration. "Sorry."

He slowed down, and the resonance faded.

She almost asked him to go on ahead to look for the children on his own, but that would be incredibly dangerous, even for Terry.

The terror bird had no defense against the subtle nudges employed by a bog hag, and the creatures were all known to be able to weaken, or even fully suppress, the magical ability of many arcanous creatures.

That was theorized to be a cornerstone of their ability to enthrall those same beasts.

Terry was monumentally powerful, but they just didn't know to what extent he would be vulnerable.

It would not be safe for him to get close to them. They might just be able to remove much of his advantage. In the worst case, they might be able to enslave him, somehow. *Now* that *would be a disaster.*

Tala tried not to grind her teeth as she kept her focus tuned outward on the surrounding trees. *Endingberries in my mouth. Biting them unwittingly would be bad.*

She moved the two bloodstars containing mirrors of perception for Alat around trees to either side to increase their field of view, just in case. The guards should be through here shortly, but she'd feel the fool if she passed the boys by and didn't notice.

And what a blessing it would be to find the two hiding nearby.

Alat chimed in. *-Their gates should be obvious, even through obscurement. But I agree, the wide field of view is still wise.-*

They had no luck as they passed quickly through the trees. In fact, they found the first confirmation of the opposite just as they reached the edge of the grove.

A burn wolf howled before bounding up, lunging off of a tree to come at Tala from the side.

It was no bigger than a large dog but was much leaner in appearance. Its eyes glowed an ember red, and the tips of its fur were each a soft, luminescent yellow. Each hair was black despite the tip and had an almost charcoal quality to their appearance. Even so, they still moved as fur would on a dog. The last thing that jumped out to Tala, upon quick inspection, was the trails of smoke rising from the lolling, fang-filled maw.

Tala drew Flow with her off-hand, holding it in a reverse grip.

She caught the leaping wolf with her right hand while funneling power into Flow, shaping it into a glaive, which skewered the closest of the wolves closing in on them from the other side.

Large pack.

Her tungsten rod rotated and shot backward, catching another wolf mid-lunge like a bit in a horse's mouth.

"Terry, quick death."

Terry became a flickering storm.

Tala dropped to the ground, her mount gone.

She crushed the neck of the wolf that she had caught before tossing it aside, away from the trees.

Burn wolves had the habit of bursting into violent conflagrations, even after death, and she didn't want the caravan to find itself in the middle of a mini-forest fire.

Millennial Mage, 6 - Fused

She had time to twist, transform Flow into a sword, and cut down two more lunging forms before the conflict was over.

The tungsten rod hadn't slowed in its streaking path backward, where it slammed the wolf it carried into a tree without slowing significantly. First, it unhinged the beast's jaw, then continued. It crushed flesh and bone, moving in an almost perfectly straight line until it impacted the tree, no part of the wolf remaining in its way.

The rod then jammed downward, embedding into the wolf corpse before flicking it away from the tree line.

With a blurring spin, the metal implement shed the gore it had picked up. Now clean, it stopped just as quickly, rigidly vertical once more. From there, it returned to its resting position at a more leisurely pace, resembling the speed of a thrown rock rather than a crossbow bolt.

In those brief seconds, Terry had slain more than two dozen of the beasts, knocking their bodies away from the tree-line.

"This is too many. Bog hags don't usually control whole packs." Tala felt building concern for the boys and the caravan as a whole.

-A coven? Bog hags have been known to function in family units on occasion. When they do that, they can control larger groups of other creatures.-

Tala did not like anything that might imply, but it made sense. One bog hag would never venture this far from the northern swamps. A group, though? They just might be bold enough to try it.

Overhead, a circling shape drew her attention, though she didn't turn her head to look.

What do you think the chances are that that blade-wing falcon is just out for an evening flight?

-Low.-

Another servant of the hags?

-Even if not, it's worth bringing down.-

Agreed. Tala locked onto the creature, without ever setting her eyes upon it.

As she jumped back onto Terry's back, and he took off once more, she activated her magics.

Crush.

The falcon overhead shrieked in surprise, already plummeting toward the earth.

Crush.

Even as the bird began flaring its own magic and straining its muscles, the second amplification hit home.

There was no recovering after that.

The large creature hit the ground with a meteoric impact, but Tala didn't divert her attention as she scanned the land around them, Terry moving northward as fast as he could without creating a resonance with his passenger.

We should look east, closer to the mountains. The thought came subtly, and she almost voiced it to Terry before she noticed that Terry was already moving in that direction.

-Tala.-

Yeah. I noticed. She shook her head. *We have to keep going due north, as fast as we can.* "Keep northward, Terry."

Terry trilled and changed his course back.

She considered for a moment, then shook her head. *They wouldn't have gone due north, we should scan to the west.*

Again, she opened her mouth to speak, but Terry was already turning toward the west.

"Straight north, Terry. They're trying to drive us off their trail."

Millennial Mage, 6 - Fused

-There.- Alat brought Tala's attention to the magic in the air. It was a ridiculously light touch. It couldn't force anything at this level of power, but it was an effective nudge.

I probably would never have noticed it if Terry hadn't started reacting first.

-Yeah, even looking for it, I missed it at first.-

When they crested the next rise to the north, Tala almost screamed in surprise.

A thunderbull surged upward from where it had been waiting just over the top of the hill, crouched low.

Time seemed to slow as Tala's eyes widened.

Power was already building, nearly to a crescendo around the bull's body.

"Terry, away!" With her instant of warning, she expanded her aura to extend well beyond her body.

Terry flickered away just as a thigh-thick bar of lightning rammed down from the sky.

Tala was flung toward the ground, but mainly because her mount was gone once again.

Thankfully, this attack was nowhere near as powerful as the griffon's attack had been, several months back, and she'd learned from that.

As the lightning entered her aura, she threw her magical weight against it. The lightning itself was being directly manipulated by magic, and that was the only reason she could sway it at all.

Natural lightning of this magnitude would have raked the entire hilltop with a scattershot of power. This was being harnessed and wrangled to hit her alone.

She broke the force which contained the lightning.

The energy shot outwards like the world's brightest, most luminescent confetti, and Tala was knocked a step backward by the concussion of thunder that followed.

I'm coming to hate lightning.

Several strikes had still jumped to her, traveling down her iron paint, but they hadn't even burnt away the portion that it had traveled through. Though, the material was hot to the point of burning her flesh beneath. At least, it would have been, if she hadn't been full of endingberry power, both from the juice and from her own scripts, which mirrored them so closely.

As it was, the greatest inconvenience was that her eyes were temporarily blinded, and she felt a little dazed from the flash and overpowering thunder that had come through both her mundane senses and those that she'd aspect mirrored.

Next time drop the aspect mirroring and close your eyes.

-Hey, you did pretty good. Don't beat yourself up over details.- After a moment's hesitation, Alat added, *-But, yeah. Those would be good things to change.-*

Terry slew the bull before Tala recovered, even as quickly as she did, and he was back under her, growing to lift her into riding position before the bull hit the ground.

Its last effect on the world was a thunderous impact.

-Bad pun, Tala. No.-

My head hurts. Leave me my puns.

Terry was already speeding along the ridge, heading north-east as the most efficient path northward when she regained her faculties.

They had already covered more ground than the children could have hoped to cover in this time, were they on foot. So they had to be close. *Or they were taken by a blade-wing falcon and are already long gone.*

Tala shook her head to clear the horrid thought.

No, not happening. She hesitated. Something was wrong.

There had to be something she was missing.

Think Tala, think... Think!

Millennial Mage, 6 - Fused

The ridgeline. Why were they going along the ridgeline? She'd asked Terry to go due north.

-There it is.- Alat brought Tala's focus to another working of magic, and she shouted to Terry.

"Into the valley, now!" She also nudged him to turn left.

But they were greeted with an empty valley, save for some tall bushes.

Do we search all the bushes?

-Tala. The magic is still there. Something is terribly wrong. I think we're missing something critical.-

Tala stopped, took a deep breath, and cleared her mind. *They are working magic.* Her eyes snapped open, and she swept the surroundings with her dual perspective, instructing Alat to do the same.

They were looking for subtle inconsistencies in the zeme of the world around them. The currents of magic should be uniform and predictable but... *There!*

Back near the grove, there was something wrong. It was in a valley just to the east of where she'd come out—as evidenced by the still-smoking bodies of the burnt wolves.

The zeme was too calm, like the eye of a hurricane.

As soon as Tala locked her focus on it, a horrific screech arose from the depths of that valley, and it was as if a sheet was torn away.

"Terry, as fast as you can. Get me over there!"

Terry crouched low and practically rocketed back the way they had come, much, *much* faster than they'd come this way.

Tala practically blazed with power as her speed instantly created a motive aura resonance, which continued to build, shouting her power to the world.

She didn't care.

Climbing up the hill toward the grove was a small army of monsters.

Don't exaggerate, Tala. There's only about a hundred of the beasts.

What had, a moment before, seemed an empty hillside was now speckled with dozens of burn wolves, terror birds of differing elements, hearth snatchers, rock spiders the size of horses, and other minor arcanous creatures.

It had been a clever tactic.

Steal children to force a search. That way, the defenders would be spread out. Ideally, the strongest could be nudged to be even farther before the true attack came.

They plan on taking everyone.

Then, as Tala and Terry came closer at incredible speed, she saw them. At the base of the hill, still nearly a quarter of a mile away, six stooped figures surrounded a wide flat hillock, on which two bodies were laid out.

"*No!*" Tala pulled out a flare and fired it off, signaling that she'd found the boys and that the danger was to more than herself and them.

She didn't let herself focus on her goal; instead, she focused on that which was in her way. She tried to lock onto the hags, but their features and locations kept shifting subtly.

-Illusion. Not mental this time.-

So, there might be more or fewer?

-Exactly, and they might not be exactly where they seem.-

Are we sure they're down there at all?

-Yes, the source is in the same area as the illusion. Look there, there, and here.- Alat drew Tala's focus to various aspects of the illusion and the surrounding magics, along with the general pattern of the zeme of their surroundings as a whole.

Millennial Mage, 6 - Fused

Alright. It's a fight, then.

The hags screeched at her, and the sound, even as distant as they were, hit her like a physical blow, the magic around her ears fighting to keep it from getting to her.

Terry flinched, letting out a sound of his own that was disturbingly close to a whimper before he seemed to buckle down and increase his speed all the more.

Tala was a flaming beacon of resonant power as they crossed the last hundred yards.

The creatures that had been advancing on the trees turned at the sound of their masters' calls, facing the new threat and charging, their own challenges added to the hags' cries.

Terry leapt high in the last moments, then flickered away, engaging the closest enthralled creatures as Tala dropped on to the nearest hag… only to pass right through the illusion.

Enough! Tala threw her aura wide, filling it with as much of her magical weight as she could.

It felt like her body was slammed by a dozen sledgehammers, but she endured, wrenching control over the zone around her from her enemies.

The illusion shattered, and Tala was left facing *ten* bog hags, all with their hands raised in her direction.

Power slammed through her eyes, overwhelming the defenses there instantly and driving into her mind.

-I've got this.- Alat took the brunt of the attack, which felt like a cold-chisel being driven into Tala's orbital cavities. The alternate interface let out a pained, whining grunt, but her goal had been accomplished.

Tala's mind was mostly uninhibited.

With fury in her eyes, Tala instantly saw which of the hags had the most power flowing through them.

Crush.

The central creature dropped to the ground, squealing in surprise. *Like a gutted pig.*

That lessened the strain on Alat, and together, they quickly targeted more, going for incapacitation on a wide scale before killing them.

Though, as Tala enacted *Crush* over and over again, sweeping through her enemies, she sprinted toward their dropping forms.

Flow will end them before they can recover. In that vein, she threw the knife forward, sending power into it to reshape it into a sword even as it tumbled toward her enemies.

It beheaded the lead hag and was already being *pulled* back to her hand as the last of the hags collapsed under the influence of Tala's *Crush*.

The thralls were going mad, and Tala had to slow her headlong rush to deal with frothing wolves, screeching terror birds, chittering spiders, and other creatures that had gotten around Terry to charge her.

In her other perspective, Tala could see Terry flickering through the mass of gathered foes, eviscerating them even as they sought to overwhelm him with the sheer volume of their power.

Unfortunately, it seemed to be working.

Tala didn't know if the savage intelligence of the hags was specifically directing the beasts or if they were just well coordinated in some other manner, but the arcanous creatures were filling the valley with hostile power to the point that Terry had very few places that he could go without immediately sustaining injuries.

Still, he wove and slashed, finding holes in the defenses and filling the low ground with torrents of blood.

But he wasn't perfect.

Even at this distance, Tala could see burned feathers and cuts on her friend's flesh.

Millennial Mage, 6 - Fused

He had taken more damage in the last minute than she'd seen him take in total through the entirety of their time together.

She needed to help him, and the best way to do that was to end the threat of the hags. If the beasts were still fighting with their masters gone, Tala and Terry would have a bloody conflict to face together, but she needed the chief devils gone first.

With that in mind, she continued to hurtle Flow at the hags and call it back, killing at least one hag with each toss. As she did that, she had to fight the enthralled with her fists, feet, and bloodstars. She was even able to crack the ending seeds and exhale dissolution power into two different foes as she fought forward. *Maybe a second weapon wouldn't be a bad idea after all...*

Even as her advance was slowed by the tide of lesser creatures, she and Flow reaped a harvest of death among the hags. Those enemies fought futilely to return to their feet and died in the attempt.

Less than two minutes after Terry had flickered away, Tala slew the last hag, and it was as if a wave of *something* passed through the assembled arcanous creatures.

They froze in place en masse for one horrifying instant, then with shrieks, and chitters, and yowls, and bellows, the animals scattered in every direction, save toward the trees. There were already noises of charging men and women coming from that direction.

Exhausted, Tala turned back toward the rocky rise on which she'd seen the two boys, even as Terry flickered to her shoulder. The terror bird was favoring one leg, smoke rising from still-smoldering feathers around several burned patches of flesh.

"We'll get you seen to as soon as we can." But her mind was on the low hillock as she raced over.

She already knew what she'd find, but she refused to let it sink in.

As soon as she could clearly see what lay atop the rise, she slowed, color draining from her face, and her chest tightening.

The two boys lay stretched out, their shirts stripped from them, their throats slit.

She'd known as soon as she'd seen them. They'd had no gates.

Now, their bodies lay before her, dead for too short a time to even have cooled off.

Even so, there was no blood around them, indicating they'd been killed elsewhere and brought here.

They were killed as soon as they were taken, weren't they... It wasn't a question, but Alat answered anyway.

-*So it would seem.*-

* * *

She was joined by a host of guards and Marnin shortly thereafter, and she updated them on what had happened.

The boys' bodies were already in Kit, and the pouch had never felt heavier.

It was a long trek back to the caravan.

The sobs and wails of the boys' parents when Tala had presented them with the bodies along with her regrets would haunt her nightmares for years.

The clearing was somber that night as everyone was faced with the stark reality of the dangers that they were all too aware of, even if just in concept.

Mistress Odera tended to Terry's injuries, and sat in consoling silence with Tala for the entire time.

Tala was grateful for the woman's presence, even more so that she didn't press. Instead of talking, Tala wrote up

Millennial Mage, 6 - Fused

her reports and passed them to Mistress Odera before volunteering to take the first shift on watch.

She couldn't imagine sleeping with her mind still filled with images of those dead boys.

The older Mage asked if she wanted to talk, but Tala had asked to wait until morning. "I need time to process this."

The woman had smiled sadly, then nodded, granting the request of first watch.

They discussed the need to move the caravan, due to Tala's aura resonance, but they both agreed that it was such a short burst that it shouldn't be an issue, not this close to Arconaven.

That city was less than a dozen miles away, after all.

They'd almost made it...

Tala sat up, late into the night, watching over the caravan.

Just as midnight was approaching, and with it the end of Tala's shift, a form appeared beside her, seemingly from out of thin air.

Tala had no time to react as Revered power seized her without effort, locking her in place physically and magically. The air was practically drowning in the deep blue of her foe's aura.

Fear gripped her down to her soul. Alat was gone, frozen just as Tala's mind and magic were. Her bloodstars couldn't move; her very soul was under someone else's power.

A too-white grin spread across the arcane's face, satisfaction as plain in his features as the blood-red of his eyes.

Within the stillness of both body and mind, Tala heard a horrifyingly familiar voice, the tone somehow bringing to mind images of blood. "Found you."

Author's Note

Thank you for taking your time to read my quirky magical tale.

If you have the time, a review of the book can help share this world with others, and I would greatly appreciate it.

To listen to this or other books in this series, please find them on mountaindalepress.store or Audible. Release dates vary.

To continue reading for yourself, check out Kindle Unlimited for additional titles. If this is the last one released for the moment, you can find the story available on RoyalRoad.com for free. Simply search for Millennial Mage. You can also find a direct link from my Author's page on Amazon.
There are quite a few other fantastic works by great authors available on RoyalRoad as well, so take a look around while you're there!

Thank you, again, for sharing in this strange and beautiful magical world with Tala. I sincerely hope that you enjoyed it.

Regards,
J.L. Mullins

Printed in Great Britain
by Amazon